BOYS, BOYS, BOYS...

What's it like to discover that you're solely responsible for one baby? Now multiply that by two—or even three—bouncing bundles of joy!

Cameron Sutton in *Little Boys Blue* and Jillian Marshall of *Three Babies and a Bargain* find themselves in exactly that predicament in these two favorite stories from Susan Kearney and Kate Hoffmann.

❤ ❤ ❤

*These little guys may be small...
but they have the adults outnumbered!*

SUSAN KEARNEY

used to set herself on fire four times a day.
Now she does something really hot—she writes
for Harlequin Blaze and Harlequin Intrigue. While
she no longer performs her signature fire dive,
she's sold over thirty novels. Included among her
five books out in 2003 were three Intrigue titles
that launched her HEROES, INC. miniseries, a
crossover between the Harlequin Blaze and
Harlequin Intrigue lines. Susan writes full-time and
lives in Florida with her husband and kids. She's
currently plotting her way through her next novel.
You can e-mail her at Sue@Kearneydev.com.

KATE HOFFMANN

began reading romance in 1979 when she
picked up a Kathleen Woodiwiss novel. She was
immediately hooked, reading the book from cover
to cover in one very long night. Nearly ten years
later, after a history of interesting jobs in teaching,
retail, nonprofit work and advertising, Kate decided
to try writing a romance of her own. Her first book
was published in 1993 by Harlequin Temptation.
Since then, Kate has written more than thirty
books for Harlequin, including titles for Harlequin
Temptation, Harlequin Duets, continuity series
and anthologies. Kate lives in a picturesque village
in southeastern Wisconsin in a cozy little house
with three cats and a computer. When she's
not writing, she enjoys gardening, golfing and
genealogy.

SUSAN
KEARNEY
KATE
HOFFMANN

FiVE TiMES TROUBLE

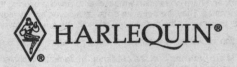

HARLEQUIN®

TORONTO • NEW YORK • LONDON
AMSTERDAM • PARIS • SYDNEY • HAMBURG
STOCKHOLM • ATHENS • TOKYO • MILAN • MADRID
PRAGUE • WARSAW • BUDAPEST • AUCKLAND

ISBN 0-373-23019-2

FIVE TIMES TROUBLE

Copyright © 2004 by Harlequin Books S.A.

The publisher acknowledges the copyright holders of the individual works as follows:
LITTLE BOYS BLUE
Copyright © 2000 by Susan Kearney
THREE BABIES AND A BARGAIN
Copyright © 2000 by Peggy A. Hoffmann

This edition published by arrangement with Harlequin Books S.A.

Visit us at www.eHarlequin.com

Printed in U.S.A.

CONTENTS

LITTLE BOYS BLUE
Susan Kearney

Prologue

"Don't be silly, Alexa," her cousin Sandra Sutton lectured. "You can watch the twins for the five minutes it'll take me to fetch us hot dogs and coffee."

Seeking to halt a rising sense of unease, Alexa Whitfield risked insulting her cousin by attempting to refuse. "I don't—"

"—know anything about babies," Sandra finished for her, an indication of how many times Alexa had used that particular excuse to avoid holding and feeding Flynn and Jason over the past few days of her visit.

Determined not to show her trepidation, Alexa neatly folded the *Boston News* and set the paper beside her on the park bench with a forced smile. "*I'll* get coffee."

"For Pete's sake. The twins are sleeping." Sandra stood, handed her the diaper bag filled with baby paraphernalia, beating Alexa to a clean getaway. Sandra's fashionable heels clicked along the pavement, but after a few steps, she turned back with a smile of encouragement. "You'll never learn to enjoy kids if you aren't willing to try."

"By the time you get back, I'll be an expert." Despite her inner turmoil, Alexa made her voice sound lighthearted.

"Just don't drop them," Sandra instructed as she fluffed her auburn hair with her hand.

"As if I didn't know that," Alexa grumbled.

Alexa Whitfield could identify a genuine Picasso from a fake at twenty paces, but if Flynn or Jason so much as burped, she wouldn't know what to do. Not that she didn't think the twins were adorable. She did. Not that she didn't want to scoop them up and bury her nose in their baby-soft skin. She'd love to.

Fate had decreed, however, that Alexa could never be a mommy. Some women couldn't stay on a diet, others didn't have the discipline to exercise regularly, some suffered from insomnia. Alexa couldn't bear children, but she didn't dwell on her inability. Not when life had so much else to offer.

While Sandra had the love of her adoring husband, Dr. Cameron Sutton, and the twins; Alexa had a passion for her work and a life most women would envy. Purchasing museum-quality art sent Alexa to Rio during Carnivale, Paris in the spring and New York City in the fall. She'd been invited to the White House for dinner, attended parties in Milan, London and Rome. European royalty often sought her advice.

Alexa stared at the Sutton twins asleep in their strollers and wished she had her sketch pad. She'd love to capture the babies' round cheeks, the dimples, the black hair they'd inherited from their brilliant father and the contrasting fair skin from their mother. Leaning down, Alexa tucked in the blanket by Flynn's feet, smoothed back Jason's hair, surprised by the satisfaction the tiny gesture gave her.

A shrill scream brought Alexa's head snapping up from the stroller.

Sandra!

Dear God, the scream had sounded like her cousin. As people ran down the path Sandra had taken, Alexa's fear shifted into high gear. Since the plane crash that had taken both sets of parents when they were youngsters, the cousins had been raised together by their wealthy Barrington grand-parents, and Alexa loved Sandra like a sister.

Don't panic. Sandra would come walking around the bend any minute, juggling hot dogs and coffee, tossing her auburn hair back from her eyes, ready to tell Alexa what the excitement was all about.

Two minutes later a siren wailed and Flynn awakened—at least she thought it was Flynn. Alexa was still having trouble telling the boys apart. With wide, frightened eyes, he looked for his mother, and when he couldn't find her, he started to cry until huge tears rolled down his chubby cheeks.

Awkwardly but without hesitation, Alexa picked him up. But not before Jason awoke and also started to howl.

"Now what? I don't have four arms." At her words the babies' cries subsided and she returned Flynn to the stroller. If she hadn't been so worried about Sandra, she would have been pleased by how easily she'd comforted the boys.

"Where's your mother?" Alexa checked her watch. Sandra had been gone more than ten minutes. Should she stay and wait? If Sandra returned to find Alexa and her babies gone, would she worry?

Alexa decided to walk the stroller up the block to the corner hot-dog stand and come straight back. Most likely she'd run into Sandra, who'd probably stopped to chat with an acquaintance.

Shoving the baby stroller into motion, she walked briskly down the sidewalk, determined to give Sandra a piece of her mind for scaring her so. Palms sweaty, Alexa rounded the corner to see yellow police tape cordoning off a crime scene.

Heart pounding, fear hastening her footsteps, Alexa hurried until her pace behind the baby stroller almost reached a jog. Shoving her way through the crowd, she took one look at the victim's cap of auburn hair and her knees turned to jelly.

"Sandra!"

A cop noticed Alexa and jerked his thumb toward the pavement where her cousin was being loaded onto a stretcher. "You know this woman?"

"My cousin." Alexa swallowed hard at the huge amount of blood on the sidewalk.

"She was mugged with a baseball bat." The kindly cop took Alexa's arm. "They're taking her to Boston Memorial but..."

At the implication that Sandra might not survive long enough to reach the hospital, tears brimmed in Alexa's eyes. "Can I see her?"

A minute later Alexa was leaning over her cousin as the paramedics strapped in her cousin. "Sandra?"

At the sound of Alexa's voice, Sandra turned her head, her beautiful clear blue eyes clouded with pain. "Tell Cam I love him."

"You can tell him yourself. I'll call him and he'll be waiting at the hospital."

Sandra convulsed, her entire body shuddering, but she kept talking. "Promise me."

"Anything."

"My boys. Take care of them."

"You'll get better. *You'll* take care of them."

Sandra grabbed her hand with waning strength. "Don't let...the grandparents...raise them."

"Hang on, Sandra. Fight. You and Cameron will raise the boys."

"No boarding schools. No nannies."

"They have their mother," Alexa insisted.

Sandra grasped Alexa's hand, refusing to let the paramedics put her in an ambulance until she had an answer. "Promise me."

Tears clogged Alexa's throat. "I promise."

Chapter One

Highview, Colorado
One year later

The telephone rang and Dr. Cameron Sutton hesitated, his hand over the receiver like a wary medical student entering the operating room for the first time. Cam had been notified of his deceased wife's mugging by telephone. Told of the upcoming custody battle with Sandra's grandparents over the twins by telephone. And ever since *Humanity Today* had named him Boston's most eligible bachelor, it seemed as if every damn reporter in the country felt they had the right to invade his privacy.

Escaping from Boston to the Sutton ranch in Highview, Colorado, had kept intruders at a physical distance. Caller ID would have helped maintain his privacy, but suppose a patient needed him? Too responsible to ignore the possible need of someone sick or injured, Cam picked up the phone. "Yes?"

"It's Alexa."

Recognizing the cultured voice of his wife's cousin, Cam relaxed in his padded leather rocker. Propping his feet on his desk, he looked out his window and let the brilliant Colorado sunshine and verdant mountains that surrounded the vast Sutton acreage of his boyhood home calm his apprehension.

"I'm calling from the airport."

Hong Kong? Budapest? Marakesh? Cam didn't ask or bother to keep up with Alexa's hectic schedule. While he commended Sandra's cousin for her monthly calls to check on the twins, he couldn't keep back a niggle of suspicion about her timing. Only yesterday, his attorney had notified him that Sandra and Alexa's grandparents had filed for custody of his boys. Despite the Barringtons' wealth, Cam wasn't too worried—not with his father, a Colorado senator, in his corner.

"The twins love it out here," he told Alexa before she could ask. On the Sutton cattle ranch, his twin prodigies could grow up with more freedom from scrutiny than in the city. "The Senator gave each of them a pony last week."

Alexa gasped. "They're only two years old!"

Cam chuckled and started to tease her, then recalled how little Alexa knew about children. And how a sharp attorney might use the ponies in court during a custody battle. Cam didn't want to give even the appearance of recklessness and did his best to keep the defensiveness from his voice. "My nephew, Keith, has been riding almost since he could walk."

"Still—"

"We never let the boys near the horses without supervision. And you know Julie grew up out here and around horses."

Alexa sighed. "Julie is a wonderful baby-sitter. You're lucky to have her."

"Yes, we are." Cam had been grateful when Julie had agreed to move back to Colorado with him and the boys. Julie Edwards had come to work for their family after Judge Stewart, an associate of his father's, had recommended her.

Although she'd grown up in Colorado, she'd agreed to move to Boston after the twins were born. And Cam was grateful she'd agreed to move back out west after Sandra's death. The adaptable nanny had eased the twins through the loss of their mother with surprising compassion for a college sophomore.

"Is Julie working today?"

"She's leaving any minute for class. Why?"

"I was hoping she could give me a lift. This airport doesn't have cab service." Cam frowned in confusion.

Alexa laughed. "I suppose I should have phoned ahead, but I wanted to surprise you."

She certainly had. Alexa, normally so clear and logical, wasn't making any sense. "You flew into Highview?"

"Straight from Rome, via New York and Denver."

What the hell? Cam scratched his head and looked around his barely framed-in home, which was still under construction and not the least bit ready for a guest—especially one accustomed to the Ritz-Carlton in Paris, Claridge's in London and the Plaza in New York City. Plumbers had yet to hook up the final water line from the well. Carpenters hadn't finished the staircase banister to the second story, and there was still a mammoth-size gap in his office window frame waiting for an oversize pane of glass to arrive. Surprisingly the swimming-pool contractor had almost finished.

From his silence, Alexa must have sensed his hesitation. "Can we discuss my visit in person? I'm afraid I didn't change enough lira into quarters."

Just as she finished her sentence, the phone went silent, then the dial tone pealed accusingly in his ear. During Alexa's infrequent but regular phone calls, she'd mentioned she might visit the twins, and he'd issued a blanket invitation, but Cam had never expected her to take him up on the offer. Not without warning. Certainly not while his house was still under construction.

With swift precision, he stood and checked his watch. When his baby-sitter had agreed to return to Highview with his family, he'd promised her he would schedule around her classes at the local college. She lived at the dorm and took classes in the afternoons and the occasional evening. If he brought the twins with him to the airport, he wouldn't have to ask Julie to miss her afternoon class.

And once Alexa saw his sons' capacity for finding trouble, Cam figured he wouldn't have to try very hard to convince her to stay at the Highview Hotel.

A year of handling the precocious twins without Sandra's help had made Cam nothing if not efficient. Within ten minutes he'd said goodbye to Julie and strapped Flynn and Jason into the toddler seats of his sport-utility vehicle, gathering toys and snacks along the way.

Flynn hated to sit still for more than ten seconds, especially when there was a yard filled with mud, interesting pipes, ditch-digging equipment and fencing to explore. He kicked his feet and pointed out the window. "Juk."

"Junnnk," Cam automatically corrected his eldest by four minutes, emphasizing the *N* sound, not in the least surprised the two-year-old remembered Cam calling the rusty equipment junk.

"Not junk." Jason disagreed. "Play toys."

"You're an optimist, junior." Cam shook his head at the younger twin, reminding himself of the need to be ever vigilant. A construction site was no place for curious toddlers. Nor was the Senator's mansion with its too many breakables. His twins didn't have the judgment to go with their incomparable intelligence.

Cam's respect for the Senator, who had raised five sons out here after their mother died, went up another notch.

Although he and his brothers had been hellions, they'd
turned into mostly respectable citizens. And he hoped to
instill the same values in his kids that his father had in
him—a love of the land, a confidence in oneself and a loy-
alty to family.

The Sutton acreage was a working cattle ranch that the
Senator had recently bequeathed to Cam and his three brothers. His brothers had watched over his portion, but after
Sandra's death, Cam had returned to Highview to build a
home, staking claim to forty acres and intent on starting a
medical practice in town. So far he'd managed to do neither.
But he had no doubt that eventually he would settle in comfortably here, and the boys seemed to thrive in the open air,
spoiled by their uncles and grandfather.

After leaving home at eighteen, Cam had always intended
to return to Colorado. But when he went East for college
and then medical school, attaining the best education money
could buy, he'd fallen in love with Sandra Barrington, great-
granddaughter of Arthur Levenger, nineteenth-century robber baron and industrialist, and the granddaughter of Boston's high-society Barringtons had captured his heart.
Sandra wouldn't consider leaving Boston and the grandparents who'd raised her and her cousin, Alexa. So Cam had
set up a practice back East and tried to appreciate the
wealthy clientele the Barrington connections threw his way.

After Sandra's murder, Cam had craved the isolation of
the ranch and the comforting acceptance of family and
friends. Out here, a man had room to breathe. And grieve.
Sandra's senseless death still clawed at him, but not only
because her murder had never been solved. In a big-city
park filled with lovers, joggers and vendors, no one had seen
anything. As the months passed without a lead, Cam had
given up on the police ever catching her murderer, but he

hadn't given up wishing that Sandra could be here to share the twins with him.

He ached to turn to her and brag about their sons' uncommon intelligence, their sheer exuberance for life. She would never see her sons grow to maturity. Never see them take their first steps, hear their first words. Not only did Cam miss Sandra for himself, it pained him that the boys would have no memory of their mother.

Cam had once asked the Senator how he'd managed to go on after his own wife, Cam's mother, had died, leaving his father to raise five sons. The Senator had squeezed his shoulder and told him that while his wife was gone forever, his memories of her would never die. At that moment some of Cam's pain had eased. The boys might not remember Sandra, but he could tell them stories about her. He still missed his wife and always would, but like his father, he had found the strength to go on. Luckily the twins kept him busy enough that he didn't have time to brood.

Even now as he pulled onto the private Sutton road that led to town, he caught sight of Jason fiddling with the strap that kept him buckled into the toddler seat. Another thirty seconds and he'd work himself free.

From experience Cam knew that the best way to control the twins was by distraction. If he could engage their curious minds, their busy fingers might stop probing, twisting and turning every button, knob, dial and switch within reach.

He tossed a spherical plastic puzzle into the back seat. "Here, you two. See if you can take that puzzle apart."

With surprisingly accurate reflexes that reminded Cam of his younger brother Rafe, Flynn caught the plastic ball between two chubby hands. "Mine."

"Share," Jason insisted.

Cam smiled at the success of his ploy, turned past the

barn and swung onto pavement just as the plumbing truck rounded the bend, heading toward his muddy driveway. Cam slowed and rolled down his window, glancing at the unclouded blue sky and the July sun directly overhead, then at the plumbers. "You guys were supposed to be here first thing this morning."

"Sorry, Dr. Sutton. We were waiting on a culvert. You said you wanted the water lines hooked up to the house today."

"Yeah, I'd like to try bathing the boys in a bathtub instead of a horse trough."

Flynn tossed the ball to his brother. "No bath."

"Like dirt," Jason agreed.

"Pipe down in the chorus," Cam ordered.

"What's a chorus?" Flynn asked.

"Us." Jason found the key and pulled out the first puzzle piece.

Cam rolled up his window and wondered if the two boys were reverting to little savages. They liked to crawl and dig in the mud. They preferred to pee outside, and without indoor plumbing, what could he expect?

Perhaps he should have kept the boys at the Senator's house until his house was complete. But Cam was reluctant to leave the boys with anyone but Julie. In the last year, the boys had been through so much, losing their mother and moving from Boston to Colorado had changed all their lives. He didn't want the twins to feel as if they'd lost their father, too. And since Cam needed to oversee the construction, he'd kept the boys at his side.

He glanced over his shoulder at the twins and reassured himself the boys were still buckled in and reasonably clean. Julie had washed their hair this morning, and if they looked in need of haircuts, at least they smelled of baby shampoo.

With their heads so close together they almost bumped, the two boys were firmly engrossed in the puzzle.

As he headed to Highview's private airport, he recalled that the last time Alexa had seen the boys, they'd just learned to crawl. Sandra had mentioned her cousin had been reluctant to hold the babies even while she'd been captivated by them. Now they were little bundles of restless energy. What would Alexa think of them?

"I BROUGHT PRESENTS," Alexa said through smiling apple-red lips as she scooped a squirming Flynn into her arms at the airport with the ease of someone accustomed to wriggling toddlers.

Cam hadn't seen her since her tragic visit to Boston last year, but he noted her new ease with the children and was fascinated by it. Her eyes sparkled with excitement as she held Flynn with a competence he'd never expected.

"Candy?" Flynn stopped wriggling long enough for Alexa to plant a kiss on his forehead and ruffle his hair.

Resting on Cam's hip, Jason's ears perked up. "Gum?"

"What did I tell you boys about begging?" Cam tried to keep the laughter out of his voice.

Alexa might not have known much about kids a year ago, but she'd learned fast, and he wondered if, in the intervening months, she'd met a man with children. She hadn't mentioned a personal relationship during her phone calls, but Alexa tended to be a private person. However, she'd already won the twins over by mentioning presents.

Cam was glad that his sons had Alexa's attention. He didn't remember her ever looking so vibrant. Highview's airport, only for small private planes, didn't boast a terminal, and Alexa shined on the tarmac like a ruby amid dark gravel. Her cherry-red suit and matching spiked heels set off her blunt-cut, shoulder-length dark hair to perfection.

Flawlessly groomed, freshly powdered and glossy-lipped, Alexa could fly for twenty-four hours straight and disembark from a plane looking ready for a model's runway.

Yet she'd come ready to do battle and win over the twins. With a vivacious face that exuded a lively intelligence, Alexa opened a red patent-leather purse, rooted around and retrieved two Chinese paper puzzles.

"Here." She handed one to each boy without a word of explanation.

"Tell Alexa thank you," Cam reminded his sons.

"Lexi, thanks."

"Me, too."

"You're welcome," Alexa told them.

Cam watched Alexa's eyes light with anticipation as she waited for his sons to stick their fingers in each end of the puzzle, saw her restrain a smile as the paper puzzle trapped their fingers.

"Sticky."

"Very sticky."

"Stuck," Cam said, his correction lost in the roar of a plane taxiing for takeoff.

Alexa swiveled Flynn onto her hip, swung her purse strap over her other shoulder to free one hand. "Push."

Carrying the always wriggling twins was never easy, but Alexa accomplished the maneuver like a professional nanny who was enjoying her task. Either she'd been baby-sitting a lot or she'd taken up juggling.

Eyes bright with amusement, Alexa guided his son's hands. As Flynn's fingertips moved together, the puzzle released his fingers. "Kew-el."

In moments Jason, too, had freed his hands and then immediately stuck his fingers back into the trap. "Do it again."

Cam steered Alexa and the boys over to the baggage area

where the pilot unloaded luggage from the small plane. "Where's your bag?"

Alexa tilted her head toward a cart of elegant black leather luggage with gold designer braid. Cam headed for the baggage, doing his best to conceal his surprise and dismay at the number of suitcases. He counted six, as well as a garment bag, a heavy-duty trunk and a computer case, and wondered exactly how long Alexa planned to stay.

Cam stowed the last suitcase into the SUV while Alexa strapped the boys into their seats. "How about lunch in town at—"

"Big Mac?" Jason asked.

"Yes. Yes. Yes!" Flynn echoed his brother's request to visit the golden arches.

Cam shot an apologetic look at Alexa. "I was thinking of lunch at the Highview Hotel." Where afterward he could leave her in a room with hot and cold running water, heat or air-conditioning and room service.

Alexa took one look at the boys' expressions and turned back to Cam. "I'd love a hamburger."

"Lexi rules." The two boys high-fived each other, a favorite gesture that Rafe had taught them while he gave them riding lessons on the ponies. As Cam stole a look at Alexa, he drove into town, grateful for the boys' exuberance and chatter. He couldn't help wondering about the reasons for Alexa's unexpected visit or how long she intended to stay, but realized it wouldn't be polite to ask.

Alexa crossed one smoothly stockinged leg over the other, distracting Cam as her skirt inched up her thigh. It must be the high-spiked red heels that made her legs look so long—or he certainly would have noticed them before now. Alexa had danced at his engagement party—been maid of honor at his wedding—wearing a stunning silver gown, and he'd seen her in somber black at Sandra's funeral. But he'd never noticed her spectacular legs before.

Once Sandra had come into his life, Cam had stopped looking at other women—at least in a sexual way. He'd loved his wife, and since her death, he'd seemed to have lost all interest in the sweeter sex. But Alexa's legs were waking him up, as if from a long, drowsy sleep, and he shifted uncomfortably.

Although he was pleased that the grief was finally lifting from his heart, Alexa was Sandra's cousin, and he felt disloyal to Sandra for even looking at another woman. Especially Alexa. His wife and Alexa were cousins, losing both their parents, who'd been on a ski vacation together, in the same plane crash. Cameron knew his wife and Alexa were more like sisters than cousins, and he'd always thought of Alexa in the same way. To think of her as a woman was disconcerting.

Besides, Alexa was merely visiting. She was passionate about her career, switching time zones and continents the way other women switched underwear. Alexa was a woman happy with her career, herself, her life. And Cam had no business thinking about her in any manner except as an aunt to his sons.

Besides, she might be here to spy on him for the Barrington grandparents who wanted to take his sons away from him. He had to remain on his guard. Now was not the time to let a sexy pair of legs distract him.

"Have you started your medical practice yet?" Alexa asked.

Was her question just friendly curiosity? Or was she gathering information to be used against him in court?

"I'm planning to start just as soon as the house is finished."

She frowned. "I thought Tyler told you it was ready to move into."

"My older brother's idea of a home is a roof to keep out the rain. He doesn't miss little conveniences like electricity and plumbing."

Cam swung onto Highview's main street, taking pleasure in the mountain range that had overlooked the whole of his childhood and youth, the great mountain chain spreading north and south of town for hundreds of miles. Highview nestled along the river in a quiet valley of lush grassland and rolling hills. The centerpiece of town was the Highview Hotel, built in the Victorian fashion and painted in soft gray and blue.

"I'll get you a room at the hotel."

"I really came to see the boys." Without creasing her designer suit, she turned to send the twins a fond glance, every hair on her head in place. "And I've camped out before."

"Where? In the lobby of the Waldorf-Astoria?" he teased.

"Try Nepal, Katmandu and Tanzania." She arched a perfectly plucked brow at him in challenge. "I'm tougher than I look."

He hadn't meant to offend her, could hear the hurt in her voice even as she dared him to send her to the hotel. "You look great."

She let out a delicate snort. "Why does that sound like an accusation, instead of a compliment?"

"Look, I'm sorry." He threaded his fingers through his hair with exasperation, knowing he should have been honest with her from the start. "My house isn't ready for visitors. I can't imagine you would be comfortable there."

"I've slept in *yurts* with the Mongols in Russia, in tents with nomads in the Sahara. They have the most fiery paintings of horses in Russia, and such delicate carvings in the desert.'' Her voice turned dreamy as she described the horsemanship captured in paintings so rich in detail that museums all over the world vied for them, and carvings of bones so ancient it was amazing they'd survived. Her passion for her finds and her work spoke to him on a level he understood. She felt about art the way he did about medicine. Ever since he'd been a kid, he'd wanted to be a doctor, couldn't imagine doing anything else.

As he swung into the fast-food restaurant's parking lot, he wondered what had brought her away from her work to Colorado. By the time the meal ended, she still hadn't answered his unspoken questions. They'd avoided grown-up talk, instead, both of them focusing on the boys. But sometime during the meal, they'd reached an unspoken truce, and he'd decided if she wanted to camp out at his house, she was more than welcome.

Alexa was good company, interesting, cheerful and easy on the eyes. He saw no reason not to enjoy the friendship or company she was offering.

The twins fell asleep during the ride back to the Sutton ranch. With the muddy driveway full of contractors' vehicles, Cam was forced to park near the barn. He turned to Alexa, who was looking around with lively curiosity. ''If you'll stay with the boys, I'll see if the stone mason will move his truck out of the way.''

''Sure.'' She glanced at the sleeping twins. ''No problem.''

THE MOMENT CAMERON disappeared behind the electric truck, Jason's eyes opened wide, the angelic look of sleep turning to mischievousness. Before Alexa could stop him, he tugged on Flynn's ear, waking his twin.

Jason kicked his feet. ''Out.''

"Out. Out. Out!" Flynn echoed.

They *had* been sitting a long time. She wouldn't mind stretching her legs and walking around, either. Cam had told her to stay with the twins, but he hadn't said to stay in the vehicle. She'd noted and admired Cam's easy competence with his children, the love shining from his eyes whenever he glanced their way. He didn't seem the kind of father who'd mind a little change in plans. What could a short walk hurt?

"If you boys promise to hold my hand, I'll take you out."

Flynn pointed to the barn. "Can we ride our ponies?"

Alexa struggled with Jason's buckle. "We can go *look* at them." Flynn had his seat belt unfastened before she'd finished with his brother's, but she blocked him from exiting the vehicle with her body, determined not to lose him.

During the past year, she'd become comfortable with children, reading books on child care and offering to watch her friends' children. The effort had cost her, but she'd been determined to overcome her reluctance and fears. Eventually she'd put aside her unease and been paid back in happiness, which she'd only wished Sandra had lived long enough to see.

In a moment she had both boys by the hand. Their little legs pumped three times as fast as hers, eagerly pulling her toward the most magnificent barn she'd ever seen on any continent. From the outside, she could see the huge building was heated and air-conditioned, immaculately landscaped with an array of wildflowers amid the verdant grasses and freshly painted yellow with golden shutters.

Flynn suddenly pulled up short. "Uh-oh."

"Holy cow!" Jason pointed.

Their excited voices shot Alexa's pulse into high gear. A

humongous bull charged around the barn's corner. For an instant, Alexa froze, staring into the animal's wild eyes.

At the sight of them, the bull pulled up short, shook his huge horns and pawed the ground. Charged.

Adrenaline rushed through her, burning her stomach with fear. With a strength Alexa didn't know she had, she scooped both boys into her arms, dashed back toward the vehicle, opened the door. She shoved both shouting children to safety on the floor and slammed the door. There was no time to climb in after them.

Horns aimed low, the bull head-butted the SUV, missing Alexa by inches, denting the passenger's front door, lifting the vehicle several inches off the ground. Then he turned toward her, about to charge again, possibly tip over the vehicle.

His head was down, his horns pointed her way. In horror, she visualized him crushing the kids, kicking in windows with those massive hind quarters and deadly hooves.

She had to protect the children. From her peripheral vision, she saw Cameron racing to the vehicle. He wouldn't arrive in time.

She had to do something now.

Something fast.

In Spain she'd been disgusted by matadors waving red capes at bulls to get them to charge. In a flash, Alexa realized her suit was cherry red. Tearing at her jacket buttons in renewed panic, Alexa whipped off the bright red garment and flung it aside—away from the vehicle. Just as she'd prayed, the bull changed direction, charging the flash of red, catching the material on its horns, then stomping it into the ground.

Slowly she moved toward the vehicle's door to check the twins. Her spiked heel snapped. Alexa tripped. At the cracking sound, the animal first raised his head, then lowered his thick neck, aiming the wicked horns at her. It was too late to remove her skirt. Too late to open the dented front door and climb inside. And if she stayed where she was, the babies would be at risk.

She had to move.

Shifting sideways, she raced away from the children, slipped in the mud, rolled. The animals' hooves pounded the ground. Alexa scrambled, crawling and kicking through the mud to her feet.

She turned, looked over her shoulder. The bull was close enough for her to see the whites of his eyes, feel his hot breath on her neck.

Chapter Two

"Fall and roll!"

At Cameron's shout, Alexa flung herself sideways, spinning through puddles and mud. Once she was out of his gun sight, Cameron fired the .410 shotgun pistol he'd just removed from his locked gloved compartment. As his gun discharged at the bull, Alexa kept rolling, a swirl of flashing red and mud.

At the pepper spray of pellets striking his hide, the angry bull bellowed in surprise and halted midstride. The widespread shot hadn't penetrated the bull's thick hide, and as several ranch hands herded him toward the paddock he'd escaped from, Cam turned to Alexa.

When he'd pulled the gun out of the SUV, he'd done a quick check of the twins, and they were fine. But Alexa was lying unnaturally still. He prayed the red he could see was material from her skirt and not blood.

"Dr. Cam, I'll take the boys up to the house," Cody Barnes offered with a shy look. The lanky young ranch hand was accustomed to watching his mother's brood, and often filled in for Cam if he got busy. Cam nodded, grateful. Cody would reassure the twins, tell them cowboy stories and make them forget their scare while Cam attended to Alexa.

"Thanks," Cam said, and ran toward Alexa, his heart

pounding against his ribs with fear that she'd sustained a mortal injury. "Bodine, fetch my bag from the house."

Bodine Stone, the head foreman, was accustomed to taking orders from Rafe, but he didn't object to Cam's hurried plea. "Where in the house, Doc?"

"Under my desk."

Cam took one deep breath to steady himself. Although he was a trained physician, taking care of Alexa was very different from treating a stranger. Cam still felt guilty that he hadn't saved Sandra. If only he'd been with her on his day off—instead of at a seminar. If only he could have put all his medical skills to use on the person he loved more than anyone else. He still blamed himself that he hadn't even been at the hospital when she'd arrived in the ambulance. Maybe if he'd been there, he could have done... something. He hadn't even gotten the chance to hold her hand. Or kiss her goodbye. It took all his objectivity and medical training to put the past from his mind. Put the last horrific minutes from his mind.

A patient needed him, and he would remain detached to do his job. Kneeling beside Alexa, he smoothed aside silky black hair caked with mud and felt for the pulse at her neck. Relief flooded through him. Her pulse was good. Strong and steady.

Gently he turned her onto her back to check her breathing. She immediately started to cough up mud and spit out dirt. Finally he heard the sound he'd been waiting for—her gasp for air.

"Easy. The wind's been knocked out of you." He knelt at her side and ran his hands over her limbs but found no obvious broken bones. He searched the rest of her for signs of injury. "Don't move."

"The twins?" Her eyes brimmed with tears.

He found no sign the bull had gored her and realized

with relief she would be fine. That her first thought was for his sons' well-being sent his objectivity flying and his admiration spiraling. Alexa wasn't just another pretty face. She had spunk and courage and as much moxie as any rodeo clown who risked his life to save endangered bull riders. And she smelled better. Much better. In spite of the mud, the expensive perfume she wore was doing strange things to his thoughts, making it difficult to concentrate.

"The boys are fine."

She coughed and turned her head to spit out a little more dirt. Her color beneath the mud was too pale, her chest heaved with spasms, her body convulsed for air. And still she asked about the boys. "You're sure?"

"Yes. Don't try to talk yet. Relax. Give your body a moment to recover."

Bodine shoved the physician's bag into his hands. "Here, Doc."

"Thanks." Cam extracted sterile water, wet some gauze and gently wiped Alexa's face free of mud. First he cleaned around eyes that were still wide and frightened, then her aristocratic nose, which flared at his touch, and finally her mouth, which trembled as she tried to contain the aftermath of her fear.

Her entire body shook. "I'm sorry I took the twins out of the—"

"Shh. Not another word. No way could you have expected a bull to charge you." He caressed her hair, using his most reassuring tone, his voice husky with the rash of emotions pouring through him at what could have happened. "You saved my boys' lives. If not for your quick thinking…" He swallowed the lump that had suddenly risen in his throat. Alexa had risked her life to draw the bull away from the twins, and he owed her a debt he could never repay. The boys were his living legacy from Sandra, their hope for the future. The idea of anything happening to them was unbearable.

He shut down the thought. He had no business worrying about his own problems when a patient needed him. "Do you hurt anywhere?"

"Everywhere." Alexa let out an unladylike groan. "I feel like a wrestler who just got body-slammed. But I don't think it's anything serious. Just bumps and bruises."

"Any sharp pains?"

"Nada."

"How's your vision?"

"Now that the dirt's clearing from my eyeballs, you don't look so fuzzy."

"Did you bang your head? Any numbness in your hands or feet?"

Alexa pushed herself to a sitting position. "I'm fine." She looked down at her silk blouse, which had once been a pristine white, and grimaced with distaste. "Or I will be fine after I've had a hot soak and…"

She must have caught the look of "no can do" on Cameron's face. Just before the bull had interrupted his conversation, Cam had learned from the plumber that the water line wouldn't be hooked to the house today. The swimming pool would remain empty, and they'd continue to drink bottled water. One of the trucks had slid off the muddy driveway into the open ditch, crushing the PVC pipe. Another delay.

"I could take you up to the Senator's house."

"Not looking like a pig who wallowed in mud, you won't."

"The Senator won't care—especially after I tell him how you saved his grandsons."

"I care." She started to place a pleading hand on his

arm, saw all the mud and pulled back. "Can you hook a hose up to the unbroken part of the water line?"

Cam couldn't believe his ears. The woman had faced down a bull with the courage of a matador, and she was worried about someone seeing her with a little mud on her face? To her credit, she hadn't complained, only offered suggestions.

Cam humored her, sure she would change her mind. "You want to wash with a hose?"

He took Alexa's hand, helping her to her feet. She squared her shoulders and tilted her chin to look up at him. "Is there another choice?"

"The Highview Hotel—"

"No."

"Well, we wash the twins in the horse trough. But I don't think you'll fit," he teased lightly.

Her eyes flared. At first he thought with anger. But when she opened her fingers and flicked mud droplets at him, he realized she was amused, laughing at her ruined designer suit, laughing at the mud, laughing with relief that the twins were okay. That she was okay.

Several ranch hands hovered around. Bodine stepped forward. "You need any help with the hose, Doc?"

"See if you can rig up a makeshift shower out by the barn and bring towels and soap," he said, keeping hold of Alexa's hand just in case she slipped or was more injured than he thought. Her hand with those perfectly manicured nails encrusted with mud felt so small in his, yet there was strength in those fingers. He recalled her ripping off her jacket, flinging it aside. His breathing had almost stopped as he'd prayed her ruse would work and give him time to retrieve his gun.

She'd survived and now he hoped shock hadn't hidden any internal injuries. "How do you feel?"

"Muddy." She kept hold of his hand and surveyed the driveway. "What was that bull doing in your front yard?"

Good point. "Either he broke out of the paddock..."

"Or?"

"Someone didn't bar the gate properly."

She looked around warily as if expecting the bull to charge again. "Do animals get loose often?"

He squeezed her hand gently but couldn't control the hardness in his tone. "It's never happened before, and if I find out who the careless S.O.B. was, I'll knock his ears down so fast they'll do for wings."

She shot him an odd look. "Excuse me?"

"I'd hit him so hard he couldn't answer St. Peter's questions."

"You talk funny when you're riled."

"You could have been killed." With one finger, he tipped up her chin, looked directly into eyes as green as the San Juan Mountains. "I'll never forget what you did. I don't know how to thank you."

She cocked her head to the side. "I can think of a way."

Once again, she made him very aware she was a woman. It wasn't just her muddy white blouse molding her body like plastic wrap that had him noticing she had curves in all the right places, but her attitude. Her sassy reply and the glint of devilry in her eyes rocked him back onto his heels.

He didn't like the way she made him notice her. Not one damn bit. Not that he could blame Alexa for looking good. Healthy. Alive. But Sandra was still in his thoughts.

Rarely a day passed by where he still didn't reach for the phone to tell her an amusing annecdote or to remind her to pick something up for the twins. In his thoughts, in his dreams at night, Sandra was part of his life. And although logic told him she was dead, in his heart, he felt looking at another woman was a betrayal.

Crossing his arms over his chest, he eyed her warily. "What?"

Her eyes misted, surprising him as they turned a soft, hazy sea-green. "You can help me keep a promise."

She started into the barn and he followed. So she was finally going to admit the reason she'd come. Had she promised her grandparents she'd try to convince him to give up the twins? If she thought he would capitulate to the Barringtons' demands to surrender custody of the boys, she'd miscalculated badly. Giving up his sons wasn't an option he would consider. Ever.

Perhaps he was misreading her intentions. Cam waited patiently, without jumping to further conclusions, leading her past the barn toward the exterior horse stalls. The woman had almost died saving his sons. He wasn't about to accuse her without hard information. Keeping his patience wasn't even a stretch, not when he really wanted to check her more carefully to reassure himself she was all right.

"Who did you promise?" he asked, stopping just outside the stall.

"Sandra." Alexa held eye contact with him as if by holding his stare, she could will him to believe her. "Before she died, Sandra made me promise her that the boys would never be raised by nannies or sent off to a boarding school."

Surprise and doubt must have flickered in his expression. "I have no intention of—"

"But my grandparents do."

Suddenly the reason for Alexa's unexpected visit focused like a microscope's lens. The woman was just full of surprises, and he felt shamed by his earlier suspicions. "You came here to help me?"

Alexa left him behind, entering the stall and talking while she stripped and threw her muddy clothing over the top of the door. Cameron had inherited the barn along with acre upon acre of rich pasture land after his father had divided up the ranch among his sons. None of the brothers had yet built their own barns, so all of them kept their horses here.

It might be the ultimate in barns, but Cam couldn't believe Alexa could so contentedly shower here. This was where the grooms washed down the animals before leading them into their stalls. Thick wooden slats lent Alexa some privacy, but the cracks were wide enough to get an eyeful if a man stood close enough.

Cameron turned his back—although Alexa didn't seem overly concerned by his presence. She must figure he was immune to nudity because he was a doctor.

But he was also a man. A man with burgeoning needs and whetted desires. Was it just his time to awaken from more than a year of mourning? Or was something inside him responding to Alexa Whitfield on a level he couldn't assess? As a man of science, Cameron Sutton no more believed in instantaneous love than he believed in little green men. Yet he couldn't deny the heat in his loins as he listened to her speak over the shower, imagined the cool droplets sluicing away the mud to reveal pink skin, slender curves and those long, long legs. And he fought hard to suppress the image, an image that didn't belong there.

"Sandra's last words should pull weight with a judge." Alexa spoke as if oblivious to the fact that only a few rails of wood and his honor were all that protected her from his eager gaze.

But his imagination left him no peace as he envisioned Alexa raising her hands to shampoo her hair, back arching delicately, face spattered with water droplets. Forcing himself to concentrate on her words, instead of the erotic images in his mind, he broke into a light sweat.

The hearing wasn't for another week. "The judge may

not let you speak. I'm sure any good attorney will claim your testimony is hearsay.''

''Exceptions are made when the children's mother is deceased.''

''You've consulted a lawyer?''

She must have heard his incredulous tone, for she responded with a self-assurance that surprised him. ''Don't you understand the enormity of what's at stake? I assure you my grandparents will spare no expense to win custody. They'll arrive with a barrage of attorneys to fight you.''

''I've never understood why they would contest a father's custody. They're your grandparents. Aren't they too old to raise children?''

Cameron really wasn't too concerned. His very competent attorney had assured him that a judge wouldn't favor the great-grandparents over the father unless some very unusual circumstances prevailed—like the father being committed to a mental institution or convicted of a crime.

The hose finally stopped running, and he heard her drag a towel off the rails and the swish as material wrapped around her body. He pictured the towel's corner tucked between her breasts, above several inches of bare thighs and shapely calves, and decided not to turn around.

''The issue isn't age. It's money.''

''I don't understand.''

''You mean you don't know?''

At the sharp edge in her voice, Cameron turned, despite his intention not to. ''Don't know what?''

With her hair slicked back off her face, water droplets spiking her eyelashes and the soft pink towel clinging to more curves than he'd remembered, his mouth went dry.

''Our great-grandfather was Arthur Levenger. Ever hear of him?''

''Of course.'' He strove to keep his voice at a conversational level. The woman had no idea how she was affecting his pulse rate. "Wasn't he one of America's last great robber barons, the industrialist who made a fortune in the shipping and oil industries during the last part of the nineteenth-century?"

She raised her arms and twisted excess water out of her hair. He swallowed hard, waiting for the towel to fall, but she'd secured it well, and he didn't know whether to be relieved or disappointed.

She reached into the bag a ranch hand had carried for her from the SUV and opened a jar of cream. Slowly she dabbed it on her arms, her elbows, her wrists, working it into her skin as she spoke. "Old Arthur set aside an enormous trust fund. While he ensured an ample legacy for his heirs, Levenger's will stated that the first *male* heirs would inherit the majority of his vast wealth."

He watched her sit sideways on a bench and smooth the cream over her toes, calves and ankles as if she was in a boudoir, not a horse stall. "So?"

"The interest has been compounding for over a century and the estate has been overseen by the shrewdest Wall Street investors."

"And?" How could he concentrate when he found her every movement provocative?

"Your sons are the first male heirs since the old codger died. Do you understand what I'm saying?"

"I'm not that interested in financial matters." He much preferred flesh and bones, genteel bones with creamy skin, although he didn't dare say so. Not when the flesh was so temptingly damp, pink and glowing. Not when the bones were aristocratic and reminded him of delicate sculptures. Not when he had no business looking at her.

"Your sons are two of the richest little boys in the United States."

Her words shocked him from his lustful thinking. Cam wasn't sure how he felt about her revelation, but he knew it would change his sons' lives in significant ways. While the Sutton family was wealthy in its own right and as a medical doctor he earned a good living, different kinds of wealth, spectacular wealth, came with a new set of problems. That kind of money made his sons a target for con men, kidnappers and terrorists, and debutantes.

Some day it would give the twins choices he wasn't sure he wanted them to have. But he still didn't understand the whole picture. "Your grandparents are already rich. What does the inheritance have to do with my boys?"

"Until the boys reach the age of twenty-one, whoever has custody of the Levenger heirs administers the trust fund."

Cam knew that vast wealth equated to power, but he still didn't understand the full implications—not until Alexa laid it out for him as she towel-dried her hair.

"The trust endows the arts, charities, medical research and makes political contributions. Whoever controls the trust has enormous power."

"Why didn't Sandra tell me?"

She didn't know. "Until recently, I didn't know, either."

"Power is what your grandparents want?"

"Power is what they don't want to relinquish." At his frown, Alexa paused in the braid she was twisting her hair into. "Apparently our grandparents administered the funds and never told Sandra about it. But that duty now belongs to you. Or it will, once the custody is finalized."

"My attorney doesn't think I can lose the boys."

"Don't be so sure."

His gut churned, but he didn't let his anger or suddenly rising fear show. Instead, he forced patience into his tone. "What do you mean?"

"Suppose the Barringtons' lawyer proves you're unfit?"

Despite his determination to remain patient, he couldn't keep the growl out of his tone. "And just how would they do that?"

Alexa faced him, her eyes sympathetic, her words hard. "You're raising your children in the wilds of Colorado, on a ranch."

"They can't take my kids from me because we live in Colorado."

"You're a busy medical doctor who almost lost his children to a loose bull…"

Was Alexa threatening him? Warning him? Or just showing him how a smart lawyer could twist things in court? Before Alexa's arrival, Cam hadn't realized the stakes. He'd thought the battle was over his sons, not his sons and their trust fund.

Should he bargain with the Barringtons? Give them control of the fund if they'd agree to drop the custody battle? Cam didn't care a flying fig about administering the trust, but was it fair to his boys to give away control of their inheritance?

"Cam?"

"Yeah?"

"You're awfully quiet."

"You've given me a lot to think about."

"Well, think about this." At the sharp edge in her tone, he paid close attention. "Could someone have set that bull loose to discredit your parenting ability?"

For a moment he wondered if the scare had addled her thinking, seeing conspiracies where none existed. But she'd been too logical, too methodical in leading this conversation where she wanted him to go for him to believe she was overreacting out of fear. He sought to reassure her.

"Most likely a hand forgot to bar the gate."

"But it could have been left open deliberately, couldn't it?" The way she kept insisting the accident had been intentional sent a chill down his spine. That little stunt could have cost her and his boys their lives.

Still, he couldn't buy her line of reasoning. Setting the bull loose was like firing a gun without aiming. No one could have predicted where a loose bull would go or whom it would attack. True, Alexa had been wearing a flapping red skirt, but how could anyone have known that before she'd arrived?

Unless someone had seen her at the airport and driven to the ranch while they'd eaten burgers in town.

Cameron looked around uneasily, wondering if someone was spying on him this minute, taking pictures with a tele-photo lens.

"If my sons don't survive—" he could barely speak the words "—who controls the trust?"

Alexa's face paled. "My grandparents. But I don't think they would resort to..."

"Murder?"

Chapter Three

Cameron couldn't believe how long it took Alexa to dry herself, dress and accompany him to the house, although he had to admit she was worth waiting for. He didn't expect a woman who seemed comfortable showering in a horse stall to be such a perfectionist about her appearance. He couldn't decide whether to be annoyed or fascinated, especially when he was anxious to check in on the twins. Soothing his impatience by telling himself the hands would shout from the house at any sign of trouble, he paced, waiting for Alexa.

Finally she joined him and he took her suitcase. She had twisted her hair into some kind of fancy braid that showed off the delicate diamonds in her ears and the lovely arch of her neck. She'd reapplied makeup, and her glossy pink lips now matched a pastel shirt, form-fitting cream slacks and sandals. She'd even switched purses to match her shoes. He supposed he should be grateful she hadn't made him wait so she could reapply matching nail polish, too.

As he walked alongside her, however, he couldn't help appreciating the reapplication of her exotic perfume. And his mouth watered.

Uncomfortable with his thoughts about Alexa, uncomfortable with the suspicions she'd planted in his head, he broke the silence, striving for normalcy. "You've become comfortable with children."

Her lips turned up with pleasure. "I've been practicing."

For children of her own? So there *was* someone special in her life. Although he couldn't imagine Alexa giving up her life of constant traveling, perhaps she'd found a house-husband amenable to staying home with children while she was away. He didn't know why the thought of her finding someone bothered him, but it did.

Seemingly unaware of his disapproval, she strode by his side, her long legs having no trouble keeping up. "Sandra once told me if I didn't try with children, I'd never learn. So this past year, I've been reading every book I could get my hands on, practicing on my friends' kids. I was surprised to have so much fun."

"They can be a hell of a lot of work, too. The way you handled Flynn and Jason, I'd say you're now a pro."

"I started learning because Sandra dared me." Alexa stopped walking and looked at him. "Does it bother you when I talk about her?"

The direct question took him aback. Alexa's forthright-ness kept catching him by surprise, and he found his respect for her upping another notch. He kept forgetting that behind the delicious-looking package was a woman with keen intelligence.

"Actually I find the memories comforting." Still, Cameron made an effort to turn the conversation back to Alexa. "So are you taking Sandra's advice and getting married? Raising a few kids of your own?"

Alexa frowned at him with as much confusion as if he were a three-headed calf. "Where'd you get that idea?"

He thought he heard a flicker of pain in the sharpness of her tone and didn't understand what caused it. "I'm sorry. I just assumed you were preparing..."

"I was preparing for my next visit with the twins."

From the closed look on her face, Cam knew he'd touched a nerve. He didn't pry. They started walking again in silence, but he refused to let it go on too long.

"Sandra hated this ranch. She always called it primitive, but I thought the boys would grow strong out here. I want them to come to love this place as much as I do."

Alexa surveyed the muddy driveway, the puddles, and then raised her eyes past the house to the verdant sun-drenched valley, the towering mountains, and breathed deeply. "There's a peacefulness here you can't find in the city." She turned to him, her mood changing with lightning swiftness. "But if you think for one moment I'm walking through that mud…"

He restrained a chuckle. "It's the only way to get to the house."

"One mud bath a day is enough for any woman." She stepped closer and placed her hands on his shoulders. "So carry me?"

There was no sexual innuendo in her tone, her demeanor or her actions. And yet every nerve in Cam's body went on full alert. He didn't want to touch that skin, flushed, creamed and perfumed after her shower. He didn't want to hold her close enough for her to feel his heart racing. He didn't want to think of her as a woman. He didn't want to want her.

But he'd be a cad to refuse her simple request. She was a tiny woman with a delicate frame. But lifting her into his arms wasn't effortless. How could it be when it took all his effort to steady his breathing, to act as if he couldn't feel the soft curve of her breast against his chest and the wisps of silky hair that had escaped her braid teasing his neck?

She placed her arms around his neck, and he started along the driveway knowing that after holding her in his arms, he'd go to bed tonight wondering what would have happened if he'd lowered his mouth to hers. And damning himself for his urges. Although Cam wasn't pleased by his newly awakened interest in the opposite sex, the timing could have been better; the woman could have been someone more appropriate.

Alexa was not for him. She was Sandra's cousin. A woman who traveled the world for her career. She was direct and sassy and trouble. He told himself not to look at her, not to breathe in her scent, not to think how good she felt in his arms.

He would react this way to any woman. He'd simply neglected certain needs too long.

He was lying to himself. He didn't know how, but she'd kindled an ember from the ashes of his heart.

Those glossy pink lips were irresistible. Impulsively he lowered his head until their mouths were inches apart. He felt her quick shiver in his arms, saw a flicker of surprise and need in her eyes, knew she could avoid his mouth if she wished. Instead, he saw interest blaze, a spark flare, which fueled him on.

He nibbled softly at her upper lip. Once. Twice. When that teasing taste warmed his blood, he crushed his hungry mouth to hers.

He'd been prepared for her to turn her head away, mutter a protest, or scream, or scratch, or slap. And he would have stopped, forced himself to be satisfied with just a quick sample. Although he'd once been a man of large appetites, he took no pleasure in forcing himself on an unwilling woman.

He'd been quite unprepared for Alexa to willingly kiss him back, creating an explosion of impressions. Searing. Sunny. Sensational. She was kissing him with a hunger that matched his own. Her arms wound around his neck and into his hair, drawing his head closer.

And their mouths fit perfectly, her lips giving and giving and giving. She radiated passion, warmth, desire, inflaming him and drawing him deeper.

A hot kittenish moan at the back of her throat demanded and surrendered. She wrapped herself tighter to him, her soft curves pressing against him, shooting waves of fire to his core.

"Ahem." The interruption came from outside the web of passion she'd woven around them.

"Go away," Cam muttered.

Alexa's hands suddenly slammed into his chest, and Cam looked up to see his brother Chase sitting on a horse and looking down at them with sheer mischief in his eyes. "I hate to interrupt."

"Then don't," Cameron growled, his thoughts hazy, dipping his head to reclaim those soft voluptuous lips.

"Stop." Alexa's hand pressed him back. "I said no."

Chase chuckled. "You'll have to forgive him—he's out of practice."

Hot blood pulsing through his veins made patience impossible. Cameron could have strangled his brother, would get rid of him as soon as he got his breath back, as soon as his hands were free.

In truth, he was angrier with himself than his brother. As the sensual haze cleared and he realized what he'd just done, Cam knew he'd mostly himself to blame for his actions. He'd been the one unable to halt his impulse to kiss her. He'd been the one who'd forgotten that Alexa had just gotten off the plane this morning and almost been killed. He'd taken advantage of her vulnerability.

Cam took most of the blame on his shoulders but the

woman in his arms had to share some of it too. She could
have turned her head away from his kiss. But she hadn't.

Even now heat rose to Alexa's cheeks as she peered at
Chase, who tipped his hat. "Chase Sutton."

"Alexa Whitfield." Although Cam still held her tightly
against his chest, she held out her hand to his brother. "This
is crazy. I wasn't kissing him."

Chase raised her hand to his lips and kissed her wrist—
no doubt to annoy Cam. "I wish I wasn't getting kissed
like that."

"I'll tell Laura you said so," Cam warned.

Chase's eyebrows rose, and he immediately dropped Alexa's hand. Cam's brother genuinely adored his wife and
sons, and Cam would never follow through on his threat.
But keeping Chase on his toes came as naturally as
breathing.

Alexa refused to meet Cam's gaze. "Cameron took me
by surprise. I had no idea, he would... I'm not interested,"
she explained weakly.

Cam eyed her skeptically. "Then why were you kissing
me back?"

Alexa sputtered, radiating indignance. "You...you—"

"—Look, I hate to interrupt such an interesting discussion," Chase said, "and you can be sure Laura will want
details when I get back, but I didn't ride over here for the
air—however hot it may be," he teased, then turned serious
gray eyes on Cam. "Keith's running a fever and Laura
wants you to take a look at him."

Cam shook his head to clear it, trying hard to think.
"We've had a little trouble around here. I hate to leave the
twins."

"I'll watch them," Alexa volunteered.

Still carrying Alexa, Cam started walking toward the

house, and his brother stayed mounted as he walked his horse beside them. "I don't know if that's a good idea."

Alexa huffed. "You don't trust me?"

Cam explained to Chase about the loose bull and finished summing up by the time they arrived at the front porch. Cam eagerly set Alexa back on her feet, anxious to break the connection between them but missing the feel of her in his arms.

Chase rubbed his chin. "I'd bring Keith to you, but I don't want the twins to catch anything. Why don't I have some of the hands come in from the pasture and work close by? Alexa can phone if there's a problem."

Nodding in agreement as they walked inside, Cam grabbed his bag. "How high is Keith's temperature?"

"A hundred and three."

Alexa looked around the unfinished house, her eyes curious. "You *live* here?"

His thoughts already on his nephew, Cameron ignored the lack of furniture, drywall, plumbing and electricity. "I told you it wasn't done. I'll take you to the hotel after I get back."

Alexa didn't seem to hear him. She peeked into the kitchen—or what would be the kitchen, once appliances and cabinets arrived. "I love the beautiful tongue-and-groove oak ceiling. Mind if I rearrange a few things? Oversee your workers?"

What could it hurt? Cam didn't have a knack for overseeing construction, and he knew it. And he hated dealing with hired help. However, the house was much closer to completion than it looked. One pipe connection would hook up water to the finished sinks, showers and hot water heater. All the electric wires had been run and just required attachment to the circuit box. The house lacked one window pane and the downstairs drywall could go up in a day. But the contractor gave him excuse after excuse. The plumber couldn't find the right parts, and the electrician never bothered to finish the job. A few ranch hands and the babysitter, Julie, were his only reliable help.

Before Cam could agree to letting Alexa baby-sit, his cook, Ray Potter, barreled into the room, mopping his sweating face with a red bandanna. His face flushed with anger, his bushy eyebrows twitching, the cook exuded rage that blasted everyone in the room.

Beads of sweat dribbled from Ray's forehead to his jowled cheek. "The contractor promised I'd have a kitchen by now." The cook pointed at Cam. "You promised I wouldn't be working under these primitive conditions for more than a week. Well, it's been a month, and I don't have a refrigerator or a stove or a sink. You have me outside in this heat, cooking over a camp stove. It's bad for my blood pressure. Bad for my heart. I quit."

Amusement twinkled in Alexa's eyes as the cook turned on his heel and huffed out of the house. To give her credit, she didn't crack a smile.

Cameron supposed Alexa couldn't make a mess of setting up a household any worse than he had. "Feel free to take over. Make yourself at home."

Alexa nodded. "I'll just check in on Cody and the twins, and then talk to your contractor."

"Uh-huh." Glad to leave the entire situation in her hands, glad to put some physical distance between them, Cam checked his medical bag, making sure he had several antibiotic samples. Keith was prone to ear infections, but his temperature didn't usually run so high.

Alexa's soft voice interrupted his thoughts. "I might buy a few things. Groceries. A shower curtain, drapes."

"Fine. Use the phone to order, and ask Cody to pick up your purchases in town." Cam snapped his bag shut and grabbed a hat off the door. "My cell phone number's nailed on the kitchen wall. Call if you need me."

Alexa snapped her fingers. "Not so fast, Doctor."

Her words stopped him and he turned to see a mischievous glint in her eye as she held out her hand to him, palm up. "You're forgetting that I need something."

Beside him, Chase restrained a smile as if he could read Alexa's mind. Cam didn't have a clue.

Slightly annoyed Chase knew something he didn't and irritated she was delaying him with talk about the sad state of construction when he needed to examine Keith and return quickly, he restrained an impulse to snap at her.

"What do you need?"

"Your credit card."

"You don't have one?" he couldn't resist asking, knowing full well how wealthy Alexa was.

"It's your house."

Cam opened his wallet and tossed it to her, anxious to be on his way. He'd avoided buying stuff. He hated making the decisions about the house when he was itching to open his medical practice. Besides, how much damage could one woman do with a credit card in just a few hours?

FOUR HOURS LATER, Alexa felt satisfied with the work she'd accomplished. Cameron's house had a masculine architecture that simply needed a woman's touch to make it home—that is, if the contractor ever finished the construction. Soaring ceilings and floor-to-ceiling windows invited the magnificent view inside.

Now all the house needed was drywall, flooring, interior carpentry, electrical hookups and plumbing. Then the real work of interior decorating could begin. Alexa couldn't help imagining how she would emphasize the massive stone fireplace with a Moulie, the only living artist to hang in the Louvre. But art should have been the last thing on her mind.

Cody had been wonderfully helpful, the lanky ranch hand bringing the groceries, furniture and supplies she'd ordered from town into the kitchen where she stacked the smaller items in the doorless pantry. She'd put Cameron's credit card to good use, and all afternoon, every time she thought of that kiss he'd stolen, she'd taken pleasure in running up his bill.

Damn him! Whatever had possessed the man to kiss her? She hadn't flirted. She hadn't been interested. For years, Cameron Sutton had belonged to Sandra and only Sandra. He'd loved her cousin, been good to her, fathered her children. And not once had Alexa ever thought of Cameron as anything but a good man, a fine catch for Sandra. But one kiss had changed everything. One kiss had knocked her socks off and she still hadn't recovered. Every time she thought about that kiss, her pulse raced. Every time she thought about that kiss, her blood heated. Every time she thought about that kiss, she got angry, confused and embarrassed all over again. Talk about dynamite. His kiss had been pure Fourth of July fireworks—the red-hot kind, with sparks that rocked almost every belief she'd ever had about men and women.

Alexa didn't believe in chemical attraction that ignited with a simple kiss. She didn't believe in falling for a tall, dark and handsome man who so obviously needed a wife and would undoubtedly want more children. And she certainly hadn't come out West for an affair with her nephews' daddy. Sandra's husband.

Yet, kisses that marvelous didn't happen to Alexa. She didn't even dream about kisses that marvelous. She couldn't figure out exactly what had happened to make her forget everything except Cameron Sutton.

As much as she'd denied her actions, she *had* kissed him back. She hadn't wanted to admit it to him, and even now she didn't want to admit it to herself. Alexa kept telling herself she wouldn't think about that kiss, wouldn't think about Cameron—not as a man with eyes of pure sterling and gilded with silver light. Or with lips that had made her so aware she was a woman.

But as the afternoon wore on and she called the general contractor, electrician and plumber while keeping an eye on the twins, she discovered that her resolution to forget that kiss was impossible.

If she hadn't promised Sandra to look after the twins, she'd have been tempted to leave the moment Cameron returned. But one kiss, no matter how devastating, wouldn't make her go back on her promise to her cousin.

Cody Barnes brought in the last sack of groceries and set them by her feet. "What should I do with the rest, ma'am?"

When she looked at Cody, he blushed. She ignored his high color, suspecting the young man would have been more comfortable outside with the other ranch hands. He might have even taken some teasing about helping with the twins, yet he hadn't complained. Alexa couldn't help noticing that Cody kept looking out the front window, seemingly anxious for Julie to return from class.

Alexa left the groceries and spied through the window the pickup truck piled high with her credit-card purchases. While she instructed the lanky hand, she caught him watching a car pull in down the road. As the blond-haired, brown-eyed Julie exited her car, Cody followed the coed's every move. Obviously he had a crush on the children's baby-sitter.

Alexa kept the knowledge to herself, knowing a comment would just embarrass the young man. "Please place the grill on the patio and find someone to hook up the propane tank. For now, we can use the pool furniture inside.''

Two hours later, Alexa looked around with weary satisfaction, grateful that Julie had returned to occupy and feed the twins so she could keep working on the house. The cheerful college student had the twins on her lap and had just finished reading them a story.

Flynn tugged Julie's hair. "Pretty."

Julie laughed and kissed the top of the little boy's head. "All right, buster. Why are you trying to butter me up?" When she spied Alexa watching her, she gestured for her to join them on the floor. "You have to watch out with these fellas. If they give you a compliment, that means they are about to ask for something they aren't supposed to have."

Jason grinned and played with Julie's hair, too. "*Is* pretty."

Alexa settled cross-legged on the rug that Cody had spread before the uncompleted fireplace. Julie, with a loving smile, gently tugged her hair out of reach. "Can you imagine these two heartbreakers at eighteen or twenty?"

"I'm sure every Harvard coed will be after them."

Julie raised a blond eyebrow. "Harvard?"

"Sandra took out one of those prepaid tuition plans when they were born."

"Wow! That's really awesome." The phone rang, and Julie turned to her charges, who were both fighting sleep and actually sitting still for a change. "Well, you guys had better be smart enough to attend an Ivy League school. And smart boys need their sleep."

She gathered them up amid drowsy protests while Alexa answered the phone. "Hello."

"I'll be back within half an hour," Cam's soft drawl purred through the phone lines.

"How's Keith?"

"Fever's down. I needed to watch him for a while before deciding whether to give him an antibiotic. But he's fighting off the infection on his own and the little tyke's going to be just fine." Just then, one of the twins let out a piercing whoop. "You managing okay?"

"We're fine."

"Julie usually leaves for her dorm around eight. Ask her to stay with you until I get home. I don't like the idea of you and the boys being alone."

While she appreciated his concern, she hardly thought Julie could protect her. Besides, Alexa had traveled the world, and while she didn't carry a six-shooter in her purse or a knife in her garter, she'd managed alone for more years than she cared to admit.

Changing the subject, Alexa twisted the phone cord around her finger. Despite her work this afternoon, she'd taken the time to change her nail polish to a soft pink. Looking good gave her courage, and she might need all the courage she could muster after Cameron realized how much of his money she'd spent.

Suddenly a little nervous and a lot guilty, she blurted, "I may have gone a little overboard with your credit card today."

"It's all right. I may not be as wealthy as your grandparents, but I'm not exactly poor. I'm a doctor, remember?"

His voice had a caressing quality that made her distinctly uneasy, since it brought back another vivid reminder of their kiss. Electricity had sparked through her. Perhaps she should take him up on his offer to stay at the hotel in town. She wasn't sure she trusted herself alone with him in this house.

By the time Cam returned thirty minutes later, she'd almost made up her mind to leave, but one look at his ex-

hausted face, his dark eyes crinkling at the corners from
weariness, and she knew she'd be selfish to make him drive
her into Highview at this late hour. He really looked beat.

"Was treating Keith that difficult?"

He shot her a wry grin. "The vet's on vacation and one
of Rafe's mares went into labor. I kept telling him I'm an
MD, not a veterinarian, but he wouldn't take no for an answer. I don't know which was worse, calming the mare who
kept trying to kick me or calming my brother who kept
threatening to punch me."

"He *didn't!*"

"He would have if I'd tried to leave. He considers the
horses his children."

Cam spied the contemporary rugs, a mixture of jute and
wool, scattered across the bare plywood subflooring. They
lent a rich texture to the foyer, and he carefully wiped the
mud off his shoes on the new mat she'd purchased. He
visibly perked up as he entered the kitchen and surveyed
the wrought-iron breakfast bar and wine rack in the corner
with two comfortable leather-seat stools that slipped out of
the way when not in use. Wrought-iron pot racks hung from
the ceiling by double hooks holding a shiny collection of
hammered copper pots with riveted brass handles.

"I left all our old stuff in Boston. Haven't gotten around
to buying new furnishings."

"Julie told me."

"You've done wonders."

Alexa walked with him into the kitchen, not quite daring
to tell him what she'd ordered from the store's catalogues
to be delivered tomorrow. She took encouragement from
the fact that at least he seemed to like the changes she'd
made so far. "Have you eaten? Would you like something
to—?"

A loud scream from outside chilled Alexa to the bone. "Julie!"

Cam's gaze turned in the direction of the stairs. He was clearly torn between running upstairs to see to the safety of the boys and sprinting outside.

"Go!" Alexa pushed him toward the door. "I'll check the boys."

She grabbed a flashlight and hurried upstairs, staying close to the wall to avoid falling on the banister-less staircase that a carpenter had promised to finish tomorrow. At least the second story had drywall and was mostly finished. She hurried into the boys' bedroom and aimed the flashlight at their beds. With relief, she saw they were still sound asleep, their chubby faces clean and cherubic-looking.

Quickly, Alexa checked the entire upstairs for intruders. Cam's room had only a rolled-up sleeping bag in one corner and open suitcase in the other. The other rooms were empty. She found nothing unusual except a kitten she suspected the boys had sneaked into the house. Picking up the lost animal in one hand, keeping the flashlight in the other, she returned downstairs to find Cam carrying Julie into the house.

Julie clutched Cam with fingers tight with tension. Her wide brown eyes brimmed with tears that she tried to blink away. Cam gently set her on the rug.

Alexa set down the kitten and hurried over, her mind teaming with questions. "What happened?"

Julie sniffed and stared at Cameron. "I was using the Porta Potti. When I came out, someone grabbed me from behind. I jabbed my elbow into him, and he threw me down."

"Did you see him?" Alexa asked as Cameron checked Julie's pupils with a penlight.

"I was so scared I just panicked. I think I screamed and

fell, then everything went black. I opened my eyes…to find Cameron carrying me in here.''

Alexa's neck prickled. ''Did your attacker say anything?''

Julie shook her head and winced. ''No.''

''There isn't any blood.'' Cameron ran his fingers over Julie's head. ''Does this hurt?''

''A little. I must have banged it when he threw me down.''

Two near disasters in one day was just too much of a coincidence for Alexa. One look at the worry in Cam's eyes told her he was thinking the same thing. If someone had deliberately let the bull loose and that same someone had then attacked Julie, what could be his motive?

Robbery, rape, murder? Nothing made sense. And what could be the reason for attacking two different women? At a new thought, the hair on Alexa's neck prickled.

In the darkness, could the attacker have mistaken Julie for Alexa?

Chapter Four

Cameron called Noel Demory, Highview's sheriff, that night, and together they decided that his visit and investigation could wait until morning. Julie's friend, Leo Harley, had driven out to the ranch and taken her back to her dorm. Alexa had settled onto an air mattress in the guest room, and the rest of the night had passed peacefully.

The morning started at seven with a tempest of activity. Plumbers busily replaced the crushed water pipe. A loader filled in the dangerous ditch. The electrician actually thought he could hook up the wires to the circuit box and they might have electricity before dark. And despite the drywall shortage, a forklift unloaded pallets in the driveway, and carpenters busily tacked more drywall to the walls, covering the framing. Assistants followed behind with spackling tape and compound.

Alexa talked quietly to the workers, and the general contractor assured her the final window would be installed that afternoon. Cameron could have kissed her for putting his life back in order. But he wouldn't. Their one kiss had been too explosive. Playing with dynamite wasn't his style. Right now, he and the twins needed stability, and Alexa would no doubt leave in the same manner she'd arrived, with little forethought and no warning.

Sheriff Noel Demory arrived at eight sharp. At five-foot-eight and 130 pounds, he made up in common sense what he lacked in bulk and stature. He'd helped Chase and Laura with a problem a while back and Cam thought he could help here too. Although the sheriff wasn't too ambitious and kept a low profile around town, he had a knack for preventing trouble before it started.

Despite her scare the night before, Julie, reliable as ever, had shown up on schedule, taking over her chores with the twins, insisting she'd rather work than have too much time on her hands to think. Alexa remained quiet, sipping the coffee Cody had brought over from the Senator's kitchen where his mother worked. The twins, incorrigible as ever, raced trucks through the living area.

As Cameron ushered the sheriff inside, Alexa and Julie each grabbed a twin and handed them over to Cody, who took them onto the back deck by the pool that was filling with water and out of hearing range. Cameron noted how the boy blushed whenever he neared either woman and wondered if the poor kid would ever overcome his painful shyness.

Not that he blamed the kid for feeling flustered. Julie oozed cowgirl sexuality in a stretchy T-shirt that bared her midriff and navel over low riding jeans. And Alexa's classy emerald blouse and cream slacks, belted at the waist, showed off her flawless figure. He restrained a smile when he noticed once again that she'd painted her nails a soft pearl color that matched a choker at her graceful neck.

The adults settled onto the pool furniture Alexa had purchased yesterday. First, Cameron recounted Alexa's encounter with the bull. Then the sheriff listened to Julie's story, taking notes and asking many of the same questions Alexa had last night.

Julie's answers remained consistent. Alexa looked

thoughtful. The sheriff frowned at both women. "Have either of you dumped any boyfriends recently?"

Alexa and Julie both shook their heads.

"Maybe Cameron has an old girlfriend, someone jealous?" the sheriff asked.

Cameron set the record straight. "There was no one special before Sandra."

Julie sighed. "It was a man who attacked me."

"What makes you think so?" Alexa asked.

"The arm that grabbed me seemed...hard. Muscular. It was just an impression, nothing I can put my finger on."

The sheriff took notes. "Do you remember his scent?"

"Like aftershave?" Julie shook her head. "I'm sorry, I was just scared. It was so dark."

"Don't be silly." Alexa squeezed Julie's hand.

The sheriff turned to Cameron. "You fired anyone lately?"

"My cook, Ray Potter, quit yesterday."

Julie snapped her fingers. "In all the excitement, I forgot to tell you that my friend Leo would be happy to have the job. I told him to stop by this afternoon. Hope that's okay."

"I'll be happy to talk to him," Cameron said. He'd have the Senator look into Leo's background. With what had gone on around here, he wouldn't take any unnecessary chances. In fact, he might have his father run checks on all the new people.

"Let's look at the spot where Julie was attacked," the sheriff suggested.

Cameron had had another portable-toilet unit installed off the pool deck. "I did as you asked and roped off the area. No one's been there since last night."

"Good."

From her expression, Julie didn't relish the idea of returning to the crime scene. She walked outside, staying close to the sheriff. "What do you hope to find?"

"I'll dust the Porta Potti for fingerprints."

"Every construction worker on this site has likely been in there," Cam muttered.

"I'll look for footprints, or anything the attacker might have dropped."

Cam suspected nothing would prove conclusive. Julie's attacker could have dropped his driver's license on the spot where she fell and claimed he did so during the workday.

Alexa walked next to Cameron, but she kept her distance so that her hand couldn't possibly brush his. She looked so poised and put together this morning, acting as if their kiss had never happened. If only he could forget it.

Outside, the house hummed with construction activity. The hot-tub decking was finished and water trickled into it from a hose that must have been run from the main line. The sheriff took Julie's elbow and Cam reached over to guide Alexa around a mud puddle. Beneath his fingers, her muscles tensed, but she didn't pull away.

They rounded the corner, walking around an assortment of construction vehicles and supplies, and almost rammed into the sheriff and Julie, who'd halted at the sight of a forklift operator lowering a dripping-wet Porta Potti back to the ground.

The forklift operator saw them, shut off the engine and jumped down. "She's all pumped out and good as new. I hosed her down, too."

The sheriff frowned. "Didn't you see the rope around it?"

"Sure did." The forklift operator scratched his head. "I figured it was full and needed pumping, but she's ready to go now."

"You figured that out—all by yourself?" the sheriff asked, his voice tinged with disgust.

The worker's face lit in a proud smile. "Yes, sir."

Stunned, Cam resorted to muttering. "Amazing. Simply amazing. The one man on the construction site who is efficient, who needn't be told what to do, just destroyed any evidence the sheriff might have found."

Alexa patted Cam's arm. "It's unlikely the sheriff would have found anything."

"What about fingerprints inside?" Julie asked, looking unhappy that there would be no clues to solving her attacker's identity.

The operator's face fell as he realized he'd made a mistake. "I used cleaning chemicals on the inside, too, Doc." He turned to the sheriff. "I'm sorry."

Not as sorry as Cameron. Damn. He'd been hoping for the impossible—a nice easy solution to the questions that nagged him. He wanted to believe that the incident with the bull had simply been a careless ranch hand forgetting to bar the paddock. He wanted a reliable ranch hand to come forward and admit that he'd accidently bumped into Julie in the dark, that her scream had scared the man into running away.

Cam's phone rang, interrupting his thoughts. Chase told him Keith's temperature had returned to normal and that Laura wanted to invite them all over for dinner to thank him. "Can I take a rain check?"

Chase laughed. "You just want to play house, or is it you want to play doctor with Alexa?"

"Very funny." Cameron snapped shut his phone, relieved his nephew had recovered, and silently cursed his brother for calling up images of Alexa that had kept him tossing and turning last night. That kiss couldn't have been as special as he remembered. Yet he had to watch himself to avoid brushing against and touching the delectable-smelling Alexa every chance he got.

The foursome walked around the house, and Chase's phone rang again, this time a real-estate secretary reminding him of his appointment in town with a realtor. As Cam confirmed his appointment to look at a medical building where he might set up his practice, Alexa seemed thoughtful.

She kept her tone casual. "Since Julie can stay with the kids, mind if I ride with you into town?"

"I might be all morning." He knew better than to think she wanted to spend time with him. She'd set her expression to convey that her request was nothing personal.

Meanwhile, the sheriff and Julie had left them behind. Cam had Alexa all to himself for the moment. He realized the only way to decide if that first kiss had been pure dynamite or an aberration of his irrational mind was a repeat performance. There was no sense wondering about it, tossing and turning all night, when he could so easily discover the truth.

But Alexa must have read the sudden flare of intent in his eyes. She stepped back, slipping a little in the mud. Cam caught her and drew her against his chest. She felt as if she belonged there. As he breathed in her incredible scent, he murmured into her ear, "You needn't keep slipping in the mud to get into my arms."

Alexa's eyes sparked with annoyance. "If you think I slipped so you would… Why, you insufferably conceited, no-good—"

Cameron brought his head down and his mouth covered hers, hungrily. Last time he'd kissed her, she'd been surprised. This time she was like a hissing kitten, all fury and unsheathed claws. For an instant she could have pushed away, kicked his shin, boxed his ears. Instead, she offered as good as she got, flooding him with the taste of mint and coffee, impatience and greed. The engine noise of the fork-lift faded, as did the steady hammering and sawing. His blood thrummed to Alexa's beat, pouring music into his soul. Her response, electric, exciting, erotic, pulled him deeper, fired him hotter than he wanted to go. Somewhere along the line, his little test backfired. He couldn't imagine falling asleep tonight without reliving it.

Their first kiss had had him off balance. So he'd kissed her again to prove the first one had been an aberration. To get her out of his system.

But two such stunning kisses in a row could be no ac-cident. Passion sizzled between the two of them and Cam had no idea what to do about it. He needed to think. But how could he think when all he wanted to do was take her back into his arms?

What the hell was wrong with him? There could be noth-ing permanent between them. She was only here temporar-ily.

And there was nothing wrong with him. He was a man with needs and hopes and a future. He'd never felt more alive and he shoved his previous feelings of guilt at his attraction to Alexa from his mind. For now, for just this moment, he wanted to be free to explore the here and now.

After he finally pulled back, forced to breathe in oxygen, her blazing eyes locked on his. Clearly furious that she had reacted to him, she quivered like overstrung barbed wire ready to snap. That she couldn't control her fervor made the memory of the kiss all the sweeter.

Now that Cam had decided to treat his relationship with Alexa as temporary, he felt lighter. Sandra would never have expected Cam to live as a monk. He no longer felt that teasing or kissing Alexa was disrespectful of Sandra's memory. Sandra would have been the first person to tell him that life was for the living. And Cameron intended to enjoy Alexa's visit while she was here.

She wiped her mouth with the back of her hand and spit words at him as if she could wipe him away just as easily. "Are you insane? You can't keep grabbing and kissing me every time we're alone."

"Why not?" he drawled, finding that he liked making her cheeks color, liked teasing until she lost the chilly poise and the simmering passion beneath was exposed. "I like the way you kiss. And you can't deny that you were enjoying yourself."

"I wasn't!"

"Then why were you kissing me back so hard my lips are bruised?" He appreciated the way her nostrils flared and her backbone straightened.

"That's not the point. We can't...we shouldn't...we aren't right for one another."

He couldn't help savoring her embarrassment as he chipped away at Alexa's poise and she fought to find words. He couldn't stop teasing her. "That kiss felt mighty right to me."

"You idiot. I'm not talking about lust."

"Nothing wrong with a little lust." Cameron cupped her chin and smoothed her lip. "You're lipstick's smeared."

"And your ego's the size of the Rockies." In one of those lightning mood changes that fascinated him, Alexa stowed her hot anger and regained icy poise. She cocked her head to the side. "Take me to town, Doctor. I have some shopping to do. And then you can take me to lunch."

Cam eyed the frustration and fury warring in her eyes and recalled that she'd never returned his credit card. Idly, he wondered how much this kiss was going to cost him. He thrust his hands into his pockets to keep from pulling her back into his arms, deciding that whatever she spent, that kiss was worth it.

Because now he knew—the first kiss wasn't a figment of his imagination. The second one had been even better.

ALEXA TOOK ONE LOOK at Cameron's expression as he entered the hotel restaurant and realized lunch wouldn't be the peaceful meal she'd hoped. Nor would they have a rational discussion over the impulsive kisses that made her pulse leap with excitement as if she'd just discovered a new Monet. There was something different about Cameron, something light and boyish that made him tease her with a freedom that took her aback. But their talk would have to wait.

Cam, too, must have fought his way past the flashing bulbs of cameras, pushed his way around microphones shoved into his face by the press, to enter the relative haven of Highview's finest restaurant.

The custody battle between the Barrington family and the Colorado senator's son made great fodder for news-hungry paparazzi. And they'd come to Highview in force.

Cam wound his way past other diners, ignoring their curious stares, and tossed a copy of a tabloid newspaper onto the table. "Who do you think took this picture?"

Alexa saw a fuzzy black and white shot of a bull charging, its horns seemingly inches from her and the twins' terrified faces. The headline read No Bulls in Boston.

Alexa perused the story, a sick feeling in her gut as she realized how much the exaggerated story could hurt Cameron in court. "Your cook, Ray Potter, is quoted heavily. He took no time in selling the story. Maybe he took the picture, too."

Cameron closed his eyes briefly and then opened them as he rubbed his forehead. "My attorney says this kind of publicity will hurt us at the custody hearing. If the judge believes my children aren't safe, I could lose them…''

At the painful thought, his voice broke, and Alexa reached for his hand and squeezed. She hated to add bad news on top of the sensationalized story, but he needed to know exactly what he was up against.

She kept her voice low so as not to be heard by other diners. ''Do you realize my grandparents' corporation, Levenger Inc., owns the subsidiary that puts out this tabloid? They also own several television-news syndicates. I expect the story may wind up on the evening television news.''

Cameron lifted his head and thrummed his fingers on the table. ''Perhaps my father could get a gag order…''

''He can't.''

Alexa looked up at Senator Sutton, who pulled out a chair and joined them without being asked. She'd been so focused on Cameron, she hadn't noticed the distinguished senator's approach. But as he looked her over, she saw that his gray eyes were clouded with worry and the notable broad shoulders beneath the designer jacket, slumped just a little.

Although they'd met briefly at Sandra's funeral, Cam made the introductions.

The Senator's eyes narrowed and she was glad she'd taken extra time with her appearance before coming to the table. Since she knew the Senator was more likely interested in her motivation than the color scheme of her outfit, she readied herself for a confrontation.

''So you're the Barringtons' granddaughter.'' The Senator kept his voice civil, but a steely undertone warned her the outward charm hid a shrewd and possibly dangerous mind. ''I heard you were…visiting.''

She wasn't surprised he'd known she was staying with Cameron. Highview was a small town and a powerful man like the Senator would keep informed, especially since she'd moved in with Cam on Sutton land. Did he think his son was consorting with the enemy?

"She's also Sandra's cousin," Cam told him, defending her before she could do so herself.

But while Alexa appreciated his help, she didn't require it. Luckily she was accustomed to powerful men. Work often took her to the homes and the businesses of the successful and the wealthy. The Senator didn't intimidate her and she let him know it.

Alexa held out her hand and the Senator took it while he perused her unhurriedly. She'd bet not much got past the sharp-eyed man and hoped he recognized honesty when he heard it. Before he could object to her presence, she let him know which side she'd chosen.

"Sandra's dying request to me was to make sure that her children were raised differently than we were. After our parents all died together in a plane crash, my grandparents took us in. But we spent our time with nannies and later in boarding schools. Sandra didn't want that for the twins. I gave her my word. And I don't go back on my word."

"Glad to hear it."

Alexa suspected the Senator was merely reserving judgment. They ordered lunch before he resumed the conversation. "A gag order is out of the question. You ever hear of freedom of the press?"

"So what *can* you do to help?" Alexa asked with a boldness that at first startled the man and then had him grinning.

The Senator's dark eyebrow arched. "She's—"

"Sassy." Cam opened his napkin and floated it over his lap.

The Senator's eyes narrowed speculatively on his son. "I was going to say audacious."

From that teasing look in Cam's eyes, Alexa knew she'd better steer the conversation to safer topics. "I'll take that

as a compliment.'' Alexa kept her tone poised, determined
not to rise to Cam's baiting her. She'd already seen how
much he enjoyed teasing her about her reaction to his kisses.
But she couldn't go there. Not now. ''Senator, answer my
question, please. We've had other trouble that hasn't made
the paper yet.''

Cam shook his head and turned the page. ''Julie's encounter is right here on page two.''

Alexa shivered at the thought that someone was watching
them so closely. ''Ray'd already left before someone attacked Julie. Another traitor on the ranch?''

''You can't blame the men,'' the Senator said. ''These
rags offer a year's wages for a good story.''

''We could sue,'' Cam suggested.

Alexa shook her head. ''That would create more publicity, and besides, your custody hearing is already on the court
docket—long before a lawsuit can be filed, much less settled.''

''She's right.'' The Senator leaned forward. ''However,
I'm doing background checks on everyone. And I've put
extra security in place around the ranch.''

''Thanks, Dad. Add Leo Harley to the list. He's applying
for the job of cook.'' Cam looked thoughtful. ''In the meantime, I'll put off opening my medical practice.''

''That may not be a good idea,'' Alexa said, recalling
her talk with her grandparents' attorney. ''The court will
want to see that you're productive and stable.''

Cam's huge fingers clenched in frustration. ''What good
is being productive and stable if my family's in danger?
Someone let loose a bull, and if you hadn't thought so
quickly on your feet, the twins could have been hurt.''

''We still don't know if that was an accident or not,''
Alexa reminded him.

''Look, I hate to accuse anyone without proof.'' The Senator sipped his water. "But your grandparents have the most to gain from the boys' injury—which would help them gain custody."

Alexa shook her head, her throat constricting. These were her grandparents they were discussing. The grandparents who had taken her in and raised her. Even if they had sent her off to boarding school and raised her with a series of nannies, they had mailed birthday and Christmas presents. Sent her and Sandra on a world tour after she'd graduated from an exclusive art university in Paris. Not once had they raised their voices to her, spanked her or even scolded her. She couldn't imagine them concocting this horrible scheme.

"My grandparents may be ruthless in business, but they aren't murderers. And I don't believe they would endanger me."

Cam ignored the food the waitress delivered to the table. "Do your grandparents even know you're here?"

She shook her head.

The Senator gestured to the tabloid picture. "They do now. Have they called to ask if you're all right?"

They hadn't. "They may own a string of tabloids, but they don't read them." Even as she defended her grandparents, Alexa knew someone would have told them about the story. Why hadn't they called Cameron's house to check on her?

Doubts filled Alexa as Cameron drove his SUV and returned to the ranch. She couldn't help but admire the way Cameron didn't badger her with questions about her grandparents that she couldn't answer. She also liked the competent way Cameron drove, as if unaware of the press following them from town. He didn't speed or curse or in any way acknowledge their presence. Cam had the ability to compartmentalize his thoughts, focusing with intensity on one thing at a time. She wished she had that ability. Maybe then her thoughts wouldn't keep restlessly circling.

Exhausted from her busy morning of shopping and weary from thinking over the possibilities, she closed her eyes and listened to the country song on the radio station. Beside her, Cameron remained comfortably silent, having no need to fill the quiet time with idle chatter.

Drowsy but not asleep, Alexa noted the reporters' cars stopping at the guarded gate after Cameron turned onto Sutton land. Thankful for the ranch's vast acreage that provided a measure of privacy, she looked forward to newly installed plumbing and a hot shower, maybe a nap.

About five miles in, Cam drove onto the bridge and over the water-swollen river that irrigated the fertile valley, watering acres of grasses. Cattle grazed peacefully along the riverbanks under a cloudless blue sky.

Peace stole over Alexa. Suddenly the SUV lurched. The bridge exploded around them, under them. She screamed, lost the sound of her own voice in the roar.

Flames from the burning bridge engulfed the vehicle. And they were falling.

Plunging into the river.

The seat belt chewed into her shoulder as the SUV, no longer level, pitched forward and downward, spinning crazily.

Startled wide awake, reeling with confusion, Alexa braced her hands against the dash. Up became down. The truck fell and fell.

Her stomach cartwheeled. Her head banged the door.

Suffocating blackness engulfed her.

Chapter Five

Alexa opened her eyes to the fearsome sight of water cascading into the SUV at an alarming rate. Groggy, as if awakening from a drugged sleep, she fumbled for her seat belt and turned to Cameron.

Eyes closed, face pale beneath his tan, blood streaming down his forehead and over his cheek he looked lifeless. He didn't appear to be breathing.

"Cameron?"

By the time Alexa released her seat belt, the river water was as high as the dash. Unstable, the SUV suddenly rolled onto its side. Still strapped behind the wheel, Cameron keeled over and disappeared beneath the icy water.

Alexa fell on top of him.

Unconscious, Cam could breathe water into his lungs, drown within seconds. Without hesitation, Alexa ducked under the water. Reaching with her fingers, she wasted precious seconds searching for his seat belt.

The frigid water slowed her thinking. She used too much air before figuring out the SUV rested sideways and the release she searched for was straight down. Finally her numb fingers found the seat belt release and pressed.

She tried to jerk Cam upward. But the straps had caught him in a web. And her stiff fingers couldn't seem to unwrap him. If he wasn't already dead, he would drown unless she freed him soon.

Opening her eyes didn't help in the dark, swirling water. She couldn't see the straps against Cam's dark clothes, had to go by feel while her oxygen-starved lungs burned for air.

Finally she untangled the straps and he popped upward. Alexa surfaced to find the water up to her neck, the top of her head pressed to the passenger window which now faced the sky. Freedom looked so close.

Yet she had no way to open or break that window.

Grabbing Cam's head out of the water, she screamed in his face. "Cam, damn you! Don't die on me! Breathe! Damn it, breathe!"

Cam didn't flinch. She had no idea if he was breathing or even if he still had a pulse.

The water rose to her bottom lip. They had to get out. Fast.

Alexa tried to open the door above her head, but she had no leverage to lift the heavy door straight up. The only other option was to swim down to the driver's door and out from the underside of the SUV.

Oh, God! Every survival instinct she had made her want to claw upward, to daylight, to air. Yet, downward led to salvation.

She tried pushing Cam aside to reach the door beneath his feet. But there wasn't enough room to slip by. He was too big. And she'd never drag him out by herself. She couldn't do this alone.

She slapped Cam between the shoulder blades, hard. He choked, spit out water, opened his eyes.

Thank God. He was alive!

She eased his head back and tilted her own chin up, too, breathing awkwardly in the last few inches of air space, praying he could hear her. "We're in the river, Cam. We have to swim down to get out."

He dragged in air in huge rasps, didn't say a word.

"Cam. Listen to me. The driver's door is below your foot. Feel around with your shoe. Use your foot on the handle. Open the door."

Cam's face, what she could see of it, looked blank. Either he was gathering his strength and saving air to make an escape attempt or he was barely conscious. Alexa had no idea if Cam heard her or even understood her.

A long moment later, Cam slipped beneath the surface. She reached to tug him back. Missed.

Water rushed over her face. The last of the air trapped with them inside the vehicle vanished in a swirl of surging water.

They would go down fast now. If they didn't get out before the SUV struck bottom, they'd be sealed inside.

They would die in this icy darkness.

An odd rush of water churned by her feet. Hands gripped her ankles and pulled her down, down. She used every ounce of courage not to fight going deeper into the water, used her hands to push past the steering wheel, out of the vehicle.

Cam slid his hands up her body and somehow she grabbed his hand. He'd found the strength to pull them out.

Now they needed air.

The light above seemed tauntingly close as her lungs turned to fire. Together, they kicked and kicked to the surface, Cam holding tight to her hand.

When her head cleared the water, Alexa sputtered and drew air into her aching lungs. Her energy spent, dizzy, light-headed and half-frozen, she gasped and swallowed water. She sank back beneath the surface, couldn't find the strength to swim.

Somehow Cam dragged her to shore, made her crawl the last few feet. They both lay on the riverbank too exhausted to move, grateful to be breathing.

It took ten or fifteen minutes for the adrenaline rush to recede, for her breathing to approach normal, for her to appreciate she was still alive. Long minutes passed before her thoughts cleared enough for her to open her eyes and look around.

Rolling onto her back, she gazed at where the bridge used to be. "We almost died."

Cam raised himself on an elbow, cleared his throat. "I never thought I'd thank a woman for screaming in my face. Are you okay?"

"Okay? I'm not okay. I'm scared, cold, wet and mad as hell." She turned onto her side, and despite the blood still trickling from the cut on his head, he smiled at her. She wanted to slap him. "What are you grinning at?"

He kneeled, opened his arms wide in invitation. "Most women would be crying in my arms right now."

She'd like nothing better than a comforting hug but refused to give him the satisfaction. "You bumped your head and aren't thinking straight. This isn't funny. Someone tried to kill us."

He stood and helped her to her feet. "You're too feisty to kill."

She stomped her bare foot. Somewhere she'd lost her shoes. Water and mud splashed over both of them. "This is no time for jokes. Someone detonated an explosion as we drove over the bridge."

His eyes narrowed and he turned to look at the bridge. "You're sure?"

She looked at his head, examining the laceration and bruise around it. "You don't remember?"

"I was driving and the next thing I remember, we were in the water. You were shouting in my face, being bossy—"

"I'm not bossy."

"—and ordering me around, as usual."

"As usual?" She made a fist, restrained herself from socking him in the gut.

"I happen to like bossy women." His gray eyes turned smoky, a look she was beginning to recognize that happened only just before he kissed her. What was wrong with the man? They'd almost died. Now they were fighting. She looked like a wet fish, and he had this look in his eyes like he wanted to swallow her whole.

When his admiring gaze swept over her, Alexa looked down at herself. Her tailored blouse molded her breasts like a wet T-shirt, and even through her bra, her nipples puckered and peaked through. She tugged her shirt from her skin, but her effort to hide her physical reaction proved futile. The material resisted all her efforts to hang loosely.

That teasing tone roughened Cam's voice. "Why are you trying to hide? You have a lovely body."

"So do you. Do I undress you with my eyes?" she snapped, humiliated, annoyed and frustrated. He couldn't just pretend she looked normal. Oh, no. He had to go and call attention to the fact that she might as well be naked.

He reached out a hand to her. "You can't fault a man for looking at what's offered."

She slapped his hand away with more force than was necessary. "You idiot. I wasn't offering. I'm cold."

Cameron sighed and threaded his fingers through his hair, winced when he touched the swelling bruise on his forehead. "And I don't suppose you want me to warm you up?"

"Sure you can."

He arched an eyebrow and stepped forward.

She planted her palm on his chest, ignoring his hard muscles, ignoring his warmth. But she couldn't ignore the beat of his heart, fast and furious, against her hand. Yet she wasn't about to let him kiss her, because she didn't trust herself. Whatever was happening between them was happening way too fast. She was off-kilter, needed to think, wasn't about to succumb to the we-almost-died-so-let's-make-love rationalization. Not when she still often thought of Cam as Sandra's husband. "If you want to warm me up, buster, you can lend me your shirt."

"You're nothing but a little tease." His eyes narrowed in mock annoyance, but his lips curved upward. "And my shirt is just as wet as yours." Still, he unbuttoned his shirt and handed it to her.

At the sight of his bare chest, her mouth went dry. Bronzed skin dappled with water droplets emphasized lean muscles in a tantalizing display of light and shadow. And she was no longer thinking of him as anything but a man. A very attractive man. She'd always known that Cameron Sutton dwarfed those around him, just hadn't realized it wasn't his height alone that made him stand out with no hint of weakness. His muscular neck emerged from brawny shoulders and a barrellike chest lightly dusted with curly black hair tapered to a flat stomach.

Alexa struggled with his wet shirt, refusing to drool over him like some bimbo. So what if he had a body Michelangelo could have sculpted? So what if she ached to run her hands over him in appreciation as she would a fine piece of art? So what if her hormones had a life of their own?

Her hormones weren't in charge.

Her brain was.

The sound of hoofbeats drew her gaze to a nearby hill. A rider on horseback approached at a canter. She had no idea if he was friend or foe. But they had no weapons, no place to hide.

Cameron squinted into the sunlight. "That's Bodine. He's one of our regular summer hands."

The cowboy neared, his gaze shifting from the torn-up bridge to them. "I heard an explosion. Thought I saw a vehicle plunge into the river."

"That would have been us." Cam, revealed his gift for understatement. "I'd appreciate it if you could lend us your horse."

"That's not necessary," Alexa interrupted. Even she could see that Bodine wasn't keen on lending them his horse. The prematurely graying, salt-and-pepper bearded cowboy's face stiffened.

Cam ignored her protest. "I'll send back another mount for you."

"Okay, Doc."

Alexa looked at the horse and her stomach fluttered. "I can walk," she insisted, avoiding his gaze.

"It's seven miles back to the house." Cam removed the horse's saddle and set it on a boulder before turning back to the cowboy. "This should save some weight. I don't want to strain his back with us riding double."

The cowboy nodded.

"And in the meantime, don't let anyone near that bridge. The sheriff will need to examine it for evidence."

"Got it. I'll see if I can fix some kind of temporary road block—at least on this side."

Cam took the horse's reins and led the animal over to the boulder, mounting with ease, his tone casual. "Don't blame you for not wanting a swim. The water's kind of cold."

Bodine looked at the shivering Alexa and laced his hands together. "I'll boost you up."

"No, thanks."

"My horse is gentle, ma'am."

It wasn't the horse she was afraid of, but if the cowboy

wanted to think so, she had no intention of correcting his mistaken impression. Letting him think she feared his horse was preferable to stating the truth.

Cameron held out his hand, gray eyes bright with amusement. "Come on, darling."

Flustered, she snapped at him. "I'm not your darling."

"Ma'am, there's nothing to it. All you've got to do is sit there and hold on."

The expensive European finishing school Alexa had attended had made sure she knew how to ride. She also knew how to entertain royalty and oversee several households. However, her etiquette teachers hadn't taught her how to cope with awkward situations like this one.

Cameron's voice teased her. "Come on, the horse won't bite you."

At his taunting tone, she spoke without thinking. "I'm not afraid of the damn horse."

"Then what's the problem, sweetheart?"

"I'm not your darling. I'm not your sweetheart. I have a name, and it's Alexa," she fumed.

It was as if he knew what effect sitting behind his huge expanse of bare back would do to scramble her senses. She didn't want to sit behind Cameron, put her arms around his waist, cradle him between her thighs, and right now, he must be guessing her reason.

"I'm afraid of heights," she lied, grabbing the first excuse she could think of, knowing it sounded lame. Cam reached down, encircled her wrist with one powerful hand and tugged. At the same time, Bodine boosted her up, and before she knew it, she was mounted behind Cam.

"Hold on, sugar."

She gritted her teeth, gingerly put her arms around him. "The name's Alexa."

"Whatever you say, kitten."

Realizing the more she protested, the more he'd tease, she clamped her lips together. Cameron urged the horse into an easy canter, and Alexa had to tighten her grip around him. Her arms barely encircled him and she had to lean closer to maintain her grip. Even through her wet clothing, she could feel his warmth seeping into her. Every step of the horse, every bounce, pressed her breasts against his back, brought her cheek sliding against bared flesh. And all the while her open thighs rubbed intimately against him.

She tried to pull back, but the horse's rhythm kept sliding her against him, his musky male scent engulfing her every breath. To distract herself, she looked around, but the cows, barbed-wire fences and fluttering butterflies couldn't hold her interest for long.

When Cam slowed the horse to a walk, she tried once again to wriggle away, gain just an inch or two of distance between them. But the horse's back, slick from their damp clothing made her efforts futile. One second later, she found herself plastered to Cam again, and the heat seeping into her hadn't just warmed her. Her stomach rippled with tiny waves of taut tension. Her breasts, sensitized from the friction, ached for more. Refusing to think about how her body reacted to his, she took the opportunity to talk.

"How well do you know Bodine?"

The Senator had dropped off copies of employment records of everyone who'd worked on the ranch. Although Cameron had reviewed them, he'd already told her that he'd found nothing suspicious. "Bodine works here during the summers. Has a small ranch of his own north of Highview that he works during his off-hours. He used to rodeo, but quit after he busted his leg."

"Was he ever in the military?"

"I'm not sure. Why?"

"Well, someone had to know how to detonate that explosion. And he was close by."

Cam guided the horse through a gate into another pasture. "What reason could *he* possibly have to want us dead?"

Frustrated, she shrugged, and her breasts moved against his back. "I don't know."

"Will you please stop doing that?"

"What?"

"Squirming."

"I'm not—"

"Woman, you're wrapped around me tighter than a blanket. Trust me. You breathe, I know it."

"Sorry." Embarrassed, Alexa released her hands from his waist. If he continued to walk the horse, she needn't hold on so tightly. But now that her arms weren't holding her against him, only her breasts rubbed his back, somehow drawing even more attention to the limited contact. "Why don't I walk for a while?"

"Barefooted?"

She'd forgotten her missing shoes. She thought it'd be nice if *he* volunteered to dismount and walk, but he didn't. She couldn't just keep sitting there, rubbing against him like a cat in heat. "Maybe if I sat in front it would be better."

He chuckled. "Not for me, darling. Just sit still and quit rubbing your sweet little body all over my—"

"Shut up. Just don't say another word."

"And you say you aren't bossy?"

ALEXA HAD NEVER BEEN so glad to reach her destination in her life. The long ride back had been sweet torture, leaving her in turn frustrated, angry and embarrassed. She wanted to sneak into the house in her still-damp clothes, take a hot shower and wash away the tension thrumming through her.

They rode up Cam's driveway, and an assortment of vehicles revealed that visitors awaited. With the pipe laid and ditch filled in, Alexa surmised that at least the plumbers had finished connecting the water. If the electrical hookups had been completed too, she could dismount, go upstairs and take that shower she'd been dreaming about.

Grateful to slide from the horse's back and free herself from the constant contact with Cameron, Alexa walked gingerly to the front porch, aching in muscles she hadn't known she had.

Cam dismounted, too, and passed the reins to a ranch hand. "Cool him down and give him extra feed, then ride over to the bridge with an extra mount for Bodine."

"Okay, Doc."

Alexa headed toward the house, head down, watching that her bare feet didn't step on any construction materials. When a shadow loomed over her, she jerked and looked up to see a young man with earnest green eyes and the hulk of a body builder assessing her progress.

He stepped down the stairs to greet her and held out his beefy hand, biceps bulging. "Hi. I'm Leo Harley. I'm here about the kitchen job."

Alexa shook the young man's hand as Cam joined them. "I'm Cameron Sutton. Julie said you can cook?"

"Yes, sir."

"Have you seen the kitchen?"

"When will the appliances be arriving?" Leo asked pleasantly, and Alexa thought him a vast improvement over the sour demeanor of Cameron's former employee.

"Daddy!"

"Daddy!"

The twins spotted Cameron through the open front door, and tiny legs pumping, they took flying leaps into his outstretched arms. Cameron caught Jason in one arm, Flynn in the other. Both boys plastered kisses on his cheek.

"You're wet," Flynn declared.

Jason eyed Alexa. "You're wet, too."

"And dirty."

"Out of the mouths of babes…" At the new voice with the clipped Boston accent, Alexa froze.

It couldn't possibly be… "Grandma?"

Mrs. Emily Barrington stepped onto the porch. Regal and thin, her white hair cut in a becoming fashion, the Boston society matriarch took one look at Alexa's disheveled appearance and frowned. "You look like a ragamuffin."

Jason giggled. "Lexi's a muffin?"

"Can't eat Lexi." Flynn smiled at Alexa.

"I'd like to try," Cameron muttered low enough for only Alexa to hear.

She had to restrain herself from kicking him. She'd barely regained control of her raging hormones, and the thought he'd just put in her head made her senses start swimming all over again.

The front door opened, and her grandfather, Dalton Barrington, his silver-handled ebony cane tapping, stepped onto the porch. He held his head and bony shoulders with a proud, aristocratic air. Alexa hadn't seen him in months, but her grandmother's white-haired husband looked exactly the same. Stern. Disapproving and in total control of every nuance of his tight-lipped expression.

Beside her, Cameron stiffened, and without looking at him, Alexa felt anger radiating off him in waves. No one shook hands. To give Cam credit, his arms were full with the twins. And Grandfather didn't budge an inch, his haughty demeanor and pale blue eyes condemning them.

Leo Harley looked from her grandparents to Cam and obviously sensed tension. "Perhaps we should do the interview at another time?"

Cam shifted Flynn to the ground, then Jason, but kept

hold of their hands. "If you could take the boys to Julie, I'll be with you in a few minutes."

"Sure thing, Doc." Leo, eager to leave, helped the boys up the steps, then disappeared inside with them.

"And to what do I owe the pleasure?" Cam asked, walking up the steps onto the porch and towering over the Barringtons.

"We were worried about Alexa," her grandmother said in her cultured Boston accent.

For a moment, Alexa thought they'd come out of worry for her safety after reading about her close call with the bull. She started to join them, actually feeling warmed.

As if reading her mind, Cam shook his head and she hesitated in confusion.

One moment later, her grandfather flung a tabloid at Alexa's feet. "Consorting with the enemy?"

Alexa's heart iced over. She should have known their concern wasn't for her, but for their precious reputations, and wondered why the newest revelation hurt so much. Her grandparents were as cold as a Boston winter, unbending, unfeeling, so sure they knew what was best for her. She'd come to grips with what they were and what they weren't a long time ago, but she'd never stopped hoping for the affection and approval she'd craved all her life.

As children, she and Sandra had never been told they'd done a good job, never been told they were loved. They'd grown up under a string of nannies and had been shipped off to boarding school at the first opportunity. Summers, they'd spent at camps and finishing schools. The only warmth in the big old gusty mansion had been Sandra and Alexa's commitment to each other.

Her grandparents had taught them that well-bred young ladies only had their names in the paper when they married and when they died. To her grandparents, having one's name plastered across the front page of a tabloid was the equivalent of committing treason.

Alexa looked down at the paper to regroup, expecting to see the photo of herself and the twins. But this article in another rag was different. Much worse. In this paper the first kiss she and Cam had shared stared up at her from page one in living color. Who had taken the picture? And how had they gotten so close to the house without being noticed by one of the hands?

She couldn't resist scooping up the paper for a closer look. She looked so young and carefree, happy to be lost in the moment. Her eyes were shut, a dreamy look on her face. Cam held her tightly, his eyes open and fierce, hungry, like a warrior claiming his woman after a long campaign.

Their private moment had been printed for all the world to see. Alexa had to stiffen her knees to keep from staggering toward Cameron. As if sensing her need for comfort, he placed his hand over her shoulders and drew her to his side, barely glancing at the photo. His warmth and support gave her the strength to keep back the torrent of ugly emotions rushing through her, emotions as primitive and harsh as this wild land Cam lived in.

She wanted to scream and shout. Pitch a fit and insist they'd done nothing wrong. But she refused to give her grandparents the satisfaction of knowing how much they'd gotten to her.

Anger flooded her at the invasion of her privacy. That someone had watched their kiss was despicable. That someone had snapped the picture and sold it made her feel dirty. Her throat tight, she fought back tears.

"I'm not the enemy," Cam said softly to her grandparents, an edge of steel underlying his polite tone. "I'm the father of your great-grandchildren. Let's all go inside and talk."

Her grandfather pointed his cane toward the house's interior. "We've seen the way you live. It isn't suitable."

Grandmother fingered the diamonds around her throat. "It's dangerous."

Rage swept away Alexa's sadness. "How would either of you know what's dangerous for children? Neither one of you has ever taken care of—"

Her grandfather slammed his cane into the front porch. "Young lady, don't you raise your voice to your grandmother."

Alexa sweetened her tone but didn't hold back her true feelings. "I'm a grown woman and will speak however I choose."

"That's enough. This man has poisoned you against us. Pack your bags. You will stay in town with us until after the trial."

Molten steel poured through Alexa's veins. "And if I don't, what are you going to do? Take my trust fund like you're trying to do with the twins?" Alexa couldn't stop the bitterness in her tone. She raised the newspaper for emphasis. "Did you plant this picture?"

Dalton Barrington's mouth dropped open in surprise. "How dare you accuse—"

"—I dare." Fury such as she'd never known spurred Alexa on. "You want to control Jason and Flynn's trust fund so badly I think you'd go to any extreme, even sending the paparazzi to do your dirty work."

"That's ridiculous."

"Is it?" Cam spoke softly, razor-sharp anger heating his words. "Someone just tried to kill us. Yet, you made it safely over the bridge. And the only *strangers* around here have the most to gain from our deaths."

"Oh, God." Her grandmother's shoulders slumped. Her

voice dropped to a whisper. "Are you accusing us of murder?"

"Come on, dear." Her grandfather started to descend the steps, his head high and expression unrepentant. "I believe we've outstayed our welcome. We're leaving."

At last. Alexa couldn't wait to see their car depart. Right now, she didn't care if she ever saw them again. Despite all her churning emotions, she knew Cam had the most to lose from the bad publicity at the upcoming trial. A sickening feeling about what could happen after this current fiasco had her shaking. Even the fairest judge might question Cam's fitness as a father after seeing that kiss plastered across the paper. People would assume Cam was a playboy, an unfit father. A good lawyer could make it appear as if he was neglecting his children and cavorting with women. And after learning about the accidents, a judge might place the twins' safety above the need to stay with their father.

Cam sighed and shoved a hand through his hair. "As much as I'd like for you to leave, you're not going anywhere."

"And why is that, young man? Do you intend to hold us hostage?"

"Nothing that dramatic. The bridge is out. And until it's repaired, you're stuck here with the rest of us."

As Alexa realized the truth of Cameron's words, she swallowed a protest. The unfolding events were worse than a nightmare. Her grandparents living in the uncompleted house, scrutinizing everything they did, would give them ammunition in court.

One look into Cam's steely eyes told her he recognized the danger. But they had no choice.

"Surely there must be another way off the ranch."

"Only by horseback."

Clearly the elderly pair couldn't ride out. On numb legs,

Alexa sank onto the porch steps. She'd come out here at her cousin's dying request to help Cam keep custody of the twins. But her actions had made the situation worse. Now her grandparents would be watching their every move. With a sigh, Alexa wondered what else could go wrong.

Chapter Six

"Don't worry." Cameron squeezed Alexa's shoulder. "I'll have the Senator put up your grandparents at his house." He looked Dalton Barrington right in the eye. "I'm sure you and your wife will be much more comfortable there."

Emily Barrington's face, pale to begin with, turned paler. "We're stuck in this godforsaken place?"

Cameron controlled his temper. The frail old lady looked as if she thought Indians might ride across the valley and scalp her at any second. "Unless you want to ride to town on horseback or swim, you're our guests here until we repair the bridge and the sheriff clears you."

Alexa cocked her head to the side, and he could have sworn he saw a hint of mischief in her eyes. "You think the sheriff will suspect them?"

She might not believe her grandparents capable of murder, but she wasn't above letting them know she'd taken his side, and her open support meant a lot to him. "After our accident, we could see for some distance and we appeared to be alone. That means a timer set off the detonation. I'm hoping there're prints on a piece of the bomb."

Dalton snorted. "A bomb? As if I would know how to set off such a mechanism."

Cameron's eyes focused on the Barringtons' burly driver,

who stood ready to help his charges back into the car. "I'll bet your man there knows all about explosive devices. He has the look of ex-military about him."

Alexa nodded. "He doubles as a bodyguard."

If anyone had even implied—never mind almost accused—someone in Cameron's family was capable of murder, he'd be ready for a fight. But Emily merely straightened her skirt and kept her protest lukewarm as if discussing which tea to serve her guests. "Paul would never—"

"Hush, Emily," Dalton said. "Don't give them any information. They'll just use it against us in court." Alexa's grandfather pointed his cane at Cameron. "You'd better go spend the time you have remaining with your sons, young man, because I've hired the best attorneys."

Alexa sighed. "Too bad your motives aren't the best."

"Alexa!" Emily's face pinched into a frown. "You should know better."

"I heard Sandra's dying wishes. She wanted her boys raised by their father, not a series of uncaring nannies followed by boarding schools and summer camps. And I've come here to tell the judge her wishes."

Dalton pointed to the tabloid picture with his cane. "You think anyone will believe you after they see those pictures?"

"Of course they will—especially after I tell them who owns those trashy rags."

Alexa's expression didn't change, except for a shadow of pain hovering in the depths of her eyes. Despite her brave front, she couldn't take much more of this venom.

Cameron had had enough. "Perhaps you would care to wait on the porch while Alexa and I go inside and make arrangements for your stay at the Senator's house."

Without waiting for a reply, he ushered Alexa inside, away from the cold stares and harsh accusations. That San-

dra and Alexa had become warm, loving women after growing up with those two ice cubes was no less than a miracle.

He swept her immediately into his arms and kissed her
soundly.

He didn't pull back until the twins started clapping.

"Kissy. Kissy."

"Daddy likes Lexi."

"And Lexi likes Daddy."

Red-faced, Alexa scooped up Flynn, and Cam did the
same with Jason. Leo and Julie looked on from the kitchen
with interest. Julie didn't look happy and Cameron guessed
she was thinking about how to explain his actions to the
twins. It was one thing to think of Alexa as a temporary
visitor; it was quite another when their actions affected his
sons. Cam knew he had to re-evaluate, but now wasn't the
time.

"Make a sandwich," Flynn demanded.

"I'm the big cheese," Jason declared.

Alexa looked puzzled and Cameron explained, "We're
the bread. Think of a four-way hug."

The two adults hugged with the squirming and giggling
kids between them. Jason tickled Flynn. Flynn tickled Cameron and Cameron tickled Alexa. The four of them ended
up on the carpet in a playful mass of wrestling bodies.

When Cameron looked up, the darkness was gone from
Alexa's eyes. The kitchen door was closed. And the two
Barringtons stared in the windows from outside as if they
were looking at animals in a zoo.

Eventually, Cameron made arrangements and sent the
Barringtons on up to the Senator's house. Alexa took her
hot shower. And he hired Leo Harley, which wasn't a tough
decision after he tasted the meal the cook had prepared on
the propane grill.

"Yummy." Jason smacked his lips, uncaring of the barbecue sauce dripping from his chin.

"Absolutely yummy," Julie agreed before turning to Cameron at the picnic table set up in the living room. "Can I borrow a horse? I really need to go to class tomorrow."

"No problem. I'll make arrangements for you to stable your mounts with the sheriff's horses. Perhaps Leo should go with you. After that attack the other night, I don't want you riding alone."

"Thanks, I appreciate it."

"The Senator hopes to have the bridge back in working order in another day or two. Apparently the explosion took out the planking, but most of the braces are sound."

"Did the sheriff find anything?" Alexa asked, digging into the ribs with as much enthusiasm as the twins.

"He found a timer right off. It was still blinking numbers on the underbelly of the bridge."

"Any prints?" Julie asked.

"Not so far, but he's hoping to trace the pieces back to where they were bought. And he tried to question the Barringtons by phone, but they refused to cooperate."

"Why not?" Leo asked, setting out a dish of baked beans with bacon and onions.

"They said they wanted to help, but needed their attorney present after the accusations we made."

Alexa licked sauce off her fingers like a dainty cat. "And their attorney will advise them to say nothing."

Shortly after dinner, Julie put the twins to bed and she and Leo left for town and her one night class at college. Alexa settled at the cleared kitchen table, poring over house plans. Under her administration, the contractor was working diligently. The house now boasted running water and electricity. Windows were done, the drywall was completed, and the kitchen cabinets were up.

But without the bridge, no work could continue. Workers from Highview couldn't return. Appliances, wall coverings, light fixtures and carpets couldn't be delivered.

Since the Barringtons' departure, Alexa hadn't spoken of them. But when a vehicle pulled into the front drive, she jerked, and he could read the despair in her eyes.

Alexa's shoulders relaxed, however, as the Senator's deep voice boomed out. "Anyone home?"

"Where would we go?" Cameron asked his father. "Pull up a chair, and I'll find you some coffee."

Alexa looked at the Senator with troubled eyes. "Are my grandparents causing you problems already?"

"Not the kind you think. Better fetch a cup for yourself and Alexa. The caffeine will help you brace yourselves."

"For what?" Alexa curled a lock of hair behind her ear, a frown drawing worry lines on her forehead.

The Senator had a look in his eyes that Cam recognized—worry, excitement and just perhaps a solution to their problems. A solution that would work but one that Cam might not necessarily like. "Those newspaper photographs could cause a lot of damage in court."

As a former attorney, no one knew that better than the Senator. His tone didn't condemn or accuse. He simply stated the facts as he saw them. But what was done was done.

Alexa sat at the kitchen table, poised and collected, seemingly unaware that Cameron's father was up to something.

While his father took his time to come to the point, Cam fixed the coffee. "There's nothing we can do about these pictures now."

"There is," his father said mildly, looking from Cam to Alexa with speculation in his eyes.

Alexa rolled up the plans, and Cam handed out mugs of coffee. "You think the papers might print retractions?"

Alexa cupped her hands around the mug. "Retractions won't change public opinion."

"Exactly."

"So what do we do?" Cameron asked. "We only shared a kiss or two. We didn't rob a bank."

"I've had some experience with the press," the Senator said, his voice even. "The problem is, once the public sees you kissing a woman on the printed page, they'll automatically assume there are lots of other women. Those pictures as good as branded you a playboy. And judges don't like to give playboys custody of their children. They might even prefer rich and stable great-grandparents. Especially if tomorrow there's a story about you and the nanny—"

"I've never kissed Julie!"

"That won't matter. We're not talking about the truth here, we're talking about perceptions. Julie's young. And pretty. While she lives at the dorm on campus, sometimes she spends nights here. There're enough facts to support innuendos. And modern photography can superimpose alien heads on human bodies. They'll have no trouble faking pictures of you with other women."

"I could move into town," Alexa volunteered.

The Senator shook his head. "It's too late for that. The damage has already been done. Now we need to put our own spin on it."

"What are you suggesting?" Cam asked, knowing he'd just taken the bait his father had so skillfully offered.

"I'm suggesting a marriage. Yours and Alexa's."

Eyes wide, face paling, Alexa sucked in air. Cameron felt as if he'd just been thrown off a bucking bronco and landed on his head. "Marriage?" he repeated, logic telling him he must have heard wrong, but Alexa's stunned expression said otherwise.

His father nodded. "A marriage would solve a multitude

of problems. The public impression can be changed with your whirlwind marriage. The judge will like that you are no longer a single dad trying to raise your babies alone. And who better to help you bring up the children than their aunt Lexi—the Barringtons' granddaughter.''

''But…but…'' Alexa was like a bird about to have her wings clipped.

''We barely know each other,'' Cam objected while letting the logic of his father's suggestion sift through his automatic protest against marrying again. It had been one thing to steal a few kisses and tell himself it could do no harm since Alexa's stay was temporary.

And while Alexa wasn't a stranger, he didn't know her well. But he did know her enough to realize it would be wrong to ask her to give up her career just to please the court and help him keep the twins.

The Senator scratched his chin and looked at the tabloid picture, a sparkle in his eyes and a hint of humor in his tone. ''Doesn't look like you barely know each other to me. And it won't look that way to the public, either.''

Cam couldn't believe his father was suggesting they marry to increase his chances of keeping the twins. But the Senator didn't often interfere in his grown sons' lives—not unless he thought he could help.

Cam also knew his father was capable of matchmaking if the occasion arose. Although the Senator had remained single since their mother had died so long ago, he stressed to all his sons that raising a family was one of the most satisfying experiences a man could know. And deep in his heart, Cam agreed. His years with Sandra had been busy, exciting, fulfilling.

But Alexa was a far different woman from Sandra. Kissing Sandra had been like sipping a smooth cognac, while Alexa's kisses reminded him of tequila straight up with a lick of salt and a bite of lime. Living with Sandra had been the comforting soft rain on a tin roof. Alexa was the lightning that struck during a spring storm. Sandra had centered her life around her family. Alexa had a life all her own.

Marrying Alexa would be like trying to tie down the wind. And yet, Cam couldn't discount his father's suggestion without thorough thinking. "You really believe we need to go to such extremes?"

The Senator leaned back in his chair, took a pipe out of his pocket and stuck it into his mouth without lighting it. "I don't know. The damage this article did to your case is immeasurable. Do you want to take even the slightest chance of losing the boys?"

"But marriage?" Cam spoke aloud even as he considered the advantages. He could claim he'd brought the twins to this unfinished house to build it for his bride. The story would have a romantic bent, and the house would no longer seem a dangerous place to raise children. And the judge would see a stable household, a family unit with two capable parents, not a single father with a busy medical practice.

The Senator turned to Alexa, his voice patient and concerned, which seemed to baffle her almost as much as his outrageous suggestion. "There's no one special in your life right now, is there?"

Alexa cringed. "My job takes me all over the world. I couldn't possibly—"

"—take a leave of absence?" Cam looked at Alexa, wondering if she found the idea of marriage abhorrent or marriage to *him* abhorrent.

The Senator shoved back his chair and stood. "If you could decide tonight, we could have the wedding...this week."

"Why so soon?" Cam asked, once again startled by his father's suggestion.

"Since the Barringtons can't leave, they'll have to attend the nuptials. And I'll have pictures taken of not just the happy event but their seeming approval by being in attendance. We'll leak the story to the tabloids, and those pictures will go a long way toward canceling the damage." The Senator nodded to Alexa and squeezed Cam's shoulder. "Please, think it over. But don't think too long. Don't get up. I'll see myself out."

Neither Cam nor Alexa said a word as his father left. Alexa avoided his gaze and simply stared into her coffee cup. Cam couldn't tell what she was thinking, didn't know his *own* mind.

To him, marriage was a sacred vow between two people deeply in love. And while he'd come to like and admire Alexa, and he felt an attraction to her—okay, a great attraction—he didn't necessarily want to spend the rest of his life with her.

Her work took her to the glamorous corners of the world. She dealt in precious art. She flitted. She didn't put down roots. Asking her to stay on a ranch in Colorado would disrupt her life, take her away from friends. He had no right to ask her to make such a sacrifice on his behalf.

"My father just made a suggestion. We don't have to—"

"I promised Sandra."

"You didn't promise to marry her husband."

At his harsh words, Alexa straightened her shoulders, and her eyes blazed with the attitude that made her so attractive to him. "Those pictures are just as much my fault as yours. I'm partly responsible for this mess."

"Maybe. But you don't have to spend the rest of your life—"

"So we marry," Alexa said. "Big deal. Divorce is still legal, isn't it?"

Her attitude hit him like a punch to the gut. "You're saying we wouldn't have a real marriage?"

"For legal purposes we would."

"And what would that do to Flynn and Jason? They'll get to know you, love you, think of you as their mother. Then you'd up and leave."

What would her leaving do to *him?*

"And if my grandparents win, how much will it hurt the boys to lose their father?" Alexa countered, her tone hard, her chin set with determination. Yet her hands shook so much, she set down her coffee cup and proceeded to twist a napkin to shreds.

"What about your work?" Cameron asked.

"I'll put it on hold." She drummed those perfectly manicured nails on the table. "After all, I don't need to work. I'm marrying a doctor."

Cam almost laughed at her sarcasm. Just like Sandra, Alexa didn't need to work. She'd inherited a trust fund larger than most lottery jackpots. She didn't work because she needed money but because she loved what she did. And if she quit, he suspected she wouldn't be able to pick up right where she'd left off when she decided to go back. Jobs like hers were rare and openings didn't come up often.

He didn't want to ask her to make this sacrifice. But he couldn't lose his boys.

Images of Alexa—protecting the twins from that bull, her ease at taking a shower in a horse stall, her screaming at him to wake up inside the SUV—all gnawed at him. She was brave and vibrant and full of life, and if she stayed here, would she wither, and blame him?

Alexa reached across the table and took his hand between

hers. "I couldn't live with myself if I let Sandra down. So call your father. Tell him we're having a wedding."

Cam swallowed hard, knowing Sandra would have wanted him to accept this courageous woman's proposal. He felt a presence nudging him toward Alexa, and a pure red flame of approval bathed him. He gathered Alexa into his arms and kissed her forehead with tenderness.

He would accept her generous offer and pay the price of letting her go if need be. Whatever happened between the two of them, he wouldn't forget her decency.

Meanwhile he'd decided not to tell the twins about the custody battle or his reason for marrying Alexa. Why worry the boys?

FIVE DAYS LATER, the wedding had been arranged. Alexa slept soundly and awakened on her wedding day to the calm certainty she was doing the right thing. She stretched, looked out the window at the inviting green ripple of grasses and the luminous clear sky. She wondered how the Senator would arrange a wedding with the bridge out.

Her peaceful feeling changed at the sound of little feet thumping up the stairs. Her door opened and the twins bounded into the room, chubby cheeks flushed with exuberance, eyes sparkling with mischief.

"Lexi!"

"Wake up. Up. Up. Up!"

The boys crawled over her sleeping bag and cuddled like wriggling puppies. Alexa put an arm around each boy, surprised by how much she enjoyed their sweet-smelling wet kisses.

Flynn whispered into her ear. "Aunt Laura brought you a present."

"Shh." Jason put his hand to his brother's lips. "Aunt Laura said don't tell her about the dress."

Flynn rolled his eyes. "You just told her."

"Didn't."

"Did."

Alexa kissed each boy on the cheek, then tickled them out of the argument. "It'll be our secret."

At the sound of a knock on her door, she looked up. A blond woman walked into the room and smiled cheerfully at the twins. She carried a delicate white wedding gown beaded with tiny seed pearls, a pair of white satin heels and a wispy headpiece. "Who's keeping secrets?"

The boys giggled and spoke in unison. "We are."

"I'm Laura Sutton," the woman introduced herself. The dress was on a hanger and she hung it on the door, then scooped up Jason.

"Hi, Aunt Laura."

"She married Chase," Flynn explained to Alexa.

"They made our cousin Keith."

"And the baby."

Laura laughed and smoothed Jason's hair. "You'll have your hands full with these two tigers."

"Grrr." Flynn barred his teeth and growled. "I'm a tiger."

"Grrr, yourself. I'm a bigger tiger."

"And tigers need their milk and cereal to grow up to be big and strong," Laura told them. "Why don't you boys go down and ask Leo and Julie to fix breakfast?"

"Do tigers like waffles?" Flynn asked.

"I'm not sure, sweetie. Cody will know. Hold his hand when you go down the stairs. After you guys eat, Uncle Chase is taking you and Keith for a ride." The boys obeyed Laura and toddled out of the room. Laura then turned to Alexa with a dazzlingly sunny smile. "That should keep the kiddies out of our hair this morning. I think this dress will fit. Do you like it?"

Not only did she like the dress, she liked Laura's friendly smile, so different from the sophisticated women she knew. Laura had calluses on her palms, hair streaked by the sun—not peroxide—and a down-home confidence in herself that Alexa found fascinating.

Alexa smoothed her T-shirt and crossed the room to the dress. "It's beautiful, and I thank you for bringing it. But isn't it too dressy for what the Senator has planned?"

"Not a chance. The Senator never does things halfway, and he has all the equipment, since he throws big parties several times a year. Tents are already up. The silver is polished and the fine china is set. Guests are already arriving."

"But the bridge is out." Alexa frowned. "Maybe it's because I haven't had my caffeine jolt to wake me up, but how can the Senator bring guests to the ranch?"

"Most people are riding in, either fording the river where it's shallow or going around the long way through the mountains." Laura took down the dress, removed the clear-plastic wrapping and handed the dress to Alexa. "Judge Stewart, an old family friend, has agreed to perform the ceremony."

Alexa suddenly turned shy with this self-assured woman, who reverently stroked the wedding gown. Knowing instinctively that Laura was offering her own wedding gown sent warm, friendly feelings through her. "Since we're going to be sisters-in-law, I'd like you to be my matron of honor."

Laura spun around, and her grin, already wide, brightened. "I was hoping you'd ask. I have this fabulously wicked dress that Chase hasn't seen yet..."

Obviously Laura and her husband, Chase, were very much in love. From the glow on Laura's cheeks and the impishness in her eyes, she was planning a seduction.

"But first we need to get you ready." Laura lifted up a canvas bag Alexa hadn't noticed before. A curling iron, a blow-dryer and other assorted items overflowed the top. Laura dug inside and removed an iron. "While you take a shower, I'll touch up the gown."

"What time's the wedding?" Alexa asked.

Laura shrugged. "I'm not sure, but everyone who is anyone within five counties will be here. The press has their own tent. The Governor's flying in and so is another Senator and possibly the head of the Department of Transportation."

"The Department of Transportation?"

"Don't worry. He eats barbecued ribs with his fingers and teeth the same way as everyone else." Laura took one look at Alexa and paused. "What's wrong, honey? The Senator said you work around important folk. You aren't going to let a few celebrities upset you on your wedding day, are you?"

Alexa took several deep breaths to steady her charged nerves. A long time ago she and Wyatt Smithee, the head of the Department of Transportation, had been friends, very good friends. When Alexa stepped into the hot shower, she leaned limply against the wall.

Wyatt had broken off their relationship when she'd told him she couldn't have children. Pain swam like a demon to the surface of her thoughts, and all the hot water in the world couldn't wash away the old inadequacies, ugly doubts and bitter regrets.

Before winning his cabinet seat, Wyatt had been the youngest congressman the people of Massachusetts had ever elected to office, and the dashing politician had swept a very young Alexa off to the glamorous parties and charity functions of Washington, D.C. The Barringtons had approved the match. All of Alexa's friends except Sandra were jealous, because everyone knew Wyatt Smithee would one day be elected to the White House.

And now he was coming to her wedding to watch her marry another man. She hadn't seen him since that terrible night when he'd cruelly told her that his career was more important to him than she was—and that career demanded a wife who could have children. And since Alexa's ovaries had been removed due to a severe infection, she couldn't ever bear children.

Since then, Wyatt had married a former Miss America and together they'd produced four children. Alexa wondered if the woman had had to present a certified document from her gynecologist before Wyatt proposed. Alexa supposed she should have been grateful to have learned of Wyatt's ruthless ambition before the wedding. After all, what woman with sense would want to be stuck with a man who saw her primarily as a breeding mare to further his career?

But Wyatt had done damage to her confidence. Since then, Alexa had never placed herself in a position where a man would ask her to settle down and raise a family. Instead, she'd made a good life for herself. She had a fascinating career, friends in almost every city in the world. And for the past eight years, she hadn't ever seriously considered staying in one place long enough to miss the family she could never have. Until Sandra had had the twins, Alexa didn't even know she liked children.

And within hours she would be a mother. If she was entering a real marriage, she would have told Cameron up front about her inability to conceive. But these circumstances were far from normal. No matter how adorable she found the twins, she had no intention of staying at the ranch to play wife and mommy for more than a few months. There was no point in letting the twins think she was more than a temporary visitor in their lives—just a fond auntie.

And Cameron? Oh, God.

She tilted her head back and let the spray of water spatter her face and neck. Alexa would have to keep their lives on a friendly footing. No more stepping over the line. No more kisses, especially no more of those devastating kisses that made her forget she was in charge of her hormones and not the other way around.

She would think of their marriage as a temporary business agreement. He'd win custody of the children at the trial and then she'd be free to leave. Maybe she'd have to stick around another month or two just to make the marriage seem real...but then she'd be free again.

Free to miss Cameron's laughter. Free to miss his easy relationship with his father. Oh, how she envied his big, warm family. Since she'd been here, she'd met only Chase and the Senator, but she remembered Rafe's charm and Tyler's steady good cheer from Sandra's wedding. The Sutton men, all tall, dark-haired and gray-eyed, drew the ladies' attention wherever they went. But it was their affection for one another that Alexa found so appealing.

Alexa stepped from the shower, wrapped a towel around her body and another around her head like a turban. She cleaned a spot of condensation off the mirror and stared at herself, suddenly full of doubts. She didn't belong in a family where everyone knew everyone's business, where the men stuck together and the women acted liked sisters. Cam and the Senator hadn't told the others that the marriage was temporary. She hated deceiving such good people.

She couldn't go through with this farce of a wedding. It might have been easier if the Senator hadn't made such a huge production out of the ceremony. Then it wouldn't have seemed so real.

Alexa now knew that she would have been making a huge mistake if she'd married Wyatt Smithee. She'd long since gotten over the man, just not the reason he'd rejected her.

Deep down, she recognized that Cameron Sutton was not the shallow excuse for a man that Smithee was—and yet, that attraction to Cameron made marrying him seem so wrong. He deserved someone better, someone who would fit into ranch life and into his loving family with the ease that Alexa collected fine art.

A knock on the door caused Alexa to jump. Laura's voice scolded, "You're not getting cold feet, are you?"

Alexa opened the bathroom door. "I'm afraid so."

"Well, come sit." Laura gently led her to a chair and pushed Alexa into it. Then she removed the towel from her hair and started to rub her hair dry with it. "I was a nervous wreck on my wedding day. It's normal."

"How did you know you were doing the right thing?"

"I didn't. I don't believe any intelligent woman is ever sure."

"Then why did you go through with the wedding?"

'I might have had doubts, but I loved Chase, and I knew he loved me. That's really what counts, isn't it? Love gets you through the hard times and makes the good times great. You'll see. Cam is wonderful husband material, and he has the same great looks all the Suttons have—dreamy dark hair and smoky gray eyes." Laura flicked on the blow-dryer, effectively ending the conversation.

If love made a great marriage, Alexa and Cameron's would surely be a disaster. They didn't know each other well enough even to know what they had in common. Alexa didn't know if he liked to read the newspaper on Sunday afternoons or watch ball games. She didn't know his favorite color, his favorite dish or his birthday. She didn't even know his age.

When Cam poked his head in the doorway, Laura shut

off the dryer and scolded him. "Cameron Sutton, it's bad luck to see your bride before the wedding ceremony."

He eyed Alexa's cleavage below the slipping towel. "She's not dressed yet."

"That's another reason you don't belong in here."

"I like her better...undressed."

"I'm sure you do."

"You're one to talk." He stepped in and swatted Laura lightly on the rear with a wrapped present. "I believe Keith was walking before his parents married."

Laura laughed, not the least bit insulted. "Chase and I were lucky to marry before the second baby came along."

Alexa listened to the easy camaraderie between them with envy, wishing she'd had a family that had allowed warmth and teasing and genuine feelings for one another. Even if the Suttons accepted her, she wouldn't fit in. Her proper Bostonian upbringing kept her separate.

Deep in thought, she'd lost track of their conversation, and then Cameron placed the wrapped box in her hands. "These were my mother's. I'd like you to have them."

Alexa opened the box and stared at a delicate diamond-and-sapphire choker set in platinum filigree.

Laura oohed and aahed. "It's gorgeous and will go great with the gown."

Baffled by the extravagant gift, Alexa held the necklace in her hand and admired it. She looked into Cameron's eyes for answers. Why would he give her a family heirloom when the marriage would be finished within months?

She was about to protest when his hands closed over hers. "The Senator wanted you to have it."

"The Senator gave me emeralds," Laura said with a dreamy smile. "And I think it's a lovely tradition."

"But—"

Cameron bent down and his lips covered hers, swallowing her protest. His kiss had the usual effect on Alexa. Fire flashed through her veins and she forgot Laura watching them with interest, forgot she didn't know this man, forgot she wouldn't be spending her wedding night in his arms. All she could think about was kissing him back—and that she'd hate herself forever if she chickened out and canceled the wedding.

Chapter Seven

"Go ahead. Open them all," Cameron insisted, looking handsome in a black tuxedo that accentuated his broad shoulders and long legs.

Alexa, dressed in a sundress while Laura made a few last-minute adjustments to the wedding gown, looked at the huge pile of wedding presents in astonishment. Prettily wrapped boxes covered the kitchen table, overflowed onto the floor and onto the back terrace.

"Where did they all come from?"

Free from baby-sitting duties since Chase had taken all the boys for a ride and had yet to return, Julie, a vision in a scrumptious gold strapless gown that set off her tan, opened a pad of paper. "Guests have been arriving all morning. The Senator sent the gifts over. After you open them, I'll record the names and addresses and note what's inside so you can send thank-you notes, and then Leo and Cody will take them back to the Senator's to put on display."

"You'll have to hurry," Laura said as she stitched closed a dart in the gown. "The Senator called and said we need to be there by four."

Alexa hadn't thought through all the implications of a wedding. People spending hard-earned money on gifts for a fake marriage didn't sit right with her. Feeling like a fraud, she hesitated, not wanting to accept the gifts. But she had no choice. Making a quick decision, she decided to open the gifts and thank everyone, but send the gifts back after the marriage ended. Meanwhile, she'd do what was expected of a bride.

Julie placed a box in her lap, neatly removed the card and made notations on her pad. "Try this one first. It's from Wyatt Smithee and his wife."

Laura must have seen Alexa's fingers shaking. She carefully put down her sewing and leaned over. "Here, let me help you."

Get a grip. It was only a gift, Alexa told herself. But the admonishment didn't calm her jittery nerves.

And Cameron was looking at her with concern. He leaned over and massaged her shoulders, his warm fingers digging into and soothing tense muscles. "Relax, sweetheart."

Alexa almost slapped away his hands and told him she wasn't his sweetheart. Just in time she realized this was her wedding day and how ridiculous she would look if she protested.

Instead, she leaned into Cam's strong hands. "Whatever you say, beefcake."

Laura chuckled. Julie looked annoyed and rolled her eyes. Both Leo and Bodine blushed. Each young man looked at Julie, and Alexa found it amusing to watch them vie for the oblivious young woman's attention who seemed to hide from them by sitting very close to Cameron.

Laura smoothed out the fancy wrapping paper, reached through the tissues and pulled out a ceramic tureen, hand-painted in the exuberant Tulavera style. "How lovely."

Alexa's stomach finally settled and she swiftly and efficiently opened chaffing dishes, hors d'oeuvre platters, silk cocktail napkins, silver-plated bottle openers, stemless hand-blown champagne glasses. A Saudi prince, a friend of the Senator's, had sent a remarkable collection of dinnerware, a set for twenty guests with each piece a different design and showcasing châteaux of the world and their gardens.

Her favorite gift was from Rafe Sutton, Cam's youngest brother. It was a framed watercolor by a local artist who had captured the spirit of a horse and its fluid speed. Against the background of Highview's snow-capped mountains, a magnificent roan stallion raced across a verdant valley. Head up, mane blowing in the wind, mighty hind quarters bunched for the next bounding leap, the animal epitomized independence, achievement and boldness.

Alexa lingered over the painting, reluctant to put it down. "It's gorgeous."

Cameron placed the painting over the fireplace, and Alexa opened the next box. Julie tapped her pencil. "I hope a card's inside. I couldn't find one attached to the box."

Her thoughts still on the painting, Alexa reached through more tissue paper and uncovered the head of a porcelain doll dressed in a wedding veil. Carefully, she unwrapped the doll's body, which wore full wedding attire. But something was horribly wrong.

The eyes had been chipped out. A hunting knife poked out of the doll's chest. Red paint had been splattered over the doll's wedding dress.

Heart icing at the sight, Alexa couldn't speak. Laura gasped. Julie dropped her pad. Bodine and Cody, unaware of the problem, remained busy carrying the unwrapped gifts to the car.

"Cameron!" Alexa held up the doll so he could see it. She couldn't believe that someone had deliberately sent such a nasty thing wrapped as a wedding gift. What kind of sick mind was stalking her? As fear twisted through her, she straightened her spine, determined not to give in. It was only a doll with red paint splashed on it. She wouldn't get hysterical. She wouldn't overreact.

From across the room, she watched Cam's eyes narrow, his lips tighten and a muscle in his jaw work. "Put it down and don't touch anything else."

As if she would. Wild horses couldn't drag her into searching through the box.

Cam had no such compunction. Leaning over her, he plucked out a card between thumb and forefinger. Touching only the edges, he read a typed message aloud: "'Don't marry him.'"

"What's that supposed to mean?" Laura asked, looking from Alexa to Cameron for an explanation.

"Someone is trying to scare me away," Alexa said softly, fear spiking through her. But along with the fear came anger. How dare someone try to manipulate her? Curling her fingers tightly into her palms, she drew a deep breath and released it slowly. If someone meant to frighten her, the scheme had worked. But she refused to give in to the fear.

"But why?" Julie asked.

Cameron looked at Alexa. "Our marriage will help me to keep custody of the twins. Obviously the Barringtons don't like the idea."

Laura peered at the doll, resting atop the tissue in the box. "I don't know, Cam. That knife looks awfully familiar. I could swear it's Bodine's."

The foreman? Bodine's? Alexa recalled how the foreman had been near the bridge after the explosion. He'd also been around when that bull had gotten loose. But why would Bodine try to stop her marriage to Cameron? She'd never met the man before coming to the ranch. Did he have a motive he alone knew? Or could he be working for her grandparents?

"Bodine," Cam called out.

Bodine came inside, and Alexa couldn't read anything but honesty in his weather-lined face. "Yes, Doc?"

"Do you have a knife with a six-inch blade and a blue handle?"

"It's missing."

"You mean you lost it?"

"No, sir. I had it last night. Took it out to clean and left it on the night stand. This morning, it was gone."

Cameron motioned the man over to the box. "Is this your knife?"

"Sure looks like it." Bodine's lips drew into a frown. "But I didn't stab this doll. What would be the point?"

"Someone doesn't want Alexa to marry me."

Bodine shrugged. "Doc, I'll pack up my things and leave if you want, but it doesn't matter one whit to me who you marry."

Alexa watched Bodine's eyes carefully. He didn't wince or avoid Cameron's gaze. He just looked surprised. Sounded sincere. But he'd as good as admitted the knife was his. Alexa wondered if her grandparents could have bribed him. Later, she'd ask the sheriff to look into his bank account, his background.

She really had trouble believing her grandparents would go to such lengths as to hire the cowboy to frighten her, but she'd never have thought they'd take Cameron to court over the twins, either.

Laura's lips pursed in thought. "The doll must have been purchased somewhere."

"I don't know," Alexa eyed the material carefully. "It looks kind of old-fashioned."

"Maybe we can trace it." Laura stood and shook out the wedding gown she'd altered and glanced at her watch. "Alexa needs to change."

Cam turned to Alexa. "You still want to go through with this?"

"Of course." With the court hearing less than a week away, she realized the timing couldn't be better. Alexa looked at her nails, then back at Cam and shot him her best grin. "I just need one more coat of nail polish first."

NAIL POLISH? How could the woman think about nail polish after she'd just received a death threat? Cam had to admit she kept a cool head. Some women might have screamed or fainted, but Alexa was made of sterner stuff. He could almost see the cogs of her mind turning, first ordering herself to be calm, then sensibly going through alternatives, options and possibilities.

His brother Chase strode in with Keith and the twins. According to plan, they'd ridden to his brother's house, where Chase had bathed and dressed the boys, then he'd driven them back in his car so they'd stay clean.

Looking none the worse for wear in his own tuxedo, Chase said, "You owe me."

Cam smiled and reached for his wallet as his sons and Keith raced by him into the kitchen. "What'd they break this time?"

"I barely turned my back on them."

Cameron took out some cash. "How much?"

"You must have eyes in the back of your head."

Cameron took out all the cash he had.

Chase shook his head. "I don't know how you do it. They found my toolbox."

Cam turned toward a kitchen drawer, figuring the cash in his wallet wouldn't cover the damage. "I'll get my checkbook. What did they take apart?"

"My computer."

"Jason! Flynn! Get your butts in here!" Cam shouted.

Not only had they caused damage, they could have electrocuted themselves.

Keith stayed in the kitchen while the twins skidded into the den, innocent looks on their faces. Jason eyed his father's black suit, black shirt, black tie. "You look pretty, Dad."

Flynn scrunched up his nose. "Men aren't pretty, they're hand...dom."

"Handsome. And don't try to distract me. What did I tell you guys about electrical appliances?"

"They shock."

"We were careful, Dad. We took the plug out of the wall."

Why didn't that news make him feel better? "Why did you destroy Chase's computer?"

"We didn't."

"Didn't."

Chase kneeled down to look his nephews in the eye. "My computer doesn't work when it's in ten pieces."

"We can put it back together, Uncle Chase."

"Maybe you can, but maybe you can't. And in the meantime, how can I work?"

Flynn took Chase's hand. "We'll help you work."

"Sorry, Uncle Chase." Jason added, his expression a mixture of sorrow and a plea for mercy. "We just wanted to see the inside."

"Look at those faces," Cam muttered. "They have this apology thing down pat."

"That's because they screw up so often. They'd make terrific actors. Maybe you should send them to Hollywood."

At Chase's words, Flynn's baby-blue eyes clouded with tears. "Don't send us away to the holly woods, Dad."

"We'll be good," Jason promised, his lower lip quivering.

"I can't afford to send you guys away." Cameron shuddered. Just the thought of his sons around all that expensive movie-production equipment was enough to give him nightmares. But he didn't think it would hurt them to be reminded that they could be punished for their actions.

Alexa, a vision of a wrathful bride, swept into the room and scooped the boys into her arms. "No one is sending you two boys anywhere." She turned angry eyes on Cam and Chase. "How could you two even suggest sending these two angels—"

"Those two angels just disassembled my hard drive," Chase complained. "And they even got Keith to help them."

Cameron enjoyed the sparkle that had returned to Alexa's eyes. Her nostrils flared and her spine straightened as if she was getting ready to fight the enemy. Although she wore Laura's wedding dress, she didn't look virginal but sexy, and for a moment he imagined planting kisses along her bare shoulders and peeling down the zipper at her back.

Would she wear frothy lace undies beneath the gown? Or nothing at all?

At least the stabbed doll didn't appear to have her too worried. But he wouldn't take any chances. He intended to stay close by her side all day. And he suddenly realized what torture that would be, breathing in her scent, pretending they were the happy couple about to share a wedding night. Cam almost groaned aloud.

"And where were you?" Alexa asked his brother. "Weren't you supposed to be watching them?"

"Dad called. He needed…" Chase threw his hands into the air. "Never mind. If we don't hurry, you'll be late for the wedding. And Laura will never forgive me."

"A fate worse than death." Cam chuckled wickedly.

"I'll bet ten bucks you haven't seen the dress she's wearing."

"And you weren't supposed to see this one until the ceremony," Alexa complained.

Cam picked up Flynn and slipped his free arm through Alexa's. "I'm not superstitious. Besides, I don't intend to let you out of my sight."

"I shouldn't have let Laura out of my sight, either." Chase's brow furled. "I suppose her dress is cut real low?"

"With a slit all the way up to there," Cam taunted, knowing the slit only came to Laura's knee, but he couldn't resist teasing Chase. "Don't worry. I thought she looked terrific."

"Keep your eyes on your own wife," Chase muttered as he picked up Keith and led them out the front door.

Behind his back, Cameron and Alexa exchanged grins. The twins high-fived, believing they'd gotten away without being punished, but Cam knew he would have to do something to contain their exuberant curiosity without stifling their creativity before they hurt themselves or created more havoc.

Perhaps Alexa would have a suggestion. That is, if she stuck around long enough after the wedding to make a difference in their lives. He supposed he should count his lucky stars that she was still willing to go through with his father's cockamamie plan and marry him after seeing that scary doll.

Her courage gave her the right to be an equal partner, and he had no business holding back evidence from her— even if it made her unhappy. Cam leaned back in the passenger seat, willing to let Chase drive. "The sheriff didn't get any prints off the bridge's detonation device. However, he did learn something interesting."

Alexa looked at him over the heads of the twins, who

were on their best behavior after the stunt they'd pulled that morning. "What's up?"

"The sheriff said that an automatic timer had been set to blow up the bridge. And it went off too early."

"That would mean…"

"It means we should have been way over the bridge and safe before the explosion."

"So now you think the scheme was meant to scare us, nothing else?"

"It's possible."

"And you think my grandparents—"

"Or someone they hired."

"—could be trying to frighten me away from you?" Alexa reached over and took Cam's hand. "Well, I don't scare easy."

Chase adjusted the rearview mirror. "Hey, you all. This is your wedding day. You two should be cuddled up and smooching in the back seat—"

"And mess up my makeup? I don't think so."

"—instead of talking about plots and schemes and—"

Cam grinned. "I wouldn't want to mess up her makeup."

"Of course not," Chase said in a tone that clearly indicated he thought Cam was crazy.

"Or her hair," Flynn piped up.

"Lexi's pretty," Jason agreed.

"She smells good."

"And clean."

Alexa smiled at the boys. "I do believe those are the nicest compliments I've received all day."

Chase shook his head. "You better hurry up and marry her before your sons get too much older and give you some competition."

Cam snorted. "Just remember you volunteered to watch these little guys for us tonight."

"Was I drinking when I offered?" Chase muttered.

Alexa turned to Cameron, her eyes full of worry. "Chase, can we take a rain check on the baby-sitting offer? With everything that's happened, I'd prefer to keep a very close eye on the twins."

"We'll be good, Aunt Lexi," Flynn promised.

Alexa smoothed a stray lock of hair off his forehead. "I know, sweetie. But I'd like my new family all under one roof tonight. That way I won't have to worry about you two boys."

Alexa seemed so poised and logical, it was as if she got married every day of the week. Cam decided she needed more color in her cheeks.

He caught Alexa's gaze. "We'll all stay together, but the only one I want you worrying about tonight is me."

ALEXA KNEW CAM was teasing her, but thoughts of their wedding night made her uncomfortable. Luckily the view distracted her. Chase drove past a ridge and made a gradual ascent to the north, passing a brow of massive cliffs and heading into the rolling valley where the Senator had built his home.

The house, although large, was not imposing on the land but blended into it. The design possessed a natural grace, a flowing grandeur that matched the vast lands and towering mountains that surrounded it. Solid stone walls, large picture windows with stunning views of the spectacular scenery lent an elegance to a house that the Senator could leave as an enduring monument to the future.

A long drive swept around an elegant curve that brought visitors beneath arching boughs of transplanted oaks, reminiscent of the Old South. As they rounded the house, the backyard spread out before them, a genteel setting of sweeping white canopies over tables spread with elegant white linen and crystal vases of lilies. A string quartet played softly and uniformed waiters served champagne to well-dressed guests.

As soon as their vehicle pulled to a stop, the Senator, looking completely at ease, opened the door and greeted them. "Right on time."

"That's because I didn't let the boys do a tune-up on my car," Chase mumbled, his gaze searching the crowd for his wife.

"Laura's making final arrangements with Judge Stewart about the ceremony." As Chase and Keith departed, the Senator took Alexa's hand. "I don't want you to worry about a thing. We have a boat ferrying people across the river. Security's very tight."

Alexa took in such subtle touches as the petals floating in a fountain, the ruby-red roses lacing the trellis and the lilac bouquet the Senator handed her. All the Suttons had gone out of their way to welcome her into this family, and the warmth almost overwhelmed her. "Thank you for arranging everything. I can't believe you managed all this on such short notice."

Julie walked over with Leo at her elbow. The young man looked about to burst with pride as he practically drooled over the blond baby-sitter.

Julie knelt and hugged Jason and Flynn. "You boys look so handsome." She straightened their ties and then took each twin by the hand. "I'll keep track of them until the ceremony. Laura thought you'd want them with you later up in front."

"Absolutely." Cam touched Jason's head. "You two had best behave or you won't get any wedding cake."

"You look terrific." Julie gazed at Cameron and Alexa, and tears rolled down her cheeks. "I'm sorry. Weddings always make me cry." Julie's emotion seemed out of proportion to the circumstances and Alexa wondered if Julie could have a crush on Cameron. She recalled Julie clutching Cam so tightly after the incident at the portable toilet, how she sat too close to Cam just a while ago. Maybe that's why Julie never looked at either Cody or Leo the way they looked at her. But then maybe Julie was just sentimental. She wiped her face with a tissue.

Leo took out a hanky and dabbed at her eyes. "There now. You'll be fine. Let's go find the twins some cheese and crackers."

Alexa caught sight of Wyatt Smithee approaching and took a moment to regroup. Pride made her stiffen her spine. She didn't want to let on that her marriage to Cameron was anything but the happiest of love matches. So when she turned to face Wyatt, she made sure that she leaned into Cameron and that she wore a polite smile.

Wyatt ignored her hand and gave Alexa a hug. "Congratulations, my dear."

In a fake tone and with a lack of warmth in his eyes, her former flame turned to shake Cameron's hand, and Alexa realized she no longer felt anything for Wyatt Smithee, not regret, not even a pang of lust, not even anger at the hurtful things he'd once said to her. She only felt lucky that she'd gotten on with her life without him.

Wyatt moved away, and Alexa noted that he'd apparently left his wife in Washington, which freed him to eye Julie, but the young woman was busy with the twins and Leo. So Wyatt's gaze swung to the stunning redhead talking to Rafe Sutton.

Alexa wanted to thank Chase's younger brother in person for the fabulous painting, but her grandparents approached. Rafe suddenly slipped away from the redhead, joined Tyler, the eldest Sutton brother, and came their way. As if by unspoken agreement, Chase and Laura joined them, too,

Chase's eyes both fascinated and disapproving of his wife's low-cut gown. And Alexa realized the entire Sutton family had surrounded her. To protect her from her grandparents?

A photographer took pictures to record the event, and Alexa wondered how anyone would believe the Barringtons were happy about the wedding. Dressed for the occasion, but looking as if she'd just swallowed a pickled prune, her grandmother greeted her coldly and with disapproval. "Alexa, I hope this is what you truly want."

"It is not," her grandfather pontificated. "She couldn't possibly want to live—"

"Careful, Grandfather," Alexa said. "You wouldn't want to insult everyone, would you?"

Before he could answer or make a scene, Cam drew Alexa away, his arm around her waist, his hand possessively on her hip. "We're about ready to begin."

His brothers, father and sister-in-law closed in around their backs, physically separating Alexa from any further Barrington disapproval. Together, the family approached the arched latticework, Laura slipping into place next to Alexa as matron of honor. Rafe lifted Flynn into his arms, Chase held his son, Keith, and Tyler took Jason.

Judge Stewart, in his rich tones, began to speak of marriage. And the crowd of guests settled into silence.

Alexa's thoughts wandered. As her gaze glanced from face to face, she realized she wasn't just marrying a man, but was becoming part of a family. And what a family. These Suttons were strong, and they showed a united front to the world. The Senator, his four sons, daughter-in-law and the grandchildren all included Alexa without question, accepted her because Cam wanted them to and had made her feel more welcome than she could ever remember.

As she looked into Cameron's warm gray eyes, she realized how much she'd missed by always being an outsider, always being alone. Her grandparents had made sure she had clothes, food and a roof over her head, but they had never known how to give her the affection she'd craved. If not for Sandra, her childhood would have been completely barren of warmth and understanding and love. And if not for her promise to Sandra, she would not be here now.

She couldn't help thinking that Sandra was watching the ceremony, smiling in approval, pleased that Alexa would look out for the family she loved and ensure her last wishes were carried out. Alexa's heart contracted, and as Cameron slipped a wedding ring onto her finger, the weight of grief lifted from her heart.

She'd lost her cousin and best friend, but she'd gained an entire family. And when Cameron's lips closed over hers and his warmth seeped into her, she flung her arms around his neck and kissed him back with enthusiasm.

Then laughter and warm wishes surrounded them, and the twins' kisses made her heart melt with delight. For a moment, the joy seemed so real Alexa wanted to grab onto the dream and believe there would be a happily-ever-after.

The soft click of the photographer's cameras reminded Alexa of her ulterior motive for the occasion. The Senator needed these pictures to counteract Cameron's playboy image. And her grandparents had to be seen looking on with approval.

Laughing, Alexa grabbed Cameron and posed him beside the Barringtons for a more formal shot. ''Please, Grandmother, Grandfather. Try to look happy. It's my wedding day.''

The flashbulb popped and then Cameron swung her onto the dance floor. She swayed against him, her feet barely moving, just content to live in the moment, to enjoy the music and Cam's strong arms around her.

Because she feared the good times wouldn't last long.

Chapter Eight

Faces smeared with wedding cake, the exhausted twins slept in Cameron and Alexa's arms as the newlyweds carried them upstairs to their beds. While Cam tucked the boys in, Alexa dampened a washcloth with warm water and gently wiped their faces.

"They were good little boys today, don't you think?" Alexa asked Cameron.

"If you don't count the pizza they threw into the goldfish fountain."

"They thought the fish were hungry."

"And if you don't count their looking up their great-grandmother's dress."

"They only wanted to see if she had a rod up her spine." Alexa grinned. "They must have overheard some adults talking."

Cam threaded his fingers through his hair and escorted Alexa into the hallway. "How about a drink?"

"Sure." She turned toward her room. "I'm going to slip into something more comfortable—and don't take that the wrong way. As much as I adore four-inch heels, after dancing all day, my feet hurt."

Ten minutes later, Alexa, wearing slacks and a casual shirt, joined Cameron downstairs. He'd stoked the fireplace with logs, and the kindling blazed, crackled and snapped. He'd dimmed the lights and soft music played on the stereo.

But the scene was casual, not set for seduction. Leo and Julie worked quietly in the kitchen, putting leftovers into the almost new refrigerator—a temporary gift from the Senator until the new one he'd ordered could be delivered. And two security guards hired by Cameron patrolled outside.

Cam spread a blanket over the rug before the fireplace and patted the spot next to him. With a sigh, Alexa accepted the glass of white wine he handed her, the same wine she'd been drinking all day. She wriggled her bare toes and winced.

Cam noticed and took her foot into his warm hands. "Let me see."

He rubbed the arch and she started to pull back. "I don't think—"

"Yes?"

"—that you should stop that for at least another hour." She plumped a pillow behind her head, sipped her wine and sighed as his fingers did magical things to her tortured arches. "Your family's wonderful."

"Mm?"

"Whenever one of the townspeople asked you a medical question, your brothers and father saw to it that I wasn't left alone for a second."

"My family's one of the reasons I brought the boys back here."

"And the other reasons?"

"I needed to get away. But I thought the boys would feel more normal out here."

Julie and Leo finished up in the kitchen and headed for the front door. Julie's gaze lingered on Cameron just a moment too long, as if she wanted to say something and then changed her mind. Leo waved, his arm around Julie's waist. "See you tomorrow, Doc. Have a good night."

"It was a wonderful wedding," Julie added.

"Thanks for helping out," Cameron told them as the young pair left.

Alexa thought they seemed anxious to be alone together. At least Leo did. His crush on Julie was so obvious Alexa couldn't understand how the baby-sitter seemed so oblivious to him. But perhaps she preferred Cody. Or Cameron. Well, if the girl had a crush on her employer, she'd just have to get over it. Whenever Julie made up her mind to settle down, she'd have no trouble attracting a mate. But Alexa didn't dwell on her impressions of Cameron's hired help.

She sipped her wine, enjoying the first private moments she'd had with Cameron all day. She still had trouble remembering that they were married, that he was her husband. But she was starting to learn little things about him. His patience astounded her. She'd known he was trying to tell her something, and yet he waited for her full attention before resuming the conversation.

After she heard Julie and Leo's horses head toward town, she gave him the opening he needed. "You're worried about the boys?"

"My sons aren't normal." Cam's voice sounded tight, and his fingers moved from her sole to the small bones of her ankle.

Alexa fought off the sleepiness that threatened to overtake her. Although it had been a long day, she didn't want to fall asleep just when Cameron seemed ready to open up to her. Not that he closed her out. One of those men so comfortable with themselves that they always appeared content, he rarely seemed to need anyone.

Alexa shifted to look into his frowning face. "I'm certainly no expert, but the twins seem fine to me. Their verbal skills are way ahead of their age group.''

"Every measurable skill is way ahead of normal. Intelligence, sensitivity, curiosity, propensity for trouble, they're all off the charts. But they *are* bundles of high energy and difficult to control.'' Cam sat up and his hands slid to her calf. "I don't want you to think they're your responsibility. I intend to keep Julie around to help out.''

"That's fine with me.'' Cameron seemed relieved by her response. She suspected he didn't want the boys to become so attached to Alexa that after she left for good, their lives would be disrupted. "This way I'll have time to finish decorating the house.''

"And I'll be free to arrange financing and deal with the real-estate agent for my office in town.'' She must have looked surprised, because he explained, "A perfect building just came on the market. It'll need renovations before I can set up my practice, so I won't be abandoning you just yet. If I have to go into town, I'll make sure one of my brothers or a security team is nearby.''

At the mention of the security team, her sleepy thoughts turned to her problems. The wedding had gone off without a hitch. No one had said or done anything suspicious, but she'd felt as if she was being watched. She'd tried to put off the feeling with logic. Who didn't watch a bride at her wedding? But the nagging feeling that something was wrong wouldn't go away.

Someone had tried to warn her off marrying Cameron. Now that she had, would the threats disappear? Or would worse things begin to happen? Somehow, as sleepiness pulled at her, her problems didn't seem that urgent.

Alexa twirled her glass between her fingers, fighting to keep her eyes open. "Did the sheriff find any proof that my grandparents paid Bodine to scare me with the doll?''

Cam shifted to her other foot and began rubbing the aching arch. "Not yet. And he says Ray Potter, my old cook, has left town. But something just doesn't sit right with me."

"What?" So he felt it, too. She wasn't surprised. Cameron wasn't only bright, he was very aware of what happened around him.

"Bodine's not the smartest cowboy I've ever met, but he's far from stupid. I don't believe if he were on the Barrington payroll, he'd be dumb enough to use his own knife."

Stifling a yawn, she sipped her wine and watched the fire flare. Cam hadn't drunk even a third of his wine, while she'd almost finished hers. If he intended to make her tipsy to steal a few kisses, it wouldn't work. She was too sleepy. "So you think someone stole the knife and tried to make Bodine look guilty?"

"It makes sense."

"Or maybe he didn't expect anyone to recognize his knife. How well do you know the man?"

"We hire him on as an extra foreman every summer. After putting in a full shift here, he goes home to work his own place on weekends and evenings."

Alexa was having trouble remembering her thoughts. "I think...I think we should go take a look at his place. Maybe we'll learn something."

Cam's eyes suddenly narrowed and he cocked his head. "Did you hear that?"

"It's probably the security guards that the Senator hired to make the rounds."

"Maybe."

The logs crackled in the fireplace. The muted glow reflected off the planes and hollows of Cameron's face. He placed Alexa's foot gently on the floor, raised a finger to his lips and stood, then motioned her to stay still.

Was that a thud she heard? To her it sounded as if the noise had come from the pool area. But as moonlight filtered through the high windows, she could see Cam headed up the stairs, his hand gliding over the banister.

Confused and sleepy, she fought to push to her feet. She couldn't fall asleep while she was upright, could she?

Alexa heard the sound of cracking wood. Saw the banister give way and Cam stumbled. He broke his fall with one hand, flipped around and, catlike, landed on his feet while the banister came down around him.

Alexa started to hurry to him. "Are you all right?"

"Stay there." Cameron leaped over the pieces of railing and dashed upstairs.

Instead of following him, Alexa walked as if in a dreamlike state to the sliding glass doors by the pool deck. Without hesitation, she flipped on the deck lights.

At first she saw only the two security guards the Suttons had hired. But they were walking oddly, arms in front as if carrying heavy objects. As she peered through the window, the guards looked at the overhead lights with surprise.

From upstairs, Cam yelled down to her, his voice full of anger and fear. "Alexa, the kids are gone! Call—"

"The security guards have them! By the pool."

Alexa didn't wait for Cam to come back down the stairs. Grabbing the fireplace poker, she raced outside, trying to think how to delay the guards. Her brain seemed sluggish. But she had to think. She knew that both guards carried guns and that their arms were occupied holding the kids. But if she or Cam threatened them, the guards could drop and hurt the sleeping kids, reach for their guns. Still she couldn't just let them take the children to their waiting vehicle.

"Stop!" she ordered. "Where're you going?"

Upstairs, she heard Cam swear. Out of the corner of her

eye, she saw him coming through the window and down the same ladder the guards must have used to kidnap the children.

Horses with riders and flashlights suddenly swung around the house. What the hell was going on? Kidnappers?

God, no! Alexa couldn't let the guards reach either car. She had only seconds to act. Keeping the poker close to her side so the guards wouldn't notice it, she raced around the pool, planting herself in front of them so they faced her and had their backs to Cam, who was descending the ladder.

"Put those children down!" Alexa demanded, fear making her voice surprisingly strong and commanding.

"Lady, move aside. No one needs to get hurt."

The guards started to brush past her. Alexa took one look at the sleeping twins' faces and acted. She stomped one man's instep and swung the poker against the other's knee.

The man she kicked swore. The other sidestepped the poker and threw a child into the pool. Knowing Cam had to be right behind her, Alexa didn't hesitate. She dived in after the child, praying Cam could stop them from taking the other.

Icy water slapped her awake. The underwater pool lights weren't turned on, and she swam frantically, arms outstretched, kicking madly. She had to find him. Soon. Her lungs started to burn. She refused to resurface. He was here in this pool. Drowning.

Something brushed her leg. Alexa instinctively pulled back, then realized her mistake. Turning around, she reached out and felt hair, then a head. Grabbing the baby, she kicked for the surface, fighting the pull of her water-logged clothes, ignoring her icy fingers and choking fear. Suppose she hadn't found him soon enough?

How long did it take for a child to drown? She didn't know. Unlike Alexa, the baby had been sleeping. He hadn't known to prepare by holding his breath before going underwater. He didn't know to keep his mouth closed.

Alexa broke the surface and dragged the child to the shallow end. Cam jumped into the pool to help her. The security guards were nowhere in sight, but a vehicle tore off down the road. And she saw Julie and Leo were holding the other sleeping twin.

Had the security guards turned into Julie and Leo? No, that couldn't be right. The guards had been men.

Too exhausted to think, too cold to move, Alexa had no idea what had happened, and now was not the time to ask. Cam took Jason from her and gently placed him on the pool deck.

The child's face looked bluish. And he was so still that ice speared Alexa's heart.

That Cameron was a doctor made Alexa feel only slightly better. She didn't know how to perform CPR on a child, didn't know if she could summon the energy if she did.

Without panic, Cam checked the boy's neck. "His heart's still beating."

Cam opened Jason's mouth, tilted back his head and with his own lips covered Jason's nose and mouth. He blew in air. "Come on, baby. Breathe."

Jason didn't move.

Cameron repeated his actions. Jason's little chest inflated and suddenly he coughed weakly. Cameron turned him onto his side so he wouldn't choke on the water. "It's okay, little guy. You'll be just fine."

Alexa still panted from her exertions, but she couldn't seem to move. As her adrenaline-induced strength faded, she started to shake and shiver. Drowsiness stole away any desire to pick herself up and move inside.

Beside her, Cameron wrapped a sleepy Jason in his shirt.

"Alexa, are you hurt? Thanks to you, Jason will be just fine."

"What about b-brain d-damage?"

"He wasn't under long enough."

It had seemed like forever to her. "Maybe we should take him to the hospital—just to be sure."

"Luckily the sleeping drug they gave him is already wearing off. He'll be fine." Cameron looked at Alexa who could barely keep her eyes open. "I suspect you swallowed some of the sleeping drug, too." His gaze swung to Julie. "Is Flynn awake?"

"Barely." Julie, her voice tight with worry, smoothed back Flynn's black curls.

Leo led her with the baby through the sliding glass door. "We should get them out of the night air. It's chilly."

"Good idea." Cameron tucked Jason close to one broad shoulder and helped Alexa to her feet with his free hand.

"I don't feel very good."

"Don't fall asleep until I get you inside."

"I won't," Alexa promised, wondering if she would do just that. She felt so tired, her eyelids so heavy. Her eyes closed, her head flopped onto Cameron's shoulder, and boneless, she let him half-lead, half-carry her inside. The warmth from the fire wrapped around her like a blanket.

Somewhere in her mind, questions tried to form and make it out of her mouth. But she could no longer fight the sleepy darkness.

ALEXA AWAKENED in her room to the smell of bacon, strong coffee and hot cinnamon buns. Cameron had brought up a tray of breakfast for two, his eyes weary as if he hadn't slept all night—their wedding night. Her cloudy thoughts suddenly cleared and last night's events rushed back to her. "The boys?"

"Are fine. I stayed up all night just to be sure. And Jason's lungs are clear. He suffered no ill effects from the water."

Cameron set the tray on the floor by her sleeping bag. Alexa realized someone had removed her wet clothes, for she was naked beneath a blanket.

Cameron must have read the alarm in her eyes. "I carried you up here and helped Julie take off your shirt and slacks. She removed your wet underwear and covered you with the blanket."

Alexa didn't like the idea of anyone undressing her, but she'd been unconscious. Wrapping the blanket around her, she stood, picked up some clothing out of her open luggage and headed for the bathroom.

She returned fully dressed to find half the breakfast gone and Cameron swallowing coffee. She helped herself to a cinnamon bun and nibbled. "Could you fill me in on what happened last night? Between the sleeping drug and the time I spent underwater, I can't seem to make sense of it."

"The security guards tried to kidnap the twins."

She'd guessed that much. "Why?"

"I don't know. They're very wealthy little boys. Maybe someone wanted to ransom them back to us."

"Or maybe this was another attempt to make it appear as if you aren't a good father. Maybe the guards didn't intend to kidnap the boys, but only to make it appear you'd lost them for a while."

"Did you get a look at their faces?"

"It was too dark."

"What about their getaway car?" Cameron asked.

She shook her head, realizing the guards had escaped. "I was underwater, remember? I don't even know how Julie and Leo got there."

"Julie forgot her backpack with her schoolbooks. She had to study for a test, so they returned to pick it up."

Alexa recalled Leo's flashlights. "But they came around back."

"After you flipped on the porch lights, they saw the guards trying to take the children and rode straight to the backyard. Leo tried to catch the guards but he tripped, and both guards managed to slip away."

"Is the bridge still out?" Alexa asked, wondering where the guards had driven. She suspected they'd ditched the car in the woods and swum across the river in the dark.

"The bridge won't hold a car, but it's strong enough for horses. Why?"

"Your father hired the guards from a firm in town. It shouldn't be too hard to figure out who they are. and then press charges with the sheriff."

WITH TYLER GUARDING the house, Cameron and Alexa left the twins under Julie's watchful eye and rode out right after breakfast. Cameron wished he could have thought of a reason to ride with Alexa again, instead of letting her ride her own mount. Their last ride together had been incredibly sexy, and despite his worry about the upcoming custody hearing and the twins, he couldn't help noticing Alexa.

The big bay mare she rode could stick to a calf like a burr on a sheep's tail, but seemed to be enjoying a morning free from its usual work. The bay pranced and Alexa rode her with an easy expertise that revealed lots of riding lessons at expensive boarding schools back East.

Alexa tipped back the hat she'd insisted on borrowing to shield her face from the summer sun and took in the green pastures they rode through, with pleasure glinting in her eyes. "I can understand why your family has become so attached to this land."

"You should see the valley from up there." He pointed to the towering mountains that made a picture-perfect backdrop for the peaceful pastureland.

"I'd like to try and paint it."

"I didn't know you painted."

"I dabble in oils." She shrugged. "When I figured out I wasn't good enough to sell my work, I started selling other artists' work to galleries, collectors and museums."

During the ride to town, she told him several amusing stories about eccentric clients, picky museum directors and her search for the perfect Dali to hang over Donald Trump's sofa. Her voice rang with a vibrancy while her words conveyed her expertise. The bottom line was that she clearly loved her work—work she couldn't do while she remained with him.

He reminded himself that their marriage was simply a convenient way for him to show the court he was stable. Nothing more than a piece of paper filed in a courthouse—and this paper gave him no right to think of Alexa in any special way. Yet, how could he not be affected by her sunny smile, her bright-eyed enthusiasm and her unflagging courage?

Once again last night she'd helped him save his boys. If she hadn't dived into the dark pool after Jason…he shuddered to think what might have happened. And she did it while drugged from some kind of sleeping tablet. Cameron had saved the remainder of her wine in a vial for the sheriff to send to be tested. And he'd wrapped the wine bottle carefully in newspaper, hoping someone had left fingerprints.

Cameron knew he owed Alexa more than he could ever repay her, and he had no right to try to convince her to stay with him and the boys. She clearly had her own life, where she was happy. It would be wrong to use the sexual attraction they felt for one another to try to change her mind about leaving. And yet, he couldn't seem to stop himself from dwelling on how he felt.

He found her too attractive. With her face pleasantly flushed from the ride, wisps of hair escaping from her braid and curling around her face, he wanted to take her up onto his horse and kiss her.

When they rode over the newly reconstructed and almost completed bridge, Cam was grateful for the distraction. Bodine had a crew of about thirty men hammering planks across the surface, a concrete truck pouring bases, while extra steel bracing had been added below. Assorted backhoes, loaders, paving equipment and rollers were working on different sections of road.

Cameron pulled up his horse to speak with his foreman. "Did any vehicles try to cross the bridge last night?"

"No, Doc." Bodine wiped the sweat off his brow. "If those security guards had tried to escape this way, they would have fallen into the river. We don't have all the braces in yet, but it'll hold your horses. If those men kept the car, they must have gone through the mountains."

"I didn't think that was possible," Alexa said.

"A four-wheel-drive could make it to town in an hour if they drove over the train tracks," Cameron answered.

Alexa shook her head. "Over the train tracks?"

"My brothers and I did it when we were young and—"

"—stupid?"

Cameron grinned and turned back to Bodine. "How long before you're finished?"

"I'm hoping we'll have it done today, sir."

"Good," Alexa murmured, shifting uncomfortably in her saddle. Clearly unaccustomed to riding for miles and miles, she would be sore later, and Cameron tried unsuccessfully to refrain from even thinking about rubbing her aching derriere. Alexa had terrific legs, smooth, lean, muscular. And his fingers itched to explore her ankles and calves and thighs. Just the thought of those legs brought erotic images of them wrapped around his waist.

Thoughts of what he'd like to do with her had his jeans tightening uncomfortably in places. To get his mind off making love to her, he urged his horse faster.

"Come on. Another hour and we'll make it to town. Last one there buys lunch."

IN SMALL TOWNS many businesses did double duty by performing two services. The local pharmacy rented bicycles to tourists, a weight loss clinic met at the health food store at night. The security agency in Highview doubled as a tourist center that offered guides. A poster on the door advertised white-water-rafting trips, four-wheel-drive vehicles for rent and camping expeditions.

As Alexa walked inside and her eyes adjusted to the dim interior, she saw mountain bikes, camping and fishing gear, wind sailing masts and boards stacked against the walls. And farther back were skis, boots and snowboards, along with the necessary clothing.

A salesclerk approached Cam with an appreciative smile that faded when she saw Alexa. "May I help you?"

"I'd like to speak to the manager, please."

"This way, sir." The clerk led them through a twisting aisle to the rear of the store. Cam took Alexa's hand in a proprietary gesture that arrowed heat up her arm and into her core. Alexa wanted to pull away, but knew if she did, it would be tantamount to admitting how much he affected her.

The clerk knocked twice on a door, then opened it. "Jess, there's some folks here who want to speak with you."

A tall, gray-haired woman with a muscular frame, peeked

over her glasses at them. She gestured to two hard-backed chairs by her desk. "Please come in. What can I do for you?"

"I'm Cameron Sutton and this is...my wife Alexa." Jess may not have noticed the hesitation in Cam's voice, but Alexa had. Not that she blamed him. She had trouble remembering she was married herself. But she was especially glad that Cameron was no longer holding her hand. Now that she was free of his disturbingly evocative touch, she could regain control of her reactions.

"Jess Parker." The woman offered her hand to Cam, then Alexa. "What can I help you with?" she asked again.

"I'd like to see the employment records of the security guards my father hired from your firm."

"I'm sorry. Employment applications are confidential. Is there a problem?"

Cameron's eyes flashed gunmetal gray. "Two security guards tried to kidnap my children."

Jess Parker's jaw dropped open in horror. "What! You're serious? I just hired two new men because your father increased security and has temporarily hired every security guard that I could find. The new men's records are impeccable. And though they insisted on working as partners, I didn't suspect anything." Jess stood, walked to her file cabinet and pulled out two folders, which she handed to Cam. "You can see they came with the best recommendations."

"Did you check these Denver references?" Alexa asked as she peered at the records while trying to ignore Cameron's spicy scent that mixed so well with leather.

"Yes, I did. We may not be a large operation, but we pride ourselves on our personnel. That's why the Senator uses my services. In all the years we've operated, nothing like this has ever happened. Are your children all right?"

"They're safe now." Cam read the applications and

frowned, his bottom lip puckering, and Alexa had the sudden thought of nipping at it until he relaxed. "Stephen Rayes and James Philbin. They shared a residence. Ms. Parker, would you mind making copies of this address, their social security numbers and references for the sheriff?"

"Not at all. I'm very sorry you had trouble. You'll receive a full refund, of course. And if there's anything else I can do, please let me know."

Alexa forced her thoughts away from comforting Cam or distracting him with a series of kisses. "You wouldn't have any pictures of the men, would you?"

"Their pictures are on their security licenses, and a copy is attached to the back of each man's file."

Alexa's hopes soared. If they had pictures of the men, they could show them around town and ask questions. They could take the pictures to the police, banks and the phone company. It was a tremendous break to have pictures of the men who'd tried to abduct Cam's children.

Cameron turned over both files, his big hands sure and agile. Neither picture remained.

CAMERON AND ALEXA left their horses in the sheriff's stable, where Noel Demory picked them up. Cam handed the sheriff the bottle of wine he'd saved and the files. After noting the addresses in the files, the sheriff swung a right and headed east toward an apartment complex west of Highview.

Alexa wanted to go straight to the security guards' apartment, but the sheriff insisted they check in with the apartment manager first. And once again, Cameron took her hand as they walked toward the site's office. She wondered if he was deliberately trying to throw her off balance by this constant touching. Or was he just being polite? Surely holding her hand couldn't mean as little to him as it appeared or he wouldn't keep doing it.

Maybe he thought married couples, newlyweds, should always be touching. If so, she found the idea sweet, but she still wished he wouldn't. His touch made her think of him as a man, an attractive man who enjoyed her touch.

A curvy redhead with big hair and a surly smile greeted them in a tiny office. She shoved fingernail polish into a drawer and fanned her wet nails to airdry.

"I'm looking for Stephen Rayes and James Philbin, ma'am," the sheriff said.

"They were in apartment 313."

"Were?" Cam asked, his voice even but edged with steel. His fingers tightened around Alexa's.

"Moved out in the middle of the night." The redhead looked at Alexa and Cameron. "They'd already paid up for the month. I can give you a deal if you want to move in..."

"I'd like to look at the apartment, please," Alexa said, hoping that maybe their suspects had left some clues, but it seemed as if the would-be kidnappers were two steps ahead of them. She could almost feel Cam's disappointment adding to her own.

The redhead dug out a key and the sheriff asked for the guards' apartment application. Alexa didn't see new clues on this form. Just the same information again.

While she, Cameron and the sheriff walked to the apartment, the sheriff called in the social-security numbers on the radio. A few minutes later, an officer called back. "Noel, the social-security numbers don't match the names. And Stephen Rayes is a seventy-four-year-old black male who reported his wallet stolen in Denver last month."

Cameron rubbed his brow with his free hand as he walked beside Alexa and spoke to Noel. "Does that mean the names were fake?"

"Yep. I'd be willing to bet the references don't check out, either, Doc."

Alexa sighed with disappointment. "So we have no idea who those two men really were."

"Or who may have hired them to kidnap the twins." Cam seemed thoughtful—and worried. And Alexa couldn't blame him. Whoever was after the twins could make another attempt. Until they figured out who was behind the scheme, they couldn't be sure of the twins' safety.

The sheriff put the key in the lock and opened the front door. One look and Alexa's hopes vanished. The apartment was completely empty. The two kidnappers hadn't left behind so much as a dirty ashtray.

Disappointment flooded her. All these questions, all the searching, and they seemed no closer to figuring out what was going on than before they started investigating. Frustrated, she turned to Cam, hugged him and looked into his steady gray eyes. "Now what?"

Chapter Nine

"We can check the phone numbers in Denver," Cam suggested, but Alexa could tell he wasn't hopeful. Still, with one arm came around her waist, he hugged her tightly for one breathless moment before releasing her.

Alexa sighed, missing his touch but glad he'd found a little comfort in her hug. "The phones are probably disconnected or bogus numbers."

Cam shook his head. "Maybe not. Jess Parker told us she called and checked the references. Someone vouched for those two men."

After calling officers to dust the apartment for fingerprints, the sheriff drove them back through town to the hotel, where they'd eat lunch. "Maybe we'll get lucky and they'll have paid the Denver phone bill by check." Noel wrote down Cameron's cell phone number and promised to let them know about the drugged wine, the fingerprints and the phone numbers as soon as he had any information.

After lunch, Cam borrowed a car from the real-estate agent who was selling him the medical building. He made a brief stop to check on the site, but soon pulled onto a road heading north out of town.

With a cocky set to his jaw, he tuned the radio. "I thought we'd pay Bodine a little visit."

"He isn't still working, is he?" Alexa asked, thinking back to the last time she'd seen the foreman that morning. He'd been busy overseeing the reconstruction of the bridge. Bodine had seemed determined to finish the job today.

But then, Colorado seemed filled with determined men, none more so than her husband. Despite their problems, he never lost an opportunity to brush against her, touch her hand, take her elbow, constantly reminding her that he found her attractive. She didn't believe he was acting to convince others their marriage was real. She could see the need simmering in his eyes, feel the tension radiating off him, knew that even a man with Cameron's patience couldn't hold back his passion forever.

But she had no idea what she wanted to do about it. She would be leaving soon after the trial. If she became any more attached to Cameron and the twins, leaving would be impossible. For just a little while, she could step into another woman's role and be a mother, a wife. This opportunity might never come again. Perhaps she should accept the invitation in Cameron's eyes and touch, and make the most of her time here. She could worry about paying the price after she was gone.

Cameron's husky voice interrupted her thoughts. "Bodine and his crew started at five this morning. They quit at three and that's a ten-hour day." Cameron checked his watch. "He should be home by now."

"See if you can work in a way to ask the man if he's ever been in the military or in mining," Alexa suggested, refocusing her thoughts on the problem with effort.

"Why?"

"Whoever blew up that bridge was familiar with explosives."

"Not necessarily. Remember the charge went off too soon?"

Cameron's patience to consider every detail annoyed her, but she couldn't fault his logic. He seemed so calm and methodical. Didn't he know how much his touches raised her pulse? Did he have any idea how much she enjoyed working with him? In all the years she'd known him, he'd never lost his temper, never raised his voice in anger. In fact, the only time he showed real emotion was when he played with his boys. And when he kissed her.

On the scale of one to ten, the man's kisses were a definite twelve. But it wasn't just his touch that sliced away at her reserve, it was his genuine courtesy. Cameron's thoughtful, simple gestures were as much a part of him as those searing kisses. Yet it wasn't manners that attracted her, but the core of the man they revealed. He thought of others with a generosity of spirit, without taking away time or love from his family. He hadn't even blamed the Senator or Jess Parker for not checking out the security guards more carefully.

Alexa knew many important men. Many were so consumed with business that they didn't have time to worry about their children. And the men who didn't strive to succeed had never interested Alexa. However, Cameron was a complex mix of hard businessman and compassionate father. He clearly adored medicine and yet he had no compunction about putting off starting his practice until he'd assured his sons' safety. She admired that trait in him most of all—his commitment to family.

And she liked the entire family. The oldest brother, Tyler, was quiet, but he'd made her feel welcome. Chase was like the brother she'd always wanted—steady, a good father and totally in love with his wife—while Rafe was the charming youngster who would someday fall hard for some lucky woman. And the Senator, a class act all his own, ran the family with an iron hand and a soft heart.

The twins couldn't have a better family to grow up in. The judge would have to see the boys belonged here with this vibrant family. And Alexa would always be glad she'd taken the time to get to know them.

Cameron pulled up to a barbed-wire gate and stopped the car. While he got out and opened the gate, she slid behind the wheel and drove through, then waited for him to close the gate and return to the car. Unlike the Sutton ranch that had the luxury of extra acreage, the majority for pastures and small ribbons of land set aside for roads, Bodine's ranch was more modest. Every inch of acreage was used for grazing, right up to the front yard of his trailer.

Boasting exaggerated eaves, the trailer ran parallel to the front yard and had a carport with saddles hanging from the ceiling at one end and a prefab fireplace at the other. The front end had a basic open-air stoop and nearby squatted a thousand-gallon cattle-watering tank that could double as a swimming pool.

Next to a row of puny poplars, a big satellite dish sat in the backyard and provided shade for cows. A faded green pickup truck was parked in the drive. Clearly little time went into the trailer's upkeep.

At the Suttons' ranch, Bodine kept a paddock of perfectly groomed horses, saw to dehorning steers and worming calves with meticulous efficiency, but inside his home, dirty laundry overflowed the hamper and dozens of marks marred the coffee table.

"Excuse the mess." Bodine's housekeeping apology, like big-belt buckles, seemed pretty ubiquitous on a small ranch. He gestured for them to take a seat on the sofa beside a dead plant. "Just move that rope and those spurs to the coffee table. I wasn't expecting company."

"I wanted to ask a few more questions about your

knife," Cam said, sitting so close to Alexa that her leg and hip and shoulder were plastered against his hard muscles.

Bodine set out a bowl of chips and handed them each a beer. "Ask away, Doc."

Cameron twisted off the cap, took a long swallow and then played with the icy bottle. "Did any of the men who worked for us ever take special notice of your knife?"

"Not that I can remember."

"That blue handle is very distinctive," Alexa said, hoping to prod Bodine's memory. She kept inching away from Cam on the sofa but sliding right back.

The foreman scratched his head. "Now that I think on it, Cody once offered to let me bet the knife, instead of a ten-dollar ante, in a poker game."

Alexa frowned. "Cody isn't old enough to play poker."

Cameron and Bodine shared a long look and shrugged in unison. Alexa chose to ignore their mockery. Gambling was illegal, and for the ranch hands to let the teenager participate just wasn't right.

"I take it you didn't wager the knife?" Cameron asked, casually looping an arm over Alexa's shoulders.

"No, sir. Ray Potter borrowed it once to fillet a fish, but he returned it that same evening. I kept good track of it. My daddy gave me that knife. And his daddy before him."

"You know the doll seemed old, too. Like an antique," Alexa commented, trying to ignore Cameron's physical closeness and his warmth seeping into her.

"What are you getting at, ma'am?"

"I'm not sure. It may mean nothing." She couldn't think with Cam sitting so near. She needed air, needed space, but he wasn't giving her any.

"All right, let's try another angle," Cam suggested. "Which men at the ranch have a military or mining background and also had access to my house yesterday?"

"I'm not sure I understand what you're getting at, Doc. Almost everyone had access to your house. It's near the stable, and you never lock it. During the wedding, anyone could have sneaked inside." Bodine paused. "As for the military background, I was a Navy SEAL."

"So you have knowledge of explosive devices?" Alexa asked, trying to figure out whether or not Bodine's freely made admission made him appear less guilty.

"Some." Bodine held her gaze, and she couldn't believe a Navy SEAL would sell out his employer for a few bucks. Cameron was right. Bodine had more sense than to stab a doll with his own knife and expect to get away with it.

"Have you heard any of the hands complaining about work lately?" Cam asked.

"No more than usual."

"Anyone speculating overly much on my personal business?"

"No, Doc."

"Have any of the hands been spending more money than normal?" Alexa asked, unwilling to let Cam do all the thinking. She crossed her legs, letting her calf rub suggestively against his leg. If he wanted to play touching games, she knew how to play, too.

Bodine's eyes narrowed, and for the first time, he seemed unsure of his answer. "What do you mean?"

"Anyone buy a flashy new car? Or gamble too much? Or uncharacteristically buy a round of drinks at the local bar?" Cameron elaborated.

Bodine closed his eyes, then opened them slowly. "Actually, that new cook, Leo Harley, just bought a spiffy new saddle. One of those expensive ones with silver inlay. And Cody's mom traded in her old Chevy for a newer model. And I just bought another hundred acres to connect to my back forty." Bodine tipped up his beer and downed the rest of the bottle. Then he wiped his mouth delicately with a cocktail napkin. "So what?"

Alexa leaned forward, letting her hair fall onto Cam's shoulder. "We think my grandparents may be paying off someone to make Cameron look foolish when he goes to court to try and keep custody of his boys."

Bodine's eyes widened in surprise. "You think your own grandparents would—"

"They think they would be better parents than Cameron," Alexa explained. "So we're looking for someone who might take a little money on the side. Maybe this person doesn't even realize the stakes. He may not intend to hurt anyone, may have been paid just to scare me away."

"No one is that dumb," Bodine said. "One other thing I should tell you, Doc. I hate to mention it, but under the circumstances..."

"What?"

"That day, when the bridge blew up..."

"Yeah?"

"I saw another horse and rider out there."

Alexa leaned forward again, practically holding her breath. "Who was it?"

"I didn't get a good look."

"Who do you think it was?"

"I can't be sure. That's why I didn't want to say anything, but I thought..."

"Thought what?" Alexa prodded as she gritted her teeth, thinking pulling information from Bodine was worse than from the twins.

Bodine finally spit out the words. "It looked like the Doc's sister-in-law. Laura Sutton."

Alexa gasped. Her beautiful sister-in-law couldn't have had anything to do with blowing up the bridge.

"Maybe Laura was out on an innocent ride," Cam said.

His stiff shoulders, tight lips and narrowed eyes said a lot more. Clearly he didn't believe Laura Sutton capable of doing such a thing, either.

"The rider would have heard the explosion," Bodine insisted with a speculative look. "And if so, wouldn't it have been normal to investigate?"

"Maybe Laura didn't hear it. Sound can travel funny over pastureland. Or maybe she was in a hurry," Cam suggested.

"Or maybe it wasn't her," Alexa said, taking his hand and giving it a gentle squeeze of support before asking Bodine another question. "What made you think it was Laura? Are you certain the rider was female? Did she have long blond hair?"

Bodine slumped in his chair. "I'm not sure. The rider was galloping, but doing a slow lope, the kind that eats up the miles, not the hell-bent-for-leather riding that winds a horse fast. The horse was dark, a deep chestnut or a black."

"That's not much to go on. Why did you think it might have been Laura?" Cameron asked, his tone even, but Alexa heard the edge of tension beneath.

"I'm telling you the truth, Doc. I just don't know. It was a fleeting impression, and that's why I hesitated to say anything at all. It could have been a man. I don't specifically remember hair color, but it may have been blond."

Cameron stood and pulled Alexa up with him. They hadn't learned much, but the more they spoke to Bodine, the more convinced she became of the man's honesty.

Cam shook the foreman's hand. "Thanks for the information and for the beer. If you think of anything else…"

"I'll let you know."

"ARE YOU GOING to question Laura?" Alexa asked Cameron once they were back on their horses and riding home, knowing they didn't have much time before they went to court, and they still couldn't prove anything.

"No." Cameron's tone turned hard. "A few years ago, Laura was accused of murdering my brother, Brent. Eventually, it all got sorted out and she was completely exonerated. But those were hard times for her and Chase. I won't cast one iota of suspicion on her."

"She could have been out there having an innocent ride," Alexa said, drawing her horse closer to his.

"Exactly."

"So wouldn't it help to know if she was out there alone or if she saw someone else?"

"We *are* looking for someone else. The subject is closed." His face, hard as flint, had a stubborn cast to the jaw, gray eyes determined to treat his family his way. For an intelligent man, he could be remarkably stubborn and close-minded when it came to his family. Usually she saw this quality as a strength, but it could also be a weakness.

Alexa reached over and touched Cam's shoulder. "Maybe Laura saw something that could help us."

"We aren't going there. Laura is a Sutton."

"And as a Sutton, she'd want to help." Alexa sighed, thinking how easily Cam could ignore her touches. "I'm not saying we have to accuse her of anything."

"We damn well won't." He moved his horse closer to hers as if his dominating presence would make her give in to his argument.

Alexa wouldn't be intimidated. "Did Laura fall apart when she was accused of murder?"

"Of course not."

"She didn't have a nervous breakdown?"

"She's a strong woman."

"And didn't your brother stand by her even when things looked their worst?"

"Of course."

"So neither of them would fall apart if we asked a few simple—"

"I said no." Cam increased the pace to a canter, his horse kicking up clouds of dust.

Alexa dug her heels into her horse, encouraging the animal to stay even with Cameron's mount. "You're being unreasonable."

"And you're being argumentative."

"That's because you're wrong."

"It won't be the first time," he said so mildly she wanted to slap him. How could she argue with him when he'd just agreed with her?

Damn him! He'd been touching her all day, making her edgy as hell. Then he tried to avoid the conversation, and when she wouldn't let him, he'd just ended it by saying he'd made the decision, and that was that. While Alexa admired his absolute faith in Laura's innocence and his determination to protect his sister-in-law from anything unpleasant, she didn't agree with his thinking.

"Maybe Laura saw something and didn't realize it might be important to us." Frustration made her reckless, and she cut off his horse, forcing him to a stop.

"We'll manage without questioning Laura."

Slightly out of breath from anger more than exertion, Alexa glared at him. "Does anyone ever win an argument with you?"

When he reached over, grabbed her waist and plucked her from the saddle, she was too astonished to do more than sputter. "Just w-what—"

His mouth came down on hers, cutting off her words. Her palms slammed into his hard chest and she jerked her head back. "I'm not kissing you back."

He gathered her closer. "Sure you are, darling."

"I'm not your darl—" His hands came up over her breasts and she responded immediately. Not only did he notice, his thumbs tweaked her aroused nipples maddeningly.

She couldn't stop her physical reaction, and that only increased her anger. How dare he treat her like this? He couldn't win the argument, so he wanted to kiss her into submission?

Not this woman. But why did he have to feel so good? He knew exactly what she liked—seemingly instinctively, his fingers found sensitive spots, his mouth was magic, and her thoughts spun dangerously out of control. Her back arched and she barely bit back a soft moan of delight.

"You want me as much as I want you." His mouth came down on hers again, taking, demanding, and shooting darts of pleasure through her.

She wanted him, all right. But she couldn't decide if she wanted to kiss him or kick him. Out of nowhere, he had her hot as a branding iron ready to burn, and that he could affect her so easily was downright humiliating.

She twined her fingers into his hair, yanked his head back and locked gazes with him. "Are you out of your mind?"

"That's the effect you have on me. You're making me crazy. Crazy for you."

"I've married a lunatic."

He nibbled on her ear. "Lucky for you, they haven't locked me up yet."

"Arrogant man." His tiny nibbles were doing odd things to her erratic pulse. She actually felt light-headed and excited. "I'm not making love on a horse."

Cameron let out a low, husky growl and dismounted. He yanked a bedroll from behind his saddle, unfurled it, wrapped his arms around her and toppled her with him to the blanket.

"Now, where were we?"

"You were about to let me tear off your clothes," she teased, unbuttoning his shirt and exposing his broad chest.

She twirled her fingers through the light dusting of curls, gratified to see his breathing change in response to her slightest caress. Beneath her white fingertips, his tanned flesh was sleek, hard and hot.

He didn't give her much time to explore, drawing her lips back to his and tugging her shirt out of her slacks, unfastening her bra. "I've been wanting to do this since the day you took that mud bath and showered in the horse stall," he muttered.

"What?"

"Didn't you know what you were doing to me?"

She nuzzled the soft skin at his neck, liked the feel of his breath by her ear. "What?"

"You were naked and I wanted to peek."

"Did you?" she murmured as she unbuckled his belt and shoved his jeans and boxers to his knees.

He kicked his pants the rest of the way off and removed her slacks and panties. "I should have. I've been wondering what you looked like with your clothes off."

"And now you know."

"I haven't seen anything yet." He pulled back and his gaze moved over her hungrily, his eyes kindled and smoked. "Wow!"

His hot look urged her on to a boldness she'd never known. She arched her back and flicked her hair over her shoulder, letting him feast his eyes on her breasts. She actually felt herself warming, swelling, under his gaze. She'd never felt so feminine. Never felt so eager to know a man. She wanted to learn him by feel, memorize the silky texture of hair over solid muscle, taste the salty musk that intoxicated her like a fine wine.

For a big man, he didn't carry a spare inch of fat. Cameron was all lean muscle and broad bones.

She breathed in his scent, a heady combination of sweet grass, leather and spice. Her tongue lapped at the soft spot between his neck and collarbone, and he bucked under her, impatient for her weight.

Then his head rose and he captured the tip of one breast between his teeth. Hot, sizzling sensation seared her. Her head arced backward as she gasped in sheer pleasure.

She straddled him, but he held her captured in limbo with his teeth and tongue, creating exquisite sensations, like soft rain on a gentle breeze. He took her bottom in his big hands, spreading her legs wider until his fingers slipped between her legs.

"Darling, you caught me unprepared. I didn't bring protection."

A fleeting sadness washed over her, only to disappear in a moment. "It's taken care of." She reached behind her and found him thick and hard and waiting.

He groaned, hot and heavy and deliciously ready for her. "Have mercy, woman."

She wanted to make him wait. She wanted to make him as wild as he'd made her. But she couldn't stand the sensations beating at her, urging her onward, making her crazy with need for him. She shifted her weight. He slid inside her smoothly, and she took him with an ease that showed how ready she was for him.

"You feel too good," she whispered, experimentally flexing a muscle.

"Hold still, sweetheart," he ordered, sweat beading on his forehead.

She grinned her most wicked grin. "Not a chance, beefcake." Rocking her hips, she gyrated, taking pleasure in how he was trying to hold back, liking the power she had over him.

Control ended all too soon. Cam's hands slid to her bottom again, and he reversed their positions in the blink of an eye. Suddenly he was on top, driving into her. She wrapped her legs around him, welcoming each thrust, urging him deeper.

His hips lunged downward and she matched him move for move, wrapping her arms around his chest, her nails clawing at his back. And when he took her over the edge, he went with her, his shout letting her know his pleasure.

But Cameron wasn't done. Although his heart pounded against her chest, although his flesh was slick with sweat, he gathered her close, holding her as if she were a fragile piece of glass. He fondled and caressed and massaged. At his tenderness, sweet emotions threatened to lift her into a state where she believed anything was possible.

She considered staying here, wrapped in Cam's arms and letting their marriage become real. As he held her gently, she knew they'd just shared something precious, something that shouldn't be wasted. Her bones felt like melted butter, and her thoughts drifted around the fact that staying with Cam might be her one chance to have a family.

She had to admit she felt remarkably content. And she sensed her cousin Sandra would have approved. But was that enough to start a life together? She'd always enjoyed her independent lifestyle, traveling, work. But she'd never before felt she had other options. After her terrible experience with Wyatt, she'd never again placed herself in a situation where she had to consider any other kind of life.

Alexa was surprised to find contentment here playing the pretend wife, sharing Cam's children. But she had no idea if these feelings for Cam could last, and even thinking about how she felt scared her. She hadn't wanted to become too attached to him and the twins, but she'd ended up making love to him, ended up adoring his children. And when the time came, leaving would just about break her heart.

Even if she wanted to stay for a while, she shouldn't let the twins become too close to her or her to them. She'd miss Cam, too. Making love to him had been indescribably delicious, and she didn't regret their actions, no matter how hard it would be to leave.

Cam smoothed back a stray lock of hair from her face. ''I'd like you to stay with us, Alexa.''

Chapter Ten

"What do you mean?" Alexa asked, a soft hitch in her voice.

"We're good together," Cam said, stating the obvious. Ever since Alexa had arrived in his life, the sky had seemed bluer, steak had tasted better, music had sounded sweeter. He felt more alive, more alert than he had since he'd been married to Sandra. And though he'd always love his first wife, he loved Alexa differently.

"I hardly think one good romp in a cow pasture qualifies as a basis for me to stay, Cam."

Beneath her tone, he heard a purr of satisfaction, but also a hint of unease. Just because she fit so well into his family didn't mean she wanted to stay, he reminded himself. Although he might not have the twins if he lost them in tomorrow's court case, he'd fight one battle at a time. Cam wouldn't let her go without a fight—not after what they had just shared.

Already he wanted to taste her again, run his fingers through her silky hair, feel her nestled against his chest. She fit him physically, her long lean legs wrapping around him, her head tucked under his chin, her fingernails lightly raking his back. She matched him emotionally, their passions equally fervent. Lord, kissing her was like having peach cobbler drizzled with brown sugar and whipped cream.

He'd merely tapped the surface of the passion he'd sensed in her. A swirling maelstrom lay below the poised veneer she presented to the world, and he couldn't wait to delve into those feelings again. But already, she was erecting walls.

He twirled a piece of her hair around his finger. "You like the boys."

"What's not to like?" Her voice remained light, but she tensed, her muscles taut across her shoulders and neck.

"And you must like me just a little."

"I like lots of men."

He bristled that she would place him in the same category as other men, implying there had been so many in her life. He knew better. Sandra had often worried that her cousin would never find the right man, because she wouldn't let any man into her life. Nor did he believe Alexa could treat what they'd just experienced as a casual encounter. Couldn't she feel the attraction between them? Surely it wasn't just one-sided.

He tried to think rationally. She'd told him he needn't use protection. Did that mean Sandra had been wrong, that Alexa kept herself prepared for a serendipitous affair whenever she had an itch? He didn't believe it. Alexa wasn't the kind of woman to be satisfied with a one-night-stand or a short-term lover.

And he was guessing she'd used that last statement to put him off. But it wouldn't work. He didn't care about the men in her past. He only cared that there would be one man in her future—him.

"But you like me the best," he concluded as his hand closed over her breast, which reacted immediately to his caress.

"Women don't rate men on scales of one to ten," Alexa told him, without pulling away. "But if you want me to tell you how good it was, I will."

"I'm not looking for a compliment but a commitment."

Alexa sat up and fumbled for her clothes, her face flushed. She avoided looking at him. "That wasn't the deal."

A moment ago, she'd been as relaxed as a cat snoozing in the sun. Now she needed clothes to put another barrier between them.

He let her dress but didn't bother doing so himself. Instead, he rolled to his back and laced his fingers behind his head. "What's wrong with changing our agreement? Making our marriage a real one?"

"You don't want me."

Of all the responses Alexa could have given him, that had to be the lamest. He damn well knew what he wanted. And he wanted her.

He rolled to his side and raised himself on his bent elbow. "Why don't you think I want you?"

"Do you want more children? A sweet little brother or sister for Jason and Flynn?"

Cam watched her pale, saw her fingers clench, noted the tight cord of distress in her tone. Anguish flickered in her beautiful eyes, and he realized she was torn up inside. And suddenly it hit him.

Alexa couldn't have children.

That was why she didn't worry about protection. And from the tense way she was holding herself, he sensed his next words were crucial to their future.

"I haven't thought that far ahead," he said slowly.

Cam wouldn't lie to Alexa, nor would he lie to himself. A big family had never been his dream, but he'd always just sort of assumed he would have more children someday.

As if she could read his thoughts, Alexa straightened her spine and fisted her hands on her hips. "I can't have children, Cam. My ovaries are gone, so don't start thinking about medical miracles. It won't happen."

She'd finished dressing and stood looking down at him. Cold, self-possessed, calm. And he wondered how much it cost her to act as if she didn't care. Cam held out his hand to her. She hesitated for a moment and then let him draw her against his side.

She sat with her back to his chest, leaning against him, and, dry-eyed, stared off at the horizon. "Don't feel pity for me. I lost the ovaries when I was sixteen, long before the age when most women decide they want kids. I simply changed my life into a direction that satisfied me. I'm happy, Cam."

She didn't sound happy. She sounded drained and emotionally spent. And all he could think about was wiping that wan look off her face.

"Jason and Flynn are such a handful it might not be fair to them to have other children. But adoption is always a possibility. I really don't see what having children or not has to do with your agreeing to stay."

"Because if you want more children, and you probably will, I won't be able to give them to you. It's hard to find babies to adopt. And could you feel the same way about them as your own—"

His voice hardened. "Don't go there. Dad adopted Brent, and I loved him just as much as my other brothers. After his murder, I sure as hell didn't console myself by saying he wasn't my biological brother. I loved him just as much as Tyler and Chase and Rafe. The good thing about love is that it's limitless. For the right people, there's always enough to go around."

"Even if you feel this way now, you may change your

mind and grow to resent me. You can't know the future. It's just not that simple. "

"It is. I want you, Alexa. If we can't have more children, I can live with that."

Cam hoped she could hear the truth in his words. He wouldn't have said them if they weren't true. He had too much respect for Alexa to lie to her about an issue this important. A family of four would satisfy him just fine.

Her fingers twisted the plain gold wedding band around her finger as if it was a shackle. "I don't want you to have to settle for less."

"Alexa, I already have two healthy boys. What I need to complete my family is a woman I love. And that woman is you."

He'd just laid his heart open to her, and she didn't say a word. The silence sliced and diced his emotions raw, but he waited through the pain, knowing that however this discussion ended, he wouldn't give up. He'd woo her, wine her and dine her and make love to her until she agreed to spend the rest of her life with him. Cameron Sutton considered his best quality to be sheer stubbornness. And no matter what Alexa said, no matter how much she denied it, she was going to like being married to him. He'd make sure of it.

She swiveled to face him, her eyes brimming with unshed tears. "I don't know what to say."

He read the confusion in her gaze and kissed her gently on the lips. "You don't have to decide now. Think about it. Think about having a family and living here with me and Jason and Flynn. We need you, Alexa. We want you."

"I need time to think."

"So I'll give you a moment or two," he teased lightly. He didn't want her to think. He wanted her to feel. To let herself go where she hadn't gone before.

One tear escaped down her cheek. "You're very good with words."

With his thumb, he smoothed away the tear, kissed her forehead, her nose, her mouth. He reached for her shirt, ducked his head under it and murmured, "That's not all I'm good with."

ALEXA REPAIRED her hair, tucked her shirt back in and reapplied lipstick, blush and mascara. However, she couldn't make her feelings return to the way they were before she and Cameron had made love. During the ride back, Cameron didn't try to sway her. In fact, he seemed content to let her think about what had happened between them and the future he'd dangled in front of her like a big juicy plum.

Alexa didn't know what to think or how to decide. Indecision swamped her. How could she believe Cameron knew what he wanted? Clearly he thought he was telling her the truth about being content with just the twins, but suppose he changed his mind? He would come to resent her. Yet because he was such an honorable man, he'd never say anything, just let regrets eat away at him until their relationship corroded.

And even if Cameron meant what he'd said, Alexa didn't know if she wanted what he was offering. She already loved the twins. But did she want to be their mother? It was a huge commitment and one she needed to consider carefully.

How much would she miss her work, and what would she replace it with? Alexa had no idea. Work had kept her too busy to develop hobbies to fall back on, and being a mother full-time wasn't enough to keep her satisfied. She thrived on the chase of a rare piece of art, the satisfaction of acquiring great art for her clients.

And she didn't know if she was falling in love with Cameron. She might be. She liked him. She respected him. And she'd never met a man who could turn her on with just a look. But was that love?

Confused, Alexa's thoughts swirled as she tried to use logic to evaluate every angle. She told herself this might be her only chance to have a family—but was that what she wanted?

Alexa had a good life, a career many envied and friends in every major city in the world. To give that up to become a doctor's wife and live on a ranch in Colorado was a drastic change. She needed to consider it carefully.

Cameron had said he would give her time, so the only pressure she had was what she put on herself. But indecision didn't sit well with Alexa. She liked to know what she wanted and then work to achieve it. This uncertainty was akin to swimming in the ocean without a place to put your feet down and rest.

Cameron rode toward the stable, and Alexa's horse needed little direction from her to follow. They unsaddled the horses and turned them over to a groom. Cam carried the tack to the equipment room, and Alexa walked behind him, breathing in the fresh scent of hay, manure and oats.

The tack room, neat as the Barringtons' Boston living room, boasted an assortment of saddles, bridles and hackamores. Stirrups, bits of leather and horseshoes hung on pegs on one wall.

Since arriving on the ranch, Alexa had learned some interesting cowboy customs from Cameron. A hand's saddle was always the best he could afford. A little stamping or carving on the leather added character. And with two-inch boot heels and jingling spurs, the cowboy's yen for flash could often be seen when they went into town.

She could probably borrow a cowboy's gun if she needed to, and for a good enough reason she could borrow his horse. But it was unthinkable to ask to borrow his saddle, since it was a part of him that was near sacred.

The Senator kept the horse that Cameron had lent her for guests. Same with the saddle. As Cameron hung the gear on pegs and slung the saddles over wooden benches, Alexa heard an odd zap. Like static electricity, only louder.

"Did you hear—"

Cam grabbed her and thrust her through the tack room's back door. "Run!"

The urgency in his tone, the force of his hands propelling her body, hastened her footsteps. Her pulse skyrocketed at the danger he sensed, but she didn't see anything wrong.

He didn't wait to see whether she listened to him. Taking her hand, he yanked her out of the barn and half-pulled, half-carried her into the yard.

A sudden roar, then a blast of hot wind, sent Alexa tumbling to her knees, her stomach. Beneath her, the ground bucked.

Then Cam flattened her, his big body covering her, protecting her from flying debris. Smoke filled her nostrils and horses screamed in fear. Alexa turned her head toward the stable and saw flames leaping skyward.

"You okay?" Cam asked, rolling off her with the agility of a mountain cat.

She stood, horrified at the flames licking their way from the tack room toward the stalls. "The horses!"

His measured look seemed to assure him that she wasn't injured, and Cam started to run toward the stable, yelling back over his shoulder, "Get help."

Alexa turned to do as he asked, but the noise from the explosion had already warned everyone of the danger. Men came running from all directions—sheds, paddocks, Cameron's house and the open range. But she and Cam were closest.

Without hesitating, she raced after Cam. Dodging fiery debris and hellish flames shooting out a window, she sprinted around to the far side of the stable.

The groom jammed open the double doors and shooed two horses out by flapping a blanket. An overhead sprinkler system came on, but instead of dousing the flames, the fire worsened and the smoke thickened. Alexa thought she saw Leo hooking up a hose, but couldn't be sure. Surely Leo couldn't have made it from the house to the barn yet, but she could have sworn she saw him through the smoke for an instant.

Holding her arm over her mouth and breathing through her shirt, Alexa ran from stall to stall, opening the doors and hoping the animals would have the sense to flee. As Alexa slipped into the stall where the twins kept their ponies, Cameron smacked a horse on the rump and sent it fleeing to safety.

"Get out of here. The roof's going to collapse," Cameron ordered.

She couldn't abandon the twins' ponies. Alexa hurried to their stall and shoved back the door. She eased toward the frightened horses, then backed them slowly out of the stall. The animals snorted at the smoke and their eyes rolled with terror.

"Come on, boys," she crooned. "That's the way. A few more steps." She kept talking reassuringly until the ponies cleared the stall, then slapped them on the rumps to shoo them outside.

Freeing all the animals was taking too long. Many of the other horses snorted in fear in their stalls, too terrified to leave. The groom headed past Alexa and shifted between a roan and a gray. "Move aside."

Alexa stepped into a nearby stall. The groom slapped the

animals on the rump, and they took off for the open doors at a gallop.

Alexa knew the hands would round up the horses later, and she'd just turned to leave when she realized that she'd ducked into the stall where Rafe kept his prize stallion. When the chestnut with white hooves and face spotted her, the frightened animal reared up, whites of his eyes rolling, hooves flailing.

"It's okay, fella. Calm down. I'll get you out of here. Just let me put a hand on your mane and I'll lead you to green grasses, cool water and mares. You'd like that, wouldn't you, boy?"

She spoke softly, knowing the words didn't matter and that the terrified horse probably wouldn't calm down from the sound of her voice, either. But she had to try. She couldn't leave him to burn. But the temperamental animal didn't want anything to do with a stranger.

Alexa ignored the crackle overhead, concentrated on the horse. She needed to throw something over the horse's head so he couldn't see the flames. The thick smoke blinded her and she gave up on finding a blanket. Quickly, she unfastened her blouse, dipped it in the water trough. As the leery animal scooted to one side, she moved in and threw the blouse over his head.

He reared, spun. Knocked her against the wall.

She sprang back and grabbed a handful of her shirt and his mane. "Whoa, boy."

The horse trembled but he didn't buck again. Alexa spared him a moment and rubbed his nose, then tugged on his mane. Inch by inch, she coaxed him out of the stall.

She could hear other voices, hooves clopping down the passageway. Help had arrived. Other hands led out horses, but she couldn't see much in the smoke. She tried to call for help, but her throat was so raw, her voice came out like a croak.

The stallion banged her against a rail, and she almost lost her grip. Overhead, a huge sheet of flames flared, eating through the roof. Beams behind her collapsed.

They had to get out. Now.

And she needed the horse's speed as much as he needed her guidance.

Knowing the animal might buck her off, knowing she couldn't hold on without bridle and saddle, Alexa made a desperate choice. In one awkward move, she flung herself onto the stallion's back, used his mane to pull herself upright and slapped his hind quarters. The powerful stallion needed no further urging.

Muscular hindquarters gathered and thrust forward. And Alexa guided him with her knees, praying she remembered the way out. The stallion lunged forward, and suddenly they burst past the double doors. She glimpsed Leo, Cody, Rafe and Cameron.

Cameron shouted her name as she and the stallion bolted out. Behind them the roof caved in with a crash.

With no bridle and no saddle, Alexa had no way to control the stallion, and he accelerated from zero to thirty in mere seconds. As his hooves pounded the pasture, she hung on to his mane for dear life, gripping his smooth flanks as best she could with her knees.

Wind whipped the hair from her face and she could barely see. The horse tossed his head and her blouse soared behind them. She had no reins to stop the stallion's wild run across the pasture and considered throwing herself to the ground.

Beneath his flying hooves, she saw rocks and reconsidered. How long would it take the animal to tire?

Yanking on his mane did little to stop his terrified dash.

She tried talking softly to him but doubted he could hear her through the sound of his hammering hooves.

She heard shouts behind her but didn't dare turn to look. The animal's back became slick with his sweat and she squeezed her knees tighter, hoping she could hang on long enough, but the horse had been bred to run. He didn't even sound winded.

She tried not to think what would happen if he stepped in a hole, tried not to think of pitching over his head and him trampling her.

"Hang on." Cameron's voice, surprisingly close behind her gave her added strength. "We're coming."

Out of the corner of her eyes, she saw two horses and riders closing on her, sandwiching her runaway horse between them. Cam neared on her right, and one of his brothers, Rafe, maybe, on her left.

"Hurry, Cam! I'm slipping!"

"ALMOST THERE." Cam rode next to her, knee to knee, and then he looped one arm around her just as Rafe threw a lasso over the stallion's neck.

Soon. Soon she would be safe.

Until the moment he'd spied Alexa on the stallion's back racing out of the burning barn, he'd had no idea she'd disobeyed him. Instead of going for help, she'd entered the burning building, and in all the confusion and smoke he'd never seen her. Until she rode out like some wild Valkyrie and almost shocked him into a panic.

He and Rafe had lost precious moments, grabbing mounts and going after her. Finally they'd caught up. The two brothers worked together, and slowly the stallion's pace wound down to a canter, then a trot and finally a walk.

In the moonlight, Alexa's face looked as pale as the rising moon. But she tossed her hair over her shoulder, straightened her back, and asked, her tone almost jaunty, "What took you guys so long?"

Rafe chuckled. "Lady, that was some ride. Did you know this horse has never had a rider on his back? I keep him for breeding."

At Rafe's words, Cam's stomach churned. She could have been stomped to death, bucked off and broken her neck. His hands started to tremble, and he felt a little sick at the thought of what could have happened.

Alexa finally seemed to realize the risk she'd taken. "I'd like to get down now."

Cam lifted her from the stallion and placed her on the horse in front of him. She was either trembling from the aftershock or shivering from the cold. He removed his shirt and wrapped her in it. Then his arms closed around her, and he kissed her behind the ear. "Better?"

"Mm."

"Whatever possessed you to climb on his back?" Rafe asked as he led the stallion behind his mount.

"At the time, it seemed the fastest way out of the barn."

"Well, I appreciate your efforts. We left him for last because he's...difficult."

"Difficult!" Cameron exclaimed. "How many times has Bodine told you to shoot the beast? He's a killer."

Alexa leaned against Cam for strength. "He saved my life. And he's as fast as the wind. I'm surprised you caught me."

"We almost didn't," Cam muttered, the fear for her still burning through his stomach. "You shouldn't have risked your life—not even for a million-dollar piece of horse-flesh."

Alexa looked behind her at the prancing stallion. "I didn't know the flames would spread so quickly. The sprinklers came on, but they didn't seem to help much."

Rafe cursed under his breath. "Someone turned off the water valve."

Another act of sabotage.

"What caused the explosion?" Alexa asked, her voice still a little shaky.

"We don't know." Cam's arm tightened around her waist. "But I'm betting the explosive device was similar to the one used on the bridge. Someone doesn't want us to make it to the custody trial tomorrow. I hate to accuse them, but the Barringtons have the most to gain from our deaths."

Cam felt Alexa stiffen and could almost feel her working up an automatic protest, but somewhere inside her, it died. Although she didn't believe her grandparents would try to kill her, he couldn't come up with a single other alternative that fit the facts. There'd been trouble since the first day she'd arrived. First the bull had escaped and almost gored her. Then those security guards had drugged her and tried to take the twins. And the bridge and barn had been blown up. Each incident could be used against them at the custody hearing in court, tomorrow.

Cam knew Alexa had never believed her grandparents would fight this dirty, endanger her life, but now she *had* to believe it since no other explanation made sense. He couldn't imagine the sorrow she must feel at the knowledge her only living relatives had turned against her. But she had a new family now. One that would appreciate her, cherish her, protect her.

As they rode back to the Sutton's stable, now a mass of smoking beams and ashes, the air reeked. The building was a total loss, but at least all the animals had been saved.

The Senator, Chase, Tyler and Laura met them on horseback as they rode up. The Senator's face was tight and his eyes glinted with anger and sadness. "Damn stable has too many bad memories."

Brent, Cam's oldest brother, had died in that stable. Tyler had had a terrible accident there, too. Perhaps it would be best to rebuild on another spot.

"I've already called the sheriff," Chase told them. "At least the bridge is back up."

A car pulled down the road and the headlights caught them in the glare before the driver shut them off. Alexa's grandparents exited the vehicle, stared at the smoking stable and then back at Alexa.

Her grandmother, Emily Barrington, frowned at her. "My dear, that shirt is too large for you."

"She's lucky to be alive," Cam practically growled. He wanted to throttle the old woman for giving Alexa any grief after what she'd just been through.

The old man, Dalton, frowned. "You aren't taking very good care of my granddaughter, young man."

"I don't need anyone to take care of me," Alexa protested. "But I'd like to know how long ago you two left the Senator's house."

"There's nothing to do at night," Emily complained. "No shows, no opera, no parties. So we went for a little drive, but there's nothing to see except cows."

At the old woman's admission that they'd been out driving, Alexa's face hardened, but her eyes burned with grief. Clearly she was thinking her grandparents could have set off the explosive device.

"Would you mind if I search your vehicle, sir?" Tyler asked politely, but flint sharpened his tone.

"Are you accusing *me* of something?" Dalton's tone rose in outrage.

The Senator stepped forward. "We think a trigger device set off the explosion and caused the fire. We'd like to make sure you don't have one on you."

Emily Barrington's jaw dropped open and she staggered

a step backward. Dalton pounded his cane into the dirt and then at Cameron. "If you accuse me again, I'll take you to court for slander." The old man's face darkened with rage. "Don't blame us if you can't protect your family." He took Emily's arm. "And let me assure you that the judge will hear about this unfounded accusation. With all the goings-on around here, you aren't fit to raise my great-grandchildren. The judge will see things my way, so I'd suggest you start packing their belongings."

"Don't listen to him," Alexa whispered. "He's all bluster."

Cameron took comfort in her words and in her soft body against him. He could only pray that the old man was wrong.

Chapter Eleven

Cam didn't sleep well the night before the custody hearing and knew dark circles underlined his eyes that morning, but as usual, Alexa, in a blue silk suit, looked luminous enough for them both. She seemed to light the courtroom. Her fair skin, lightly tanned, glowed with well-being, which protected her from the scowls and frowns of her grandparents.

The Barringtons' attorney presented his case first, and even Cam had to admit the evidence against him sounded damning. Their attorney, a sophisticated smooth talker with a dignified air, twisted the facts, bringing up numerous incidents that had occurred since Sandra's death and painting Cameron darker than a moonless night. Apparently the Barringtons' strategy was to smear his name until the judge ruled him unfit.

When the judge heard how the twins had repeatedly been in danger, Cam's heart sank. He'd known these issues would come up, but he hadn't realized how bad they would sound.

Beside him Alexa squeezed his hand, her chin cocked with confidence. "Just wait for our turn."

Cam feared that the damage done to his reputation couldn't be reversed. Although Alexa had spent an inordinate amount of time talking with Cam's attorney in private, his hopes started to plummet.

His entire family sat on his side of the courtroom, and Cameron appreciated the solid show of support. But the thought of losing the twins left his palms sweaty and his pulse unsteady.

Finally Alexa took the stand. She didn't rush and kept her gaze on Cam as the bailiff swore her in.

Cam's attorney, Drake Francis, one of Denver's top lawyers had flown in this morning. He offered Alexa a glass of water, then asked her what her relationship to the twins was.

Alexa's voice was cool, direct and businesslike. "I'm their mother's cousin and their mother by marriage."

"What prompted you to marry the week before the custody hearing, Mrs. Sutton?" Francis asked.

"I promised my cousin I wouldn't let our grandparents raise the twins."

"So married the father?"

"We thought a couple would have a better chance of keeping the twins than a single father."

"Tell me about the promise you made to the former Mrs. Sutton."

"She was dying and she knew it." Alexa cleared her throat and pain flared in her eyes. "She begged me to make sure our grandparents would never raise her boys."

"And why is that?"

"The Barringtons were our grandparents and they raised Sandra and me."

"Were you abused?"

Alexa shook her head, a lock of her dark hair falling forward onto her cheek, and Cameron couldn't help but recall the soft silky texture of it. "Sandra didn't want her children to be raised with nannies and then sent to boarding school like we were. She wanted them raised with love.''

''Do you love the boys?''

''Yes.''

''If you have other children, will you be able to love Flynn and Jason as much as your own?''

''That won't ever be a problem because I can't have children.''

''Please, tell us about the man you married. What kind of father is he?''

''He's the kind of father every child could wish for. He's smart and generous with his time. He keeps the boys in line with a kind heart and a loving soul. Sandra wanted Cameron to raise their children, and no one has the right to take that away from him.'' Alexa stared down her grandparents. ''No one.''

''Now these incidents that opposing counsel brought up, could you tell us what's happening out at the ranch?''

''We don't know.'' Alexa's honesty and integrity rang in her tone, and the judge paid attention to her every word. She kept her chin up, her shoulders squared. ''Because the trouble began around the same time as the custody battle, we could only assume that someone needed to make Cameron look bad so my grandparents could use the evidence against him in this court.''

''Your grandparents are getting on in years, Mrs. Sutton. Why do you think they are fighting for custody?''

''The boys have a very large trust fund. The Barringtons don't wish to give up the administration of such a vast amount of money.''

Emily Barrington gasped aloud as if the mention of money was akin to muttering a curse.

''And why is giving up administration of the trust such a big deal?''

"For one, because they are courted and entertained due to the contributions to charity they make in the boys' names. And second, they don't like to give up anything. They consider it a defeat."

"Are you worried about the boys' safety?" the attorney asked.

"Yes. But once this issue is settled, I expect the danger to be over."

"Thank you, Mrs. Sutton. No more questions, Your Honor."

Opposing counsel for the plaintiffs stood and stepped forward. "Well, I have several."

"Go ahead, sir," the judge said.

Alexa's demeanor didn't change. Although opposing counsel appeared ready to tear her to shreds, she kept her composure.

"How do you feel about your grandparents, Mrs. Sutton?"

"What do you mean?" Alexa asked, her beautiful blue eyes wary, her hands clasped together, each glossy nail a perfect foil for the agitation Cam sensed beneath her calm poise.

"They raised you, and you turned out okay, didn't you?"

"Yes. And if you want to know if I think my grandparents did the best they could, again my answer is yes. But Cameron and I can raise the twins better."

"Do you love your husband, Mrs. Sutton?"

Cameron saw her eyes flicker, and she hesitated for just a second. Clearly she didn't want to answer the question under oath.

But she spoke smoothly and he'd doubted anyone but him could guess how much she didn't want to answer the question. "I love seeing Cameron play with the boys. I love listening to him talk about his passion for medicine. And the love between him and his brothers colors everything the family does. The twins won't be getting just a father and mother, they'll be getting loving aunts and uncles, cousins and—''

"Do you love your husband, Mrs. Sutton?" The attorney pressed her, sensing a weakness he could capitalize on.

Cam's attorney stood. "Objection, Your Honor. I fail to see the relevance—''

"Overruled. Answer the question Mrs. Sutton," the judge said.

When Alexa didn't answer immediately, the courtroom fidgeting stopped. No one whispered or coughed, rattled a paper or so much as shifted in their seat. It was quiet enough to hear a pin drop.

"Let me remind you that you're under oath, Mrs. Sutton," the Barringtons' attorney said.

"I'm aware of that," Alexa snapped. She looked at her grandparents and then back at Cameron and his gut clenched. "Yes. I love my husband."

After that, the case moved easily through each of his brothers' testimony, and by the time the Senator took the stand, it was practically a done deal. However good Alexa had been on the witness stand, her words gnawed at Cameron. Was Alexa telling the truth when she'd said she loved him? The doubt disturbed him. He'd thought they were on their way to a good and passionate marriage, but suppose Alexa had lied so he could keep the twins?

He'd found her courage admirable. And yet he'd wished she could have responded without hesitation. Cam liked being a husband. He liked being part of a family and he liked being married.

Those poor determined-to-remain-bachelors, afraid-to-commit men didn't know what they were missing. Family was everything, and without it, a man had no place to root himself in the world. Even though Cam was a doctor, he simply couldn't imagine delivering a baby or saving a life and never having someone to come home to and share the joy with. He liked intimacy, liked sharing, liked loving.

And he'd married a woman who didn't know what she wanted.

THE SENATOR HAD INVITED the family over for a celebration dinner after the judge ruled the twins would stay with their father and new mother.

The parting scene with her grandparents had been painful for Alexa. No hugs. No goodbyes. Just hurtful glances because she had implied they were behind the series of problems on the ranch.

And now Alexa stood in front of her newly finished closet, her nose screwed up at the scent of fresh paint and wallpaper paste, deciding what to wear. Her silk black skirt and black wraparound top seemed too casual for the occasion, her white beaded pantsuit, too formal.

Cam stuck his head through the door to her room. "Hurry up, sweetheart. The twins will need another bath if you don't decide soon."

Alexa groaned. "I should have called Laura and asked her what she was wearing."

"Something sexy. She wants another child, and she's determined to make Chase so crazy he'll forget how hard the last childbirth was on her."

"You're a big help."

Cameron stepped into the room, wearing a black sports jacket that emphasized his broad shoulders over a black sweater with black jeans that made his long legs seem even longer. His gray eyes perused hers, and then his sooty lashes swept down to hide his thoughts. "I'm sorry. I shouldn't have thrown Laura's wanting a third baby in your face."

Taking her cue from Cam's elegantly casual attire, Alexa finally pulled out a red blouse and the black skirt and donned them over her slip. "I'm not that sensitive. I suspect the twins are just about all I can handle. So you don't need to tiptoe around the subject of children, okay? If Laura has another baby, I'll be happy for her."

Cam's nostrils flared just before his eyes turned to smoke. And she knew he was going to kiss her. Anticipation heated her. Cam's kisses were worth waiting for, and he'd been remarkably generous with them since the custody hearing last week. If he'd been another man, she'd have been sure his mind was bent on seduction.

But Cam had more complicated thoughts. He seemed to have some kind of campaign mapped out to woo her. And she found his intentions not only sexy but invading her dreams at night. Lately her dreams had been erotic, and she kept wondering if he was waiting for her to seduce him.

So she was more than ready for his kiss. A slow heated kiss that had her throwing her arms around his neck and pulling him against her. His spicy aftershave mixed with the scent of his jacket and his natural masculine musk, invading her senses until she wanted to drag him onto her bed and rip off his clothes.

The patter of hushed voices finally wiggled through her consciousness.

"Told you they were kissing." Flynn's loud whisper traveled right through the open door.

Jason sounded as if he'd made a new discovery. "He put his tongue in her mouth."

"That's yucky."

"I saw Uncle Rafe breeding a stallion. The stallion's yang pointed at the moon and he put it right—"

Cam broke their kiss, a smile on his lips. "Boys, we don't discuss the details of breeding horses in front of a lady."

Flynn's little face screwed up with confusion. "But, Dad, Aunt Laura talks about breeding."

Alexa could see that Cameron was at a loss. His inquisitive sons asked the darnedest questions. Restraining a laugh, she decided to help him out.

She smoothed Jason's hair and straightened Flynn's collar. "It's okay to talk about breeding—but only if the lady brings up the subject first."

"Okay, got it." Flynn grinned up at her mischievously. "Are you ready yet? Dad says ladies take a real long time to put on their faces, but yours looks all done and I'm hungry."

Alexa chuckled. "My face doesn't come apart into pieces like one of your puzzles."

"It doesn't?"

"Your father meant it takes me a long time to fix my hair and makeup."

"Your hair is clean." Jason tugged her hand. "Can we go now?"

Cam drove them over to the Senator's, claiming if they went by horseback they'd be late. But Alexa knew the real reason. The kiss had inflamed her senses and aroused Cameron so much that sitting on a horse right now would be uncomfortable.

Alexa liked the passion that sizzled like lightning between them. But what did she really want? Her life had taken a different path the day she'd learned she couldn't have children. She'd made the most of her skills and abilities, but now that a new direction offered itself, the chance to have children and a family, did she want to take it?

Would she have wanted children if she could have had them? Maybe. Alexa didn't know. She most certainly enjoyed the twins. Every time she considered leaving them she thought about how much she'd miss their carefree smiles and delicious hugs, their antics, their curiosity. She loved them.

But did she want to live in Colorado, give up the reputation she'd built for herself in the art world? Then again, she'd always dreamed of retiring and opening her own art gallery in a tourist town, and Highview certainly had enough tourists to support such an endeavor.

During the drive to the Senator's house, her thoughts drifted as the boys argued over a puzzle in the back seat. It seemed just minutes before they pulled into the Senator's drive.

"Look!" Flynn's excited voice drew Alexa's attention to Rafe, who was leading a frisky colt onto the driveway.

Sunlight gleamed on the colt's black back, but it was the delicately arched neck, the proud lift of the head and the intelligent eyes that drew the entire family out of the car to admire the animal.

Rafe, whipcord lean, and elegant from his gleaming black boots to his freshly combed dark hair, held out the hackamore lead to Alexa. His eyes lit with a rakish twinkle and his mouth quirked. "He's yours."

Alexa gasped.

"He's awesome," Jason said.

Flynn patted his nose. "And friendly."

Alexa stared at the colt's finely shaped head, the ears pricked forward. The animal's graceful neck arched down to well-defined withers, which were in direct line with the croup, the highest point of the rounded and muscled hindquarters. But it was the legs that told her the colt's value, the feet matching one another in size and shape, the legs muscular and lean and long.

Rafe tipped his hat and placed the lead in her hand. "My gift to you for saving his sire."

Surprise took her aback. "I can't accept such a valuable—"

"Take him," Cameron urged her with a slight smile. "My brother will be insulted if you don't."

"But, but…I don't know anything about training such an animal."

"You can learn," Cam said.

"I wouldn't want to make any mistakes with him. He's gorgeous but…"

Alexa tried to give the lead back to Rafe. Rafe only refused it and shook his head. "The cost of boarding shouldn't be much. 'Course there's feeding, shoeing, veterinarian fees, insurance, tack and the costs of traveling to the shows—"

"Shows?"

"—and entry fees if you wish to compete."

"Compete?"

Feeling overwhelmed and knowing she didn't have the knowledge to do this horse justice, she scratched the animal behind the ears, enchanted with the idea of owning a living thing of such beauty. "I'll accept him on one condition."

Rafe and Cameron raised identical eyebrows.

"Is she dumb?" Jason asked. "She can't give him back."

"She's not dumb," Flynn argued. "She's scared."

"Boys—" Cameron's voice turned stern "—what did I tell you about calling anyone dumb?"

"It's rude. Sorry, Lexi." The twins said in unison.

Cameron shrugged. "They have that down a little too pat."

Were her emotions so obvious that two-year-olds, granted extra bright two-year-olds, could see the fear on her face? Alexa refused to accept so valuable an animal when she had no conception of the responsibilities required to care for him.

"What's your condition, Alexa?" Rafe finally asked.

"We go partners on him, fifty-fifty." Alexa held out her hand for Rafe to shake.

Rafe hesitated, looked at Cameron, who nodded slightly, then took her hand. "Partners."

They shook on the deal, and then Rafe motioned for a ranch hand to take the foal back to his mother. Alexa watched the proud prance of the animal and knew, regardless of whether she stayed as Cam's wife, she would come back often to check on the colt's progress.

"She's looking at the colt like she looks at you," Rafe teased Cameron.

"You're just jealous," Cam teased right back.

"Of a horse?"

"Very funny. Now that the partnership's settled, let's go eat." Cameron steered Alexa toward the front door.

Behind them, Rafe took each of the twins by the hand, shortening his long steps to allow them to keep up. "Do you boys know what a partner is?"

Jason frowned. "She gave you back half the horse?"

Flynn's high-pitched voice asked, "Why, Uncle Rafe?"

"Because sometimes when you give away half, you get more than if you kept everything for yourself," Rafe answered patiently.

"I don't get it."

"Me, neither."

"The horse will be more valuable if I train him, because I'm an expert," Rafe told them.

"I want to be an expert."

Alexa took Cam's hand and they entered the house together. Once, she'd felt a stranger here, but now as Laura and Chase, Tyler and the Senator greeted them, and the kids raced toward the dining room, feelings of contentment stole through Alexa. This was the family she'd always wanted.

"Would you like to freshen up?" Laura asked her. "I'll take you upstairs."

After petting the horse, Alexa did want to wash her hands, and she also appreciated the chance to speak to Laura alone. They climbed a carpeted staircase lined with family portraits. No stuffy pictures for the Senator. His pictures were framed shots of little boys riding and playing and growing up on the ranch.

Alexa vowed to study them another time. "There's something I've been wanting to ask you…"

"About Cameron?" Laura's bright green eyes turned to Alexa with a twinkle.

"As a matter of fact, Cameron would be furious with me if he knew I was discussing this with you."

Laura's face broke into a friendly grin. "Sounds interesting. I adore gossip."

Alexa slipped into the first bedroom they came to. "It's something that's bothered me for a long time, and Cameron forbade me to say anything to you, but…"

Laura seemed to realize that Alexa wasn't going to ask some deep secret about Cameron's past but about the recent problems on the ranch, because her face turned serious. "The men in this family tend to be overly protective of me. Sometimes it's great. More often it's a pain in the ass. Talk."

"The day the bridge exploded, Bodine said he saw someone who looked like you riding in the distance." Alexa hesitated. "I just wondered if you saw anybody or anything unusual that day."

Laura's eyes darkened. "Why didn't Cameron just ask me?"

"He didn't want you to think we were accusing you of anything."

"That's ridiculous. I'm not made of glass." Laura stared unseeingly out the window at the green mountains, and Alexa could almost envision her memories turning back to that day. She twisted her fingers through her gorgeous blond hair as she concentrated. "I didn't hear the blast because Julie and I had taken the twins and Keith out for a ride, and Julie had the radio turned up. Leo brought us a picnic basket for lunch. But I didn't see anything unusual."

"Would you have noticed my grandparents' car?" Alexa asked, hoping to put her doubts behind her.

"Maybe. Maybe not. When the twins and Keith get together, you need eyes in the back of your head." Laura repeated Chase's favorite expression with a sigh. "Sorry I can't be more helpful."

"Helpful about what?" Chase wandered into the room, and both women jumped.

Laura gave him a bright smile. "Just woman talk."

Her sister-in-law wasn't a good liar, but Chase seemed inclined to let it go. He winked at his wife. "I like woman talk."

"And pillow talk," Laura teased him right back, took his arm and led him downstairs.

Relieved at their departure, but jittery and a little ill at ease from going behind Cameron's back to question Laura, Alexa took in several deep breaths. To calm herself, she washed her hands and freshened her makeup, then joined the others for dinner.

As she looked across the table at Cameron and into his shadowed gaze, she knew he suspected the subject of her conversation with Laura. But it wasn't until they'd gone home and tucked the kids into bed that he stopped her at the upstairs landing overlooking the first floor, cornered her and asked, "So what did you and Laura talk about?"

Ignoring his question, she gestured to the finished living area below. The painters and wallpaperers had done a fine job, and the comfortable leather furniture she'd ordered fit in well with the elegant but snug look she'd been striving for. Cam hadn't mentioned whether or not he liked the finished product, nor had he complained about the bill she'd rung up on his credit card.

"You did a great job and I like the way you've turned this place into a home. Now tell me about your conversation with Laura."

Although he was making her feel as if she'd betrayed him, she didn't bother lying. But the conversation was going to cost him. She had a few very expensive pieces of art she wanted to hang on his walls. "Laura told me she and Keith met up with Julie, Leo and the twins for lunch the day the bridge exploded."

Cameron stiffened and anger radiated from him like rain clouds coalescing across a midnight sky. "I specifically asked you not to—"

"Laura didn't mind." Although Alexa trembled inside at the sharp edge in his tone, she kept her voice breezy.

His eyes flashed rare annoyance. "That's not the point. We agreed—"

"You think my grandparents could have hired Leo? He brought them all a picnic lunch."

"You're trying to divert me by changing the subject."

"We aren't going to agree on this one. Besides, I don't find it pleasant when you're angry with me," she admitted, hoping her words would make him realize that she did care about his wishes—even if she went against them.

Just then, Cameron's cell phone rang. "Sorry, someone

might need me." He flipped open the phone and listened for a moment, then snapped it shut. "That was the sheriff."

"And?" There was something he didn't want to tell her. Something he was considering that he wanted to protect her from.

"Remember the references those security guards used in Denver?"

"Yes."

"The phone bills were paid by money order."

"So they can't be traced."

"Probably not, but we did learn something interesting."

"What?"

"You aren't going to like it."

"But I should know, right?"

"The phone bills were sent to a post-office box…in Boston."

Chapter Twelve

At the raw pain in Cameron's voice, Alexa embraced him, her hands curling up his back, her chest, hips and thighs pressed to him. He gathered her close, breathing in her scent as she tipped her head back and looked into his eyes.

Alexa nibbled her bottom lip. "I don't understand what you're thinking. My grandparents live in Boston and Sandra died in Boston. But they had no reason to murder Sandra, since she didn't know about the trust fund."

The fact that she had accepted that the grandparents who had raised her could be capable of such a deed pained Cameron. He couldn't imagine how it must be for her to suspect her only living relatives of such ugliness.

"Exactly. But if those bills were sent to Boston, perhaps we've been looking in the wrong direction." Heat filled him, and deep inside, muscles tightened around a kindled ember. He ached to kiss her. He had trouble concentrating and dipped his head until his lips almost touched hers.

"Wait a minute. Sandra was mugged in the park. You think it might have been premeditated? That whoever murdered Sandra caused the trouble here? What makes you think that?"

"The possibility hadn't occurred to me before now." His fingers traced slow, lazy circles at the base of her neck. He enjoyed his effect on her, enjoyed watching her pupils dilate and feeling her pulse quicken. Enjoyed watching her lose to the pull of desire.

She trembled at his caress. ''Did you have any enemies in Boston?''

He drank in her response and ran his hands through her hair. ''There are lots of crazy people in this world. Maybe some patient's relatives blamed me when their loved one died.''

''That's crazy.''

''Whoever let that bull loose, blew up the bridge and the stable isn't exactly what I'd call sane.'' She shivered against him, and he rubbed her arms to warm her, but he knew he wouldn't succeed. Despite her passionate nature, cold fear had taken over as she considered the possibilities.

She shivered again. ''Don't forget the stalker didn't just attack us, he went after the twins. It's almost as if someone has a vendetta against your entire family.''

Cam didn't want to think about his family right now. Nor did he want to think about danger and intrigue.

He often found a solution to a puzzle would pop into his mind if he relaxed. And he could think of no better way to take his mind off his problems than a little relaxation with Alexa.

''Come on, let's get you warm.'' He led her downstairs, past the fireplace to the hot tub off the pool. The hot tub had been designed deep and wide to hold four to six people. He was glad for the privacy fence, glad to have Alexa alone. He left the lights off, except for one pink underwater light that reflected through the water in enticing rays.

As the night air blew across the privacy fence, goose bumps rose on Alexa's flesh. ''I thought you were going to make me warm?''

''Oh, I am—right after you take off your clothes,'' he

teased as he started to strip. He couldn't wait to try out his new toy with Alexa. "Last one in has to…"

He jumped first into the hot tub without finishing his sentence. Letting the warm water swirl over his bare flesh didn't change his temperature much. His skin, already heated from thoughts of Alexa, adapted easily to the water.

Cameron rose to the surface and flicked on the whirlpool jets. He turned to watch Alexa slide into the water, her back arched, her breasts high and aroused in the pink water.

She tilted her head back on the ledge with a contented sigh. "This feels wonderful."

He shifted his body close to hers and claimed her lips in one possessive swoop, let the heat chase away the cold, let the soft light banish the shadows. She kissed him willingly, pulling him to her, her mouth fitting his perfectly, making the ache spread through his body until he needed her with a force that shook him.

Refusing to deny himself, he drank deeply from her mouth, letting his tongue move over hers. Then he felt the liquid movement of her hips against his sex.

"Not yet." Ending the kiss caused him pain. Backing away cost him. But she was worth every bit of patience he could summon, worth the savage pleasure she gave him with her eagerness. Worth waiting to bury himself in her heat.

Without his body to block her, her toes floated to the surface, and he nipped the arch of her foot. His hands kneaded her feet as he ignored his aching arousal.

She giggled and tried to pull away, watching him with a breathless combination of wariness, excitement and pleasure. "That tickles."

Urgency roughened his tone but he kept himself under control. "Too bad. You have to hold still. You lost the bet."

"What bet?"

"You were the last one in, so you have to do whatever I ask for the next hour."

Her breath drew in sharply. "I never made any such bet." Her protest, lazy with indignation and a hint of curiosity, lacked conviction.

"Hold still," he demanded as his lips traced a path from her pearly pink toenails, past her delicate ankles to her parted knees.

"Oh."

"What's wrong?"

"The whirlpool…"

He swallowed a knowing grin and returned to exploring the tantalizing softness of her legs, the gleaming ripeness of her thighs. She had a terrific body, and her legs called to him, the smooth silky muscles quivering as he parted her legs wider and raised her hips to his mouth.

"Cameron—" Surprise and hunger made her tremble with anticipation.

"It's all right." He fully intended to taste all of her— and he would wait until she wanted him as much as he wanted her.

Cameron knew his patience would reward both of them. Although she wriggled and squirmed, he avoided the spot where they both desired his lips most. He tasted her thighs, her hips, the hollow at her waist as she floated in the water, open to him and content to let him have his way.

Only content wasn't quite the right word. Little moans of pleasure came from deep in her throat, a sound he could become quite accustomed to hearing. Holding back had never been so difficult. He wanted her badly. Wanted to thrust into her heat and feel those silky thighs around his waist, hear her purr turn to a shout of satisfaction.

But not yet.

Water glistened over her skin. Pink shimmers of water

lapped at her flesh. She had no idea how much he wanted her.

But he waited, wanting to show her how good they were together, and he'd hold back until he'd done so—even if it killed him.

"Cameron?"

"Hmm?" She wasn't hot enough yet.

Slowly he maneuvered her parted legs over a jet, adjusting the pressure and direction of the spurting water until she tensed in pleasure.

"Relax, darling. We have all night."

She lifted her head, her eyes dilated with need, her voice urgent. "I can't...relax. I'm not sure I can wait one more second."

"But you'll wait for me, won't you? I want to be inside you when you explode. Tell me, you'll wait."

"I'll try."

"Not good enough." He eased her away from the water jet. "Promise me," he demanded softy.

"I promise. But you don't know how good I feel."

"Tell me." He floated her back over the jet.

"My skin is hot and hotter. It's hard to breathe. And my heart is beating too fast. And if I don't move, I'm going to die."

"Don't move, sweetheart. And remember your promise." Then his mouth came down over her and she tasted so sweet, he wondered how he'd ever recover if she left him. Her hips bucked and he supported her legs with his arms, pinning her open for him against the hot tub's wall.

She flailed and reached for his hair to tug his mouth away and drag him upward. Gently he replaced her hand on the pool's edge. "Patience."

"I'm...going...to get...even."

He breathed more sweet torment into her. "I can hardly wait."

But he couldn't wait. Not another second.

Breathing brokenly, he thrust into her and she welcomed him with a throaty whimper. Her breath rushed out, his name on her lips.

He paused to angle another jet onto her sweet flesh. And she arched upward.

"Wait. Wait, just a few more minutes," he coaxed.

He pumped back and forth slowly, enjoying the exquisite sensations of silky heat and burning nerve endings. And when he could hold back no more, he moved his hips faster.

She clutched his shoulders, frantic, her hips meeting his, matching him move for move, thrust for thrust. Giving herself to him completely, she shuddered against him, her nails raking his back as she dragged him with her into a fiery intimacy, rocking them both with a series of explosions that left him weak, breathless and very much in love.

ALEXA AWOKE in Cameron's bedroom. They'd made love several more times last night, leaving her satisfied and lazy and just a bit sore. She desperately wanted coffee and a shower, but Cameron's arm across her hip kept her pinned to the bed.

She moved his arm without waking him and wondered if he normally slept this deeply or if his exhaustion was due to his strenuous activities last night. Alexa hurried to the shower, wondering why she didn't smell breakfast being made. Had Leo slept in? She'd kill for a sip of caffeine but would settle for brushing her teeth, a hot shower, soothing body lotion and a quick manicure to make her feel human again.

After her long shower, Alexa returned to her room for a fresh set of clothes. Although the shower had revived her, she still wanted coffee and again wondered if Leo had slept in for she still didn't smell any food. Perhaps she'd try her hand in the kitchen and serve Cameron breakfast in bed.

Alexa eased open her bedroom door and stepped inside. Hundreds of big fat scorpions marched across the wall like an army of invading soldiers. With a shriek, Alexa backed into the hall and slammed her door.

She rammed into something hard and let out another yelp.

"Steady." Cameron's strong arms gripped her and she realized she'd bumped into him. He'd run naked into the hallway without taking a moment to pull on his pants. And his main concern was for her. "What's wrong?"

She forced her throat and mouth to work past her fright. "My room is full of scorpions." Turning, she hurried to the twins' room. "Let's make sure they're okay."

Cameron got there first and opened the door. The room was empty of scorpions and children, and he let out a sigh of relief. "Julie must have taken them for breakfast and a ride."

Alexa tried to control her shaking. If she had gone to her room last night, instead of Cameron's, she might not be alive right now. "Cam, there're too many scorpions in my room for them to have gotten there by themselves."

Cam gathered her into his arms and ushered her back to his room. Alexa dressed in yesterday's clothes with a grimace. Cam's silence grated on her nerves, but she knew him well enough by now to know his mind was busy sifting through possibilities and alternatives, and he would make a connection she couldn't in her frightened state. So she waited.

"This is the first attack on you alone. I always assumed you'd been in danger because you were with me or the twins. But it appears as if we are all in danger."

Alexa shivered. "You're supposed to be making me feel

better, not worse. Our problems were supposed to be over after the custody hearing.''

"Maybe we were wrong and the dangers had nothing to do with the hearing or your grandparents,'' Cam suggested.

"Maybe. Look, I just can't think without coffee. And I'd rather put a full flight of stairs between me and those scorpions.'' She glanced toward her room with a shudder and wondered if the deadly creatures could travel under the door.

Cameron put on jeans, a shirt and boots, then they both went down to the kitchen. There were no signs of Julie and the twins or Leo. The house was so quiet Alexa could have heard a tear dropping on the kitchen floor.

There were no dirty cereal bowls in the sink, not even a hint of the aroma of coffee or bacon. But then, both Julie and Leo kept the house spotless. Alexa opened the dishwasher, looking for signs of breakfast. The machine was empty, and panic replaced her feelings of unease.

"Let's go see if the ponies are still here.''

Cameron looked up from the coffeemaker, his eyes dark with concern. "I thought you wanted coffee.''

"Something's wrong. I don't think Julie and Leo have been here.'' Alexa gestured at the dishwasher. "There aren't any dirty dishes around.''

"Leo could have washed the dishes and unloaded it,'' Cam suggested, but he was already moving toward the back door. Ever since his old stable burned down, they'd kept the children's ponies and Julie's horse in a hay shed out back. Most of the other horses were let loose in open pastures to graze on the summer grasses until the stable could be rebuilt.

Alexa and Cam hurried to the shed. Cameron shoved open the door and looked inside. "Julie's car is here. So are three of the four kittens. Both ponies and Julie's horse are gone. She must have taken them for a ride."

Alexa frowned, unable to banish a niggle of worry. "She didn't say anything to me about a ride."

"The twins may have talked her into it." Cam pulled out his cell phone. "I'd feel better if she'd left a note or we could check with Leo. Remind me to buy Julie a cell phone."

"We're probably worrying for nothing. They'll likely all come riding in within the hour," Alexa agreed as she scanned the horizon for two little boys and their sitter.

Cam dialed the phone, then ended the call without speaking to anyone. "Leo's not home, either."

An hour later there was still no sign of Julie and the boys, and Cam had alerted all the ranch hands to be on the look-out. Four hours later they were positive something was very wrong.

"Maybe they stopped for a picnic and the horses ran off," Alexa suggested.

"Maybe."

Alexa admired Cam's calm, but she could see the worry in his eyes, hear the tension in his voice. He'd notified the sheriff, Tyler had mobilized a group of neighbors to help, and Rafe had gone up in the helicopter to do an overhead search. There was nothing left to do but wait.

The ranch was huge, a full four days ride from east to west and almost that from north to south. The land encompassed rivers and mountains and ravines and creeks. By early evening it was obvious that Julie would never have voluntarily kept the twins out so long. And where was Leo?

And as the sun fell behind the mountains, so did their hopes of finding the boys before morning. Alexa brought Cam a sandwich and coffee. He accepted the drink and ignored the food. All afternoon they'd searched the area where the boys and Julie usually rode and were finally forced to come in and rest their weary horses.

Alexa sat beside Cam on the front porch, knowing he burned to continue a night search—on foot if necessary, but knew it was foolhardy. "At least it's warm tonight."

"The Senator's bringing in more help tomorrow." Cam told her. "I just wish I could do something more. I feel so helpless."

The waiting was eating away at her. Alexa had filed her nails down to nubs, blistered her feet from pacing and had trouble controlling her tone to keep from snapping at everyone who was trying to help. Cody had cleaned out the scorpions in the bedroom, but she couldn't even consider sleeping with the twins still missing. Her place was here with Cameron.

"No one's found Leo in town. Do you think that's suspicious?"

"I don't know. Maybe he and Julie are together with the boys."

"Can you think of anywhere else Julie may have stopped?" Alexa asked. "Maybe a nearby cabin, a neighbor's, a cave?"

"She never rode out for more than an hour or two. The boys can't sit still in the saddle longer than that."

"Maybe Julie mentioned something to her roommate," Alexa suggested. "Why don't we ride into town and check? If we find nothing there, we should check with Leo's neighbors. Someone may know where to find him."

Cameron's voice wasn't argumentative or commanding or angry. It was as if the loss of the boys had created a dead icy spot inside him that made his eyes into gray pools of despair. "I'm not leaving."

She couldn't bear to see him in such misery. She knew better than to urge him to eat or sleep. How could he when she couldn't, either? "You have your cell phone. The sheriff and his men have taken over the kitchen. They'll call if there's news. Wouldn't you rather do something?" she coaxed.

JULIE LIVED in a dorm by the community college. Cam drove over without much hope of finding anything that would help. He knew Alexa was simply trying to keep him busy, but it made sense to cover all the bases.

Perhaps Julie had mentioned something useful to her roommate. Perhaps the roommate had noticed someone following Julie. Perhaps Julie had mentioned being frightened. Ever since she'd been attacked on the way back from the portable toilet, he'd felt responsible for her safety. But Leo had always been there as an unofficial guard.

And after the fiasco of hiring the security team, Cameron had preferred not to bring more strangers onto the ranch. Another mistake. Although the sheriff thought the twins and Julie might have run into trouble with the horses, Cam suspected their trouble was the human kind.

Tomorrow they would find them. Alexa had to be correct. It was warm, and the twins and Julie would survive the night—even without food and water. And Julie was no fool. She always packed boxes of juice and snacks for the boys in her saddlebags. They would be fine. Once they returned safe and sound, the twins would be talking about their adventure for months.

Alexa looked at Cam worriedly and knocked on the dorm door. Alexa had shadows under her eyes, her cheeks were hollow, and her lips raw from nervously biting her lips. She wanted the twins back every bit as much as he did, and that knowledge made him love her all the more.

Loud country music blocked out her knock. Cam pounded harder, and finally a young woman answered the door. She wore heavy eye makeup, and her hair was teased out around her head in a most unbecoming fashion.

Cam forced himself to smile pleasantly. "Can we talk to you about Julie?"

"Julie?"

"Julie Edwards. I'm afraid she and my boys may have met up with an accident. They're missing."

The woman let them inside the dorm and turned down the stereo. "You must be Cameron Sutton. I'm Patricia Truitt." She frowned at Cameron and Alexa. "How long has Julie been missing?"

"Since this morning," Cam explained.

Alexa looked around the cheap apartment. "When was the last time you saw her?"

Patricia glanced at the ceiling as if seeking an answer there. "Last week?"

Cam and Alexa exchanged puzzled looks. Before Cam could ask another question, Patricia volunteered Julie's whereabouts. "She's been staying with Leo Harley at his camper."

The sheriff had already checked Leo's address. He was gone, too. Cam's stomach started to churn. If Julie and the twins had just had a mishap while out riding, then Leo's being missing didn't make sense. But if Julie and Leo had taken off somewhere with the twins...

Cam could hardly believe he was thinking that Leo had betrayed him. Julie had vouched for him and he and Sandra had always thought of Julie as part of the family. He suddenly recalled that Julie had been in Boston when Sandra had been killed. Julie could have sent the telephone bills for the fake security guard's reference to a Boston post-office box. And Julie could have faked her own attack to gain their trust and allay their suspicions.

But although she'd had the means and opportunity to

commit the crimes, she didn't have a motive. Nor did Leo have a motive, unless he was trying to force Julie to do something against her will by threatening the kids.

"Would you mind if we looked around her room?" Alexa asked.

"I don't know." Patricia hesitated. "Julie doesn't like anyone to go in there."

"We won't touch anything," Alexa promised.

Patricia walked over to an ashtray and plucked out a key. "I guess she won't have to know."

"We won't tell her." Cam tried not to get his hopes up as he opened the door and flicked on the light.

Beside him, Alexa drew in a breath. Horror tingled down Cam's spine at the sight of the wall by Julie's bed. His baby-sitter was insane. She had pictures of Cam and Sandra—with Sandra's face cut out and a picture of Julie's face replacing it. Julie had thrown darts at a picture of Alexa and Cameron taken at the wedding.

And now he knew Julie's motive. She had a sick crush on him.

Over her dresser, she'd blown up a poster of Cameron's face, tacked one of his old shirts under it and attached a pair of his jeans he'd forgotten he'd lost. On the ceiling were pictures and stories about the twins and the Levenger legacy that made his sons two of the richest little boys in the world.

Her voice shaky, Alexa grabbed his arm. "Don't touch anything."

Shaken and more worried than ever about his sons, Cam took out his cell phone. "I'm calling the FBI."

IT TOOK MOST of the night for the FBI, the sheriff and Cameron to put the pieces of the puzzle together. Back at Cameron's house they went over the facts.

Leo Harvey was Julie Edwards's friend. He wasn't too bright, but he'd had a crush on Julie and would do whatever she asked. He'd been dishonorably discharged from the military special forces after he'd failed to take enough care during his training on explosives.

The information about Julie made Cameron shake with anger and frustration. She had grown up in a series of foster homes and been sponsored by Judge Stewart, who'd recommended her to the Suttons as a baby-sitter. Unfortunately the judge had believed that Julie's troubles with the law during her teenage years were long over, and he'd sealed her files.

Her college entrance exams showed Julie to have an exceptionally high IQ. Personality profiles showed her stable. But once the court ordered documents were revealed, several disturbing facts came to light.

Cam and Alexa read the file with the FBI over a pot of coffee in his living room. When Julie was fifteen her foster mother died under mysterious circumstances, and her foster father claimed Julie had made sexual advances on him. Julie claimed *he* made the advances, and in court Judge Stewart believed her.

Cam wondered if this was the second time she'd gotten away with murder after developing a crush on a man. That he had trusted her made him ill. That she had taken his sons made him frantic.

He tossed the file onto the table. "It still doesn't make sense."

Alexa squeezed Cameron's hand. "She may have killed Sandra, thinking you'd turn to her. When you didn't, she decided to try and get rid of me."

Cam thought about the explosions at the stable and on the bridge. "And when that didn't work, she became so enraged she tried to kill us both?"

"Maybe." Alexa sighed. "You may not ever have been her target. Leo bungled the explosives. They may just have gone off at the wrong time. It was *me* she wanted to scare off, and when that didn't work, she wanted me dead—so she could have you."

"And now she's taken the boys. But why?" Cam dropped his head into his hands. She could be anywhere by now, and the twins could be terrified...or worse.

Alexa tugged Cam to his feet. "Come on. You need a walk to clear your head."

He followed her onto the porch. "Why did she take the twins?"

"I don't think she'll hurt them. She loves those boys."

Cam knew that Alexa was trying to look on the bright side, but it wasn't helping. "She loved me, too, in her sick way, but that didn't stop her from almost killing me. I was an idiot to trust her. What kind of doctor am I that I couldn't see she had problems?"

"You aren't a shrink. And beating yourself up won't bring the boys back." Alexa pulled him down the drive as if compelled to keep moving. "No one suspected her. None of us."

"She was right here in the house almost all the time. She seemed so innocent."

"Where would she take the twins?"

Alexa was thinking more clearly than he was. The past couldn't be changed. He had to let go of his mistake, concentrate on getting the twins back.

Cam's cell phone rang. He answered it listlessly. "Hello."

At the sound of Julie's voice, Cam held the phone so both he and Alexa could hear. "If you want to see the boys alive, bring one million dollars in unmarked bills to the Bird's Nest at noon tomorrow. Bring Alexa. If we see the law, your brothers or anyone but you and Alexa, you'll never see the twins again.''

Cam's heart pounded. ''How do I know the boys are still alive?''

''Hi, Daddy.'' Jason's voice came over the phone and Cam's heart clutched.

''I'll see you soon,'' Cam promised.

''I miss you,'' Flynn said, and Cam knew he was crying. The boys sensed something was wrong. He'd never let them go away overnight before—not even with Julie.

''I miss you, too.''

The phone clicked before Cam even finished his sentence. He looked at Alexa and knew he couldn't risk going back inside to the FBI. She wasn't a good liar, and hope was written all over her face.

''Oh, God.'' Alexa gripped his hand, her nails digging into his flesh. ''Where's the Bird's Nest?''

''It's an old silver mine in the mountains.''

Alexa frowned. ''I can have my bank wire the funds. But can we get that much money changed into cash by noon?''

Chapter Thirteen

It turned out that dipping into Alexa's trust fund wasn't necessary, but Cameron appreciated her unselfish offer. The Senator kept a safe on the ranch's premises, with cash for emergencies. Between that and Cameron's withdrawal from the bank, they'd come up with the funds necessary to ransom the twins.

Cameron worried about the twins, hoping they weren't terrified. Julie's voice had sounded so tense and wild he couldn't be sure she wouldn't hurt them.

And he also worried about Julie's request for Alexa to accompany him. If Julie wanted just money, there was no need for her to specify that Alexa should be there to make the exchange. So he didn't say a word of protest when Rafe slipped Alexa a semiautomatic pistol.

In all likelihood, if anyone checked them for weapons, they'd only check Cameron. And if the weapon made Alexa feel more protected, he wanted her to have it. He knew her well enough to realize she wouldn't have accepted the gun if she didn't know how to use it. No doubt her exclusive European finishing school had taught marksmanship, as well as riding.

As partners went, he had every confidence in Alexa. She might be a bundle of simmering passion hidden by cultured poise, but in a pinch, she could think straight. And with the way his nerves jittered, he wanted all the calm around him he could get.

"How much farther?" Alexa asked. She pulled up, took a swig from her water bottle and tipped back her hat to look at him.

As usual, every hair was in place. Her lipstick and makeup were perfect. She'd even used makeup to hide the dark circles he knew were under her eyes.

Cam took his bearings from the ranch below and the mountains above. They rode a narrow trail toward the rugged high country. With trails this steep, they had to use cutbacks and couldn't go in a straight line. "Several more hours."

To her credit, Alexa bit back a groan. Instead, she glanced at her watch. "We better get moving."

"You think I'm making a mistake, don't you?"

"By not calling in the law or your brothers?" Alexa shrugged. "It's your call, Cameron. They're your boys."

She'd said "your boys," not "our boys," and that bothered Cam almost as much as second-guessing Julie's intentions. The more he knew of Alexa, the more he saw in her to love. She had a sassy way about her, but wasn't too pushy. She had sense when it counted, and her prim attitude disappeared when he removed her clothes.

And she adored the twins. She might spend his money with a heavy hand, but she hadn't thought twice about offering *her* money to save the boys. Complex, confident and interesting, she may not have been the right woman for him, but nonetheless, she'd stolen his heart.

She rode beside him without complaining, although he knew she had to be sore. Back straight, eyes bright and curious, she looked eager to meet up with Julie Edwards.

"What's the plan?" Alexa asked him.

Cameron shrugged. "We give Julie the money. She gives us the twins."

"I want to see the twins first."

Cameron shook his head. "Julie holds all the cards. I won't put my sons in danger."

"And she has no reason to give them to us, unless you demand to see the boys first."

Cameron nodded. Alexa had a point. He might not care about the money, but he wanted to keep his boys safe. If that required playing the hard-ass, he could do it. All he had to do was recall his boys' last words to him, and anger fired through him. How dare Julie put his sons through such an ordeal? There could be long-term emotional consequences. Nightmares. Pain.

Damn her. Why hadn't he noticed Julie's attraction to him? She'd held on to him too tightly after he carried her from the portable toilet, but he'd thought it was fear that made her clutch so. And at his wedding when she'd burst into tears, he should have seen that her tears weren't of joy, but heartbreak.

He'd been too involved with Alexa to notice or think about Julie Edwards—especially since he'd never had a romantic thought about her. He'd never encouraged her craziness. Another woman would have gotten over her crush and moved on.

He clenched and unclenched his fist as he led his horse around a hummock. Up ahead the trail leveled off for a mile or two before it climbed again toward the mine. He forced thoughts of the past away and surveyed his surroundings. Even up this high, the mountain grasses were green, the forest lush. A stream, an offshoot of a waterfall, trickled nearby, and he saw a white-tailed deer pause to drink from the stream. Startled by the deer, a rabbit scooted for cover. A blue jay took flight. It was hard to believe that in all this peace, his children were in danger. He would never forgive Julie for frightening his babies.

Stop it.

He needed to keep his wits about him. Enough about revenge and could-have-dones and should-have-seens. Berating himself wouldn't help the twins.

He smelled smoke long before they rounded the final bend and saw smoke curling from the mine entrance. Eager, he pushed forward. He wanted the exchange over with and the boys back in his arms.

"Hold it right there, Doc." Leo Harley stepped out of the trees, a rifle aimed at Cameron's chest.

Cameron eased his mount to a halt. "Whatever you say. I just want the twins back."

Leo ignored Alexa. "Climb down, Doc. I need to make sure you aren't armed."

Cameron held his arms wide and tried to appear harmless. "I don't have a weapon."

"Let's make sure, Doc." Leo came forward and frisked Cameron efficiently. Then he motioned them toward the cabin. "You can walk the rest of the way."

Alexa dismounted and started to loop the horses' reins to a low-hanging tree branch.

Leo shook his massive head. "Bring the horses."

Alexa did as he ordered. "What do you want me for?"

Leo shrugged. "Julie's orders."

"You take orders from a woman?" Alexa asked in an attempt to drive a small wedge between the accomplices.

Leo snarled, and fear and pride lit his tone. "Julie always gets what she wants. Anyone who stands in her way gets hurt."

Cameron didn't make any threatening moves and did as Leo asked. "Are the twins hurt?"

"Naw." Leo shook his head. "She keeps the brats sleeping so they won't be any trouble."

Alarm zapped through Cameron. Although sleeping boys couldn't be frightened, the danger of overdosing two-year-olds was very real. Judging medication for children was done by weight, but it wasn't an exact science. A little too much could cause brain damage, lead to a coma—even death.

He'd brought his medical bag with his bedroll, but out here in the wilderness, he could do very little. He consoled himself with the knowledge that Rafe was standing by with the helicopter. A quick call from the radio or cell phone would bring his brother flying in within minutes.

As they walked up to the mine entrance, Leo eyed Cam's bulging saddlebags greedily. "You brought all the money?"

Remembering Alexa's concerns, Cam kept his voice reasonable but firm. "You can count it *after* I see that the twins are safe."

Leo pushed him forward with the gun. "That's not Julie's plan."

Cameron held his ground. "I don't give a rat's ass about Julie. Can't you see that she's using you?"

Pointing a gun at Alexa, Julie stepped out of the mine, her face angry, her cheeks wet with tears. "You never did care about me, Cam. I took care of your children and you never even thanked me for all I did for you."

At the wild look in Julie's eyes, Cam damned himself for his careless words. He'd let anger and fear do his talking, and he had to try to repair the damage. Try to start a fight between Leo and Julie. He chose his next words—an outright lie—to the unstable Julie with extreme care. "I thought you loved Leo."

Julie wiped away her tears, but her gun stayed pointed at

Alexa. The college student's voice rose an octave, almost to a screech. "You thought wrong."

Leo's meaty lips turned down. "But you said—"

"I said what I needed to say to get you to help me," Julie boasted. "And I don't want to hear any complaints out of you. We're going to be rich, Leo. Now—" she faced Cameron "—bring me the money."

"First we want to see the twins," Alexa insisted.

Leo started toward the mine.

"Forget it. I give the orders." Julie held up her hand, stopping Leo. Her voice turned eerily calm. "No way is she taking *my* babies and *my* man. Kill her, Leo."

Leo looked from Julie to Cameron, his face red with rage. Eyes lit like a fuse, lips twisted with humiliation, he looked ready to explode.

Cameron waited, balancing on the balls of his feet, bunching his muscles, ready to attack.

Leo had finally figured out that Julie had used him. Julie didn't love him. And the knowledge boiled into fury.

Cameron watched Leo's eyes fill with hatred. Then Leo raised his gun, pointed it at Alexa, tightened his finger on the trigger.

Cameron shoved Alexa aside and lunged for Leo's weapon, knocking Leo's wrist into the air. A bullet whizzed by his head, and then the two men rolled onto the grass, pummeling each other with their free hands.

Cameron focused on the hand holding Leo's gun. He took a blow to his chin, but he didn't release pressure on Leo's wrist. His knowledge of anatomy came in handy. Leo's wrists might be massive, but the bones could only take so much pressure.

At the sickening snap, Leo roared like a bull, slamming his forehead down. Cameron ducked at the last second, avoiding a broken nose. He brought his knee up, hard.

Straight into Leo's groin. Leo twisted, and Cam's blow glanced ineffectively off Leo's massive thigh.

Somewhere Leo found a rock. He raised it over Cam's head, ready to strike a killing blow.

Several gunshots sounded, and simultaneously, a huge red spot stained Leo's shirt. The rock dropped harmlessly to his side and he keeled over, unconscious.

On shaky legs, Cameron stood and took his bearings. Alexa lay on the ground, the gun she'd shot Leo with resting on her thigh. She motioned with the gun for him to go. "Julie's getting away with the twins. Go."

Cam heard Jason and Flynn cry out sleepily from the mine. He paused halfway between his sons and Alexa. Alexa looked a little pale, but then, she'd just shot a man. Torn between helping Alexa to her feet and going to the twins, he hesitated. "Are you okay?"

"I'm fine. Get the boys."

Figuring Leo was no longer a danger to Alexa, Cameron scooped up Leo's gun and followed Julie into the mine. He burst inside, and his eyes took a moment to adjust to the darkness. Empty tin cans of food, candy-bar wrappers and sleeping bags littered the floor.

A cot stood in the corner. It was empty.

But Cam had explored the mine with his brothers when they were boys and knew there was a second entrance, just off the main artery. He hurried inside and rounded the bend, then raced outside again, sure that Julie had taken the boys out the mine's side entrance. Cameron suspected she'd hidden a four-wheel-drive vehicle there for her escape.

Fear for his sons' safety urged his feet faster. He raced after Julie and skidded around the bend and back out into open air.

Sure enough, she was lifting the sleepy twins into the

back seat of a Jeep. Cam's relief that the boys were semi-conscious tempered his fury.

He reminded himself Julie was unbalanced—just as she spun around and aimed her gun at him. His fist connected with her wrist and threw off her aim as she pulled the trigger. The bullet spit by harmlessly.

In pain from the force of his block on her arm, she dropped the gun.

Rage and tears combined, she attacked him with her hands. "You should have loved me. *Me*. Not Sandra. Not Alexa. *Me!*"

Her raving made her violent, dangerous and unpredictable. Cam had never struck a woman in his life, couldn't bring himself to do so now. He shifted to the side and swept her feet out from under her. She fell hard and he scooped up her gun, placed it in the waistband of his jeans.

"We could still make it work," she pleaded with him, proving once again how unbalanced she was.

He checked his boys' pulses and kept a wary eye on Julie. "You murdered Sandra, didn't you?"

Julie raised her chin. "I did it for us. So you could inherit her money and we could be together."

"I didn't care about Sandra's money. I loved her."

"And I killed Alexa, so now you are free."

"What?" Cam's heart stopped and skipped several beats. Alexa was fine. She'd told him she was fine.

Julie smoothed back her hair, oblivious to his confusion. "You're free to marry me. She's dead. Or she soon will be. I shot her in the gut. After all the trouble she caused me, she deserves a slow and painful death."

Horror stabbed him, made his hands shake. He took the keys from the Jeep's ignition and slipped them into his pocket. He picked up Flynn, then Jason, and hurried back to Alexa. Julie wouldn't get far on foot.

He suddenly recalled Alexa's pallor and weak voice, which he'd attributed to her having shot Leo. He hadn't seen any blood, but then, she'd twisted away, so he hadn't gotten a good view.

Cameron needed to call Rafe and the chopper, but he didn't have a free hand. It seemed to take him forever to reach Alexa. He gently placed the sleepy boys on the ground beside her and reached for the cell phone.

He turned her over and paled at the wound. There was blood. Too much blood. He tried to staunch the bleeding while he called Rafe on his cell phone.

The helicopter ride was a nightmare. At least the boys slept through it. Cameron knew Alexa wouldn't make it to the hospital without a transfusion. Luckily he matched Alexa's A positive. He started giving her his blood until he barely remained conscious.

Then he slumped, vowing that whatever happened, if Alexa lived, he wouldn't pressure her to stay. She'd practically given her life to save the twins. It would be selfish of him to ask more of her.

He loved her so much. He loved her enough to let her go. But first—she had to live.

ALEXA OPENED HER EYES, and the first thing she saw was Cameron. "You look terrible." Her voice came out in a croak, and she licked her dry lips and looked around the room.

A bright light glared at her. Machines beeped, and she figured out she was in a hospital bed.

Chin dark with stubble, eyes darker with worry, Cam leaned over her. "Don't try to move. You're hooked up to a few monitors and an IV's in your wrist."

She felt his hand holding hers and squeezed. "Love you."

"Sounds good, but I won't hold you responsible. You're on heavy-duty drugs. But you're going to make it."

She recalled rising out of her body, a long tunnel filled with light. And Sandra hugging her. "Sandra told me it wasn't my time. She sent me back. And I do love you."

His brow rose skeptically. "Uh-huh."

She could tell he thought she wasn't lucid, but she'd never been so sure of anything in her life. As she'd lain on the ground, her life's blood leaking out of her, all she could think about was Cameron and the twins. Not some precious job that took her all over of the world. Not unearthing a piece of art from some dusty attic. Not pocketing a finder's fee.

She wanted Cameron. She wanted the twins. She wanted her family.

She wanted to tell Cam, but she couldn't find the strength. Her mouth was dry, her throat parched. He seemed to realize her need and lifted a glass with a straw to her mouth. Two small sips wasted her. The effort sent her to sleep.

When she awoke again, she felt stronger. A nurse hovered over her bed, checking the IV in her wrist. "How do you feel?"

"Like I've been shot."

"Are you in pain?"

"Not if you're going to put me back to sleep again." Alexa turned her head and took in the flowers spilling over from the nightstand and the dresser to the floor. The room smelled like heaven, and she breathed in deeply. A mistake. Breathing hurt.

"If you're up to it, you have visitors. But the doctor says they can only stay five—"

Cam strode into the room and glared at the nurse. "She's awake and you didn't tell me?"

"Where's my hairbrush?" Alexa asked, knowing she must look a wreck.

Cameron laughed and then he danced the frowning nurse around the room. "Now I know she's going to be all right."

At the commotion Chase and Laura stepped into the room. Laura ignored the dancing, crossed to the bed and gently used her own brush on Alexa's hair. Laura pulled out a small pink bottle and held it up. "I brought nail polish."

"Good. Maybe once I look more like myself, the big oaf will believe that I love him enough to stay in Colorado."

Cameron stopped dancing with the nurse who left the room. "I thought that was the morphine talking."

Laura handed Alexa the hairbrush and nail polish and tugged on Chase's arm. "We should leave."

Chase resisted her tug. "This is just getting interesting."

Cam shoved his brother toward the door. "Get out."

"I want to hear this," Chase protested.

"Hear what?" Rafe had apparently heard the commotion and entered the room, curious to know what was going on.

"Is anyone else listening outside?" Alexa asked, barely containing her grin. Grinning hurt. Yet with all the love shining out of Cameron's eyes, the concern in Laura's, the humor in Chase's and Rafe's, she figured that the Senator and Tyler couldn't be far behind.

Sure enough, the Senator and Tyler crowded into the room, each of them holding a twin. Keith ran to his father, and Chase lifted him into his arms. The only one missing was Laura and Chase's newest baby, and only because he was too young to expose to hospital germs.

"Okay, we're all here now," Rafe teased. "What's so important?"

"First," Alexa demanded, "someone tell me what happened to Julie and Leo."

"Leo's recovering while incarcerated in the county lockup," Cam told her. "Julie's in a Denver psychiatric hospital. She'll probably be judged unfit to stand trial."

"What's *incarpatrated?*" Flynn asked.

"What's a *sytrick?*"

No one answered the boys, and Alexa grinned, wondering how long the adult vocabulary could continue to keep the twins in the dark. Alexa helped change the subject. "So how did I get to the hospital?"

"Rafe flew you."

"Then I donated blood," Rafe bragged.

"Really?" Alexa looked to Cam for an explanation.

"You needed more blood after we landed at the hospital and I'd already given you what I could. So Rafe volunteered."

"What did we do in the helicopter, Uncle Rafe?" Jason asked, his tiny face screwed up into a frown. "I can't remember."

Rafe ruffled his hair. "You were blessedly quiet and followed my directions to sleep."

Flynn scratched his head. "And that helped?"

"We got Alexa to the hospital, didn't we?"

Alexa motioned for the twins to come closer and took their hands in hers. "Thanks for the help." Clearly they didn't remember much—if anything—of the entire incident, and she was relieved. They were bright enough to figure it out from all the talk, but they wouldn't remember being separated from their father, wouldn't remember their fears.

Rafe slapped Cam on the shoulder and looked at Alexa. "Now what made Cam so happy he was dancing with a nurse?"

"This is private," Cam growled.

"We're all family here," Chase said innocently.

"I love him and I'm staying," Alexa told them, knowing the words felt right.

Laura and Chase exchanged knowing grins. Tyler looked at his feet. Rafe chuckled. "Now that she's half-full of Sutton blood, she can't think straight."

"It must be the morphine," Tyler added, getting into the spirit of teasing Cameron.

The warmth and love surrounding her was incomparable to any feeling Alexa had ever known. She belonged with this man, with this family. She knew it in her heart and she knew it in her soul. "It's not the morphine. I know what I'm saying. I love him."

At her repeated announcement, Flynn and Jason exchanged high fives.

Rafe rolled his eyes. "Is that all?"

Tyler dug his elbow into Rafe. "Shh. Don't interrupt."

Alexa saw Laura wipe a stray tear from her eye. But Alexa was focused on Cameron.

Cameron leaned over her. "You don't have to leave your job. You can—"

"I won't be a part-time wife or part-time mother. I'm not ever going back to my job."

Cameron protested halfheartedly, probably to test her. "But you love your work."

"I've been thinking about opening a gallery in Highview." She winked at him, "It'll be expensive."

"Better hide your credit card," Chase warned.

"—But I'm staying here with you and the twins."

"For good?" Flynn asked.

"Forever?" Jason echoed.

"For as long as your dad wants me," Alexa agreed.

Flynn whispered to Jason, "Dad's smart."

Jason whispered to Flynn, "He won't ever let her go."

''That means we have a mother,'' Flynn told Jason, his voice full of awe.

''And we'll get more hugs and kisses and chocolate-chip cookies?'' Flynn's voice rose on a hopeful note.

Without needing adult confirmation, the twins exchanged high fives again, big smiles and round eyes making them look, for once, more innocent than mischievous.

The nurse returned with another frown. ''It's been more than five minutes. Everyone must leave.''

''Good.'' Cam kissed Alexa gently on the mouth. ''Everyone can leave except her doctor.''

''Is that so?'' The nurse raised an eyebrow.

''Yes, Nurse.'' Cameron leaned over Alexa protectively. ''This doctor's going to keep kissing his wife until she's all better.''

THREE BABIES
AND A BARGAIN
Kate Hoffmann

1

"Ayyyeeee!"

The high-pitched squeal hit Jillian Marshall's ears just as sticky fingers grabbed at the hem of her skirt, and she bit back a cry of dismay. She glanced down beneath the breakfast bar at the messy face of her two-and-a-half-year-old nephew, Andy. Dressed in his Dr. Denton's with the little elephants and the plastic feet, he held onto a soggy piece of toast covered with grape jelly.

"Jibby ee toad," he said, his mouth full of food. Slowly, he pushed the glob of half-chewed bread out of his mouth with his tongue and Jillian caught it just before it joined the jelly on her skirt.

"Jillie eat toast," he repeated, plopping the slice of bread facedown on her knee and rubbing it around for good measure.

The toast slithered down her leg and landed on her sandal before dropping to the floor, the jelly dripping between her toes. Jillian forced a smile, then pushed back from the counter. "I found Zach's missing breakfast," she said, holding the evidence up to her sister, Roxanne.

Roxy sighed. "I wondered where that went." She bent down and looked under the counter, growling playfully. "What else is down here? Are there monkeys under here?"

The other two members of her sister's terrifying trio giggled at their mother's silly faces, tumbling around amidst spilled Cheerios and colorful Legos beneath Jillian's feet.

Zach, the most rambunctious of the identical triplets, wielded a wooden spoon and was about to bang on the bottom of a battered aluminum pan. Wearing the saucepan as a hat, his brother Sam sat placidly. A quiet, serious child, Sam was unaware of the enthusiastic military tattoo about to be played on top of his head until his mother plucked the pot from his head.

"You're not serious about taking care of the boys while Greg and I are in Hawaii, are you?" Roxy asked.

"Of course I am," Jillian replied.

Roxy looked up at her from the floor. "Jillie, you don't have to prove anything to me. I know you probably could do it. You can usually do anything you set your mind to."

If only that were true, Jillian mused, as she slid off the stool. She walked to the sink and tried to scrub the jelly stain from her skirt, her mind occupied with her sister's comment. She'd spent her entire life trying to carve out a place of her own in the Marshall family, trying to prove that she was as good as her sister. Roxy was the popular one, the cheerleader, the prom queen, the daughter who married a fabulous man and gave their parents not one, but three, grandchildren! Roxy was beautiful and witty and self-assured, a perfect copy of Jillian's mother and their father's pride and joy.

Jillian was the other daughter, painfully shy and gawky, a complete geek in high school. She had only one quality that had set her apart. She was smart—brilliant, by most standards. While Roxy had charmed boys and set fashion trends, Jillian had occupied herself with advanced calculus and computer programming, serving as president of the Math Club. By her sophomore year, she'd already begun taking college credit math courses. And she had graduated a whole year early, sitting next to her sister at commencement—the ugly duckling next to the gorgeous swan.

Though she'd outgrown her gawky body and was now passably attractive, she still carried the scars of a clumsy and socially inept teenager. And she was still trying to prove herself to her parents. According to Sylvia Marshall, a husband and a family were the only true measures of success.

Unsure of herself in the social realm, Jillian hid behind her formulas and equations. Mathematics had become her life, bringing her recognition around the country as one of the foremost experts on number theory. She'd been the youngest person ever to be offered a tenured professorship at the New England Institute of Technology.

Though her mother still hoped for another wedding in the family, Jillian had grown satisfied with the course her life had taken...until now. Lately, her career was leaving her feeling strangely unfulfilled. She dabbed at the jelly stain on the cotton skirt, then gave Roxy a sideways glance. "Don't you think I'd make a good mother?"

"Maybe," Roxy said. "But you'll need to learn to roll with the punches a little more."

Punches? Roxy looked as if each day with her sons was a severe pummelling. At that precise moment, the Hunter home could have qualified for government aid as a national disaster area. But then, the house was always in a shambles—toys scattered everywhere, the sink piled high with dishes, the laundry room belching dirty clothes into the hallway and her beautiful sister looking like she'd slept in a wind tunnel.

"I'm sure if you put your mind to it, you could regain control of your life," Jillian murmured. She had wanted to speak her peace on that matter for such a long time. It was clear Roxy had lost her ability to maintain any semblance of household order. In just an hour with the boys, Jillian could see a thousand simple ways to improve the living conditions in the Hunter household, starting with the judicious use of grape jelly.

Roxy laughed out loud. "Triplets defy organization, the same way they defy eating their vegetables and taking a nap. It's genetic." She gave Jillian a shrewd look. "Why do you want to do this? Are you thinking about getting married and having a few monsters of your own?"

Jillian paused before her next words, wondering if she should tell Roxanne about her plans. She *had* been thinking about children. A husband, on the other hand, wasn't a necessary factor in the equation. All that was required was a visit to a sperm bank, a test tube with a high IQ, and a simple withdrawal. "No," she lied. "I just want to spend more time with my nephews, that's all."

In truth, there were three people in the world she felt completely comfortable with, three people who never judged her—Zach, Andy and Sam. Though she didn't always understand them, or the havoc they wreaked, they loved her unconditionally. They accepted her for the person she was and she returned their love in full measure.

Jillian sighed softly as she dried off her skirt. Perhaps if her life had taken a different path, she might have had her own children by now. But she was twenty-nine years old, with few prospects for marriage, though that was probably her own fault. When she'd finished her doctorate six years ago, she'd developed a list of standards for a potential mate—an IQ equal to or greater than hers, a successful career in the sciences and a belief that her work was as important as his. He'd have to be an extraordinary man, perhaps a Nobel prize winner.

She'd had a respectable number of male friends—successful intellectuals, most of them colleagues at the New England Institute of Technology. But after three or four dates, she found herself losing interest. Something was missing from her list, some element she couldn't describe, and Jillian was beginning to believe she'd never find it, even if she dated every Mensa member on the planet.

"It's hard work," Roxy warned. "It would be a big mistake for you to think it's easy. And ten days will seem like a lifetime."

"It just takes organiza—"

"I know, I know," Roxy interrupted. "Organization. Your answer to every problem. You're the only woman I know who keeps a schedule of housekeeping chores on a computer. Heck, if it's messy, I clean it. And if it's not, I catch a quick nap."

Jillian tipped her chin up stubbornly. "I'll bet if you gave me ten days with your boys, I'd have this house running smoothly." At first, she wanted to take the words back, knowing the statement might hurt Roxy's pride. But then, as the notion sank in, she began to realize that this would be an excellent opportunity to test her mettle as mommy material. And preempt any concerns Roxy might have over her baby plan.

"Mom said she'd take the boys," Roxy countered. "She's hired extra help, fortified the house, put away the good china and told Dad he can't play golf for an entire week. She's expecting her grandsons. It took me two months of cajoling to get her to agree so that Greg and I could go on this second honeymoon."

"I'm sure she won't be disappointed if you changed your plans," Jillian replied. "I'm not teaching my seminar on transcendental numbers at the institute this summer. I've got my Goldbach research to work on, but I can do that in the evenings after the boys are in bed and while they're playing."

Babysitting the boys would also give her an excellent opportunity for empirical research. By the end of the week, she'd know just how her work and children mixed. "If I need help, I can always call Mom," Jillian added. "She's only ten minutes away. I know I can do this, Rox. Just give me a chance."

Roxy's expression softened and she nodded. "All right. But you have to promise, if things get bad, you'll call Mom immediately."

Jillian knelt down and the boys gathered around her, hanging off her arms. She gave them each a kiss, wincing at sticky fingers and dirty faces. "I promise. But I know we'll get along just fine. We'll have a wonderful time, won't we, guys?"

"ZACHSAMANDY! Put that down!"

Jillian groaned, then raced over to the entertainment center in the family room. Cereal crunched beneath her shoes as she dodged a pool of spilled milk and the sleeping form of Duke, the family's long-suffering Golden Retriever.

"You'd better stop that right away!" she warned. "That doesn't go in there!"

The little tyke watched her shrewdly, his mind calculating his odds of shoving the graham cracker into the VCR before she reached him. Jillian scrambled for a name, frustrated with her inability to tell her nephews apart. Roxy had taken care to identify each of the boys before she left for the airport, but, in a disciplinary pinch, "Zachsamandy" had become her generic name for them all. She'd always thought Zach was the troublemaker. But after spending just one day with the boys, that theory had been disproved time and time again. They all had their destructive moments—together and separately.

She snatched the cracker from… "Zach," she muttered, putting a name with the red shorts he wore. "This is for tapes." She grabbed a Thomas the Tank Engine tape and pushed it into the VCR, only to hear the unmistakable sound of crumbling crackers.

"Poop!"

Jillian spun around to find another hellion standing behind her. By process of elimination, he had to be Andy or Sam. "Andy," Jillian murmured, recognizing the blue T-shirt. "Poop? Now?"

"Poop!" he repeated, patting his backside with a chubby hand. "Dirty diaper!" He punctuated each word with a hearty slap. "Change! Change! Change!"

"How could you do this to me?" Jillian cried. "I just changed you ten minutes ago." She crossed the room and grabbed Andy's hand, ignoring the strangled sounds coming from the VCR. "We are going to have to work on this," she muttered. "You're supposed to tell me *before* the actual act."

Andy looked up at her and grinned again. She was certain he understood her, but took some perverse delight in staring at her like she was speaking in some bizarre alien dialect.

She reached behind him and grabbed one of his toy trucks, then rolled it across the floor in front of him. A metaphor would be in order here, she mused, trying to gather her patience. Dr. Hazelton, the noted pediatrician and bestselling author of *Successful Child Rearing*—a book she'd read from cover to cover the night before last—recommended making potty training fun for the child with interesting examples.

"Pretend you're the dump-truck driver," she said, "and Auntie Jillie is the customer. You're supposed to let me know when you're coming so *Jillie* can tell you where to dump your load. The driver doesn't get to decide. And Aunt Jillie would really prefer only one load a day. All right?"

"Aw right," Andy replied, nodding, holding up his hand for a high five.

Jillian gave his paw a playful slap and struggled to her feet. But just as she was congratulating herself on her successful intervention, she saw Sammy wander into the room, a big piece of paper stuck to his cheek. Jillian plucked it off, then frowned. The pattern on the paper was oddly familiar. In fact, it looked just like—she groaned softly—the wallpaper in the powder room.

"What did you do?" Jillian asked. She raced to the bathroom, all three boys hard on her heels, only to find another disaster. The pretty wallpaper border that circled the room midway up the wall was now in shreds, tiny pieces scattered all over the tile floor. "I can't do this," she murmured, backing out of the room. "I give up. I can't keep track of all of you at once. You win. I surrender. I'm calling my mother!"

After only six hours as primary child-care provider to the Hunter triplets, Jillian was ready to give it all up. She felt as if she were the captain in a pediatric version of *The Poseidon Adventure,* trapped in an upside-down house that was about to sink to the bottom of the lake outside. If she didn't call her mother now, more serious disasters might await them all.

Of course, just when things couldn't get worse, they did. The phone rang.

"Phone!" Zach screeched, his attention diverted from unrolling yet another roll of toilet paper. He grabbed the end in his hand and ran toward the kitchen, a trail of white following him the entire way.

"I get it!" Andy shouted in delight, taking off after his brother.

Sam plucked another piece of wallpaper from the wall and handed it to her with an innocent smile, before joining the parade. Jillian sighed softly, her heart melting a bit at

Sammy's little gift. How could she be angry at such a sweet child?

"Phone!" they all shouted.

Jillian palmed the scrap and took off after the boys, reaching the phone before they had a chance to climb up on the counter. "Hello?" she said breathlessly.

"Jillie? Jillie, is that you?"

Jillian winced at the sound of her sister's voice. Of all the times for Roxanne to call, why did she have to call in the midst of yet another calamity? Not that there'd been a break in the string of disasters that day.

Jillian schooled her voice into the essence of calm and control. "Hi, Rox. How are you? Are you there already?"

"Yes," her sister shouted, as if the distance between Hawaii and New Hampshire hadn't yet been conquered by the phone company. "It's incredible. Beautiful. I can't believe we're actually here!"

Jillian held the phone away from her ear. "I can hear you fine, Rox. You don't have to yell."

"How are the boys?" she asked. "Is everything all right?"

"Everything's just fine," Jillian lied. "We're all getting organized. It's going quite smoothly. No problems at all."

"Yeah, I bet," she said. "Let me talk to the little monsters."

As the boys took their turn with the phone, babbling their greetings to their parents, Jillian's thoughts wandered back to the conversation that had gotten her into this mess in the first place. "It's all a matter of organization," she had told her sister. Good grief, how could she possibly get organized when she couldn't even tell the boys apart?

"Jillie? Is everything all right? Jillian, are you there?"

Startled out of her contemplation, Jillian looked down to find Zach at her feet, bashing the handset of the phone against the leg of a kitchen stool. Her sister's voice was barely audible as she called out in alarm.

She snatched the phone from her nephew's hands, eliciting a shriek of disapproval from him. "I'm here," Jillian said over his cries. "Everything's fine. Don't worry."

"I'm not worried," Rox said. She paused. "Well, maybe a little. It's just that I've got the nagging feeling that I've forgotten to tell you something."

"I have an entire notebook full of instructions," Jillian said. "And I've practically memorized Dr. Hazelton's book. I can recite the phone numbers for the fire department, the police, the pediatrician and the poison control center and I have enough Huggies to last until the boys enter high school. Everything is fine. You and Greg have a wonderful time. And don't worry!"

She could almost see her sister's reluctant smile on the other end of the line. "You have our number," Roxy said. "Call if you have any questions. If not, I'll call back tomorrow or the next day."

"You and your husband should be spending time thinking about each other," Jillian insisted. "I don't want you calling for at least three days."

"All right," Roxy said. "I'll try. Kiss the boys for me. And make sure Sam has his blankie before you put him down. And Zach won't sleep unless—"

"Good night, Rox. Go have wild hot sex with your husband now. And make sure you use protection or you may end up with another set of triplets on your hands." Jillian hung up the phone, then let out a tightly held breath. She glanced down at the boys. "That went well, don't you think?"

They all looked up at her and once again, she tried to put names to identical faces. With a soft oath, Jillian grabbed a laundry marker from the drawer beside the phone, then turned to the boys. "Sit," she said. They obediently did as they were told and Jillian smiled in satisfaction. She grabbed Zach's leg, tickling him behind the knee, then carefully wrote an initial on the top of both of his feet in thick black marker. She did the same for each of the boys. *Z* for Zach, *A* for Andy, and *S* for Sam.

Though the forehead might be better for quick identification, blond bangs would hide the initials. At least now, as long as they were barefoot, she'd be able to tell them apart. "See? Who needs Grandma now? Organization. That's the key."

JILLIAN WASN'T SURE what woke her, but some instinct deep inside told her something wasn't right. Her eyes snapped open and she listened for a long moment, holding her breath as she lay on the couch in the same spot where she'd thrown herself after finally getting the boys to bed. She tried to determine the time. Had it been minutes or hours since she'd lain down?

She expected to hear one of the boys crying or the dog barking, but that was not what she heard. She heard footsteps. Not the little patter of pajama-clad feet or the click of dog nails, but the distinct sound of heavy feet on a hardwood floor. Stifling a scream, she sat up and searched the family room for a weapon. But every item that might cause harm had long ago been put out of the reach.

She silently stood and tiptoed toward the phone, her mind racing to remember the number of the police station. But all she could recall was the number for poison control. If she could force the intruder to swallow Drano, she might be all right. On her way to the phone, she stubbed her toe on one of the boys' toys. Biting her bottom lip, she forced back the tears of pain, then realized she'd stumbled on exactly what she'd been seeking.

Jillian picked up the small xylophone and measured it for its heft and balance. For a weapon, it would have to do. And after she'd rendered her prowler unconscious, she could play a chorus of "Twinkle, Twinkle, Little Star" while she waited for the police.

The police! She had to get to the phone and call for help. But the instant she headed for the phone, she heard the footsteps coming nearer. Jillian crouched in the shadows beside the sofa and held the xylophone out to the side.

When the tall, dark figure passed, she seized the moment. Jumping up from her hiding place, she swung the instrument. The very highest note grazed his temple, then the xylophone smashed up against the wall in a bizarre chord. Duke, the guard dog, looked up from his spot in front of the fireplace, yawned, then put his head back on his paws.

The blow caused the prowler to stumble backwards. When he caught his heel on the oriental rug, his feet flew out from under him and he landed on his back with a thud. A great whoosh of air left his lungs and as he gasped for breath, Jillian fumbled for the light switch.

Bright light flooded the room and he winced holding up his hand. It was at that moment that she realized she was staring at one incredibly handsome prowler. He had warm brown hair that was streaked blond by the sun. His face, all smooth planes and angles, was tanned and clean shaven. He wore a faded work shirt that revealed well-muscled arms. Blue jeans covered long legs. He looked up at her with surprised hazel eyes. Once he caught his breath, he tried to struggle to a sitting position, but she raised the instrument over her head again.

"Stay right there," she warned in a trembling voice, "or I'll sic my dog on you."

He groaned, then forced a smile and scoffed. "Duke? Unless you expect him to drown me in drool, I wouldn't bother.'' He flopped back down, placing his arm across his forehead. "What the hell did you hit me with?'' he asked.

"A Toony Tots xylophone," she said. "And I didn't hit you. The high C just grazed your temple. Who are you? And what are you doing in my house?''

"This isn't your house," he said. "I know the people who live here and you're not one of them, lady.''

Jillian shifted uneasily, then swallowed. "N-neither are you, so I guess I had every right to hit you.''

"Maybe you'd better tell me who you are," he said.

"I'm Jillian Marshall. I'm Roxanne Hunter's sister.''

He touched his temple and cursed, then pulled his fingers back and examined the traces of blood. "Ah, so you're the infamous Jillian," he muttered. "The math whiz. Your brother-in-law said you hated men, but I didn't think you'd take your feelings quite this far.''

Jillian gasped. Of all the nerve! "I don't hate men! I can't believe Greg said that. When did he say that? And who are you that he would say something like that to you?''

He pushed himself up to a sitting position again, groaning as he moved. "Let me ask you something, Jillian. Do you make a habit of whacking your dates with musical instruments, too? No wonder you're still single.''

How dare he speak to her so rudely? Was she now expected to defend her social life—or lack of it—to a complete stranger? "Who are you? And what are you doing in this house?''

"They didn't tell you I was coming?" He rubbed his head. "I'm Nick Callahan. I'm building bookshelves for Greg and Roxy in their library.''

"Well, this is the first I heard about it," Jillian said. "How did you get in?''

"They gave me a key. I thought everyone would be gone. What are you doing here?''

"I'm taking care of the boys," Jillian replied.

Nick studied her for a long moment. "Did the rug rats do that to your hair or is that the way you usually wear it?" he asked.

Jillian's free hand fluttered up to touch her hair, the shoulder-length style now spiked up like she'd taken a bath with a plugged-in toaster. "I was just taking a—a nap." She frowned. "What time is it?"

"Around eleven," he said.

"Why are you here so late? Don't you—you carpenter guys work during the day?"

"Hey, I've got other jobs. I'm doing these shelves as a favor to Greg and Roxy and they're letting me stay in the guest house. Now, are you going to put down that xylophone and let me get up, or am I going to have to find a trombone and challenge you to a duel?"

Jillian reluctantly lowered the xylophone. "How do I know you're telling the truth? How do I know you're not some deranged psychopath who will murder me and my nephews in our sleep?"

"What do you want?" he asked. "Identification? I'll show you my hammer. Or how about my drill?"

"Your driver's license will do just fine," she replied.

Nick Callahan rolled to his side and withdrew his wallet from the back pocket of his jeans. Jillian watched him suspiciously, then realized that she was staring a bit too hard at his backside. She dragged her gaze away and met his eyes. A sardonic smiled curled his lips, a smile that told her he knew exactly what she had been staring at. He tossed his wallet at her and she caught it.

With fumbling fingers, Jillian found his driver's license and confirmed that he was indeed Nick Callahan from Providence, Rhode Island. She also confirmed that he was the only person in the United States who looked good on his driver's license picture. Very good. Incredibly sexy and handsome and—

"Are you satisfied?" he asked.

She snapped the wallet shut and dropped it on his chest. "You can wait on the porch while I call Roxanne. And don't try anything weird."

"Don't worry," he muttered, as he pushed up to his feet. "Right now you've got the corner on that market." He stood and stretched sinuously in front of her, the muscles of his chest bunching and rippling beneath the taut fabric of his shirt. Then he walked to the back door, rubbing the back of his neck. She slammed it behind him, making sure it was locked securely.

Fifteen minutes later, after frightening Roxanne half to death and disturbing her sister's late afternoon siesta on the beach, Jillian had confirmed that Nick was the "little something" Roxanne had forgotten to tell her about. Roxanne also added that this "little something" was handsome and available. But when Jillian opened the back door to let Nick back in, the carpenter was nowhere to be found.

She tracked him down in the library, where he'd already set to work. He'd moved most of the furniture to one side of the room and had begun to measure the empty wall. "I thought I told you to wait outside," Jillian said.

"I got tired of waiting," he replied through the pencil clenched in his teeth. "So I used my front door key." He snatched the pencil out and scribbled something on a piece of paper. "Did Roxy certify that I'm not a..." He turned to look at her. "What did you call me...a deranged psycho?"

Jillian tipped up her chin defiantly. "I was only protecting my nephews' safety. And she told me you were a good friend of Greg's and that you're supposed to be doing exactly what you said you are."

"Good," he replied. They stood there for a long moment, staring at each other. "Was there something else you wanted?" he asked. "Or do I have permission to get back to work?"

Jillian blinked, once again the first to look away, then shook her head. "Just try to keep quiet. It took me two hours to get the boys to sleep."

"I'll do my best," Nick said, giving her a devastating smile before returning to his measurements.

Jillian shot him an icy look before she walked out of the library. This was all she needed. Not only did she have to keep an eye on three energetic little boys, now she had to deal with Nick Callahan hanging around the house as well. How was she supposed to get things organized when all these unexpected events interfered?

Well, she'd just have to factor in Nick's presence. Perhaps he'd be an asset to her research. She could pretend he was a husband. He'd be there, but he wouldn't offer any help with the children, which probably would provide an average empirical model. She'd consider Nick Callahan the typical male. While he was working on the bookshelves she could make believe he was watching football or taking a nap on the sofa. In the end, he'd only serve to confirm what she already knew—that she didn't need a man around to raise a child.

An image of him flashed in her mind, broad shoulders and narrow waist, and she brushed it away. All right, there were other advantages to having a man around. But she shouldn't even be attracted to a guy like him. After all, he wasn't her type. Jillian preferred men with more brains than brawn, men who were a match for her on an intellectual level.

Sure, she had to admit that she could understand the fascination with a man like Nick Callahan. All that muscle and masculinity wrapped up in such a pretty package. So confident, almost arrogant, in his power over women.

But unlike the other weak-willed women in the world, Jillian knew what she wanted from life, and it wasn't Nick Callahan, or any other throwback to the Neanderthal age, who expected his women to be warm and willing and obedient. No, Nick Callahan definitely was not her type. She'd much prefer a pale, introverted Nobel laureate than a gorgeous Greek god with an inflated ego.

Jillian pinched her eyes shut and fought back a yawn. It was nearly midnight. The boys would be awake in six hours and she was exhausted. If she knew what was good for her, she'd leave Nick to his work and get some sleep.

But as she lay in the guest room, tossing and turning and trying to relax, thoughts of Nick Callahan teased at her mind. She pushed up and punched at her pillow, then flopped back down and began to methodically recite the prime numbers between one and five hundred.

Somewhere after eighty-nine, she fell asleep, drifting into restless dreams of muscled male bodies and crying children.

2

NICK STOOD at the kitchen sink, slowly sipping at his mug of coffee as he stared out the window. The rising sun sparkled on the surface of the lake and the trees blew in the soft morning breeze. Of all the houses he'd designed, he'd always liked this one best. Even better than his own house—or his ex-house. Though it rankled to admit it, for the near future, he was homeless.

His ex-house was currently inhabited by his ex-fiancée, Claire, and her son, Jason. It was the house he'd designed and painstakingly built on a vacant city lot in a trendy neighborhood of Providence, the house he'd thought had finally become a real home, inhabited by a real family.

Nick had never really wanted children, a fact he'd made perfectly clear to Claire early on in their relationship. But along with Claire, he'd gotten her seven-year-old child. At first, they'd kept a wary distance, Jason adamant that he didn't need another father and Nick certain that he didn't want a son. But it didn't take long for the walls to come crumbling down and for Nick to realize he'd been wrong about children, wrong about Jason. So, after going together for several months, Nick asked Claire to move into his house with her son.

They'd lived happily for nearly a year, but when he'd brought up the subject of another child to Claire, she'd steadfastly refused to consider the matter. This was not part of the agreement, she insisted. She had her child and no matter how much she loved Nick, she didn't want to have his. What had started as a minor disagreement over their future suddenly became a wedge, sharp enough to drive them apart.

It wasn't long before the fickle Claire had moved on to someone else, someone willing to give her exactly what she wanted—a glamorous, baby-free life. Nick sighed softly, then took another sip of his coffee. He'd walked out the instant he found out about the other man, unable to stay in a house full of anger and regret. He said a somber good-bye to Jason, the boy who had nearly become his son and told Claire she had two months to vacate. Luckily, the cottage on Greg and Roxy's property was vacant for the summer. Hoping that some solitude would put some perspective back into his life, he'd moved in about a month and a half ago.

Soft footsteps sounded behind him and he slowly turned to find Jillian Marshall standing in the doorway. She looked so soft and sweet-smelling, dressed in a pretty white nightgown and a robe with tiny flowers embroidered around the scooped neckline and around the cuffs of the wide, flowing sleeves. When she wasn't glaring at him, or whacking him across the head with children's toys, she was actually quite beautiful. He felt the faint stirring of desire, then brushed it aside. Though Jillian Marshall was pretty, he'd sworn off women, at least for the rest of the summer, and he was determined to keep that promise to himself.

She blinked, then frowned sleepily. "What are you still doing here?" she murmured, rubbing her eyes with her fists.

"Good morning," he said softly.

"I asked you a question," Jillian grumbled, hurriedly combing her hair with her fingers. "Why are you still here?"

He bit back a sarcastic reply. Jeez, the woman was

prickly twenty-four hours a day! "I just finished up for the night," he replied. "Would you like a cup of coffee? It'll do wonders for your mood."

Her brow shot up in surprise. "You—you made coffee?"

Nick turned and poured her a cup, then handed it to her. "Sleep well?" he asked.

She glanced at him over the rim of the mug. "No, not particularly."

He watched her gradually throw off her sleepiness. This was what he'd always imagined family life to be, sharing the first cup of coffee in the morning, starting the day together, quietly, with the little ones asleep upstairs. Not that he'd imagined a wife like Jillian Marshall—or triplet boys. It was just that Claire had always started her day fully dressed, makeup artfully applied, clothes neatly pressed.

"What about you?" she asked. "Don't you ever sleep?"

"Sometimes," he said. In truth, sleep had been hard to come by lately.

"You should always try to get eight hours every night," she murmured between yawns. "Usually, I keep a very strict schedule. I go to bed exactly at eleven and wake up exactly at seven. Once I get this household organized, I'm sure I'll be able to get back to my normal schedule."

"Really," Nick said. "Tell me, do things always go exactly according to your plans?"

"Of course," Jillian said. "It's all a matter of organization. For instance, the boys are supposed to sleep until six o'clock. It is now five-thirty. I'll have just enough time to eat my breakfast and take care of some household tasks before I go and get them dressed."

The words were barely out of her mouth when Nick heard a wail coming from the direction of the boys' bedroom. He grinned. "I guess you forget to tell the boys about your schedule."

She shot him an irritated glare, then drew a deep breath and closed her eyes. "They're supposed to sleep until six," she said. "He'll just cry for a few minutes, and then go back to sleep." Another wail joined the first. "Roxanne assured me they sleep until six." Soon the duet became a trio and Jillian covered her ears.

"Why don't you let me get the boys dressed?" Nick suggested. "Sit down and finish your coffee."

She frowned at him in disbelief. "You know how to change a diaper?"

"I grew up in a big Irish family," he said. "The oldest of ten children. I think I can remember enough to get by."

She studied him for a long moment, then shrugged. "Go ahead," she said. "They're yours, dirty diapers and all."

Nick grabbed his coffee mug and headed upstairs. He found all three boys standing just inside their bedroom door, their faces screwed up in frustration, ready to start the day but unable to work the doorknob.

"Hi, guys," he said. "You're up a little early."

"Nick!" Andy cried, his arms outstretched. "Nick, Nick! Go up!"

"I want out!" Zach cried. "Now!"

Sam watched Nick from a safe distance, wide-eyed, his thumb stuck firmly in his mouth.

He picked Andy up and placed him on the changing table, then took a quick survey of the situation. A search for diapers turned up a stack of Huggies with dancing bears across the front. "Disposable diapers," he muttered. "All I remember is plastic pants and pins." Plucking at the little tabs, he unfolded the diaper. "You've got a masters degree in industrial engineering, Callahan. You can certainly figure out a Huggies."

Nick went through six diapers before he managed to get Andy off the changing table and into a pair of shorts and a

T-shirt. By the time he finished with Sammy and Zach, the mangled diapers made a rather impressive pile. He gathered them up and shoved them into a dark corner of the closet. The dirty diapers were another matter. After five minutes of tinkering, he managed to unlock the secrets of the Diaper Disposal, a finely engineered gadget that he found fascinating in its simplicity and practicality.

The moment he opened the bedroom door, the boys made a beeline to the kitchen, screaming all the way. Nick was the last to appear in the doorway, just in time to see Jillian's eyes widen with what appeared to be sheer terror.

"Come on, guys, let's give Auntie Jillian a chance to finish her coffee. I don't think she's ready to handle you until she's had a big dose of caffeine."

Jillian pushed up from the kitchen table, a look of exhaustion already flooding her face. "They're hungry."

"Sit down," Nick said. "I'll get them their breakfast."

She shook her head. "But you don't know what they eat. They have to have a nutritious balance and you have to cut up the food so—"

Nick chuckled. "I'm sure I can figure it out. It's got to be big enough to pick up with their fingers and small enough so it doesn't choke them. This isn't rocket science, Jillian."

She watched him suspiciously, her hands wrapped around her coffee mug. He plopped the boys into their booster seats and placed a bowlful of dry cereal, sliced bananas, and a spill-proof cup of milk on the breakfast bar in front of each of them.

"You're really good at this," she murmured.

He warmed under her unexpected compliment. "It just takes a little common sense," Nick replied.

"I'm not good at this," Jillian said, exhaustion tinging her voice. "Take the diapers. I figured if I fed and watered them all at once, they'd *go* all at once. But I changed diapers every half hour yesterday. By now, Dr. Hazelton says, they should be open to potty training.''

"Who the hell is Dr. Hazelton?" Nick asked.

Jillian shot him a warning look. "Don't curse in front of the children," she whispered. "Dr. Hazelton says cursing can have a detrimental effect on their emotional well-being. And Dr. Hazelton happens to be the nation's leading authority on child rearing."

"Forgive me," Nick teased, snatching a cup out of Zach's hand an instant before he hurled it at Jillian's head. "But aren't they a little young for potty training? They don't even know how to pull their pants down yet."

"My nephews are more advanced than the average two-and-a-half year old."

Nick watched as Zach tried to stuff a piece of cereal up Sam's nose. "Yeah. I can see that."

The boys took only ten minutes to wolf down their breakfast. Nick wiped their faces and hands, then sent them off to play. All the while he felt Jillian's eyes on him, watching his every move.

"Tell me," she asked, after the boys had scampered out of the kitchen, "how much do you carpenter guys make? What's your hourly rate?"

Nick raised a brow at the sudden turn in conversation. "Carpenter guys?"

"Guys like you," Jillian said. "How much?"

He shrugged, too amused to be insulted. Though he'd always found great nobility in men who worked with their hands, his talents with a hammer and saw were merely a hobby. "I don't know. Union scale is around thirty dollars an hour for a journeyman carpenter. More for a master."

She gasped. "You make thirty dollars an hour?" He watched as she mentally did the calculations. "That's sixty-thousand a year for a job that requires absolutely no college education. That's half what I make and I've got a Ph.D.''

"Supply and demand. I guess there are a whole lot more people that need carpenters than mathematicians. The invention of the calculator really cut into your business, huh?"

The color rose in her cheeks, and he smiled. God, he loved pricking her temper. She was such a snooty little thing when she wanted to be, full of herself and her prejudices. Just what would she say if he told her he held a master's degree in both industrial engineering *and* architecture and brought home ten times what a "carpenter guy" did? Right now, Nick thought it best to keep that information to himself. He might need it later to bring her down a few more pegs.

"For your information, number theory is a very complex science," she said.

"Something us working-class guys would never understand, right?"

"And I hardly ever use a calculator. All my calculations are done on a mainframe computer."

"Then why are you interested in my wage?" Nick asked. "Are you thinking of switching careers?"

Jillian shook her head and gave him a shrewd look. "No." She opened her mouth to speak, then snapped it shut.

"What?" he asked.

"Nothing." Jillian paused. "It's just that the boys like you so much and I thought it would be nice if you stopped by later this afternoon and visited—if you can spare the time."

"If you find caring for them so difficult, why did you ever agree to it?" Nick asked.

She shifted in her chair, straightening her spine. "I have

my reasons. Besides, you said it. It just takes a little common sense. You watch, by the end of today, everything will be fine."

"I think you're being overly optimistic. Caring for three toddlers is very tiring."

She frowned, and then tipped up her chin, a stubborn gesture that had already become familiar to him. "I'm a highly intelligent woman, Mr. Callahan. Now, if you'll just be on your way, I can get started with my day."

A shriek split the air and Jillian's face went pale. She froze, her white-knuckled hands gripping the edge of the counter. Nick walked over to her and pulled her up out of her chair, then pointed her in the direction of the noise. He slowly rubbed her shoulders, like a trainer about to send a boxer back into the ring. "I've got some work to do," he said. "I can come back around three, if you'd like."

Jillian glanced over her shoulder and forced a smile. "I— I'm sure the boys would love that."

Nick steered her toward the stairs. When she'd taken the first step, he walked to the front door and opened it. He chuckled, wondering what scene would greet her when she reached the source of the scream. He suspected that by the time he returned, Jillian Marshall would be more than happy to see another adult. After all, common sense didn't always accompany a post-doctorate education in mathematics. And when it came to child care, Jillian seemed woefully short of common sense.

By MID-MORNING, Jillian had managed to forget her earlier encounter with Nick Callahan, putting him and the memory of his hands on her body completely out of her mind. She'd never been touched by a man in such a casual, but powerful manner, and the thought of it disturbed her.

But by lunchtime, Jillian could think of nothing *but* Nick

Callahan. She found herself counting the minutes until he reappeared, in between wiping macaroni and cheese and soggy saltines off the floor and walls. She'd taken great pains to prepare a nutritious, homemade sauce, a cheesy béchamel served with whole-wheat pasta, rather than feed the boys the boxed variety that Roxanne had recommended.

An hour later, after she'd cleaned the last trace of cheese sauce from the last little face, Jillian realized that the box probably was a better alternative—especially since half of it ended up on the floor anyway. Duke was the only one who got a nutritionally balanced meal! The dog plodded off for his nap, macaroni hanging from his left ear, and Jillian followed, looking for the boys.

She found them in the nursery. Sammy had already climbed into bed and was arranging his stuffed animals around his pillow. Andy was yanking books off the bookshelf, determined to find his favorite or make a mess trying. Jillian looked around for Zach and found him in the bathroom just off their bedroom, drenched in water and holding a tiny toy car over the toilet. Zach looked up at her as she came in, a devilish glint in his eye. "Boat," he said. He made a buzzing sound with his lips as the car circled the toilet seat.

Jillian glared at him. "That is not a boat and it doesn't belong in the toilet."

"Boat," he repeated stubbornly.

"Car!" Jillian insisted.

Zach watched her for a long moment and she could almost see the wheels turning in his mind. She crossed the bathroom in three short steps but before she had a chance to grab the little car, he dropped it in the toilet with a resounding "plunk" and yanked down on the handle. With a delighted giggle, Zach peered over the edge and watched the little red sports car circle the bowl for the last time. "Bye-bye, boat. See you later."

Jillian reached into the bowl and tried to catch it, but it was no use. The car was gone, along with her patience. "That was very bad," she said to Zach. "And you won't ever see that boat—I mean car—again!"

He nodded, frowning intently. "Very bad," he said, shaking his finger at her.

Jillian didn't have the energy to resort to Dr. Hazelton and his methods of discipline. Instead, she grabbed Zach by the hand and drew him back into the bedroom, firmly closing the bathroom door behind her and making a mental note to start closing doors more often. She changed his clothes, not even bothering to contemplate how he'd gotten so wet, then raced through *The Cat in the Hat* and *The Little Engine That Could*. Thankfully, they all retired without much fuss. Exhausted, she flopped down on the floor beside their beds and closed her eyes.

How would she ever make it through another eight days of this? Every time she thought she might have a moment to catch her breath, some new domestic tragedy rained down on the Hunter household. If she could just get a few steps ahead of the boys, she might be able to get things organized. But she always seemed to be lagging behind them, there to clean up after the latest disaster, yet never anticipating the next.

The only bright spot was the prospect of a visit from Nick. An image of him drifted lazily through her mind. Jillian rubbed her shoulders where he'd touched her, wondering at the warm tingle that still lingered on her skin. She'd nearly asked for his help that morning, but her pride had stood in the way. That, and the unbidden attraction she felt toward him.

She could rationalize the attraction, even ignore it. But it was the basics of child rearing she couldn't seem to get a grip on. No doubt if she asked for his help, he'd lord his superior skills over her. But she refused to admit failure so quickly. And calling in reinforcements, namely her overbearing mother, was not an option. At least not yet.

If only she could get him to stay in the house. Maybe she could fiddle with the plumbing in the cottage. Or cut the electrical line. She'd then magnanimously offer him a guest room and he'd be here when she got up in the morning and he'd be here when she and the boys went to bed. With another adult around, she'd at least be able to maintain a small measure of her sanity.

A shiver skittered through her at the thought of having Nick Callahan around twenty-four hours a day. She silently scolded herself. So he was attractive. Why not admit it? There was certainly nothing wrong with admiring perfection in the masculine form—broad shoulders, hair streaked gold from the sun, beautifully muscled arms and...

Her thoughts focused on more intimate territory. She'd had lovers in the past, but she'd never had one with a perfect body, a narrow waist and flat belly and a backside that just...

This time the shiver shot clear to her toes. "Nick Callahan is not your type," she muttered to herself. "He's arrogant and overbearing. He acts like a know-it-all. Besides, he's a carpenter. He works with his hands, not with his head. You've always preferred a great mind to a great body."

But, oh, what hands, she mused. Strong and warm. Jillian closed her eyes and thought back to the moment that those fingers skimmed along her shoulders, brushing briefly at the nape of her neck. Though his touch had been a purely innocent, casual gesture that meant nothing at all to him, she couldn't help but wonder what his touch might have done to her if he'd had other intentions, if he had really *wanted* to touch her.

She opened her eyes and sighed, then pinched them shut again, blocking out the handsome face that teased at her mind—and the mess that surrounded her. The nursery looked like a typhoon had roared through. She tried to push herself off the floor, knowing she should pick up the mess before Nick arrived. But she couldn't move and could barely keep her eyes open.

When she awoke some time later she wasn't sure how long she'd napped or what actually woke her up—whether it was the sound of Nick's voice calling from downstairs or the little face that stared at her from close range. She blinked, then reached up and rubbed her eyes. But when her vision cleared, she could do nothing more than scream.

Zach held out a colored marker which he'd already liberally applied to his face. "Red," he said, holding it beneath her nose. "Smells like juice."

Jillian snatched the marker from his hand thanking the heavens Zach hadn't been suffering from severe facial lacerations. At the very same moment Sam and Andy jumped on top of her. They also clutched watercolor markers in their fists, only their faces looked much worse than Zach's, both sporting a collage of bright colors and swirling patterns to rival van Gogh.

"Jillian? Where are you?"

She jumped from the floor, frantically searching for the Baby Wipes. They were hidden under Sam's bed and once she retrieved a handful, Jillian immediately set to work scrubbing all three faces clean. She finished just as Nick appeared in the doorway of the nursery. Stuffing the crumpled Baby Wipes into the pockets of her sundress, she turned and gave Nick a nonchalant smile. "Hi! Look who's here! Uncle Nick!"

The boys screamed his name, then ran right past him out of the nursery, leaving the two of them alone. He gave her an odd look, part frown, part grin. "Is everything all right?" he asked.

"Just fine," Jillian said. "The boys had their nap and we were just…playing. I—I think we're finally starting to get organized."

He nodded, then looked around the room, his brow quirking up. "I can see that."

"In fact, you probably could have stayed away. I've got everything under control here." Why couldn't she just admit she was overjoyed to see him? She had nothing to prove to this man, to this stranger. She caught an odd expression on his face, half-confusion, half-amusement. Slowly, he reached out, as if to touch her cheek, but Jillian stepped out of his reach, afraid of the contact.

Nick forced a smile. "I'm sorry, I was just trying to—you have something on your—"

She reached up and smoothed her mussed hair, then straightened the neckline of her dress, disturbed by her reaction to his unbidden advance. This casual touching was completely inappropriate. "I realize we're in rather close quarters, Mr. Callahan, but I—I don't think we should…I mean, for the sake of the boys, we shouldn't…"

"I wasn't making a pass," he said with a grin. "You just have something on your face."

Jillian swallowed, heat rising in her cheeks as she rubbed them, finding a Cheerio stuck to her temple. "I know. It's fine," she said, popping the cereal into her mouth with as much nonchalance as she could muster. Dropping to her knees, she gathered the markers and started shoving them back into the box.

"So," Nick said, glancing around. "What would you like me to do?"

She looked up at him for a long moment, all manner of possibilities racing through her mind. He could touch her the way he had earlier that morning. Or he could stare into her eyes in that way that seemed to make her blood run warm. Or he could always just stand there and let her look at him until she had her fill of handsome carpenters with flat bellies and nice backsides.

"Well?" he prodded.

"I hadn't really thought about it," Jillian replied with a shrug. "Maybe you could play with the boys. Keep them out of trouble while I get some work done. It's a beautiful day. Why don't you take them out for a walk?" A long, exhausting walk, she thought to herself.

He grabbed her hand and helped her up from the floor, then slowly reached out and brushed his thumb along her cheek. Her body trembled, but this time, Jillian didn't pull away, but just savored his touch. He allowed his fingers to linger for a long moment, then he grinned. "Why don't you come with us?" he suggested.

She smiled hesitantly, tickled that he enjoyed her company enough to ask. "All right. I think I will. I could use some fresh air and exercise."

"And I suppose I could use an extra pair of eyes and hands," he said.

Oddly, it took Nick only five minutes to get the boys into their shoes, a half-hour ordeal for her. He grabbed a ball and headed outside, the boys at his heels and Jillian following close behind. She watched him as he strode up the drive to the narrow road that circled the lake. The boys romped after him, kicking the ball and running along to catch it, the sun bright on their blond heads.

Her gaze moved to Nick and fixed on his wide shoulders, on the muscles that bunched and stretched beneath the taut fabric of his work shirt. Slowly, she let her eyes drift downward until they stopped at his backside. She took a long, slow breath as she admired the fit of his faded jeans, his long, muscular legs and easy athletic stride. Scolding herself, she hurried to catch up.

They strolled along the winding road, the five of them causing mild curiosity for the people in the passing cars. They waved at a few neighbors along the way and by the time they'd turned back for the house, the exercise had invigorated Jillian and brightened her mood.

"You really have a way with them," she said as Nick hoisted Sam up onto his shoulders. The other two boys walked at his sides. He was completely at ease with them, as though acting the part of a father came naturally. Maybe it was a male thing, boys bonding with boys.

A sudden thought shot through her mind. "Do you have children of your own?" She groaned inwardly. Roxy had said he was single, but she'd never considered the possibility he might be a father.

He gave her a sideways glance, then shook his head. "I like kids, but no, I don't have any of my own."

"Have you ever been married?"

"Almost, once," he said. "But that didn't work out."

All the warmth had left his voice. Jillian crossed her arms in front of her, sorry for her curiosity. "Well, the boys certainly seem to like you." She cleared her throat, then glanced at him. "I've never been very good with children. I guess you've noticed that. That's why I decided to stay with the boys. I do like children. All it takes is time and practice."

"And organization?" he teased.

"Yes. I believe that," she said firmly. "Children need structure in their lives. Dr. Hazelton says that structure creates an atmosphere of safety and harmony in a child's life. You'll see, by the end of Roxy and Greg's vacation, I should have this household running like a well-oiled machine.''

''And you think the boys are going to cooperate with this plan?'' he asked.

''Why wouldn't they?''

He shrugged. ''I think you might have overestimated your organizational abilities, Professor Marshall. Unlike those numbers you're so fond of, triplets defy organization.''

She straightened her spine and gave him a stubborn look. ''I'm perfectly able to achieve my goals with the boys. I've done my research and if I lay the groundwork properly, I'll—''

''If you're so capable, why did you invite me over for a play date?'' he teased.

''You're good with the boys,'' she replied. ''I'm not too proud to admit that.''

Nick chuckled. ''Gee, and I thought it was because you liked the way I wore my jeans.''

She gasped and felt heat flood her face.

''Don't act so surprised,'' he said. ''I noticed you looking.''

''I was not!''

''Yes, you were,'' he countered.

''Why would I waste my time looking at your backside? You're hardly the type of man I'm attracted to.'' With that, she spun on her heel and headed back in the direction of the house.

''And what type of man *are* you attracted to?'' he shouted, as he gathered the boys to follow her.

She turned around. ''Certainly not a man with such a high opinion of himself—and his backside.''

He laughed then, loud and deep, the sound echoing through the woods. The three boys giggled and clapped right along with him. Cursing beneath her breath, Jillian picked up her pace. By the time she reached the end of the driveway, they were nearly fifty yards behind her.

When she reached the house, she headed for the nursery, determined to clean up the mess that awaited her there. Dragging her fingers through her wind-tangled hair, she glanced at herself in the bathroom mirror, then stopped dead. The image that stared back at her brought a groan of mortification.

No wonder Nick had been looking at her so strangely! Her cheeks were covered with red and blue marker, the results of Zach's nap-time artistry. She looked like a reject from clown school! "You'll pay for this, Nick Callahan," she muttered. "Don't think you can make me look the fool and get away with it."

Jillian grabbed a bar of soap and scrubbed at her cheeks with a spongy bathtub toy. She dried her face with a wad of tissue, then dropped it in the toilet and flushed before scrubbing off a second layer of skin. But as she worked, the toilet gurgled and sputtered beside her.

She turned and watched as the water rose, higher and higher, until it began to flood over the rim. Screaming, she grabbed a towel and tossed it on the floor, then pulled a stack from the closet and scattered them at her feet. But nothing she did could stop the torrent. She clambered to the open window and shouted for Nick. To her relief, he'd reached the driveway.

An eternity later, Nick appeared at the door with the boys and calmly surveyed the situation. The floor had at least an inch of water on it and the flood had seeped out into the hallway. She didn't bother to chastise him for the marker incident. The disaster of her wildly colored face had now been replaced by a disaster of greater proportions. "Do something!" she cried as she mopped at the floor.

"Water!" Andy cried, patting his hands on the floor.

"Auntie Jillie make a mess," Zach added. "Clean up, clean up."

Duke appeared and began to lap up the water with great gusto.

"It looks like you need a plumber," Nick said, stepping over to the toilet. "I'm just a carpenter. Union rules prohibit me working on the toilet, unless you're willing to pay union wages."

"How much?" she asked through clenched teeth.

"Fifty dollars an hour should do it," he said.

Jillian stood up and tossed a soaked towel at his chest. It hit him with a loud "thwap." "Fix it," she said, as she shoved past him.

JILLIAN WAS SITTING at the kitchen counter when he and the boys came back downstairs. A bottle of wine was open in front of her, but Nick saw no evidence of a glass. *She must be feeling pretty badly to drink right out of the bottle,* he mused.

"You could have told me I looked like an idiot," she muttered, taking a slug of the wine.

"I tried," Nick said. "But then I figured you'd done it on purpose while you were playing with the boys. Besides, you looked kind of cute with scribbles all over your face."

Jillie groaned and cupped her chin in her palm. Sammy crawled up on the stool beside her and pointed to the wine bottle. "Juice?" he asked.

"Grown-up juice," she murmured, patting him on the head. She glanced over at Nick. "So, what was the problem with the plumbing?" she asked in a weary voice, no longer interested in blaming him for her short stint as a clown.

Nick held out a handful of toy cars he'd recently extracted from the toilet. "Major traffic jam," he said.

Zach screeched and reached out for the toy cars. "Boats!" he cried.

"Cars," Nick said, giving him a stern look. "And toys do not belong in the toilet. These are mine now."

Zach watched him suspiciously, deciding whether to pitch a tantrum or accept his punishment. He finally shrugged and wandered off to find another source of entertainment.

Jillian looked at her watch, then sighed. "Two hours at fifty dollars. I owe you a hundred." She slid off the kitchen stool and grabbed her purse from the counter. "Will you take a check?"

"Actually," Nick said. "it's going to take more work. The water leaked through the floor into the ceiling below and the drywall needs to be replaced, along with the wallpaper border." He instantly regretted his words. She looked like she was about ready to cry. Instead, she grabbed the wine bottle and took another swig. "But, don't worry. I can fix it so Roxy and Greg will never even know."

Jillian lowered her head to the counter. "Have you ever heard of chaos theory?" she murmured, her cheek pressed against the granite, her glazed eyes staring off into space.

Nick's gaze was drawn to her hair. At first, he'd considered it a very ordinary color. But upon closer observation, he noticed how the warm brown hue glinted with red and blond. He reached over and plucked at a strand that threatened to slip into a puddle of orange juice. It felt like silk between his fingers. She moved slightly and he snatched his hand away.

"I'm not sure," Nick lied. In truth, he had read about chaos theory in one of his graduate classes, but he couldn't recall the particulars. All he knew was that, standing so close to her, he was certain chaos theory was at work in his body. He wanted to reach out to her and draw her into his arms, to bury his face in the sweet smell of her hair and run his hands over her soft skin, capture her mouth with his.

But his common sense told him that these protective feelings toward Jillie Marshall would only get him in trouble. Sure, he could play the hero for her, helping her with the boys, unclogging toilets and taking diaper duty. And she might need him, but not in the way he really wanted. "Why don't you explain it to me?" he murmured, unable to take his eyes off her.

Jillian looked up at him. "It's a modern area of mathematics. It tries to explain the erratic or irregular fluctuations in nature. When a system is chaotic, its behavior is only predictable if the initial conditions are known to an infinite degree of accuracy."

"In other words," Nick said, "you'd have to know precisely how many Hot Wheels a toilet could handle before you could predict whether it would overflow and ruin the ceiling?"

Her expression brightened and she straightened, managing a tiny smile. "Exactly! You see, I think this is where I've made my error. I neglected to apply chaos theory to child-rearing. I'm an expert in number theory. It's very orderly and predictable. Naturally, I wouldn't have considered chaos theory."

"So, what does this mean?"

"It means that it's not my fault that things seem to go wrong all the time!" Jillie cried. "It also means I should be prepared for things to lapse into chaos every now and then. It's all part of the natural order of this universe." She drew a deep breath. "I shouldn't let myself get too concerned about my mistakes. To this end, I'd like to pay you."

For a moment, he wasn't sure what to say, stunned by

her direct statement. Hell, he'd be willing to do anything she wanted for free. "I'm not that kind of man," he teased.

A faint blush colored her cheeks through the faint streaks of marker still on her face. Nick couldn't help but notice how pretty she was—even when she was talking math. It wasn't just her body he found attractive. She had a curious and fascinating mind as well.

"I've got a deal I'd like to propose," she continued, "and I'm willing to pay you very well."

"What kind of deal?" Nick asked, curious and cautious at the same time.

"I want to hire you," Jillian said. "Just for a few days, until things get organized."

"Roxy and Greg already have hired me. Besides, I can incorporate the cost of the new ceiling into the price of the bookshelves. It's just a piece of drywall and some fresh paint."

She shook her head. "I—I'm not talking about the ceiling or the bookshelves. I want to hire you as a nanny."

Nick frowned. A nanny? He'd been propositioned by a fair number of women in his life, but he'd never heard this variation. And the fact that Jillian Marshall considered him on par with Mary Poppins certainly didn't do much for his ego! "I don't understand."

"It's quite simple. You appear to have a way with children, a way that I am still in the process of perfecting. Until I do, I'd like to hire you to help me care for the boys."

"Why not call your mother?" he asked. "She was supposed to take care of them in the first place, wasn't she?"

Jillian squirmed uneasily. "I have my reasons. I'll pay you six hundred dollars for three days. You'll come at three and work for me until eight, when the boys go to bed. After that, you can complete your carpenter duties."

Nick smiled. He'd been presented with a valid excuse to

spend time with the beautiful, yet prickly Jillian Marshall and her exuberant nephews. And he'd get paid for it, to boot. He really couldn't afford to take the time away from work, but hell, he could work in the mornings and consider the afternoons a vacation. And what better way to spend a few free hours than with a gorgeous—and brilliant—brunette. This might be good for a few laughs, and God knew, he hadn't had a lot of laughs in his life lately.

He whistled softly. "Six hundred dollars for three days. Five hours each day. That's forty dollars an hour. You must be desperate."

"Actually, it represents a thirty-three percent raise above your normal wage. Fair compensation. And I am not desperate. I simply need an extra hand—or two. Just until I get organized."

He looked down into her indifferent gaze. She was trying hard to maintain an aloof air, but he could tell how much she needed his help. Should he agree now, or should he make her beg a little? Perhaps he might ask for a few fringe benefits to go with the hourly wage. A simple kiss, a quick taste of those perfect lips, one of which she was chewing on at the moment.

"All right," Nick said. "It's a deal." He held out his hand and she hesitantly placed her fingers in his palm. A warm tingle worked its way up his arm and without thinking, he reached out and touched her face. She blinked in surprise and drew back, her fingers fluttering to the very spot where his hand had just lingered. "You still have a little marker on your face."

Again, she blushed, her gaze flitting from his eyes to his toes. "Oh. I—I'm sorry."

"No," he murmured. "I'm sorry." He grabbed her hand and dragged her out of the kitchen. "Since I'm officially on nanny duty, I think you can spare an hour to soak in a hot bath." She trudged up the stairs after him and he threw open the door to the master bathroom he'd designed especially for Greg and Roxy. Without a word, he bent over the whirlpool tub and flipped on the faucet, and then grabbed a bottle of purple bath salts and added a generous amount.

He turned and placed his hands on her shoulders, looking down into her eyes as he gently massaged her stiff muscles. "Relax," he murmured. "I'll scrape up something for dinner and get the boys fed. You have nothing to worry about now that I'm on the job."

Jillian gave him a grateful smile and nodded. "I don't think I'm paying you enough," she said.

"We can discuss a raise over dinner." With that he strolled to the door and pulled it closed behind him. Nick would have preferred to remain and scrub her back, but he'd have to wait to be invited into Jillian's bath.

3

JILLIAN STOOD IN THE SHADOWS of the hallway, wrapped in her robe, watching Nick and the boys playing on the nursery floor. The boys were dressed in just their diapers and Nick lay on the floor, shirtless. They were all so engrossed in make-believe, they didn't even notice her. Cars and trucks were spread out all around them and her nephews ran the little toys up and over Nick's body, giggling when he captured a little arm or a racing car in his hand. "So much for chaos theory," she murmured.

She distractedly rubbed the damp from her hair with a towel, feeling relaxed for the first time in two days. She felt as though she'd been on a forced march, exhausted and battered, scarred by battle. But the moment she'd sunk into the tub, her worries took flight and her aches were eased. *What a nice man Nick Callahan is,* she mused, listening to his deep laugh.

At first, she'd thought him to be a cad, a man concerned only with tweaking her temper and making her look like a fool. She scolded herself for jumping to conclusions. Now that their deal was in place, she found him to be completely charming. He'd been happy to offer his help with the boys and he'd generously drawn her bath. Sure, she was paying him for his help, but he could have refused her offer of employment.

Jillian frowned. Six hundred dollars was probably a lot of money to a guy like him. Maybe he hadn't accepted just because he wanted to be nice. Perhaps he had bills to pay, pressing financial obligations. It must be tough to make a living building bookshelves.

Whenever she met a man, she automatically held him up against her list of criteria. But since she'd met Nick, she'd begun to believe the list was just getting in her way. Though Nick didn't have the extraordinary, scientific mind she sought, he had his own special qualities, qualities she found very—

Jillian sighed softly. It wouldn't do to continue these silly fantasies. A sexy body and a smile that melted every bone in her body wasn't enough! For a relationship to be a success a man and woman had to be intellectually compatible as well. As for his intelligence, so far, she knew he could build bookshelves, change diapers and make coffee.

She watched as he grabbed Zach and held him above his head, pushing him up and down like a barbell, his biceps taut, the muscles in his shoulders rippling. He hugged the little boy to his bare chest and growled playfully, then tucked him under his arm and stood up. Andy and Sam each took a leg and Nick lumbered toward the bathroom, all three boys in tow. "Time for a bath," he said in a gruff voice.

Jillian's breath caught in her throat and she closed her eyes as she imagined the scene. Of course, Nick would look incredible with his clothes off. Just the thought of him naked sent a secret thrill through her body. She sighed softly and the boys faded from the scene, replaced by an image of herself, soaking amidst the Mr. Bubble with Nick.

He'd probably bathed with lots of women. With his experience, he'd know exactly where and how to touch her. He'd start slowly washing her back, kissing her neck, caressing her soap-slicked skin. His hands would be strong and firm on her body, his touch assured. And when she moaned his name, he'd...

She clutched her robe around her neck and opened her eyes. The thought of a little affair with Nick Callahan was tempting. Sex had always been rather uninspiring for her, ordinary, even. If she'd been more physically attracted to her partner, it might have been better. And she couldn't deny that she found Nick very attractive in that way. But Jillian had never chosen her companions for their physical appearance. She'd always looked for intellect first.

Jillian wandered back to the master bathroom and stood in front of the mirror, staring at her reflection. Good grief, what could she be thinking? She wasn't ready to throw herself into an affair with a complete stranger! Especially with a man as unsuitable as Nick Callahan. She frowned. Besides, though she might find him attractive, he hadn't shown any sign of returning the sentiment.

She padded over to the wall and stared at herself in the full-length mirror. With hesitant hands, she opened her robe and looked at her naked body the way a man might. There wasn't much to recommend her. She had small breasts and narrow, almost boyish hips—but she did have a slender waist. With a soft oath, Jillian wrapped the robe back around her body. "You're seriously deluded," she muttered. "How can you even be thinking such a thing? He'd never find you attractive."

Putting all erotic thoughts of Nick Callahan out of her mind, Jillian grabbed a brush and began to tug it through her damp hair. She heard shouting and laughter from the boys' bathroom and smiled, wondering if Nick was as wet as the boys were. It really was sweet of him to give them —

A sudden realization hit her. "Oh, no," she murmured. Nick was giving them a bath!

Jillian adjusted the gaping front of her robe, then ran down the hall and through the nursery, stubbing her toe on a vicious Tonka truck and leaping over a pile of dirty clothes. Cursing under her breath, she hopped along, rubbing her sore foot. When she reached the bathroom door she sucked in a sharp breath at the sight of Nick, his hair drenched, his chest damp.

Nick glanced over at her and grinned, oblivious to the splashing of the three little naked boys in the tub. "Did you enjoy your bath?" he asked, raking his hand through his hair.

She knelt down beside the tub and reached into the water, snatching up a right foot from the nearest triplet. Jillian searched the water for another foot and when she saw six immaculately clean feet, she groaned, then sat back on her heels. "You washed their feet," she murmured.

Nick stared at her, his gaze drifting down to the gape in her robe, then back up to her face. She didn't bother to alter the view. She had other things on her mind besides modesty. "They were dirty. There was marker all over them."

"I—I put the marker there," Jillian said.

"You scribbled on their feet?"

"Roxy always dresses them in different colors so she can tell them apart. I didn't want to get them mixed up, so I–I wrote their initials on their feet. Oh, God, Roxy's going to kill me. We'll never know which is which. Dr. Hazelton says I have to make sure I never call them by the wrong name. It could cause irreparable harm to their developing individuality. Maybe we could take them to the hospital. They must have fingerprints or footprints or—"

"I know which is which," Nick interrupted. "This is Andy," he said, pointing to the triplet on the left. "This is Zach and this is Sam."

Her gaze darted from boy to boy to boy, seeing absolutely no difference in appearance. They all looked like little drowned rats. "How can you be sure?"

Nick shrugged. "I can tell. Sam hasn't said a word since I put him in the tub. Zach tried to shove Andy's hand up the faucet. And Andy told me that Aunt Jillie is the most 'bootiefull' aunt in the world." Nick smiled. "Either he means you're nice looking or that you have a pretty... backside."

Jillian couldn't help but laugh, his joke easing her worry.

"Besides, just ask them," Nick continued. "They know the difference." He bent over the tub. "Where's Sam?" Two of the boys pointed to another. "Where's Andy?" This time, they chose another triplet. "By the process of elimination, we can figure out who Zach is."

Jillian plopped down on the wet tile floor and sighed in relief. Once again, Nick Callahan had ridden to her rescue and saved the day. She was starting to become dependent on his help. He provided a calming influence in the house, a rational mind when hers was going haywire. "I can't tell them apart," she said. "If it weren't for the labels on their feet and the different clothes, I'd be lost."

"Just watch them," Nick replied, turning back to his job. "And use your instincts. If you'd stop trying to organize, Jillie, everything would become clearer."

Jillian did as she was told, sitting against the wall and observing as Nick bathed the boys. She listened as he talked to them, participating in their conversations as if he truly understood what they were babbling about. When they got too rambunctious, a single warning was all it took to bring them under control. And when it was time to get out of the tub, they didn't whine or pitch a fit as they'd done for Jillian. They scrambled out and danced around Nick, three happy little naked boys waiting to be dried off.

"Look at how they respond to you," Jillian murmured. She drew a deep breath. "I'm such a failure at this."

Nick finished drying the last triplet, then sent them all

running to their bedroom for their pajamas. When they were alone in the bathroom, he sat down beside her, leaning his back against the tub. He took her hand in his, giving her fingers a gentle squeeze. It was such an innocent gesture but it revived her quickly sinking confidence. And she liked the rush of warmth it sent through her bloodstream.

"Somewhere along the line, you've made the mistake of thinking that child-rearing should be easy." He chuckled softly as he toyed with her fingers. "It isn't. And you don' learn it all in one day. It's a talent that comes by degrees. But you do have one thing that a good mother needs in abundance."

"What's that?" Jillian asked.

"Tenacity," he said. "You're not the kind of woman to give up, Jillian." With that, he bent closer and brushed a quick kiss on her cheek. Then he pushed up from the floor and wiped his damp hands on his thighs. "I better go see what the boys are up to."

Jillian sat in the bathroom for a long time after he left, staring at the empty doorway, her fingers pressed to her cheek. No matter how she tried to wrap her mind around his kiss, she couldn't seem to figure it out. Did he feel sorry for her? It could have been a pity kiss. Or maybe it was just a friendly gesture. It couldn't possibly be romantic, she mused.

Jillian buried her face in her hands and moaned softly. Trying to figure out the mind of Nick Callahan was almost as difficult as trying to figure out the minds of two-year-old triplets. Some things were simply beyond her capabilities.

"WHAT DO YOU MEAN you might not be able to come?"

Jillian stood in the kitchen, the boys sitting in their booster chairs, lined up along the breakfast bar. They'd been chattering away, guzzling orange juice from their tippy cups and stuffing their mouths with buttered toast. But when she'd screeched out her question to Nick, all three had stopped and watched warily, concerned by the desperate tone in her voice.

"I'm sorry," Nick said. "I've got an emergency at work. It can't wait."

"This is exactly what I should have expected," Jillian said with an edge of sarcasm. "You carpenter guys are all the same. Start a job, then disappear when it's half finished. When can I expect you back, next month?"

Nick gave her an irritated glare and she immediately regretted the comment. All right, perhaps she had been a little harsh, but they'd made a bargain and after only one day, he was reneging! She was his boss and she had a perfect right to be upset. After all, she'd come to count on him and the prospect of getting through an entire day alone with the boys was...daunting at best. Things went so much better when Nick was around.

She drew a ragged breath. "Can't you tell them you've got another commitment?" she pleaded.

"I would if I could, but I can't. I promise to be back by five or six. If you're that worried, call your mother. Have her take the boys for the day."

"No," Jillian said stubbornly. "I don't need my mother to bail me out."

Nick reached out and grasped her shoulders, catching her gaze with his. "Jillie, this isn't brain surgery here. You feed them, you change their diapers, you feed them, you put them down for a nap, you feed them, you put them to bed. You're a smart woman. Trust your instincts. Besides, you've weathered the worst of it. What else could happen?"

"All right, I'll trust my instincts!" she said. "And my instincts say that I don't need your help. In fact, the bargain's off! You can forget your career as a nanny and you can go back to your nails and your boards and your—your thing that makes holes in wood.''

''My drill?''

''Yeah, your drill.'' She crossed her arms over her chest and leaned back against the edge of the counter, refusing to meet his gaze again. How could she ever have thought Nick Callahan attractive? And charming? And sweet? When the chips were down, physical perfection was no match for honor and trust. They'd made a bargain and a good man would have respected their deal. Nick Callahan was not a good man!

''Go ahead,'' she finally said.

Nick glanced at his watch, then looked over at the boys. ''I'll try to get back as soon as I can.''

Jillian turned to the sink and began to scrub at a stubborn grape-juice stain. ''Don't bother. I'm sure we'll be just fine.''

She thought he'd left, but then she felt a hand on her shoulder, his strong fingers branding her skin beneath the thin cotton of her dress. ''I'm sorry,'' he said, his voice soft and warm. ''But I wouldn't leave if I thought you couldn't handle it. You'll be just fine, Jillie.'' With that, he turned and walked out.

Jillian rubbed away the traces of his touch and bit back an oath. ''Jerk,'' she muttered.

''Jerk!'' Andy cried.

''Jerk, jerk, jerk!'' Zach shouted.

''I heard that!'' Nick called from the foyer.

She felt a blush warm her cheeks, then smiled at the boys and placed her finger over her lips to shush them. Just then, the doorbell sounded and all three of the boys shouted out loud, ''I get it!'' They scrambled down from their chairs, falling all over themselves as they raced to the front door, but Nick had already opened it.

"Nana!"

Jillian groaned inwardly when she saw her mother standing on the front porch. Dressed impeccably in designer golf clothes, she looked like she'd just walked off the pages of *Town and Country* magazine. Jillian frantically ran her fingers through her tangled hair, then tried to wipe an orange juice stain off the bodice of her dress.

But Sylvia Marshall didn't notice. After kissing each of her grandsons, she fixed her attention on Nick. Jillian could see her mind working, drawing the only conclusion that a nosy mother could. "And who are you?"

Nick smiled and held out his hand. "Mrs. Marshall. It's so nice to see you again. Remember me? I'm Nick Callahan."

Caught off guard by his charm, her mother took Nick's hand and gave it a feeble shake.

"We met a few years back when Greg and Roxy were building the house," he offered.

Jillian knew her mother didn't remember, but she acted like she did. Sylvia Marshall was always the picture of social grace. "Oh, yes. Nick, it's nice to see you again."

"I'm sorry I can't stay," he continued, moving to the door, "but I've got business in Providence. Say hello to Mr. Marshall for me." He nodded, then sent Jillian an apologetic look. "Good luck," he mouthed.

The door closed behind him, leaving Jillian to explain his presence and her general state of dishevelment. When her mother turned and stalked toward the kitchen, she grabbed her dress and tried to suck off the orange juice stain, then hurried after her. "Mother, it's not what you—"

Her mother had no patience for explanations. "I simply cannot believe what I see," she muttered, bending down to attend to the boys' appearance. She rebuttoned shirts and turned down socks and tied shoes. Before she finished, she fished a comb out of her purse and ran it through tangled hair. Then she sent the boys off to play and sent Jillian a withering glare.

She sighed. "Mother, he's just—"

"In front of the children! You're supposed to be caring for these boys, not entertaining your—" she lowered her voice "—male friends."

"He's not a male friend," Jillian said. "I mean, he is a male. An acquaintance. But he's not my friend. He's here building bookshelves in the library for Greg and Roxy. And he's staying down in the guest cottage. He just came up to the house for coffee."

Her mother slid onto a stool at the counter and stared at Jillian for a long moment, an aristocratic arch to her eyebrow. "Then, there's nothing between you?"

"Of course not!" Jillian lied. She wasn't about to tell her mother the truth. That he'd kissed her on the cheek and told her she was cute, and that she'd spent most of last night in fitful dreams of his hands skimming over her body and his tongue following close behind. She drew a deep breath, banishing the residual images from her brain. "There's nothing going on."

Her mother sniffed, then heaved an impatient sigh. "And why not?"

Jillian gasped. "Why not?"

Sylvia clucked her tongue and shook her head. "He's a perfectly charming man, Jillian. And so handsome. And if he's a friend of Greg and Roxy's, then you know he's not some bum. You could do much worse. In fact, you have been doing much worse. How long has it been since you've had a date?"

"Mother, would you like some coffee?" Jillian turned and grabbed the pot from the counter, sloshing a fair amount on the front of her dress. But she was past caring. She'd almost welcome a domestic disaster with the boys right around now. At least she had a chance of handling that. But she'd never been able to handle her mother. To Sylvia Marshall, a successful career meant nothing unless there was a husband and children as well. In the pursuit of more grandchildren, she was ruthlessly outspoken and mercenary.

Jillian poured a mug of coffee for her mother, then handed it to her. "Why did you stop by?" she asked.

"Roxy called last night and she sounded worried. I wanted to see how you were doing."

Jillian glanced around the kitchen, then nodded at the boys who were gathered in the family room, watching the latest episode of *Barney* on television. "We're doing just fine."

"I could give you a break," she suggested. "I'll take the boys and you could go into town and get your hair done. Maybe get a manicure. There's a new little dress shop on Main Street." Her gaze drifted down to the huge stain on the front of Jillian's dress.

"Why would I need a new dress?" she asked.

Sylvia rolled her eyes as if she were talking to the village idiot. "He's coming back, isn't he? I really think you'd make a nicer impression on him if you weren't dressed in rags. You could cook him dinner, let him see the real you." She plucked her comb out of her purse and circled the breakfast bar. "Did you even bother with your hair this morning?"

Jillian brushed her hand away. "Believe me, Mother, he's already seen the real me. And it wasn't pretty. If you have any fantasies about Nick Callahan and me living happily ever after and providing you with additional grandchildren, then I'd warn you not to hold your breath. He's not my type."

Her mother looked at her long and hard. "Darling, I'm

not a fool. That man is every woman's type. Those shoulders and those eyes. My goodness, I—''

"Mother! Stop!" Jillian gathered up the remains of breakfast and tossed them in the sink. She was so tempted to accept her mother's offer to care for the boys, but after Nick's challenge, she was determined to prove that she didn't need his help. She could get through the day. If worse came to worse, she could lock the four of them in the nursery for the next eight hours to avert disaster.

She wiped her hands on a dishtowel and turned to her mother. "I've got a busy day today, Mother, and I'd really love to sit and chat. But the boys and I are going outside to play. Why don't you get your hair done today?"

Sylvia reached up and patted her perfectly coiffed hair. "Do you think it needs to be done?" She grabbed her purse, pulled out a mirror and examined her reflection. "Perhaps you're right." With that, she stood and bustled over to Jillian, then gave her a kiss on her cheek. "If you need anything, don't you hesitate to call. There's nothing wrong with admitting that you aren't the motherly type. Your father and I love you anyway."

Jillian walked her mother to the front door, then softly closed it behind her. "Of course you do, Mother. But you'd love me more if I had the husband and kids."

Why was it that her mother still had the capacity to make her feel like a failure? She was one of the most brilliant mathematicians on the east coast. She'd written two books and countless papers. She was on the verge of a major breakthrough in her Goldbach research. And just because she couldn't snag a wealthy husband and crank out a few babies, she was somehow worthless.

"Nag," she muttered at the closed door.

"Nag!" Andy shouted from the depths of the house.

"Nag, nag, nag!" Zach screamed.

Jillian giggled, then hurried back into the family room. She frowned at the boys. "Who said that? Zach? What did you call Grandma?"

Zach pointed to Andy and Andy pointed to Sam. A sudden realization hit her, a bolt from the blue. She knew who they were! She didn't even have to look at the initials she'd redrawn on their feet. Jillian bent down and gathered the triplets up in her arms. They squealed and wriggled, but she managed to hold on to them. "Listen to Auntie Jillie. Since Nick welshed on our bargain, I'm going to have to make a bargain with you." They all looked at her with angelic smiles and devilish eyes. Jillian took a deep breath. "No trouble today, all right? I want you to be good."

Zach nodded. "Be good," he said. He wagged a finger at his two brothers. "Be good."

Jillian sat back on her heels and watched them run off in three different directions, leaving a mess of toys scattered on the floor. If she couldn't trust a grown man like Nick Callahan to keep his promises, how was she ever supposed to trust two-and-a-half-year-old triplets?

She plopped down on the floor and leaned back against the wall. The coffee had seeped through her dress to her underwear and she just noticed she was wearing two different sandals. "Nick's desertion, my mother's visit and a ruined dress, all before 10 a.m. The day can't get much worse."

THE BOYS HAD BEEN way too quiet for way too long. Jillian had tried to keep them in the family room to limit the area of destruction, but they'd taken to running through the house, screaming like banshees. She'd attempted for the third time that day to clean up the mess, but it was impossible to collect all the Legos, Lincoln Logs, puzzle pieces and blocks before they came roaring back into the room to wreak havoc. If Greg and Roxy wanted to live in a perfectly clean house, Jillian suspected that they'd simply have to move and leave their sons behind with the mess.

They made it through lunch and nap time without any major disasters, and though she was exhausted, Jillian was starting to feel pretty proud of herself. She didn't need Nick Callahan! This mothering business wasn't that hard. In just three days, she'd nearly mastered it.

She'd learned to anticipate trouble and head it off before it blew up in her face. For lunch, she'd prepared hot dogs and sliced apples, very neat, very clean. She'd closed all the doors to the bathrooms to ward off toilet troubles and had hidden every marker and crayon the boys owned.

Jillian glanced at her watch. "Four o'clock," she murmured. "Four more hours until bedtime." And two more hours until Nick returned, she added silently. She pushed up from the floor and stumbled to the hallway where she found Zach and Andy sitting on the floor in front of the bathroom, shoving Hot Wheels beneath the door. Duke lay beside them, his nose pressed against the crack beneath the door. Jillian looked around for Sam, then called his name.

Jillian walked down the hallway and shouted up the stairs, but there was no answer. Her heart lurched and she ran to the front door, but she found it locked and secure. "Sam? Sammy, where are you?" She checked all the doors and windows, then ran upstairs and looked under every bed. But he was nowhere to be found. It wasn't like the boys to wander off. If they weren't playing together, they were usually in plain sight.

She raced back downstairs, then slid to a stop in front of the bathroom. "Where's Sammy?" she asked. "Tell Auntie Jillie where Sammy is."

Andy pointed to the bathroom door. "Sammy in there," he said.

"In the bathroom?" Jillian asked. "Sammy's in the bathroom? How did he get in there?"

Andy glanced over at Zach, then pointed to his brother. "Zach did it."

Jillian pressed her palm to her pounding heart. "How did you get that door open?" She reached out and turned the knob, but it wouldn't budge. Frowning, she gave the door a shove, then rattled the knob. Her stomach sank to her toes as she realized that the door was locked—from the inside.

"Sammy, honey, unlock the door for Auntie Jillie."

There was no sound from inside.

"Sammy, are you all right?"

Still no sound. With a groan, Jillian scrambled to find her shoes then slipped out the back door. She imagined all sorts of scenarios—Sammy unconscious from hitting his head on the toilet, Sammy munching on aspirin and guzzling cold medication, Sammy facedown in the bathtub.

The window to the bathroom was just above her reach, so she pulled a lawn chair over, shoved it through the bushes and climbed up. Through the screen she could see Sammy, sitting on the floor near the door playing with the Hot Wheels his brothers had offered up. Jillian called his name and he turned and waved at her, a wide smile on his face.

As if a ruined ceiling and torn wallpaper wasn't enough, Jillian contemplated breaking through the screen and crawling through the window. Nick could certainly fix a screen, and she had another hour or two to come up with a plausible excuse for why it had suddenly become broken. Drawing back her hand, she punched the mesh out of its frame, but the motion upset her balance and the chair beneath her wobbled.

Before she could catch herself, Jillian felt the chair tip and her body fall backwards. She had just enough time to scream before she landed hard on the ground between the bushes. Her ankle buckled beneath her and the sharp branches scraped her face. For a long moment, Jillian couldn't move. Then she heard Sammy's voice. He stood at the window, smiling at her from above.

"I—I'll get you out," Jillian called in a weak voice.

She managed to drag herself back into the house and, over the next hour, tried everything she could think of to free her nephew. She'd removed the doorknob to no effect, tried to jimmy the latch with a credit card, attempted to saw a hole in the door with Nick's tools, and finally began to pry the moulding off the door frame.

But Sammy was getting impatient and Jillian's ankle had swelled to the size of Andy's Nerf softball. When Sammy began to cry, she realized she had no choice but to call for help. She punched in the number for the fire department, then patiently explained the problem, asking that they send over a couple of discreet firemen with a short ladder. Then she limped back into the hallway to wait. But she didn't have to wait for long.

Within minutes, the sound of sirens drifted through the open window. Zach and Andy jumped up and ran to the front door, peering out through the screen. Jillian hobbled to the door and moaned. A long line of emergency vehicles snaked up the driveway. Two fire trucks, an ambulance, three police cars and the SWAT team had all turned out to witness her latest disaster, lights blazing.

A few moments later, they all hurried into the house with ropes and axes and handheld radios. Jillian explained the problem, then was shuffled aside. Within minutes, Sam was freed. Zach and Andy revelled in the excitement, falling all over the firemen and curiously examining all their equipment. Duke decided to take his guard dog duties more seriously and began an endless aria of howls and barks.

"Jillian? Jillian, where are you?"

She looked up from the chair in the family room, where a female paramedic had insisted she sit while she wrapped Jillian's sprained ankle and tended to her cuts. Nick stood in the kitchen, dressed in a suit and tie and wearing a troubled expression. A tiny moan slipped from her throat as she stared at him and the paramedic stopped what she was doing.

"Did that hurt?" the paramedic asked.

Jillian smiled in embarrassment, then shook her head. She wanted to sink down into the chair and disappear into the upholstery. How would she ever explain the mass of emergency personnel that had descended on the house? Or the crowds of neighbors that stood on the lawn with concerned curiosity? Or the ravaged bathroom door and the broken screen? Her pride hurt worse than her ankle.

A policeman murmured a few words to Nick, then pointed to Jillian. He rushed over, then bent down and took her hand, lacing his fingers through hers. A frisson of electricity tingled through her arm. Why did it always feel so good when he touched her? She should have been angry. This mess was partially his fault for leaving her alone. But the genuine concern in his eyes banished the last trace of anger from her body and replaced it with a warm, cozy, safe feeling.

He reached up and gently touched the scratches on her face. "Are you all right? I saw the fire engines in the driveway and I—"

"I'm fine," Jillian said. "I just twisted my ankle."

The warmth of his fingers caused her heart to skip a beat and the paramedic who was now taking her pulse glanced up at her. She turned to look at Nick and then grinned at Jillian with silent understanding.

"Jillie, Jillie. What kind of trouble did you get into

now?'' His thumb brushed across her lower lip. ''It seems I can't leave you alone for a second.''

Jillian gave him a weak smile. ''It—it wasn't that bad. A simple little problem. Sam got himself locked in the bathroom and I tried to get him out. And then, things just got worse and worse and before I knew it I had another disaster on my hands.''

Gradually, the house cleared, and before long Jillian and Nick were left with just the boys for company. Nick took her arm and helped her out of the chair. She winced, the pain in her ankle much worse than it had been.

''I think you need to lie down and elevate that foot. You've had a very hard day.'' He slipped his arm around her waist, pulling her body up against his and taking some of the weight from her foot. If there was an upside to her sprained ankle it would have to be this, she mused—Nick touching her, his hands sliding over her, her body pressed to his.

''I'm just no good at this,'' Jillian murmured. ''The more practice I get, the worse I do.''

They passed the bathroom and Nick peeked inside, then frowned. ''What's the toast doing on the floor?''

Jillian turned her embarrassed face into his shoulder and groaned. ''When Sam started crying I thought he might be hungry, so I slipped him some food.''

''See,'' Nick said, touching the tip of her nose. ''You're using your instincts. I'm sure Dr. Hazelton didn't mention that in his book, did he?''

Jillian had expected to feel like a complete fool once Nick saw what she'd accomplished in his absence. But to her amazement, he was doing his best to make her feel better. She glanced up at him. ''You look very handsome in that suit. When you first walked in, I thought you might be from the FBI.''

Nick chuckled as he helped her up the stairs. "Promise me you won't do something so bad that it would bring the FBI down on us."

She paused on the stairs. "When chaos theory is at work, I can't make any promises."

With that, Nick scooped her up and carried her the rest of the way up the stairs. And when he set her gently down in bed, Jillian allowed her arms to linger for just a few moments longer, wrapped around his neck. When she drew away, her fingers brushed the hair at his nape and she fought the absurd temptation to pull him down onto the bed with her. She'd almost resolved to ask him to stay. But then he heard a scream from one of the boys and turned for the door.

"Don't go anywhere," he teased, his smile warming her blood. "I'll be back."

Jillian sank into the down pillows and sighed, pressing her palm to her chest. Her heart beat a rapid rhythm and she felt flushed all over. She wondered how long a sprained ankle took to heal. She'd never been one to malinger, but the chance to spend a little more time in Nick Callahan's arms seemed too good to pass up.

4

WHEN NICK FINALLY got back to Jillian, she was comfortably ensconced in bed, her laptop computer resting on her thighs and stacks of computer paper spread out around her. He pushed the door open with his foot and carried the tray inside. Jillian looked up and quickly took her glasses off, hiding them beneath her pillow.

"Men don't make passes at girls who wear glasses," he teased.

She blushed as Nick set the tray down next to her and sat on the edge of the bed. "The boys are already asleep and I surveyed the damage downstairs. It shouldn't take much to fix. I even found some extra wallpaper in the basement."

She chewed on her bottom lip as her expression turned serious. "I—I want to pay you. Whatever it costs. Just so Roxy and Greg don't know what happened."

"Jillian, this is a small town. I'm sure they'll hear from someone. Half the town was standing on the lawn and the other half was here with the volunteer fire department." The look of mortification on her face gave him pause. "It could have happened to anyone," he said.

A soft moan slipped from her lips. "But why does it always happen to me?" She grabbed her laptop and turned the screen toward him. "Look at this. I've been working on a computer model of my disasters. I've assigned a numerical value to each factor—time of day, severity of problem, length of predicament, cost of repairs. You'll see that things aren't getting better. They're getting worse. If the model is extended over the course of the week, I can expect to burn down the house sometime on Thursday. I may also be the cause of the first major earthquake New Hampshire has ever experienced.''

Nick held back a laugh. She looked so serious and solemn—and so incredibly sexy. Even with her scratched cheeks and her mussed hair, he fought the urge to push her computer aside and yank her into his arms. After all, they were in a bedroom and, right now, he was having some serious bedroom fantasies.

He wondered what the pulse point right below her ear might taste like. And whether the hair at the nape of her neck was as soft as the tendrils that framed her face. And whether her breasts would mold perfectly to his hands when he slipped off her cotton nightgown.

"And what if you factor me into your model?" Nick asked, his gaze falling to her mouth. That incredibly sweet and tempting mouth, shaped like a perfect Cupid's bow.

"You?" ·

He could kiss her again, kiss away all her doubts and insecurities. He'd grown used to his role in the house— rescuing Jillie from her disasters, then reassuring her that she wasn't a complete failure. But words didn't seem to do the trick anymore. If he kissed her, then maybe she'd believe what a wonderful woman she was. She wouldn't have to turn to her formulas and charts and mathematical models for comfort. She'd turn to him.

But an ordinary kiss wouldn't do. This time he'd try a real kiss—long and wet and deep. A kiss that would bring a fierce blush to her cheeks and a breathless tone to her voice.

"Me," he said, letting his eyes drift along her neck to

the spot at the cleft of her collarbone. "What if I help you out with the boys? How would that change things?"

She ignored his gaze and quickly typed the information into her computer, then studied the results. A slow smile curved her lips. "It would help. Look. The coefficient of disaster severity is nearly cut in half. But of course, I'll have to factor in the cost."

"I won't charge you." It wouldn't be the worst thing in the world to have Jillie Marshall indebted to him, Nick mused.

She blinked in surprise. "Oh, but I have to pay for your time. It wouldn't be fair. You have other work to do."

If accepting her money was the only way he'd get to spend more time with her, Nick wasn't going to quibble. "All right," he said. "What did we agree on? Fifty dollars an hour?"

"Forty," she said, her eyes turning suspicious.

"Right. Forty." He glanced down at the tray. "Forty dollars an hour for a jack-of-all-trades. Nanny, carpenter and general go-fer. At that rate, I probably should have spent more time on your dinner." He reached over and picked up the plate. "Grilled cheese, Tater Tots, and lime Jell-O."

"Umm, gourmet fare," she said, returning a bit of his teasing. With delicate fingers, she grabbed the sandwich and took a bite. Nick handed her a goblet. "Fine wine?" she asked.

"Fine grape juice," he replied. Watching her eat was almost as much fun as watching her try to diaper the boys. She did both with such concentrated enthusiasm that he made a mental note to provide better meals. Perhaps he could stop at one of the trendy delis in town and pick up something tasty for tomorrow night. Something suitable for eating by candlelight.

"What are you working on?" Nick said, anxious to continue the easy conversation. "I mean, besides your disaster model."

"An article on perfect numbers," Jillian said, glancing at her laptop.

"Tell me about it."

"Really?"

He nodded. She took a slow sip of grape juice while she collected her thoughts. "Perfect numbers are…well, they're perfect. A perfect number is a number whose factors add up to that number. Like six. One, two and three are factors of six, but they also add up to six."

"Is that what you study?"

"It's part of what I study. My area of expertise is number theory, which has to do with the properties of integers. Whole numbers. Like one, two, seven, thirteen."

"Were you always good at math?"

Jillian nodded, snatching up a Tater Tot and popping it into her mouth. "I was a real geek in high school. The smartest girl in the county. It didn't make me very popular with the boys."

"You've grown up," Nick murmured, mesmerized by the sound of her voice. He couldn't imagine that voice shouting over a roomful of college students or rapping out some mathematical formula. Her voice was made for more intimate encounters, soft conversations in bed and ragged moans in the throes of passion. "You must have plenty of men in your life."

Jillian smiled and leaned back into the pillows. "When I first started working with perfect numbers, I had this silly theory that love was like a perfect number. You know, each person brings different factors into a relationship and when they all add up, they're…perfect."

"And do you still think that?"

She frowned and shook her head. "Now I think maybe love is more like an irrational number. Or a transcendental number. Like pi, it's unfathomable. And if you try to figure it out, you just go crazy."

Nick plucked a Tater Tot from her plate and considered her view on the matter. His opinion of love wasn't much different. After he'd left Claire, he'd driven himself mad trying to figure out where it had all gone wrong. "Have you ever been in love?"

She shook her head. "Not the perfect number kind of love. How about you?"

Nick considered her question for a long moment. He'd thought he was in love with Claire, but now he wasn't sure. He'd said it enough times, but looking back on it all, it seemed like another man's life. The intensity of his feelings for her had faded over the weeks they'd been apart, so much so that he hadn't thought of her in—in forty-eight hours, exactly the same amount of time he'd known Jillian Marshall. "No," he finally said. "I don't think I've ever been in love."

A long silence grew between them and Jillian focused her attention on finishing her dinner. He wanted to kiss her again, but for some reason, the time didn't seem right. Thoughts of Claire nagged at his mind. How could he have forgotten so quickly? He was supposed to have loved her! And now, all he could think about was Jillian and her sweet lips and tempting body.

"I should go," he murmured, when she'd finished her meal. "You need your rest. You've had a very busy day." He stood up and took the tray. "I'll make breakfast tomorrow morning. Why don't you sleep in?"

"But you're not due to stay with the boys until three."

"Call it a favor. You'll have to factor favors into your computer model."

A winsome smile touched her lips and she snuggled down in the bed, tugging the comforter up to her chin. "If you were a number, you'd be a perfect number."

Nick turned and walked out of the room, balancing the tray beneath his arm as he shut the door. When he reached the solitude of the kitchen, he slid the tray onto the counter and stared out the window above the sink. The full moon glimmered gold on the black surface of the lake. He wandered over to the door and pulled it open, then stepped outside to draw a deep breath of the balmy night air.

He'd promised himself that he wouldn't jump into another relationship. He'd been burned badly by Claire and he never wanted to go through that again. A relationship with Jillian, however short and sweet, promised to be complicated. She was Roxy's sister, for one. And—and she didn't like carpenters. And—he tried to come up with another reason. She'd make a horrible mother?

Nick knew that wasn't true. Though luck hadn't been with her the past few days, he had no doubt that she'd treasure her children and make a wonderful home for them. But he just couldn't picture her children as *his* children, too.

So if he couldn't imagine a future with her, what was the attraction? Maybe it had to do with her helplessness, her vulnerability. He liked rescuing her. Claire had never needed anything from him. She had her own money, her own friends, a great job and a son she adored. That's probably why he'd been so determined to have children with her—it was the only thing he could give her that she didn't already have. Jillian, on the other hand, seemed to spontaneously combust every time he walked out of reach. She needed him.

How could such a brilliant woman have so little common sense? Nick should have found that trait irritating, but in truth he found it quite charming. He pulled the door closed behind him, then strolled down the lawn toward the lake and his cottage. When he reached the water, he turned around and looked back at the house. Her window was still illuminated and he wondered if she was working or if she was dozing off to sleep.

Nick closed his eyes and imagined himself lying next to her, touching her, inhaling her scent and listening to her soft and even breathing. He saw her kneeling before him on the bed, the hem of her nightgown bunched in his hands. Slowly, he'd pull it up, the fabric brushing along her thighs, skimming her backside and belly, rising to reveal the soft swell of her breasts. And then, he'd tug it over her head and her hair would fall loose and free around her naked shoulders.

His fingers clenched with instinctive anticipation and he allowed a long breath to slip from his lungs. Nick opened his eyes and the vision was still there, behind the lacy curtains. But then, her bedroom light went dark, startling him out of his reverie.

He cursed softly, then turned away, frustrated by the errant path of his thoughts. If this was the way he put women out of his life, then he was doing a damned poor job of running his life!

THE NEXT DAY DAWNED hot and humid. As he'd promised, Nick appeared before breakfast. After bringing her coffee in bed, he got the boys dressed and fed, then suggested they all spend the morning down at the beach. Hobbled by her sore ankle, Jillian was looking forward to the solitude. She'd been far too anxious for a few stolen moments with her nanny, caught up in disturbing fantasies that always involved a semi-naked Nick.

Later, from her spot on the family room sofa, she watched him finish cleaning up the remnants of the boys' breakfast.

A morning all alone would do her some good. She had planned to spend the time with her computer on her lap and an ice pack on her ankle. But after Nick had slathered sunscreen on every body, snapped every life jacket, tugged on every beach shoe and blown up every water wing, he had scooped her up in his arms and carried her down to the water's edge, the boys racing ahead of him.

She hadn't realized that "they all" included her as well. Secretly pleased that he expected her company, she didn't bother to protest. After all, she was supposed to be in charge of the boys. She couldn't abdicate all responsibility. Nick settled her on the cushions of a chaise lounge just a few yards from the water, fetched her a glass of iced tea from his cottage, then raced into the lake with Zach, Andy and Sam. Jillian laughed as she watched the four of them splashing and shouting and jumping up and down.

At any other moment, Jillian might have considered sunning herself in a lawn chair to be the ultimate waste of time. But here, in the eighty-degree heat, her sundress clinging to her skin and her iced tea sweating in her hand, she didn't even want to think of work. Her research on the Goldbach conjecture could wait. Her paper on perfect numbers didn't need to be done for a month. Right now, she'd much rather enjoy the sight of Nick Callahan, dressed in a pair of baggy shorts and nothing else.

The wide brim of her straw hat shadowed her face, hiding the fact that her eyes remained on Nick. He had incredibly broad shoulders and finely muscled arms, probably from carrying all that wood, she mused. His smooth chest gleamed in the sun and Jillian allowed her gaze to drift downward, following the narrow dusting of hair that began at his collarbone and ended beneath the waistband of his shorts.

She continued her survey of his physical attributes with

a study of his lower body. A flat belly, narrow hips and long legs. Jillian had always believed only women could boast of attractive legs, but she'd now be forced to change that opinion. Nick Callahan had great gams.

Her mind flashed back to the moment when he'd tugged his T-shirt off, the way the muscles in his torso bunched and twisted. A silent thrill had raced through her at the notion of watching him undress. Now, as he emerged from the water like some Greek god, Jillian grabbed his T-shirt from the blanket beside her chair and stuffed it beneath her. If he wanted to cover that wonderful body, he'd have to use a towel.

Jillian sighed softly. What was this sudden obsession with the physical? Did all women go through this when they came across a stunningly handsome man? Or was she a special case? She'd just never noticed the male physique before and like a child deprived of sweets, she was now stuffing herself with candy.

The boys stayed in the shallow water and Nick kept a careful eye on the triplets, easing her mind. If she knew nothing else about Nick Callahan, she knew he could be trusted to take care of Zach, Andy and Sam. And the boys revelled in his attention. They'd made a game of Nick grabbing each boy around the waist, tossing him up in the air a few times, then suddenly dunking him. Though they coughed and sputtered and wiped water from their eyes, they came back for more with cries of "Do again, Nick, do again!" And he was happy to oblige.

There were times, when Nick was with the boys, that she saw such childish exuberance in his face, such joy for the simple act of play. And then, she'd see him in another light, as a man, strong and sexy and completely aware of his charms. Such a contradiction, Jillian mused. A woman would never be bored by him.

The splashing stopped and Jillian watched as Nick and the boys stumbled from the water. He paused when he reached the sand and raised his arms to rake his fingers through his wet hair. Her eyes fixed on his chest, on the tiny rivulet of water that ran down his belly. Nick bent over and grabbed a stack of beach towels. He handed one to each of the boys, then took one for himself, draping it around his neck.

Jillian knew she shouldn't stare. But from beneath the brim of her hat, who would know that she'd developed a lustful nature? Or that she possessed such voyeuristic tendencies? Nick looked over at her and she quickly closed her eyes, pretending to nap.

"The water is great, Jillie," he called.

She looked at him just in time to see him rubbing the towel over his sun-streaked hair. It stood up in spikes, making him look as cute and boyish as Zach, Andy and Sam. "You should go in," he added, slowly approaching her.

"I didn't bring a suit," Jillian said, grateful that she'd managed to forget that little item. In truth, she didn't even own a bathing suit, at least not since high school swimming class. She'd never had the courage to put one on after that.

"I'm sure Roxy has one you can borrow," Nick said.

Jillian chuckled. "I don't think we want to expose the boys to the sight of me in a bathing suit. It might scar them for life."

He plopped down on the blanket beside her chair. "Why?" he asked, surprised by her comeback. "You have a great body. You'd look incredible in a bathing suit."

He said it so casually, as if it were a known fact throughout the civilized world. "Jillian Marshall" and "great body" had never appeared together in the same sentence to her recollection. She opened her mouth, ready to brush aside the compliment with a silly joke. But then she merely smiled. If Nick really thought she had a great body, who was she to disabuse him of that notion? She rather liked the thought that he considered her sexually attractive.

Nick crossed his arms over his bent legs and stared out at the water. "I don't ever want to go back to Providence," he murmured. "I'm beginning to get used to this place. An endless summer."

"Is that where you usually work?" Jillian asked. "Providence?"

Nick nodded. "My office is there, but I work on projects all over, mostly up and down the east coast."

"A lot of people must want bookshelves, huh?" Jillian said.

He glanced at her, frowning, then broke into a soft chuckle. "Yeah, lots of bookshelves just waiting to be built."

"Actually, bookshelves are a very important thing. Look at libraries, universities. I have some very nice bookshelves in my office. Where would the world be without bookshelves?"

"I never really thought about it," he said, rubbing his palm over his damp chest. "Although with the advent of the Internet, I guess my job might be obsolete before long."

Her eyes followed his every move, imagining the contours and curves of his body beneath her own hands. "Oh, I'm sure you could do something else," Jillian said, her voice cracking slightly. He glanced her way and she quickly averted her eyes, ashamed to be caught gawking.

An odd silence hung between them for a few moments, then Nick called out to the boys and they scurried over. He grabbed up a bottle of sunscreen and liberally applied it to every inch of exposed skin, then sent them on their way to build sand castles on the narrow strip of sand at the edge of the water. "You should put some of this on yourself," he suggested.

"I'm all right," Jillian replied. "What about you?" His skin was already burnished a deep shade of gold. As he leaned forward to wipe his hands on a towel, she noticed the contrast between his tanned back and the skin that peeked from beneath the waistband of his shorts. He'd obviously spent a fair amount of time outside, with his shirt off.

He sat up, then twisted to look over his shoulders. "Maybe I ought to put some on." But rather than squeeze a blob of lotion into his hand, he handed her the bottle. "Do you mind?"

Jillian swallowed hard. Had it sounded like she was looking for an invitation? "No!" she said, her voice cracking again. The bottle nearly slipped from her trembling fingers.

"No?"

"I—I mean, no, I wouldn't mind. Where would you like it?" She said a silent prayer that he didn't sunburn in intimate spots, places on his body that she wouldn't be able to touch without swooning.

"Shoulders," he said, turning his back to her.

With shaky hands, she flipped open the top and squeezed the bottle, but it had been sitting in the sun for too long and the lotion squirted out, spraying all over her hand and arm and the front of her dress. "Oh!" Jillian cried.

Nick glanced over his shoulder. "Is there a problem?"

Of course, there was a problem! She been invited to touch him, to run her palms over the taut muscles of his back, to enjoy the smooth expanse of his naked skin. And she wasn't supposed to enjoy it! Slowly, she moved her hand toward him, then with a silent oath, slapped the lotion on his back and began to rub.

At first, she moved frantically, as if desperate to finish as quickly as possible. But then, as her fingers became aware of the pleasant warmth of his skin, the hard muscle and sinew beneath, she slowed down, grazing her hands over his shoulders and memorizing the feel of him.

She couldn't remember the last time she'd touched a man the way she was touching Nick now. In the past, foreplay had always seemed so perfunctory, the touching and caressing an obligation to be performed before the actual event could take place. Perhaps she'd ignored it all out of nervousness, or the knowledge that she probably wouldn't enjoy the encounter as much as she was supposed to.

But now, as she touched Nick, every nerve in her body stood on edge. Her skin crackled with strange new sensations, like tiny electric shocks racing from her fingertips through her arms and ending somewhere deep inside her, in that place where desire had lain dormant for so long. Gently, she kneaded the muscles near his neck.

"That feels nice," he murmured.

Jillian wasn't sure what to do next. She could lean closer and let her hands slip over his shoulders to his chest. Or she could allow her fingers to drift lower on his back to his narrow waist and tempting backside. She'd never seduced a man before, never felt bold enough to try. Maybe she should just kiss him, brushing her lips along the skin below his ear. She closed her eyes and bent forward, but before she could reach her target, his voice startled her.

"Are you almost done?" he asked.

Jillian's eyes snapped open and she drew back, snatching her hands from his skin as if it had suddenly turned hot to the touch. "Yes," she murmured. "You should be fine."

The expression on his face was uneasy yet intense and, for a moment, she thought he might be angry with her. Then, he sighed softly. "I—I think I'm going to go back in for a swim." He grabbed his towel and levered to his feet, then walked away from her without looking back.

When he reached the pier, he dropped the towel. Jillian's breath caught in her throat as she caught a glimpse of the bulge in the front of his shorts. A mortified moan slipped from her lips and she pulled her sunhat lower over her eyes. Good grief, what had she done to him?

Jillian slouched down in the chair and tried to quell her humiliation. She'd just assumed that her touch wouldn't have any effect on him at all. She'd never been adept at the sexual arts. But then men did have involuntary responses to…stimulation, whether intentional or not.

She watched him swim laps from the pier to the small raft that floated a good distance out into the lake. "Oh, God," she muttered. "What must he think? I've completely embarrassed him."

Jillian thought about making her escape, but the boys were playing a few feet away in the sand, and Nick was too far away to watch them. She'd just have to stay and face him again. Perhaps if she pretended she hadn't noticed his…discomfort, everything would be all right.

"From now on, just keep your hands off him," Jillian muttered to herself. Though that vow might be hard to keep, she had no choice. Nick Callahan already believed she was a complete nitwit when it came to child care. She didn't want him thinking she was a sex-starved spinster as well.

THE SUN WAS HIGH in the sky before Nick could finally pull the boys away from the water for lunch. They'd put up such a fuss that he decided to scratch up something to eat from his refrigerator instead of heading back up to the main house. The boys usually weren't allowed to play in the cottage, so when Nick pulled the screen door open, they tumbled inside, sandy feet and all. Jillian preferred to wait on the threshold, hesitant about entering.

Since Nick's rather deflating dip in the lake, an uncomfortable silence had descended around them. Hell, his reaction had surprised him as much as his hasty retreat had surprised her. He'd always had such ironclad control around women. But the feel of her hands on his skin, the warmth of the sun and the slippery lotion, had been more than he could handle. At least he'd managed to hide the evidence of his arousal with a well-placed towel.

"Come on in," Nick murmured, snatching up rolls of blueprints and tossing them in a corner. "Sorry about the mess."

"What are all these?" Jillian asked, limping as she entered. To his relief, she'd refused his offer of transportation across the lawn and had tested her ankle instead. If lotion application had caused such an unbidden reaction, he wasn't sure what having her in his arms might do.

"Just some plans. For a new project."

She picked up a blueprint and stared at it. The design for a new auto assembly line probably looked like Greek to her—or maybe like bookshelves, Nick mused. But when she picked up his sketch pad, he held his breath.

"What's this?" she asked, pointing to a drawing of the front facade of a house.

He'd been thinking about building another home, ridding himself of the place that he and Claire had shared. Sleeplessness the previous night had produced a few interesting ideas, in between fantasies of Jillie. This home would be different, set on a wooded lot, perhaps beside a lake, constructed of stone and natural woods with a wide porch and a spacious, but cozy interior. "Just a hobby," Nick replied. "I like to draw houses."

"This is very good. You should think about becoming an architect—you know—go back to school and study."

Nick took the sketch book from her and shoved it beneath a stack of blueprints. Though he basked in her compliment, he knew it was based on a perception of him that was less than accurate. To Jillie, he remained a simple carpenter. How could he possibly possess the talent to design a house? "Nah, I think I'm finished with school."

He really should tell her the truth. At first he'd kept his background from her on purpose, hoping to use the revelation to tweak her temper. But now his decision to hold back the truth just stood in the way. Deceiving her about who and what he was would only cause trouble in the future. She'd been completely open with him and he hadn't returned the favor.

But then, what future did they have together? He'd been to hell and back trying to come to terms with Claire's desertion. He didn't want to go through that again. And the fastest way to repeat his mistakes was to fall in love with another woman—with Jillie Marshall. It was better to let her believe he was a working-class guy, the kind of man she could never love. His little lie could be used to his advantage, to protect his heart from more hurt. For if Jillie had any lustful fantasies the reality of his professional prospects would make her quickly push them aside.

"Sit down," he said, shoving the rest of the blueprints off the table.

She did as she was told, perching on the edge of her chair and folding her hands in front of her. It felt so odd to have her here, in his temporary home. He'd imagined her here a number of times, when he'd lain in bed and let his mind wander. He'd pictured her sitting across a candlelit table from him, seen her slow dancing barefoot with him on the porch. And he'd also imagined her lying on his bed, wrapped in his embrace, her naked body pressed against his.

Nick turned away from the table and began to busy himself with lunch preparations. Why couldn't he stop fantasizing about her? Every shred of common sense told him Jillie wasn't his type—and he certainly wasn't hers. Hell, Claire *had* been his type and look at what happened to them. Falling for Jillie Marshall was a one-way ticket to heartbreak.

"Can I help?" she asked.

"I think I have everything under control. How about SpaghettiOs and hot dogs?"

"You have SpaghettiOs?"

Nick smiled. "I've always considered them one of the major food groups. A boon to bachelors everywhere." He held up the can. "Nutritious and great-tasting. Plus they only take a minute to heat up in the microwave."

"You need a wife," Jillie teased.

Nick knew she'd meant it as a joke, but when his eyes met hers, he couldn't keep himself from speaking. "Are you volunteering?" A deep blush stained her cheeks and he instantly regretted provoking her.

"You wouldn't want me as a wife," she said. "I'm a terrible housekeeper, I don't cook very well and I put my work before everything else. And you've certainly been witness to my skill with children."

Her words should have confirmed his feelings, that Jillie wasn't his type. But instead, he found himself even more attracted to her, to her plain-spoken honesty, to her ability to recognize her flaws and face them. "I think any man would be lucky to find a woman like you."

She smiled uneasily, then glanced around the room. "Don't you think it's a little quiet?" She pushed to her feet and when he moved to help her, she waved him off. "I'll go find the boys. I don't want disaster to strike your house, too.''

She limped across the tiny living room and peeked inside the bedroom door. A few moments later, the boys came running out, smelling of Nick's cologne. Jillie appeared hard on their heels, the empty bottle clutched in her hand. ''Disaster on a small scale,'' she said. ''They dumped this all over your bed. It's so strong in there, it'll make your eyes water.''

''No problem,'' he said. ''I've been sleeping on the screened porch lately. In the hammock. I like listening to the sound of the water and the night birds.''

''Maybe if we drag the bed outside and air it out, the smell will—''

''Don't worry about it,'' Nick said with a shake of his head. ''If it doesn't go away, I'll buy Greg and Roxy a new bed. This wasn't your disaster.''

Jillie took her place at the table, keeping one eye on the boys, who were hitting each other with rolled-up blueprints.

''How's your ankle feeling?'' he asked.

She held out her leg, turning it from side to side. ''It's feeling better, but it's still a little swollen. It doesn't hurt too much when I walk. By tomorrow I should be back to normal.''

He took a moment to admire the trim curve of her calf and her pretty ankle, before turning back to the SpaghettiOs. He'd grown so used to having her near that he'd begun to look forward to any situation that might put them together. Baby-sitting the boys was just a convenient excuse. But what would happen when Greg and Roxy returned? Would she just walk away, never to see him again?

Nothing in her manner gave him a clue as to how she regarded him. Even when he'd kissed her, he'd been met with an uneasy silence. He was tempted to kiss her again, right here and now. They'd grown closer since that night in her bedroom, yet it was becoming harder and harder to make a move, more difficult to predict her reaction.

Why? Was it because now there might be some real desire behind his kiss? Or was he just afraid? Hell, he wasn't sure what he wanted. Rejection would be impossible to handle, yet capitulation would be even worse. Perhaps it would be more sensible to stop thinking about kissing Jillian Marshall altogether.

When lunch was ready, Nick gathered the boys and set their bowls on the plank floor of the porch. He and Jillie grabbed a pair of wicker chairs and sat down to iced tea and ham sandwiches. "I was thinking, if your ankle is better by tomorrow, we could take the boys into town. The volunteer fire department is having their picnic this weekend and they have pony rides and cotton candy and clowns."

Jillie smiled. "That would be nice." She took a tiny bite of her sandwich, then set it down. "I want to thank you again for helping me with the boys. I don't know what I would have done if you hadn't been here. I can't chase them down with this bad ankle."

He leaned back in his chair. "Why were you so determined to take care of them?" Nick asked. "It's hard enough for Roxy and you haven't had any experience with kids."

"That's why I volunteered," Jillie said. "Because I wanted to see what it was like."

"Why? Are you thinking of adopting triplets? If you are, I'd seriously question your sanity."

Jillie paused. "Actually, I have wondered what it would be like to be a mother. But after this week, I think it's pretty clear that I should put it out of my mind."

"I wouldn't use this week as an example. Most women don't have to care for three. Three boys are even worse. I grew up in a family of ten and we didn't enjoy as many disasters in an entire year as you've had this week. It just takes—"

"Organization?" she asked, a grin curling the corners of her mouth.

Nick laughed. "Yeah. Organization."

Slowly, the easygoing banter between them returned and the morning's events were forgotten. But Nick knew his desire for Jillie Marshall lurked just below the surface. All it would take was another touch, an inadvertent caress, and he'd be faced once again with the inevitable proof that when it came to Jillie, he wasn't sure where friendship ended and passion began.

5

_____

BY THE NEXT DAY, Jillian's ankle felt almost normal. The scratches on her face had faded and Nick was hard at work fixing the window and the ceiling of the downstairs bathroom. Had Roxy and Greg walked in that evening, they'd have believed that everything had run smoothly during their time away.

Only she and Nick knew differently. And maybe the boys, although they wouldn't be doing any talking. She planned to brainwash them with as many pony rides as possible at the Firemen's Picnic so the experience would be the only thing they'd talk about for days. Nick had promised he'd finish up after lunch so they could all head into the village for the festivities.

She wiped her hands on a dish towel, then followed the sound of a power drill as she went to find Nick. But she was stopped by the ring of the phone. She grabbed the receiver before the boys noticed a second ring, then froze when she heard her sister's voice.

"Roxy! I didn't expect you to call again," Jillian said.

"It's been four days. Is everything all right? I've just had these strange feelings, like something was wrong."

Jillian put on a light-hearted tone. "I told you I'd call if anything went wrong. I didn't call, did I?"

A long silence travelled over the phone lines from Hawaii. "Are you sure? I mean, you haven't had any experience with babies," Roxy said. "Things can't be going that well. There must be at least a few problems. What about Zach's allergies? And Andy had that scrape on his knee. That's not infected is it? And Sammy can never sleep when it's windy.''

Jillian detected the desperate edge in Roxy's voice. Her sister wanted to know that she was irreplaceable, that no one could take care of the boys as well as she could. Guilt niggled at Jillian's mind and she considered telling her the whole truth—that the past five days had been one disaster after another, punctuated only by interludes of lusting after the family carpenter.

But then, knowing Roxy, she and Greg would be on the next plane home if she told the truth. Maybe it would be best to soften it just a bit. ''Well, I did slip and fall while I was playing with the boys,'' she said. ''I twisted my ankle. But I'm fine. The boys are fine. Here, I'll let you talk to them.''

Jillian called the boys from the family room where they'd been watching *Sesame Street*. Zach grabbed the phone first and began to babble to his mother. Jillian sat on a stool and listened distractedly as she sipped her coffee.

''Jillie fall down,'' Zach said. ''Jillie have owwee.''

She set her cup of coffee on the counter where it sloshed over the side, then pried the phone out of Zach's hand. ''Roxy, I'll put Andy on now.''

Andy grabbed the phone and laughed as he listened to his mother's voice on the other end. Then he went silent for a moment. ''Jillie fall down,'' he said. ''Fire truck. Fire truck!''

Jillian took the phone again and pushed it into Sammy's hand. At least she could trust Sammy not to talk. He just listened to his mother, nodding and saying ''Uh-huh.'' When he finally handed the phone back to Jillian, she figured her secrets were still safe. The boys ran back into the family room and she prepared for damage control with her sister.

"Jillie, what happened?" Roxy demanded. "Andy was talking about fire trucks."

Jillian cleared her throat. "Yes. I—I tripped over his little toy fire truck."

"The boys don't have a fire truck," Roxy said.

"They didn't," Jillian said, her voice cracking slightly, "until I bought them one. Tell me, how is Hawaii? Are you having fun?"

"Sure, sure," Roxy said. "Palm trees, white sand beaches, flowers everywhere. It's a damned paradise. I miss my boys. I want to come home."

"Don't be silly," Jillian said. "We're all getting along so well. In fact, we were about to go down to the Firemen's Picnic in town. Nick says they have pony rides."

"Nick? Nick Callahan?" Jillian could almost see the sly smile curling the corners of Roxy's mouth. "So, how is Nick?"

At that very moment, the man in question strolled into the kitchen, shirtless, his jeans and his tool belt hanging low on his hips. He smiled at her, then moved to the sink to get a glass of water.

"He—he's been great with the boys," Jillian said distractedly, admiring the smooth expanse of his shoulders, the fascinating curve of his back. "And he's a wonderful carpenter. Your bookshelves are looking just...fine. Everything's just fine."

"So what do you think of Nick?" Roxy asked. "You know he's not just a—"

"Roxy, I've got to go," Jillian said, unwilling to discuss Nick Callahan's particular attributes in front of the man himself. She wasn't sure she'd be able to hide her true feelings about him, or keep her voice from trembling. "We'll discuss this when you get home. I've got to get the boys ready for the picnic. Bye-bye. See you soon.'' She hung the phone up, then sank down onto a stool and drew a shaky breath.

Nick watched her from over the rim of his water glass. ''How's Roxy?'' he asked.

''Fine,'' Jillian replied.

Nick nodded. ''Did you tell her about the water problem? And the twisted ankle? And the—''

''Of course, I did,'' Jillian lied with a weak smile. ''Right before you walked in.''

He chuckled. ''So when does her plane come in? Should we leave for the airport now or do we have time for lunch?''

Jillian couldn't help but laugh at his gentle teasing. ''All right, so maybe I didn't tell her everything. She'll find out soon enough. There's no need to ruin a perfectly lovely vacation.''

He sent her a smile so charming that she wondered if she'd be able to stand upright again.

''Are you ready to go?'' he asked.

She nodded. ''Are you planning to go like that?'' Her gaze drifted down his body and her fingers twitched as she thought about touching him. The feel of his warm skin still lingered on her fingertips and, standing so still, his hip cocked against the edge of the counter, he looked like he'd been sculpted by Michelangelo, muscle carved from fine marble.

''I'm going to run down to the cottage and take a quick shower,'' he said, interrupting her little fantasy. ''I'll be back by the time you have the boys' shoes on.''

Jillian grabbed the damp dishtowel and tossed it at him as he walked to the back door. Determined to prove him wrong, she rounded up the boys, lined them up on the sofa and pushed their shoes on, one after another. Then she went back down the line and tied the laces. "See. It's just a matter of organization," she murmured, her hands braced on her hips. "Time for pony rides!"

Andy looked up at her and frowned. "No ponies in van," he said.

"Ponies go *nnnnneeeeeeaaaay*," Zach shouted.

"I kiss ponies," Sammy said.

Jillian smiled. "No ponies in van. We're going to ride on top of the ponies, not drive them around in the van. And as for kissing the ponies, we'll have to see about that, Sammy. Now let's go. We don't want to keep Nick waiting."

The boys jumped down and ran to the front door. Grabbing her sun hat, Jillian followed after them. They only waited outside for a few minutes, before Nick appeared from around the corner of the house. His hair was damp and he wore a fresh T-shirt and clean jeans. Jillian couldn't help but think, dressed as he was, he was the handsomest man she'd ever met.

He grabbed Sammy and swung him up on his shoulders. Zach and Andy climbed into the wagon and they set off on the short walk toward town. The tiny village of Dunsboro was only a mile down the road, set on a serene inlet of the lake. The boys were so filled with excitement that Jillian couldn't help but be caught up in it as well. That is, until she recognized some of the firemen who had rescued Sammy from the bathroom. She expected some joking and teasing, but to her surprise, the volunteer firemen considered her emergency the most excitement they'd had since Ed Ridley's horse got loose in the town square.

Nick and Jillian strolled through the arcade, observing the games and trying to keep the boys from running off. There were pennies to throw into goldfish bowls and balloons to pop with darts. There was even a sledgehammer challenge with a weight that flew up a pole and measured masculine strength in terms of "Mama's Boy," "Girly Man" and "Hercules."

A volunteer fireman she didn't recognize lured them over with a colorful pitch and a wave of his hand. "Come on, lad. Show your little wife the limits of your strength. Hit the bell and win a teddy bear."

Jillian opened her mouth to correct his mistake but Nick stepped up to accept the challenge. He plucked Sammy off his shoulders and handed him to Jillian. With a playful grin, he spit on his two palms and rubbed them together, then offered his palms to each of the boys so they might participate with a good spit of their own.

They all watched Nick heft the sledgehammer over his shoulder. And then with one smooth motion, he brought it down on the anvil. The ball rose like a rocket and struck the bell and the boys squealed in delight. Nick paid four times and each time, he hit the bell. In the end, he presented them each with a tiny stuffed bear.

"You've got quite a husband there," the fireman called, slapping him on the back.

"He's not my husband," Jillian said.

The fireman looked at the boys, then back up at her, a questioning arch to his eyebrow.

"And they're not my children," she added.

"You're not the little lady staying out at the Hunter house, are you? My goodness, I heard all about your little emergency. Sorry I couldn't respond, but me and the missus was over in Nashua visiting her sister. Heard it was quite the to-do."

Jillian politely listened to a recap of her "emergency," before Nick found a way to excuse them. But again and again, as they walked through the amusements at the picnic, people either assumed she and Nick and the boys were a family or they knew the truth and had heard about her disaster at the lake house. She couldn't seem to escape embarrassment, no matter which way she turned.

But oddly, she didn't feel the need to defend herself or to retreat behind the facade of the esteemed Professor Jillian Marshall. Perhaps it was because Nick was holding her hand, giving her confidence. Or maybe she was beginning to "roll with the punches." There were even times when she laughed along with the stories, finding her actions genuinely amusing.

After three hours at the picnic, they started for home. The boys, filled with cotton candy and corn dogs, were placed in the wagon where they dozed, a tangle of arms and legs and sticky faces.

Jillian and Nick walked along the road, hand in hand, commenting on the flora and fauna they passed and enjoying the late afternoon sunshine, dappled by the trees overhead.

The air buzzed with insects and birdsong filled the woods. Though Jillian's ankle ached, she barely noticed. Instead, she enjoyed the perfection of the afternoon, the easy camaraderie that had developed between Nick and her, the feel of her fingers laced through his.

It was no wonder people assumed they were married. She'd even caught herself pretending they were a couple a few times during the afternoon. It wasn't hard, with Nick treating them all to games and food, gathering up the boys like a watchful father and inquiring about her comfort like a doting husband.

She'd seen so many sides of Nick over the past few days. The carpenter who competently cleaned up after her disasters, the father figure who looked after the boys, the sexy male who piqued her passion and the boy inside the man who played with her nephews in the lake. And now, she saw him as he might be—as a husband.

How strange that her little list of criteria for a mate now seemed utterly ridiculous. She'd always thought she'd have the power to choose the man she'd fall in love with. But it had become obvious to her that she had no more control over her feelings than she had over the rising of the sun and movements of the moon.

She was falling for Nick Callahan and there was nothing she could do about it.

JILLIAN SAT at the long table in the mahogany-panelled conference room at the Institute. She was dressed in a tailored suit and a silk blouse, her typical wardrobe for work. Yet, she felt oddly uncomfortable. She fought the urge to kick off her shoes and wiggle her toes, to unfasten the buttons of her blouse and free herself from the tight collar.

She'd been summoned back to Boston by a phone message, left for her while she and Nick and the boys had been at the picnic. At first she'd thought about ignoring the message, but then her professional ethics overruled her initial reaction. Nick had graciously offered to watch Zach, Andy and Sam, but Jillian had adamantly refused and called her mother instead.

She glanced at her watch and wondered what the boys were doing at home. It was just about nap time and Sylvia had probably put them to bed. Nick was no doubt busy in the library. Or perhaps he was fixing the evidence of her disasters.

As soon as the interview was over, she'd find a phone and call home, just to check on everything. Though she'd learned to expect the unexpected from Zach, Andy and Sam, her mother hadn't a clue as to what the boys were capable of. Jillian smiled, thinking back to the sticky kisses the boys had pressed on her cheek that morning. The thought that they missed her, even a little bit, warmed her heart. She also imagined that someone else in the house might notice her absence. Would Nick think of her while she was gone?

She'd certainly thought about him more than a few times over the past hours. On the drive down to Boston, she'd been caught up in a careful review of their time together, from the moment she'd hit him on the head with the xylophone to the quick kiss she'd brushed across his cheek before he'd returned to the cottage the night before.

She now listened with only halfhearted interest as the chairman of the Committee for Academic Excellence droned on and on about the merits of an association with the institute. The entire committee was there, dressed in their very best suits, determined to impress Dr. Richard Jarrett. Jarrett, a well-known physicist, had expressed an interest in a faculty position at the New England Institute of Technology and had promised to bring considerable research money with him. The committee had convened to discuss the possibility of a tenured professorship and to interview the candidate.

As Jillian listened to the committee's questions and the physicist's answers, she realized how quiet the room was. Besides the soft-spoken voices, the only thing she could hear was the whir of a ceiling fan. She'd grown so used to the chatter of childish voices that she almost missed it.

In truth, Jillian should have been captivated by this entire process. Here was a man that fit all her criteria for a husband. Richard Jarrett was relatively attractive, although not nearly as handsome as Nick Callahan. She scanned his curriculum vitae, noting the long list of publications and awards. He was obviously brilliant and with a teaching position at NEIT, he'd be close at hand.

Jillian groaned inwardly. So why did she find him so

incredibly boring? Why did she find this entire meeting excruciatingly dull? Everyone in the room seemed to operate in slow mode, their questions carefully worded, their answers deliberate. She'd been operating at such a high speed lately that her co-workers, men and women she admired, now appeared almost lifeless.

"Dr. Marshall?"

Yanked out of her thoughts, she looked up. "Yes?"

"Do you have any questions for Dr. Jarrett?"

"Ah...no," Jillian said. "Actually, all my questions have been answered. Thank you...sir."

The chancellor frowned at her for a moment, then went back to his agenda. Jillian felt a trace of embarrassment. She probably should have asked something, just to appear interested. But it was patently clear that Richard Jarrett was eminently qualified and anyone who didn't think so didn't have a bit of sense. The interview was simply a formality and had she been in charge, she might have stood up and adjourned the meeting.

A few minutes later, the chancellor did just that. Jillian got out of her seat, but rather than join the group gathering around Dr. Jarrett, she wandered to the door, hoping to sneak back to her office and call her mother. But the chancellor caught her eye and before she could make her escape, she found herself cornered.

Dr. Leon Fleming's ruddy cheeks were flushed with excitement. "Well, Dr. Marshall, what do you think? A fine addition to our staff. No doubt about it. Now we just need to hope he accepts our offer."

Without giving her a chance to render her own glowing recommendation, he drew her aside and spoke in a hushed tone. "Dr. Marshall, the committee would like to ask a favor of you. Dr. Jarrett is staying the night in Boston and, as he's unfamiliar with the city, we'd like you to show him around, take him out to a nice restaurant, maybe for a stroll along the Charles.''

Jillian forced a smile and tried to appear grateful that she'd been chosen for such an important task. ''I—I'm afraid I can't, Dr. Fleming. I've got…family responsibilities.''

''Family?'' the chancellor asked. ''I don't understand. I didn't think you had a family.''

''Oh, I don't,'' Jillian replied. ''It's just that I'm taking care of my nephews for a few days while their parents are away and they're quite a handful. I really don't like leaving them with someone else.''

''I'm sure they'll be fine. They won't even realize you're gone.'' He cleared his throat. ''I don't think you understand how important this is to the committee, Dr. Marshall.''

''Why don't you send someone else? Dr. Wentland is much more familiar with the city than I am. And he and Dr. Jarrett are both graduates of Stanford. Or Dr. Symanski. She's quite a gourmet. I'm sure she'd choose a wonderful restaurant.''

''But we all think you would be the better choice,'' Dr. Fleming insisted.

Realization slowly dawned as her gaze flitted amongst the members of the committee. She was the better choice because she was a young, relatively attractive, single woman! Good grief, wasn't this against some institute policy? Using her as bait to lure in a hot physicist with loads of research money? Jillian weighed her options. Refusing the request would probably result in her being dropped from the prestigious committee. But then, she never really wanted to serve in the first place.

Still, what harm could it do to take Dr. Jarrett to dinner? On any other day, she'd be thrilled to spend time talking research work and grant proposals and Nobel prizes. ''All right," she said. "But it will have to be an early evening. I've got a long drive back to New Hampshire."

The chancellor grinned and gave her hand a squeeze. "Now, I've heard that Dr. Jarrett is quite the ladies' man. I expect you to keep things strictly business. Try to pump him for information about his time at Oxford. I'd like to know the real reason he decided to leave, not the reason Oxford is peddling."

"I'll do my best, sir. Now, if you don't mind, I really should call and make sure the baby-sitter can stay with the boys."

"You do that," the chancellor said.

Jillian glanced over at Dr. Jarrett and he looked up at that very second and sent her a warm smile. Her heart should have skipped a beat, but instead, it sank. This promised to be a very long evening, an evening that could have been spent with Nick and the boys.

She found a pay phone just outside the meeting room and Jillian quickly dialed the lake house. Her mother answered on the third ring. She expected to hear chaos in the background, but the line was silent. "Mother, it's Jillian. How's everything going?"

"Oh, everything is just fine, dear. I'm just having a cup of tea."

"And the boys?"

"They're with your friend, Nick. He's got them in the library."

Jillian sighed. "Mother, you really shouldn't let them play around in there while he's working. He has to finish those bookshelves for Greg and Roxy before they get back."

"He's not working, dear. He's reading to them. They've been so quiet, like little angels." She lowered her voice. "Your friend is such a nice man, Jillie. So kind and patient with the boys. You'd never guess that he didn't have children of his own. Or that he's not even married.''

''And how do you know that mother? Did you interrogate him?''

''We ate lunch together. I made him chicken salad with roasted pecans and grapes. He was very appreciative. And he's got wonderful table manners.''

Jillian groaned. The last thing she needed was her nosy mother pumping Nick for information—or trotting out all of Jillian's personal and professional accomplishments for a potential husband, which she could just imagine her doing. ''The reason I'm calling is that I need you to stay a little longer. I've got to take Dr. Jarrett out to dinner and show him the city.''

''Dr. Jarrett? Is he single? Handsome? Rich?''

''He's not married, marginally attractive and we're not close enough yet for me to ask to see his stock portfolio.''

Sylvia sighed. ''Oh, dear, I can't stay. Even though I'd love to give you and Dr. Jarrett an evening to yourselves, Daddy and I have plans at the club. But I'm sure Mr. Callahan would agree to watch the boys. Here, I'll let you talk to him.''

''Mother, no, I can't—''

''Jillie?''

She drew a ragged breath. An image of Nick flashed in her mind. He was probably dressed in his jeans and a T-shirt. And his hair was probably mussed from rolling around on the floor with the boys. She could picture his smile, the easy way he moved. ''Nick. Hi, how are things going?''

''No problems. When are you coming home?''

''Actually, that's why I was calling. I'm going to be late. I have to go to dinner with Dr. Jarrett. Hopefully, I'll be back by nine or ten. Mother can't stay. I hate to ask you but—''

"Sure," he said. "We'll be fine."

"Roxy would probably have a fit that I asked you. You signed up to build bookshelves, not to ride herd on the boys. But I trust you and you're so good with them and I can't get out of this dinner date."

"Date?" he asked.

Jillian sucked in a sharp breath. "Not exactly a date."

"You're going with a group?"

"No," she said. "Just me and…him. But it's not a date. It's strictly professional."

"He's bringing his wife?"

"He doesn't have a wife," Jillian said.

Her statement was met with a long silence. Was he angry? Or just curious? Jillian couldn't gauge his mood over the phone, but she couldn't imagine that he'd be jealous. "Nick?"

"I'll see you when you get home. Have a good time, Jillian."

She slowly hung up the phone, letting her hand linger on the receiver as she tried to figure out what had just happened between them. He'd called her Jillian. To her memory, he only called her that when he was angry or frustrated. Lately, it had been the more informal "Jillie."

"Well, Professor Marshall, I understand we're going to dinner. Are you ready?"

Jillian jumped slightly as Richard Jarrett touched her shoulder, then she turned and forced a smile. She tried to summon some enthusiasm for spending an evening in such illustrious company. But in truth, she'd much rather choose a root canal over an endless evening with Dr. Jarrett. Jillian grabbed her purse. Maybe it wouldn't be so bad, she mused. He might even turn out to be a nice guy.

Twenty minutes later, after a quick stop at her nearby apartment to change, they were comfortably seated at a trendy restaurant just off Kendall Square. The waiter hovered over them as he explained the evening's specials and, though Jillian insisted she didn't care for wine, Jarrett ordered a bottle anyway. She soon found out that his lengthy perusal of the wine list was only to show what good taste and exacting knowledge he possessed. She tried to pay attention as he catalogued the qualities of every single wine the restaurant offered. But instead, she busied herself with pulling a dinner roll into tiny bits.

"Wine is a great passion of mine," Jarrett said. "I just bought a case of '90 Chateau Margaux at an auction that is simply marvelous. At $5000 a case, it should be. You must share a bottle with me sometime. It has a deep plum color with an exquisite bouquet. Aromas of roses, cherries and blackberries. Opulent, full-bodied and harmonious. A very nice structure. The first time I tasted it, I knew I had to have it." He reached over and covered her hand with his. "And when I see something I want, I go after it."

Jillian pulled her hand away and tried to steer the conversation toward more innocuous subjects, like the weather. But Jarrett continued his monologue and somewhere around the time he began talking about the silky texture of his favorite wine, Jillian's mind began to drift away from the droning one-sided conversation and back to the lake house. She glanced at her watch and noticed it was about time to put the boys to bed.

After just a few short days, she'd grown accustomed to the ritual and actually believed she might be getting more efficient with the drill—wrestling the boys into their pajamas, gathering them all on Sammy's bed for stories, then tucking them each into their own beds with a kiss goodnight. Suddenly she longed for those chubby little arms around her neck, for the sweet smell of their bodies after their baths, for their silly, fractured sentences.

How easy it was to love them, Jillian mused. Even through all the trouble, she couldn't stop caring. The disasters had all been her fault, due entirely to her lack of preparedness. She had already learned to anticipate problems at mealtime and playtime. And though chaos theory could never be completely discounted, she was beginning to understand the conditions that created chaos—open doors, messy food, available art supplies and little boys with too much energy.

Jillian smiled to herself, then let her mind drift to Nick, to the moments after the boys went to sleep, when she'd wander downstairs and hope to find him waiting for her. It had never really happened that way, except in her imagination. She imagined him waiting now, wondering when she'd get home, ready to yank her into his arms and kiss her "hello."

Had the cool tone of his voice really indicated jealousy? Perhaps he'd just been maintaining an indifferent attitude toward her because her mother had been standing right there. "That's it," Jillian murmured to herself.

"I thought so, too," Jarrett said. "Three hundred dollars a bottle was my top price for that Bordeaux."

Jillian groaned inwardly and willed the waiter to hurry with the entrées. The sooner she got out of this restaurant, the sooner she'd be on her way back to Nick and the boys. She wondered about the reception she'd receive when she got home, wondered how Nick really felt about her "date."

Only a lovesick fool would be jealous of a dinner with the esteemed but pompous Dr. Richard Jarrett. And if Jillian knew one thing about Nick Callahan it was that he was no lovesick fool.

SOMEWHERE, DEEP in the house, a clock chimed midnight. Nick set his level down and stepped back from the shelf he'd been hanging. Every hour on the hour, the clock reminded him that Jillie was out with another man, sharing an intimate dinner, perhaps dancing—and God only knew what else.

Nick cursed beneath his breath. Hell, by this late in the evening, they could have hopped into bed as well! He shouldn't have felt anything at the prospect of Jillian Marshall with another man. He'd already written her off as a woman wholly unsuitable to his tastes. Yet even the mere consideration of her kissing this—this Dr. Jarrett caused his gut to twist and his temper to flare.

He raked his hands through his hair, brushing out the sawdust. This was his fault! He should have refused to baby-sit for the boys—then she would have had to come home directly after her meeting. He thought he'd been doing her a favor, for professional reasons. But after he'd hung up, Sylvia Marshall had informed him, with great relish it had seemed, that Dr. Jarrett was just the type of man Jillie found attractive—a brilliant scientist, who just happened to be single and handsome.

Nick stepped away from the bookshelves that now lined an entire wall of the library. He'd thought to do the project slowly, but in his anger, he'd been working for nearly four hours without pause. At this rate, if he stayed angry with Jillie, he'd have the project finished sometime tomorrow morning.

Wiping his hands on his jeans, Nick headed for the door. He'd check on the boys, then get himself a beer before he finished installing the crown moulding along the top of the cases.

He walked silently up the stairs. Jillie couldn't stay away the entire night. Not without calling. He mentally calculated the time it took to drive from Boston to the lake house— two hours by his count. Dinner with a business associate shouldn't last any longer than nine o'clock. That meant she was already an hour into something much more than pure business.

When Nick reached the bedroom, he found the boys sound asleep, curled into impossible positions, their faces sweet and innocent, their breathing even. Outside, the distant rumble of thunder signalled an approaching storm. His thoughts went immediately to Jillie, wondering if she was driving home in the dark, on the winding road that led to the lake. Driving would be more dangerous with a storm upon her.

He bit back an oath, resolving to put Jillie and her safety out of his mind. She was adult. She could make her own choices. And if those choices included an affair with Dr. Jarrett, so be it.

Nick carefully covered each boy with the light blankets they'd managed to kick off, then tiptoed to the door. Watching Zach, Andy and Sam sleep brought a stark realization to his mind. He had no right to worry. These were not his children, no matter how much he wished they were.

And Jillie Marshall was not his wife. He had no claim on anyone in the house. And no reason to be angry with Jillie.

He took the stairs slowly, and when he was nearly to the bottom, he looked up to see the front door quietly swing open. Nick froze, standing in the shadows that kept the stairs in near darkness. By the feeble light from the porch, he could see that she'd changed out of her prim suit and into a form-fitting black dress with a scooped neck and short sleeves. Her hair, which had earlier been pulled back into a neat knot was now loose and falling in soft waves around her shoulders.

He wasn't surprised by her beauty, though the dress and her hair did take his breath away. The woman he saw en-

tering the house was not the Jillie Marshall that he'd come
to know. This woman was almost a stranger, aware of her
beauty and willing to use it to her advantage.

"I bet that dress wowed them at the institute," he said.

The sound of his voice coming out of the darkness star-
tled her and she jumped, then pressed her hand to her chest.
"Nick?" Jillie squinted up the stairs as she stepped nearer.
"What are you doing?"

He slowly descended the last five stairs, emerging from
the shadows to stand in front of her. "I could ask you the
same. It's past midnight. Awfully late for a business dinner,
isn't it?"

Jillie gave him an uneasy look, confusion mixed with an
apologetic smile. "It did go on a lot longer than I thought
it would. I almost decided to stay in the city, but then I
knew you were here alone with the boys. I figured you'd
want me to come home."

"This isn't your home," Nick said, his voice cold and
dispassionate. "And why should I care whether you spend
the night here or at your place in Boston? Or even in a hotel
room with some stranger you just met?"

Jillie gasped. "What? Some stranger? What are you talking about?"

Nick brushed by her and stalked back to the library, ready
to pick up where he had left off. But Jillie wasn't about to
let his comment go by without a response. She hurried after
him, tossing her purse onto a hallway table as she passed.

When she reached the library, she braced her hands on
her hips and glared at him. "Are you angry that I stayed
out so late?"

"I didn't say I was angry."

"Then why won't you look at me?"

Nick glanced up at Jillie to find her expression filled with
apprehension. But it didn't dilute his anger. Damn, she was

so beautiful and so vulnerable. Yet she was also a woman and, right now, he wasn't sure he could trust his feelings about any woman, especially Jillie. "Did you enjoy your dinner?" he asked, his words sharp and biting.

She blinked, unnerved by his tone. "Not really. I found Dr. Jarrett egotistical, self-aggrandizing and boorish."

"Did you kiss him?"

A faint blush worked its way up her cheeks and her gaze darted to her feet, then back up again. "Kiss him? No, not exactly."

"Ah, here we go. This wasn't exactly a date. And he didn't exactly have a wife. Come on, Jillie, you're a mathematician. What can you tell me that might be exact?"

She narrowed her eyes, apprehension slowly replaced by indignation. "All right. He kissed me. It lasted exactly 3.8 seconds, he used exactly this much of his tongue—" she held out her fingers to demonstrate "—and on a scale of one to ten, I felt exactly zero attraction to Dr. Jarrett." She paused. "But why should that make a difference to you?"

Nick stared at her for a long moment, his anger subsiding with every passing second. And then, without thought, he crossed the room in three easy strides and yanked her into his arms. His mouth came down on hers, first punishing, then probing and then sinking into pleasure. This was more than just a kiss. It was an end—and a beginning. An end to the little dance they'd been doing since the night they'd met. And the beginning of something real and passionate between them.

He pulled back and look down into her flushed face. With his thumb, he slowly traced the remains of the scratches on her pale complexion, then moved to touch her bottom lip, still damp from his kiss. "It makes a difference," he murmured before kissing her again.

But this time the kiss didn't last for long. With a soft cry,

Jillie pulled away, squirming out of his embrace until she stood a safe distance away. "What are you doing?"

"I thought it was obvious," he said with a satisfied grin. "Would you like me to do it again, just to clear up any confusion?"

"Stop it!" she snapped. "You—you just can't kiss me and expect me to forgive you."

"You're the one who stayed out late, wining and dining another man."

"And you're the one who was angry! You have no right to be angry. And certainly no right to kiss me."

"I didn't hear you complaining," Nick said, sauntering toward her.

"It's a little hard to talk when you're—when you—when I—"

His arm snaked around her waist and he pulled her hips to his. Then he bent lower, until his lips were just inches from hers. "I think we've said everything that needs to be said. At least I have."

"Then let me go." Her gaze met his, defiantly, daring him to try again and warning him that he'd be rebuffed. But Nick wasn't about to give her the last word. He waited, his breath soft on her lips, his eyes scanning her face. Then he suddenly let go of her and stepped away, glancing around the room.

"I think I'm done here," he said.

With that, Nick slowly walked from the room. He smiled to himself as he heard her moan of frustration. Hell, he didn't care what she thought of him. One kiss was all it had taken to change the stakes between them. And whether she wanted a man with a Nobel prize or an Einstein IQ, Jillie Marshall was about to find herself caught up in an affair with a lowly carpenter. Because, if Nick had anything to say about it, there would be more to this than just one or two passionate kisses.

Maybe they didn't have a future together, but that didn't mean they couldn't have a present. He wanted Jillie Marshall more that he had ever wanted a woman in his life. He wanted to kiss her whenever the mood struck, draw her into his arms on a whim.

And he wasn't going to let the chance to have her pass him by. From now on, the gloves were off. There was going to be so much more between them—just as soon as Jillie faced the fact that she wanted him as much as he wanted her.

6

JILLIAN STOOD in the middle of the library, stunned into both silence and immobility. Her breath had caught in her throat when he'd kissed her and she wasn't sure that she had drawn another breath since. Slowly, she raised her fingers to her lips. "Oh, my," she sighed, her heart pounding in her chest, her mind spinning.

If she had any doubt at all about Nick Callahan's feelings, those doubts were erased the moment he kissed her. This hadn't been a kiss between two friends. There was passion and need, an almost desperate will to possess her. A shiver ran down her spine.

Wasn't this exactly what she'd been fantasizing about? Jillian racked her brain to recall some of those fantasies. How had she responded? If this were one of her fantasies now, what would she do? Would she follow him and throw herself back in his arms? Or would she wait in the library until the house grew silent and she could sneak up to bed?

Even with her limited experience with the opposite sex, Jillian sensed that the next move was hers. Nick was probably waiting for her to follow him, waiting for her to make her own feelings known.

"This would never work," Jillian muttered. "We have absolutely nothing in common."

She could just picture it now. Walking into a faculty reception with Nick Callahan. Everyone might act pleased to meet her new escort, but she knew the gossips would start speculating. "What could Professor Marshall possibly see in a man like that?" they'd say. "A great body and even better sex," they'd say. "Outside of the bedroom, he's probably a crashing bore."

But that wasn't true! Jillian had spent five days in the company of Nick Callahan and she hadn't once been bored. In truth, she found him exciting and interesting and enormously intriguing. They never ran out of things to say to each other and even when they weren't saying anything, he was the most fascinating man she'd ever met.

"So what does this mean?" Jillian murmured, still frozen in place. "Does this mean that you like him? That you're falling in love with him?" She moaned softly, then covered her face with her hands. She drew a ragged breath and straightened. "Maybe it's about time you found out."

Jillian hurried to the library door, then raced through the house to the kitchen. But Nick was nowhere to be found. She yanked the back door open and saw him, his head bent to the rain, heading toward the cottage. She stepped out onto the deck.

"Nick Callahan, we need to talk!" she shouted over the sound of the rain.

He stopped, but didn't turn around. "I'm tired," he called over his shoulder. "You're getting wet. And we're done for the night."

Jillian's temper flared and she walked to the edge of the deck. "Damn it, get back here! I'm not leaving the boys alone to chase you!"

Nick turned to face her, walking backwards as the rain soaked his jeans and washed the dust from his bare shoulders and chest. He held his hands up in a nonchalant gesture, his T-shirt clutched in his fingers. "Then you're stuck, aren't you?"

Jillian knew if she didn't go after him, this thing would

lie unresolved, nagging at her all night and keeping her awake until sunrise. She needed to know where things stood between them and she needed to know now! Jillian glanced up at the boys' bedroom window, then stepped off the deck. She'd seen Roxy work in the garden when the boys were napping. Taking that as her cue, she strode across the slick grass, her heels sinking into the soft turf. With a vivid oath, she kicked off her shoes and proceeded in her bare feet until she reached Nick.

"This can't wait until morning?" he asked with a self-satisfied smile.

"No, it can't," Jillian replied.

"You don't want to hear what I have to say, Jillie."

"I'm not afraid of you," she said.

Nick stared into her eyes, causing a shiver to skitter down her spine. "Maybe you should be."

As if it wasn't raining hard enough already, water began to come down in torrents. Thunder cracked and rumbled and Jillian was certain the storm was right on top of them. She stared up at the sky, the raindrops pelting her face and drenching her hair. "We're going to get struck by lightning standing out here!"

"Go back in the house, Jillie."

Jillian didn't listen to him. In truth, she wasn't even listening to her own common sense. She didn't want to listen, she just wanted to feel—the warm rain on her skin, the heat from his body as she moved closer, the damp of his naked chest beneath her palms. Without speaking another word, she wrapped her arms around Nick's neck and pulled him nearer. And then she kissed him as if it were the most natural thing in the world for her to do.

The rain poured over them as their mouths searched and their tongues probed. Jillian's blood ran like liquid fire through her veins, tingling the nerves in her fingertips and toes, and warming the gooseflesh from her skin. If she hadn't known better, she'd think that lightning had struck them both, sapping the breath from their lungs and causing them to gasp.

"We shouldn't stay out here," Nick murmured, his mouth tracing a damp path from her lips to her jawline.

"I've heard that you're supposed to stay low," Jillian replied. She grabbed his hand and tugged him down on the slick grass. Nick rolled until he'd pulled her beneath his body, their legs tangling, his hips pressed against hers. With a low moan, he grabbed the neckline of her dress and tugged it off her shoulder, then softly nipped at the skin he revealed.

"What do you want from me?" he asked, his voice tinged with anger.

This was exactly what she wanted, this fire and lust, this uncontrollable passion that seemed to consume them both. She'd never felt more alive in her life, the storm raging around them, his body heavy upon hers. "Just this," Jillian murmured, arching against him as his mouth drifted lower. "All I want is this."

"But you don't want a man like me," he said, his breath hot on the skin above her breast. His teeth grazed her flesh, causing a flicker of pain. Did he mean to punish her, or had he been swept away by pure sensation as she had?

"And you don't want a woman in your life," she challenged, nipping at his neck.

"You want someone brilliant and driven," he said, nuzzling at her cleavage. "Someone with a scientific mind."

"And you want someone sweet and compliant," Jillian countered. "A woman who'll let you be the boss."

"A man who'll play second fiddle to your work."

"A woman who'll be at your beck and call, in bed and out."

"Then we're agreed," Nick said, his hand slipping beneath the neckline of her dress. "There can't possibly be anything between us."

She furrowed her fingers through his hair, then pulled his mouth against hers. "Except this," she said against his lips.

The sounds of the storm faded into the background and all Jillian could hear was his breathing, harsh and quick, and her pulse pounding in her head. The rain made her sense of touch even more acute and as she ran her hands over his naked chest and back, she could feel every taut muscle beneath his smooth skin.

She didn't care about the consequences of what they were going to do. She just wanted to feel his hands on her body, to taste his mouth and to hear the sound of his moans, soft in her ear. Why bother thinking about the future? For Jillian, this was enough.

Nick slipped his fingers under the edge of her bra, following an inexorable path. A moment later, he cupped her breast in his palm. And then his mouth closed over her nipple and Jillian cried out. But the sound was swallowed up by the storm.

Time seemed to slow, measured only by the exquisite sensations that pulsed through her body. Jillian ached to be possessed by him, giving herself over to his touch, to the power of his hands and his lips on her body. Any inhibitions that she had were gone, replaced by undeniable need.

She no longer wanted to resist, no longer cared what loving him might cost her. Nick held her heart in his hands and even if they only shared this one moment, Jillian knew it would be a moment that defined the rest of her life. There would never be another man like Nick Callahan.

"Is this what you want, Jillie?" he murmured, his mouth pressed against the curve of her breast. "Do you want me to make love to you right here? In the rain and the wind?"

Though Jillian wanted to shout out her assent, his words tripped a circuit in her mind, an instinct all but forgotten beneath his gentle seduction. Faced with the choice, apprehension stole into her thoughts. Was this really what she wanted? Overwhelming lust followed by meaningless sex followed by ultimate desertion? She swallowed hard and closed her eyes. *Yes, yes, yes.*

But her single moment of indecision was all it took for Nick to roll off her. "Maybe we should go inside and check on the boys," he murmured.

Jillian tugged at her dress and sat up, the fire between them suddenly doused by the rain. Why didn't he want her anymore? Why had he been so willing to put a stop to it? And where had this wanton behavior come from? Was it simply a physical reaction to his touch or were these feelings racing through her true and real? "Maybe we should."

Nick levered to his feet, then reached down for her hand. He gently pulled her up and began to walk toward the house, silent, indifferent. He pulled the door open and stepped aside to let her pass.

As Jillian stepped inside the house, she rubbed the water from her face and ran her fingers through her hair. "I'll just go upstairs and see how they are," she murmured, glancing over at him. "And I'll bring us a few towels."

Nick smiled, then nodded. But as Jillian walked through the darkened hallway, she knew when she returned to the kitchen, he'd be gone. Her tiny moment of indecision had ruined everything. She stopped halfway up the stairs and listened, just in time to hear the back door open and then close. With a soft sigh, she walked back down to find the kitchen empty. All that was left of him was a puddle of water where he'd stood.

She blinked. Droplets of rain blurred her eyes and ran down her cheeks. With a soft oath, she brushed at the water, determined not to give in to tears. Instead, she sighed softly and tried to banish every memory of his touch from her mind.

"Well, Jillian, you wanted to know if you were falling in love with him," she murmured. "I guess now you have your answer."

HE COULDN'T SLEEP. The rain continued on through the night, driving away the humidity and freshening the air that blew through the screened porch. Nick lay in the hammock, his arm thrown over his eyes, his mind occupied with thoughts of Jillie Marshall. The taste of her damp skin still lingered on his tongue and the feel of her warm flesh had branded his palms.

Every instinct had told him to make love to her there in the grass, and then later, in the house. But when it came to Jillie, he couldn't trust his instincts. He had to walk away or risk making a mistake he could never take back. A mistake he'd regret for a long time.

After Claire, he'd believed that no woman would ever hold the power to hurt him. But then he'd met Jillie, a woman determined to keep him at arm's length, and all that had changed. With a soft curse, he swung his legs over the edge of the hammock, then furrowed his hands through his damp hair. The light from her bedroom window had gone dark hours ago. Nick wondered if she, too, lay awake with thoughts of what they'd shared.

Now, in the deepest dark of night, he could almost believe it had all been a dream. That first kiss, borne of frustration, her passionate response, and the desire that had driven them to grasp and gasp as the rain poured down on top of them. Her flesh in his hands, her hands on his body, her body beneath his. And then, that tiny moment of hesitation, the doubts and insecurities apparent in her eyes.

Though he'd wanted her in the most intimate way, Nick knew, in the end, he couldn't have made love to her. With Jillie, he needed more than just a one-night stand, more than a night of meaningless passion. He needed her to want him, the *real* him. Hell, if she couldn't accept him completely, both body and soul, then he couldn't have her at all.

It wasn't an easy thing to admit, this power she unwittingly held over him. But Jillie was special, a woman who hadn't been molded by the same forces that other women in his life had. She was the most intelligent woman he'd ever met, yet she lacked basic common sense at times. And though some men might pass her by as too plain, Nick had immediately seen the beauty in her features.

He smiled. She was opinionated and independent, yet sweet and vulnerable at the same time. Every time he advanced, she'd retreat, hiding behind the proper facade of Professor Marshall, refusing to acknowledge the passionate side of her nature. But tonight he'd seen it, felt the fire that burned deep inside of her. And he knew in a single moment, that he wouldn't be satisfied with just one night.

He pushed to his feet and paced the length of the porch, his bare feet cool on the painted floor. "This will have to stop," he murmured. "Needing Jillie Marshall has already cost you more than you can afford." Every minute of every day had been consumed with thoughts of her, questions about her desires and speculation about what they might share.

With a sigh, he shoved the screen door open and stepped outside. As he strode down to the lake, Nick unbuttoned his jeans, then kicked them off, along with his boxer shorts. The moon was just beginning to break through the clouds when he jumped off the end of the pier and sliced into the black water.

The lake was still warm from the hot day and he swam

back and forth between the end of the pier and a raft that bobbed thirty yards away. If only he could exhaust himself, perhaps he could sleep. He swam and swam, the water rushing by his body until his breathing grew labored. When he couldn't go any further, he pulled himself up onto the raft and lay on his back, naked in the moonlight, the cool breeze drawing a shiver over his skin.

He closed his eyes and images of Jillie floated in his brain. But this time, he didn't push them aside. What if he had no control over his fate? What if he and Jillie were meant to have this undeniable passion? Stranger things had happened.

Nick sighed, then raised his hands over his head. His muscles were tired but his mind was even more exhausted. Every ounce of his energy had been used to walk away from Jillie and the intimacies they'd shared. It would have been so easy to make love to her…so easy, he mused as he closed his eyes.

The sun was just beginning to lighten the eastern sky when he finally dived off the raft and swam back to shore. Nick grabbed his jeans and boxers, then strode into the cottage, sleep now unnecessary. The sooner he finished the library, the sooner he could go back to his life in Providence. He'd gotten over Claire. Hell, he'd even managed to ward off a wicked case of lust for a near stranger. Surely, he'd had enough of women by now, hadn't he?

He quickly dressed, then walked up to the house in the dark. When he opened the back door, he'd expected silence to greet him. But instead, he found Jillie, perched on a stool, sipping a cup of coffee and lost in her thoughts. She was illuminated only by the light from above the sink and, for a moment, he was afraid to make a noise. She looked so tiny, so alone, wrapped in her robe and clutching her mug as if it offered some solace.

"I didn't think you'd be up," he said softly.

Startled, she turned to him, her eyes wide. He remembered that first night, when he'd walked in on her and she'd hit him with the xylophone. Had that really only been six days ago? Lord, it felt as if he'd known Jillie for a lifetime.

"I—I couldn't sleep," she murmured, flustered by his appearance, her hands fidgeting with her hair.

Nick shrugged. "I couldn't either. I thought I'd get an early start in the library." In truth, he didn't care when he got the library done. The moment he saw her, he knew he didn't want an excuse to walk away.

"I—I'm glad we have a chance to talk," she said. "I mean, while the house is still quiet." She picked up an envelope from the counter and held it out to him.

Nick took it from her fingers. "What's this?"

"It's your pay. For your services as a nanny. I've included extra for the overtime you worked yesterday evening."

Nick tossed the envelope down in front of her, his jaw tight, anger surging up inside of him. Was this supposed to solve everything between them? A quick paycheck and a pink slip. "I don't want your money."

"We had a bargain," she said in a small voice.

He cursed softly, trying to control his fury. "What is this really about?" he demanded. "Is this about our bargain? Or is it about last night? Are you angry because I wanted to make love to you? Or because I wouldn't."

She toyed with the handle of her coffee mug, refusing to meet his gaze. "I don't even want to talk about last night," Jillie said. "We made a mistake. We got carried away. Both you and I know that."

"I don't know anything," Nick said. "I don't think you do either. Except that from the moment we met, we've been heading toward this."

"I know that you're not the kind of man I belong with," she said, her words lacking complete conviction.

"Why? Because I'm just some carpenter guy who makes a living with his hands instead of his head. Is that all you care about, Jillie? Because if it is, then I'm glad we didn't make love. Because you're not the woman I thought I knew. And you don't know me at all."

She sighed deeply, then met his gaze. "I'm just being realistic," she said, her chin tipped up defensively. "Admit it, Nick. You don't really think I'm your type either. I'd make a terrible wife and a worse mother. You couldn't want that, could you?"

He cursed softly. "I don't know what I want right now. Except to get those bookshelves finished so I can get the hell out of here."

"I think that would be best," Jillie murmured.

Nick gave her a long look, trying to see past the indifferent expression and the icy composure, looking for some sign of the passionate woman he'd kissed last night, the woman who had moaned his name and arched against his body. But she wasn't there—she'd hidden herself behind the condescending facade of Professor Jillian Marshall, calculating female and cold-hearted realist. He shook his head and walked out of the room.

When he reached the library, he closed the door behind him and leaned back against it. He still had at least a day, maybe two, of work ahead of him, though he could always leave and come back after Roxy and Greg were home. They'd given him the cottage for the entire summer if he wanted it that long, so there was no need to put himself through this torture.

But he'd started a job and Nick knew if he didn't finish it now, he'd never come back. He glanced around the room. This wasn't the only thing left unfinished. Though Jillie had given him his walking papers, he still felt as if there was something left between them unresolved.

Had Nick known building a set of simple bookshelves would completely mess up his life, he might have chosen a different project. He still had a new house to design for himself. Next month, he was due to travel to Tennessee to firm up plans for the new auto plant he was designing. In two or three months, he had a canning plant in Florida that he'd have to start. There was plenty to keep his mind off Jillie Marshall once he escaped her presence.

But he'd gotten a taste of something here, something he never thought he'd have. He and Jillie and the boys had fallen into the rhymes and rhythms of a makeshift family. It wasn't surprising that everyone at the picnic believed Jillie to be his wife. And Zach, Andy and Sam, his sons. He'd imagined it that way himself. So much, that now he could barely picture a family that didn't include Jillie Marshall at his side.

But he'd thought the same of Claire and Jason, that they'd be his family and his future. And how quickly they'd been forgotten. And this from a man who, until a few years ago, had been determined to remain single.

"I don't need a woman in my life," Nick murmured, as he reached for a shelf bracket. "There are some numbers that aren't meant to be perfect. And I'm one of them, Professor Marshall."

JILLIAN STOOD in the kitchen, watching the boys as they picked at the hot dogs, apple slices and Cheese Nips she'd offered them for lunch. They'd passed the entire morning without catching sight of Nick. He'd shut himself in the library and hadn't come out. Zach had knocked on the door, then tried the knob, but found it locked. Jillian had even prepared a sandwich for him, certain he'd emerge for lunch.

But the only evidence that he was still in there was the occasional sound of a hammer or a power drill.

With a soft sigh, she reached out and stole a Cheese Nip from Andy's plate. He giggled in delight, then offered her a soggy one from his mouth. Jillian smiled to herself. At one time, she would have recoiled in horror at the offer, but now, she bent down and let Andy put the cracker in her mouth, smacking her lips and sending him a rapturous smile.

"It hasn't been so bad, has it?" she asked. "None of us has been seriously injured or emotionally scarred. We've managed to follow most of Dr. Hazelton's advice. And we're starting to know each other pretty well, don't you think?" All three of the boys nodded in unison.

"So what if Nick is mad," she continued. "We're better off on our own anyway. There won't be anymore disasters, will there?"

They nodded their heads again, clearly confused by the question. Jillian laughed. "What shall we do today?" she continued. "I thought we could play outside, perhaps a little ball toss to work on your eye-hand coordination. Dr. Hazelton says that's very important at your age."

"Play ball," Andy said, milk dripping from his upper lip.

Jillian reached out and swiped at his mouth with a damp paper towel. "Now that you're the only men in my life, I guess you have my full attention."

She slipped off the stool, then helped them down from their booster chairs. They ran to the back door and Zach worked at the doorknob. "Go out," he cried.

"Out, out, out!" Andy shouted.

Jillian collected the shoes and socks which had been scattered around the family room during the morning playtime. When she managed to get them all on the correct feet, she sat back on her heels and grinned at the boys. "Zach,

Sammy and Andy,'' she said, pointing to each one in turn. ''How could I have not known the difference?''

She opened the back door and the boys went tumbling outside, tripping over themselves as they ran. Jillian grabbed a ball from the bin on the deck and tossed it out on the lawn. They kicked it back and forth, then fell on top of it in a pile of legs and arms. Jillian ran over to them, ready to pull them apart. But when she saw how much fun they were having, she fell into the pile, tickling and teasing them.

Their play was rough and tumble, nothing like the sedate dolls and puzzles that she'd enjoyed as a child. The boys seemed to push themselves to near exhaustion, then, somehow, find a bit of reserve energy to go even further. After fifteen minutes with the ball, they moved on to the sandbox, then back to the ball, then to the tire swing hanging from a huge maple. Like little bees buzzing from flower to flower, they never seemed to light for more than a few minutes.

As Jillian stood off to the side, watching the boys chase a butterfly, she felt someone watching her. She slowly turned and looked up at the library window only to see the curtains flutter slightly. Had it been her imagination, or had Nick been looking down on them? Everything had been settled between them. There was no room for regret or doubt. So why couldn't he just leave her alone?

Jillian thought about all that had passed. It seemed like weeks ago when she'd arrived to care for the boys, not just a few days. Nick had walked into her life as a stranger, but in such a short time, they'd nearly become lovers. But what had she really learned about him? And could she trust her judgment when desire affected every thought of him?

This week was meant to be an experiment in motherhood, not in moral fortitude. She'd expected it to be so easy. But now she realized she'd been a fool to believe anything involving a lifelong commitment could be simple. Falling in love, having children, building a future with a family. None of it was meant to be easy.

She'd lived in her protected little world of numbers and theories and formulas. In truth, she'd hidden herself there, away from love and commitment. Now, for the first time in her life, she'd met a man who stirred her senses and made her heart soar. And she didn't want to go back to her orderly little life. Instead, she wanted to rush headlong into chaos.

"There is another man out there for you," Jillian murmured. "A man who fits into your life-style." But was that what she really wanted? Order and predictability? Settling for half-hearted passion and unfulfilled desire with a man like Richard Jarrett?

"I always have my work," she said. In truth, she'd barely thought of work in the past few days. Her time had been consumed by Nick and the boys. She'd always thought it weak when a woman gave up a career to raise a family and take care of a husband. Why couldn't all women have both—career and family life?

But now she saw that it wasn't necessarily a choice made for lack of time or energy to do both. It came from priorities, from listening to the heart. She now understood why Roxy had given up her career in law to raise her boys. Zach and Andy and Sam were a piece of Roxy's soul come to life and watching them grow was a miracle unfolding before her eyes.

"Chaos theory," Jillian murmured. "One never knows what to expect."

The boys came running toward her and she braced herself for an assault on her knees. But when they raced right by, Jillian turned to see Nick striding across the lawn.

"Nick! Nick!" the boys shouted, then threw themselves against his legs. His expression, at first fierce, softened and then broke into a grin. He placed Zach on his shoulders, poking and grabbing at Andy and Sam as they frolicked alongside. When he reached the spot where she stood, he set Zach down.

"Hi," she murmured.

"Hi," he replied.

Jillian took a deep breath and pasted a bright smile on her face. "You've been working hard," she said, nerves making her voice a little breathless. "We haven't seen you all morning."

He shifted his gaze from her eyes to a point somewhere over her shoulder. "I've nearly finished in the library. I just have a little more work to do this afternoon and that will be it."

"Well," Jillian said, twisting her fingers together and staring at her toes. "That's good, then. I'm sure Greg and Roxy will be pleased."

She groped for something more to say. How had they suddenly become strangers after all the time they'd spent together, the intimacies they'd shared? The barriers that had first stood between them had been rebuilt in less than a day.

"They've hired someone else to do the finishing," Nick continued. "I'll collect my tools from the house after I'm done and I'll be leaving tomorrow morning."

Jillian shouldn't have been surprised by his revelation, but she was. Her heart twisted in her chest and, for a moment, she couldn't breathe. "Then you'll have to have dinner with us tonight—seeing as it's your last night with the boys." She didn't ask for herself, preferring instead to issue an invitation that couldn't be refused.

But Nick shook his head anyway. "I've got too much packing to do. And I have to clean up the cottage."

"Don't you have the cottage for the rest of the summer?"

His gaze met hers. "I've had enough of vacation," he said. "I need to get back to Providence."

Jillian clutched at the skirt of her cotton dress, bunching the fabric in her fists. "It doesn't have to be this way," she murmured. "This hostility between us isn't necessary. We're both reasonable adults."

"I think that's the problem," he said with a dry laugh. "We're adults and we're entirely too reasonable. I'll be out of your way before you know it." With that, he continued to walk toward the lake, leaving Jillian and the boys to stare after him. A few moments later, he disappeared into the cottage, the crack of the screen door splitting the air.

"Nick mad," Andy said, taking her hand.

"Jillie bad?" Zach asked, looking up at her with questioning eyes.

Jillian shrugged, then sent them a little smile. "Nick is just preoccupied," she said. "Busy," she amended, noticing their blank looks. "Very, very busy."

"Sad," Sammy said.

She reached down and ruffled his hair. "No, not sad."

She sat down in the grass and the boys, sensing her mood, gathered around her. They held her hands and curled up beside her in the warm sun. Jillian stared out at the lake, watching a small sailboat glide by on the soft breeze. She'd come to love this place, the quiet, the serenity of the woods and the water. But how would she ever be able to come back without thinking of him?

Could she walk through the house and not remember the disasters he'd saved her from? Could she stand on the lawn and not recall the touch of his hand or the warmth of his kiss? Maybe she ought to think about getting back to her real life, her research and her plans for next semester, and resolve to put this week in the past.

She looked down at the boys. "We only have a few days left," she said. "I say we should have all the fun we can.

What would you say if I filled up the pool and we could go for a swim?''

"Fill the pool!" Andy cried.

If only life were so simple that a summer afternoon splash in a plastic pool could solve all her problems. Jillian wondered if she'd ever come to terms with what had happened between her and Nick. These ten days at the lake house might very well haunt her for the rest of her life.

7

JILLIAN SLEPT FITFULLY, completely exhausted, yet on edge at the same time. She'd close her eyes, certain that this time she'd drift off, only to be frustrated with hazy images of Nick teasing at her mind. Again and again, she found herself reliving the previous night, when they'd nearly made love in the storm. And each time the memories came back so vividly that she could almost feel the cool rain on her face and his warm hands on her body.

Her thoughts were interrupted by a quiet cry from the boys' room. Jillian pushed up from the bed and listened. Over the past six nights she'd learned to wait, rather than run in. They often woke from a dream, then fell back asleep again a few minutes later. She glanced at the clock—it was just past midnight.

When the crying continued, Jillian rolled out of bed and pulled on her robe. She turned on a small lamp on the dresser in the boys' room and moved to the bed against the wall. To her surprise, all three boys were curled up in Sammy's bed. They wore only their Huggies, pajamas discarded sometime after she'd put them to bed and closed the bedroom door. "What's wrong?" she murmured, picking up the triplet closest to the footboard. He looked like Sammy, but Jillian couldn't be sure.

She placed her hand on his cheek, then snatched it away. His face was hot and as she walked him around the room, he began to cry inconsolably, a plaintive sound that woke his brothers. "Are you sick?" she murmured, putting him down on the changing table and pressing her lips to his forehead.

Her brain scrambled to remember Dr. Hazelton's advice as she ticked off his symptoms. Flushed cheeks, glazed eyes, warm to the touch, tugging at his ear. Could he have an earache? Jillian looked into his eyes. "Does your ear hurt?" He burst into a fresh round of tears without answering.

She glanced around the room. Should she call the pediatrician? What if it was just a little sniffle? Maybe she should take him to the emergency room. "I don't know what to do," Jillian said. The only thing she really did know was that she needed help. She couldn't possibly take care of a sick child and watch the other two boys at the same time. There was only one place to turn for help.

Jillian put the boys back in their own beds, kissing each on the head. "I'll be right back," she murmured. "I promise."

She hurried downstairs and slipped into her sandals before stepping outside. The night air was warm, but a shiver still rocked her body as she ran toward the lake. The cottage was dark, and though going to Nick for help rankled her pride, the boys were the most important thing on her mind. Nick would know what to do. When it came to the boys, he always knew what to do.

A bright moon illuminated her way and when she reached the cottage, she knocked on the screen door, but after a few long seconds, there was no answer. Jillian turned to look back at the house, but a movement caught her eye. She stared into the darkness at the edge of the lake and watched as a figure rose from the water in slow motion, then levered up onto the pier.

Moonlight gleamed off wet skin and a tremor of fear

raced through her body. But then she realized it was Nick who had emerged from the water, long limbed and slender hipped—and completely naked. She stepped into the shadows near the doorway, her gaze transfixed by the sight. He grabbed a towel and ran it over his body before draping it around his shoulders and she held her breath as he made his way toward the cottage.

When he was nearly to the porch, Jillian stepped from the shadows. Her heart pounded in her chest and she shifted uneasily from one foot to another, clutching at the front of her robe and trying to keep her eyes on his face.

"Jillian?" He peered through the dark at her. "What are you doing out here?"

"I—I need you," she said, her voice trembling.

"Jillian, we talked about this. I—"

"No!" she cried. "I need you because one of the boys is sick and I don't know what to do. I don't know if I should call the doctor or take him to the hospital. He's so hot and I think his ear hurts. Please, can you help me?"

He took a step toward her, unfazed by his nakedness, then cupped her cheek in his hand. His cool touch immediately soothed her nerves. "Just let me get dressed. I'll come right up."

Jillian nodded in relief, then turned and ran back to the house. On her way upstairs, she grabbed Dr. Hazelton's book and was frantically paging through it outside the bedroom door when Nick appeared beside her. An image of his naked body flashed in her brain, but she pushed it aside.

He took her hand and, together, they slipped into the boys' room. "Over here," Jillian whispered, moving to the bed in the far corner. "I—I think it's Sammy. They took off their pajamas, so I can't be sure." She clutched the book in front of her. "I don't even know who it is. What am I supposed to say to the doctor? How is he supposed to treat him if he doesn't know which triplet it is?''

Nick bent down beside the bed. "It's Sammy," he said softly. He reached out and stroked Sammy's tousled hair. "He does feel warm. Find a thermometer and let's take his temperature first.''

Jillian rushed to the bathroom. She struggled with the child-proofed cabinet door before she managed to get it open. A few moments later, she returned with the thermometer. She held it out in front of Sammy's mouth but he turned away, whimpering in protest.

Nick smiled and shook his head. "Jillie, that's the wrong end.''

Jillian frowned and flipped the thermometer around, the silver end pointing toward her. "That can't be right, can it?''

"No," he said, taking it from her hand. "The wrong end on Sam." He grabbed a jar of Vaseline from the dresser and took off Sam's diaper.

"Do you know what you're doing?" she said, peering over his shoulder, wincing.

"Pretty much. Why don't you read me directions out of Dr. Hazelton just to be sure.''

Jillian held the book up and slowly recited the section on thermometers while Nick calmly responded. His composure both surprised and steadied Jillian. When she'd found Sammy ill, she'd panicked, but now she knew with Nick at her side, everything would be all right.

Sammy watched them silently, his characteristic quiet interrupted only by the occasional whine. Zach and Andy were both lying in their beds, observing the action with their eyes half-closed. "Well?" Jillian said. "The book says a normal temperature...er, on that end is 99.6.''

He held the thermometer up to the light. "It's high,''

Nick said, placing it on the dresser before fastening the tabs on Sammy's diaper.

She grabbed up the thermometer and squinted to read it. "It's 103.4. That's bad."

"What does Dr. Hazelton say?"

Jillian scanned the book. "Temperatures of up to 102, monitor closely. Between 102 and 104, give medication, a sponge bath, and call a pediatrician if it persists. Over 104, take to doctor or emergency room immediately."

"Do you have the pediatrician's number?"

"No," Jillian said. "I mean, I do, but I don't want to take any chances. I think we should take Sammy to the emergency room."

Nick took her hand and gave it a squeeze. "If that's what you want to do, then that's what we'll do, Jillie."

"You don't think I'm over-reacting?" she asked, her mind spinning with indecision. "I just don't think I can trust a book to tell me what to do. He looks so flushed and what if he gets worse? We're a half hour away from a hospital. By then, it might be too late. Do you think I'm over-reacting? Dr. Hazelton says there can be convulsions. If you think we should keep him here, we won't go."

Nick stood, then pulled her over to the door and placed his hands on her shoulders. He gazed down into her eyes. "I can stay with the boys, while you take Sammy in. Or I can take Sammy in while you stay with the boys. What do you want to do?"

"I—I want to go and I want you to come with me. We'll take the boys with us."

"All right," Nick said. "I'll get Zach and Andy up and dressed, you take care of Sammy. See if there's any Children's Tylenol in the medicine cabinet, and if there is, give him a dose. Then get him dressed." He bent lower and gave Jillian a gentle kiss, his thumb hooked beneath her chin.

Time seemed to stand still and, for a long moment, neither one of them moved. Jillian risked a look up at him, expecting to see desire in his eyes. But instead, she found concern and care, and what she'd always thought love might look like. She wanted to break down and cry, to throw herself into his arms and have him assure her that everything would be all right.

Nick brushed his hand over her cheek and smiled. "Kids are resilient, Jillie. Everything will be all right. I promise."

"Roxy is going to kill me," Jillian said, fighting back tears. "Nothing was supposed to go wrong."

He smiled. "This happens with kids. It's not your fault. You didn't give him a fever."

"I let him play too long in the pool. He got cold water in his ears and now he has an ear infection. It *is* my fault." She drew a ragged breath, needing him to kiss her just once more. "I'm sorry to get you mixed up in this. I should be able to handle this on my own. What if you weren't here? What if you'd finished the library and left? I should be able to handle this."

"You would have. And you are, Jillie. Now, go get dressed and then find the Tylenol for Sammy. I'll get the boys ready."

The next few minutes passed in a blur. Zach and Andy weren't too happy about being roused from sleep a second time and fussed as Nick pulled on shorts, T-shirts and shoes. She gave Sammy the medicine, then quickly dressed him, wrapped him in a light blanket and brought him downstairs. Nick had already fastened Zach and Andy into their car seats and took Sam from her arms to do the same.

Jillian hopped in the front seat and closed the door. She took a deep breath and Nick started the van. "Wait!" she cried. "I should go back and call Roxy. What if she calls and we don't answer?"

"Sweetheart, it's past midnight. I don't think she'll call. And we can call her after we find out what's wrong. If we call her now, she'll just worry."

"You're right," Jillian said. She sent him a nervous glance. "Did—did you just call me 'sweetheart'?"

Nick shrugged as he pulled away from the garage and steered the van down the driveway. "Yeah. Sorry. It just slipped out."

"No," Jillian said, secretly pleased with the endearment. No one had ever called her sweetheart before—besides her father. It made her feel safe and cherished, something she needed right now. "It's all right. I—I liked it."

They drove silently for a long time, all three boys drifting off to sleep in their car seats. She reached back and stroked Sammy's cheek and he felt cooler to her touch, but Jillian didn't know whether the fever had subsided or she was engaging in wishful thinking. "Did I thank you?" she murmured.

"Yes, you did," Nick said. He reached over and slipped his arm around her shoulders, gently massaging her nape. "But I don't need thanks. I want to help you, Jillie. You and the boys are important to me."

She sank back in the seat, all the emotions welling up inside of her. Tears pressed at the corners of her eyes and she fought them. She didn't deserve a man like Nick, especially after she'd been so cold to him. He was kind and thoughtful and any woman, including her, should be happy to have him in her life. "I—I just feel so helpless. Sammy can't tell me what's wrong and my mind is coming up with all these terrible possibilities. And—"

"You're getting a taste of what it's like to be a mother," he said.

"I don't think I like it," Jillian said, shaking her head.

"My stomach is in knots and my head hurts and I feel like I'm going to throw up. And I can't stop shaking."

"I think that's normal."

"But I'm not even Sammy's mother. What would it be like if he were really my son?"

Nick drew a finger along her jaw. "You love Sammy. You have every right to be worried."

Jillian stared out at the road in front of them, wishing they were already a the hospital. Nick easily maneuvered the van around the sweeping curves and she sank down in the seat and crossed her arms over her chest, trying to still the tremors that wracked her body.

All her problems with Nick had dissolved in the midst of this new crisis and she took comfort in his touch, in the gentle way he consoled her, in the warmth of his fingers laced through hers. He drew her hand up to his mouth and kissed her wrist. Jillian glanced over at him and smiled.

"Everything will be all right," she murmured. But she wasn't talking only about Sammy. Things had been set right between her and Nick as well. The anger and confusion that had marred their last day together was gone and, once again, they were friends.

THEY ARRIVED at the hospital in thirty minutes, a quick ride from the lake house to the small city of Rochester. They could have driven another twenty minutes to Dover and a regional medical center, but Nick thought Jillie might not survive the ride. Though she tried to maintain her composure, beneath the surface she was a nervous wreck. He saw it in the way she gnawed on her fingernails and checked on Sammy every five seconds, in the way she kept glancing at the clock in the dashboard, then at the speedometer, mentally calculating their exact time of arrival.

Nick had offered encouraging words, but he knew they'd

gone in one ear and out the other. He was tempted to pull over to the side of the road and yank her into his arms until she quit trembling. Instead, he kept driving, nodding whenever required. In truth, he was glad Jillian had decided to take Sammy to the emergency room. Once a qualified medical professional pronounced him out of danger, she could stop beating herself up. Had they kept Sammy at home, Jillian probably would have driven him crazy second-guessing Dr. Hazelton.

The emergency room was empty when they arrived, but getting Sammy examined was a complicated affair. Jillie had forgotten to bring health insurance information for the boys and had also left the number to Roxy and Greg's hotel at home. The admitting nurse hassled her over parental permission but Nick suggested they call the boys' pediatrician whose number Jillie had committed to memory. A quick phone call and the emergency staff was satisfied with the medical permission slip Roxy had left with the pediatrician.

A few moments later, another nurse appeared to whisk Sammy away. The little boy was barely awake and put up no fuss. Jillie wanted to accompany him, but the doctor assured her that they would call her if she was needed. In truth, Nick could understand why they didn't want her in the examination room. She was nearing the edge of hysteria caused, in part, by the pamphlet on encephalitis she'd picked up as she paced the waiting room. Zach and Andy, on the other hand, seemed to be taking the whole night in stride. They'd discovered a play area in the corner of the waiting room and were busy poring over new and exciting toys and puzzles.

Nick drew Jillie over to a pair of chairs near the boys and they sat down. He held her hand, gently stroking the inside of her wrist with his thumb, hoping to divert her attention, yet also happy just to touch her. "Don't worry," he said. "I think Sammy looked better already."

"You're just saying that to calm me down," Jillie replied morosely.

"No, I wouldn't lie to you. He felt cooler to the touch and he wasn't so flushed. Little kids get fevers, sometimes for no reason."

"Maybe we should call Roxy and Greg. You could drive home and get the number."

"Let's just wait and see."

Jillie drew a ragged breath. He slipped his arm around her shoulders and pulled her against him. She pressed her face into his chest and closed her eyes, her teeth chattering. "I can never be a mother. This is just too hard." She glanced up at him and gave him a rueful smile. "Maybe I should get a cat."

Finally, a smile, Nick mused. Physical contact seemed to soothe her so he rubbed her arm, her skin like silk beneath his fingertips. "You'd always have a husband to help."

"No," she said.

Nick pulled back and looked down at her in confusion. "No? What do you mean?"

She laughed and shook her head. "Nothing. It was just...stupid."

"Tell me," Nick said.

Jillie sighed softly. "Actually, *I* was stupid. Stupid enough to believe I could have a child on my own. That's why I volunteered to take care of the boys. I figured if I could handle three boys for a week, then I could take care of one child for eighteen years. I worked it all out on my computer, work hours, home hours, school expenses, college fund. I wanted to show Roxy I could have it all."

Nick stifled a chuckle. He never knew what to expect from Jillie. The way her mind worked was sometimes a complete mystery, yet he found that quality endlessly intriguing. He could spend a lifetime with her and never be bored. "Your computer told you you could have a child of your own? I hate to tell you this, but I think it takes more than just you and your computer to have a baby."

"I know that," Jillie said. "I would have gone to one of those banks…and made a withdrawal. They have them, you know, where all the…depositors are Mensa members."

"There are much more interesting ways to make a baby."

She sighed. "It's a moot point, anyway. I thought I could do it, but this past week proved me wrong. Don't you agree?"

Nick pressed a kiss to her forehead. "You're an amazing woman, Jillie Marshall. I think you could do pretty much anything you set your mind to—including becoming a mother."

"Mr. and Mrs. Hunter?"

Jillie jumped out of her chair, nearly clipping Nick's chin. He rose to stand beside her, then grabbed her hand so she wouldn't twist her fingers together. Instead, she shifted from foot to foot. "I'm Jillian Marshall. This is Nick Callahan. We're not married—"

The young female resident glanced around the waiting room, frowning. "Mr. and Mrs. Hunter?" she repeated.

"They're in Hawaii," Jillie said. "And we're the babysitters, not the parents. We're not married. A lot of people make that mistake but we're just…"

"Friends," Nick finished, putting an end to her babbling.

"Yes," Jillie said. "Friends." She swallowed hard. "Is—is Sammy all right?"

The doctor nodded, glancing down at her chart. "He's fine. He doesn't have a fever anymore. The Tylenol must have done the trick. But he does have a little ear infection. I've called his regular pediatrician and he suggests that you monitor him for the next day or two. If the fever returns or the ear seems to give him problems, then we'll put him on antibiotics. But let's give it a little time to clear up on its own.''

Jillie sagged against Nick and he caught her around the waist, certain her knees were about to give out. "Then he's all right?'' she asked. "It's not pneumonia? Or encephalitis?''

The doctor chuckled. "No, his lungs are perfectly clear. You probably didn't have to bring him in, but if it eased your mind, then it was the right thing to do. You can talk to the admitting nurse about the bill. I'll just go get Sammy and you can take him home.''

When the doctor disappeared behind the automatic doors, Jillie moaned softly. "The bill. What does an emergency room visit cost? Two, three thousand dollars. Roxy is going to kill me. What if their insurance doesn't cover this?''

"Don't worry, I don't think it's quite that much. And I gave them my credit card,'' Nick said. "Everything will be taken care of.''

Jillie turned to him, suddenly frantic. "No! You can't keep rescuing me like some white knight. And you can't afford this. By the time you're finished paying for my mistakes, all your profits from the bookshelves will be gone. I have to learn to handle my own problems.''

Nick hooked his thumb under her chin and forced her gaze to meet his. Her eyes were rimmed red with exhaustion and her face was pale and drawn. The sooner he got her home and to bed, the better off they'd all be. "Jillie, if you haven't noticed yet, I like helping you. I like being around you. And I'm getting used to your little disasters. I can certainly afford to help you out. That's what friends do.''

She frowned. "You find this all entertaining?'' Anger flickered in her eyes. Considering the stress she'd been under, he wasn't surprised by her behavior. Just then, the automatic doors opened and another nurse emerged with a sleeping Sammy in her arms. "Mr. and Mrs. Hunter?" she whispered.

This time Jillie didn't bother to correct her. "I'm Mrs. Hunter," she said, her anger suddenly evaporated. The nurse held her finger up to her lips, then put the boy into Jillie's arms. "He'll be fine," she said. "The nurse at the desk has his discharge papers. You'll need to read them and sign. And make sure to call us if there are any further problems. Or you can call Sammy's pediatrician."

Jillie pressed her lips to Sammy's forehead, but he continued to sleep. "He feels nice and cool. Thank you. And thank the doctor for us."

They completed all the paperwork, Nick collected Zach and Andy from the play corner and they headed back out to the van. It was nearly two in the morning and the parking lot was silent, the town around them asleep. They settled the boys in their car seats, then Nick reached out to open Jillie's door, but at the last minute she turned to him.

"I'm sorry I snapped at you," she said, staring up into his eyes. "I should thank you for helping me. And tell you that you're a—a good friend, Nick Callahan." They stood looking at each other for a long moment, then she pushed up on her toes and kissed him, softly, sweetly, her lips warm against his.

Nick's hand drifted from the van door to her face and then to the nape of her neck. When she pulled back, he wasn't ready to let her go and he leaned forward and captured her mouth again. She seemed to melt into him and he slipped an arm around her waist and drew her nearer.

The kiss spun out, growing more passionate with every passing second. For a moment, he forgot where they were and what they'd just been through. All he could focus on was the taste of her, the way she fit perfectly in his arms. But what he really wanted from Jillie he couldn't have here in the parking lot of a hospital at two in the morning with three sleeping boys in the back seat.

He wanted time—minutes and hours, days even. The time to slowly undress her, to learn the angles and curves of her body, to memorize her scent until he could recall it at a moment's notice. He wanted to make her gasp and moan at his touch, to bring her to the edge, then carry her over.

Nick brushed his lips against hers, then looked down into her eyes. "I think we better get you and the boys home."

Jillie nodded, then turned to climb into the van. He closed the door and drew a long breath of the night air. Though Jillie might think of him as a friend, he just couldn't reciprocate. In truth, he'd stopped thinking of her as a pal a long time ago. She was a woman he needed. A woman he couldn't afford to lose. And a woman he'd grown to love. Nick knew it like he knew his own name.

But there was one thing he didn't know. He didn't have a clue whether Jillie Marshall felt the same way about him.

JILLIAN DIDN'T REALIZE she'd fallen asleep until she woke up in Nick's arms. He was gently lifting her from the van when she opened her eyes. "Are we home?" she asked, raising her hand against the soft glow of the porch light.

He nodded. "I took the boys upstairs and got them to bed. They're already sound asleep. You drifted off right after we left the hospital."

"I—I can walk."

"And I can carry you," he said. "You've had a rough night and I don't want you to trip and sprain your ankle again. Then what would we do?"

She wrapped her arms around his neck and snuggled against him. After what she'd been through tonight, it felt good to be indulged. And she wasn't certain she would be able to walk into the house and up to her room. She felt as if she'd been run over by a cement truck, every muscle in her body completely spent.

He carried her, as if she weighed nothing more than a feather, to the porch, then through the door and up the stairs. He didn't pause until he'd dropped her gently on the bed. "My hero," she said sleepily, lying back against the down pillows.

"Can I get you anything?" he asked, taking a step back from the bed.

She stared up at him in the dim light from the bedside lamp. Lord, he was handsome. Her mind drifted back to the moment he'd stood in front of her naked, dripping with water. A shiver ran over her body and she remembered the sheer masculine beauty of his physique, the unbidden desire it awakened in her.

But there was more than just physical perfection to Nick. He wasn't her Nobel prize-winning scientist, but he was strong and kind and capable, a man she could depend on in a crisis, a man who truly cared about her. He watched over her and the boys when everything seemed to be falling apart. And she could trust him like she'd never been able to trust a man before.

How had she managed to overlook these qualities? She'd been so set on maintaining her silly standards, certain that only a man who fit her criteria would be worthy of her love. But here was a man who protected her, who cherished her, and she'd so steadfastly refused to see him for what he was. Nick Callahan was a man she could love. In truth, he was a man she *did* love.

"There is something I need," Jillian murmured, suddenly emboldened by her revelation. She needed to touch him, to brush aside his clothes and revel in the sight of his body.

Jillian pushed up on her knees, then motioned him to come closer.

He did as she asked and before Nick had a chance to react, Jillian wrapped her arms around his neck and kissed him again. But this time there was no gratitude in the kiss. Instead, it was filled with unrestrained desire, passion that had simmered inside of her for so long. "Stay with me tonight," she whispered, her lips trailing along his jaw.

"Jillie, I don't think—"

"Don't say anything. I don't need to hear any promises. I just want to be with you. We don't have to—you know."

His eyebrow arched. "We don't have to?"

Jillian sighed. "When you're with me, I feel safe. I don't worry and obsess. I'm not going to be able to sleep if I'm alone. And right now, I just want to be with you."

Nick hesitated for a moment and Jillian's heart sank. But then he kicked off his shoes and socks and sat down on the edge of the bed. Jillian lay down on her side and softly stroked his back. "Did you mean what you said, earlier in the emergency room?"

He glanced over his shoulder. "What was that?"

"That we were friends?"

He bent his head and she heard a soft chuckle slip from his lips. "I suppose so."

"Good," she replied. "I'm glad." It felt good knowing that the man she loved was also her friend.

After a long moment of silence, Nick reached down and grabbed the hem of his T-shirt, then yanked it over his head. When he turned to Jillian and stretched out beside her, she couldn't help but notice the pained look on his face. "Are you all right?" she asked.

"Fine," he said in an edgy voice. "I guess I'm just tired, too."

He slipped his arm beneath Jillian's head and she snuggled up against him, pressing her face against his bare skin, the soft dusting of hair on his chest tickling her cheek. "This is nice," she murmured, raking her nails softly along his collarbone.

Jillian splayed her hand over Nick's chest. Beneath her fingers, she felt his heart beating, strong and sure. She tipped her face up to look at him and found him staring at her, a look in his eyes that she'd never seen before, fierce, unyielding, predatory. A shiver raced down her spine and she wasn't sure what to do.

Then ever so slowly, he brought his mouth down on hers and kissed her with such tenderness she could do nothing but respond. As his tongue gently invaded her mouth, Jillian mused at how right this felt. Different than the frantic passion they'd shared that night on the lawn. All her apprehension vanished, all her inhibitions receded and she allowed herself to enjoy the taste of his mouth.

She ran her hand along his chest, skimming her fingers lightly over his skin. The male body had never intrigued her as much as it did now and she relished the feel of muscle and bone, his broad chest and his washboard belly. Her fingers trembled slightly as she accidentally brushed the hard ridge of his desire, evident through the worn fabric of his jeans.

Jillian sighed softly. She didn't think of herself as a sensual person, but with Nick's hands on her body, she was more of a woman than she'd ever been, acutely aware of her power over the man beside her. But all her power seemed lost when he began a lazy exploration of her body. His lips trailed after his fingers, first to her collarbone, then to the cleft between her breasts, and then to her stomach, her clothing pushed aside to reveal bare skin for Nick to taste.

Jillian knew this could only lead in one direction, but she

was past worrying. She'd been fighting her feelings for him since the moment they'd met and she simply didn't have the strength to continue the battle. They'd been moving toward this moment all along and she was glad it had finally come.

Before long, her top became a barrier and he gently tugged it over her head. Jillian expected to feel embarrassed, but then she saw the pleasure in his gaze as he fingered the lacy edge of her bra. Jillian reached up and slipped the satin straps off her shoulders. He took his cue and nuzzled at her breast, capturing her nipple through the damp fabric of her bra.

Jillian's breath caught in her throat at the intimate contact, a current shooting through her body, setting her nerves on edge. How could she have lived for so long and never experienced this with a man? This pleasure was so intense it bordered on pain. "Oh," she murmured, furrowing her fingers through his hair.

Nick looked up and gave her a sleepy grin. "Does that feel good?" he asked, teasing at the nub with his thumb.

"Umm," Jillian murmured, arching beneath his touch.

"Jillie, maybe we should—"

She pressed her finger to his lips and shook her head. "You don't have to ask me if this is what I want. It is."

Perhaps she'd been waiting for this her entire life, for a man like Nick. She felt scared and reckless and completely exhilarated, as if she were about to step off the edge of a cliff without knowing what lay below. Her life up until this point had been so carefully planned that she'd even imagined a moment like this. But nothing in her past had prepared her for the sheer power of his touch, the warmth of his body next to hers, a raging need to make him ache for her touch.

For the first time in her life, she didn't have a plan. Logic had been discarded and she now operated on pure instinct. She couldn't reach for her computer and predict how this was all going to turn out. Would this be the first of many nights together? Or would it be all over tomorrow or the next day, when their time at the lake house ended? She should have been more concerned, but Jillian didn't care. All she cared about was the flood of exquisite sensation that surged through her body every time he touched her.

With hesitant hands, Jillian smoothed her palms over his shoulders. Muscle rippled beneath her fingers as he moved above her. Jillian's eyes drifted over his body, mesmerized by the sheer perfection of his broad chest and narrow waist. "I—I'm not sure what to do," she murmured. "I've never been—I mean, I have done this before but—"

With a low groan, he grabbed her around the waist and rolled her over on top of him, pulling her legs alongside his hips. He pushed up, then nuzzled the soft cleft between her breasts. "We'll just take it slow and figure it out as we go along."

A flood of relief washed over her and she smiled at him. Reaching around her back, Jillian unclasped her bra, then let it slide down her arms. A long sigh slipped from his lips as he took in the sight of her. Suddenly, she wasn't nervous anymore. The trust she'd come to have in Nick wasn't limited to their lives outside the bedroom.

"You're so beautiful," he murmured. Tenderly, he cupped her breast in his palm, his touch so stirring it took her breath away. "I knew you'd be beautiful."

Jillian closed her eyes and tipped her head back, enjoying the caress of his hands. Nick made her feel cherished and protected, and she could believe that he loved her, even if it wasn't really true. But it didn't matter, for nothing could make her turn back now. This was what mattered, this was what she needed. "Love me," she murmured. "Now."

''Now,'' he repeated, drawing her back down to the soft folds of the sheets. His mouth covered hers, his tongue urgent, his kiss insatiable. They fumbled with each other's clothes, hands frantic, limbs tangling, breathlessly anxious to do away with any barriers between them.

When they were finally rid of the last barriers, Jillian stilled, letting her gaze drift over his naked body, stretched out beside her. Her gaze fell on his hard shaft, fascinated by the beauty of his desire.

''Touch me,'' he said, his voice low and ragged with need.

She reached out and drew her fingers along the length of him, lingering there as his breathing quickened. Nick moaned softly as she closed her fingers around him and began to stroke him gently. This was how she'd always imagined true passion to be, inhibition tossed aside, desire like wildfire out of control.

Nick drew in a sharp breath, then grabbed her wrist. At first, Jillian thought she'd done something wrong, but the look on his face told her she'd brought him too far, too fast. He smiled then pulled her arm over her head. He raised the other one, then cuffed her wrists in his hand.

With a low growl, he let his other hand drift down along her body, lower and lower until he reached her moist core. Patiently, with exquisite tenderness, he touched her there, teasing at her until Jillian arched against his hand. If she'd been surprised by the powerful sensations before, those that coursed through her body now made her nearly mad with need.

As gently as his seduction had begun, it now slowed, as he twisted on the bed, reaching for his jeans and pulling a condom out of his wallet. He tore the foil packet open with his teeth, then watched, eyes half-hooded as Jillian sheathed him.

His eyes fixed on hers as he pulled her beneath him and settled himself between her thighs. Jillian had lost herself in his gaze so many times, but now she felt as if he'd opened the doors to his soul. As he gently probed at her entrance, she watched as raw emotion glittered in their blue depths. He loved her and though she'd never expected to hear the words, the feeling was evident in his eyes.

A soft moan slipped from her lips as she wrapped her legs around his waist. He began to move inside of her and slowly she lost touch with reality. But one clear thought still remained in her mind. Jillian loved Nick. And whether they parted for good in a few days or became lovers for a lifetime, it didn't matter. She'd always know, in her heart, that he'd loved her, too.

8

AFTER MAKING LOVE to Jillie until the predawn hours, Nick should have fallen into a deep and dreamless sleep. But instead, he lay awake, Jillie wrapped in his arms, her body tucked in the curve of his. The first light of day had just begun to illuminate the windows and he knew they'd have only an hour or so before they'd have to face the morning and three sleep-deprived boys.

These were their last hours together. Nick had no choice but to head back to Providence and the responsibilities of his work there. Had he known he was going to meet a woman like Jillie Marshall, he might have passed on some of the projects he had pending. Another day with her was all he wanted—all he needed.

Though they'd given in to their passion, things still remained unsettled between them. Where would they go from here? She'd been clear last night that she didn't expect any promises. And with any other woman, Nick might have been relieved. But if Jillie really thought their lovemaking was all about physical gratification, she had another guess coming. When he touched her, when he moved inside of her, it only confirmed what he knew. He was in love with Jillie Marshall. But did she love him?

At first he'd thought his little deception was standing in the way of something more serious between them. But now he was glad for it, glad that they'd made love while she still believed he was a working-class guy. What better way to test the strength of her feelings? He wanted Jillie to want him for who he was, not for what he'd made of his life. He didn't want to be just a line of check marks on her list of requirements for a husband. Acceptable job, decent education, good professional prospects, passable manners. His IQ and his bank account had nothing to do with the man he was.

Nick sighed softly, a strand of Jillie's hair tickling his cheek. But now that he knew she cared enough for him to make love with him, it was time to tell her the truth. When she woke up, he'd come clean. If she truly loved him, then the deception wouldn't matter. He was still the same man, just with slightly better prospects. She might be angry, but she'd understand why he'd done it. Hell, look at his history with long-term commitment. He hadn't taken the time to be sure of Claire's feelings before he proclaimed his own.

This time he'd be sure. If Professor Jillian Marshall could love a simple carpenter, capitulate to an emotion that went against everything she'd ever wanted, then maybe there was a chance she could love Nick Callahan for the rest of her life. And that's what he wanted with Jillie—a lifetime.

Settled on a course of action, Nick closed his eyes and tried to fall back asleep. But lying in bed with Jillie naked in his arms didn't exactly promote healthful rest. He slowly slid his palm over her hip and down her thigh, enjoying the feel of her skin beneath his fingers. Memories of their lovemaking teased at his brain. Flashes of sensation still pulsed through his body.

Loving Jillie had been a revelation. It was obvious that she'd never had a lover who had taken time with her, who had let her passion unfold slowly. She was nervous and clumsy, then eager and excited, and finally bold and unbridled. And though she knew the technical workings between a man and a woman, she had no idea of what she'd missed beyond that.

The first time, it had been all about need and release. But the second time they made love, Nick had shown her the true depths of her passion. He'd brought her to the edge again and again, before gently retreating. And when she finally came, any memories she had of previous lovers had been permanently erased from her mind.

Nick smiled to himself. He wanted to be the only man in her life, the man she woke up with in the morning and fell asleep with at night. He'd always thought falling in love would be difficult, finding a woman who captured his heart and his mind. But loving Jillie was so simple, so natural.

He pushed up on his elbow and peered over her shoulder at her face. She was beautiful. He'd never known a woman who could stir his senses with just a coy look or a simple smile. Reaching out, he gently skimmed his fingers over the dark circles beneath her eyes. He'd let her sleep, confident in the fact that they'd make love again very soon.

A soft cry broke the morning stillness and Nick glanced at the bedside clock. The boys were up. He pressed a soft kiss to Jillie's shoulder, then rolled out of bed. If he could keep them quiet, maybe she'd have a chance to catch up on all the sleep she'd missed the night before. Nick grabbed his jeans and tugged them on, not bothering with underwear. Then he softly padded out of the room.

Though he tried to keep the boys quiet over the next hour, lack of sleep and childish energy made that nearly impossible. He was just about to take them outside when Jillie wandered downstairs, her hair tousled and her slender body wrapped in a disheveled robe. She headed right for the coffeemaker and poured herself a mug.

"Good morning," Nick said.

She glanced up at him over the rim of the mug. He saw

wariness in her eyes, as well as a good measure of exhaustion. "Morning."

"I made French toast for the boys. There are a few pieces still warm in the oven if you're hungry."

"Thank you," she said. "I—I am a little hungry."

Nick grabbed a pot holder from the hook near the stove and removed the plate from the oven. He set it in front of her on the breakfast bar. "Syrup or jam?"

"Syrup," she said.

"Butter?"

Jillie nodded. He stood back as she picked up her fork and sliced into the French toast. Geez, what was wrong with them? They'd just shared the most intimate moments of their lives together and all he could talk about was condiments! He strode around the end of the breakfast bar and spun Jillie's stool until she faced him. She stared up at him with wide eyes as he grabbed her fork from her hand and set it behind her. Then he cupped her face in his palms and gave her a gentle but passionate kiss. "There," he said, when he pulled back. "That's the way we should start the morning."

A pretty blush slowly stained her cheeks. "About last night, I—"

"I know," he said, slipping his arms around her waist. "It was pretty amazing." He kissed her again, this time on the tip of her nose. "You were pretty amazing."

"That's not what I—"

"Jillie, we don't have to discuss it to make it real," he said, nuzzling her cheek. "What happened between us happened for a reason. It was meant to happen all along. And I'm glad it did."

He took her hands and wove his fingers through hers. "We do have to discuss a few things, though." He slipped onto the stool beside her. "I have to leave this morning," he said. "I've got a business meeting early tomorrow and I've got a presentation to prepare. But before I leave, I wanted to tell you something."

"I don't need to hear anything," she said. "There's nothing to talk about."

"Actually there is. And it's kind if important. You might be upset and I—"

She forced a smile, then jumped to her feet and began to wipe off the counter. "You—you don't have to worry about me," she said. "I'm perfectly capable of taking care of the boys on my own now. Besides, my mother said she'd come over tomorrow morning to watch the boys until Greg and Roxy get home. I—I have to get back to my life, too. I have some important...meetings tomorrow myself."

Nick sat back. Did this mean she wouldn't talk to Roxy before he saw her next? If that were true, then maybe he could delay a bit, lay a little more groundwork before confessing to his little lie. "Jillie, are you all right?"

"Of course," she snapped.

"Are you angry with me?" he asked, trying to capture her gaze with his.

"Don't be ridiculous! You have to leave. So do I. We both knew this would all come to an end sooner or later."

"It's not coming to an end, Jillie. We will see each other again."

"Sure," she said in a cheery voice. "We'll probably run into each other at Greg and Roxy's Christmas party. Maybe sometime next summer. It's not like we're going to go back to being strangers. That's not what I meant."

"It's not what I meant either." Nick shook his head. "We're damn well going to see each other again—and within the next twenty-four hours."

Jillie blinked in confusion. "What do you mean?"

Nick bit back an oath. "What the hell have we been doing here, Jillie? Playing house?"

"I—I don't understand," she said. "We've been taking care of the boys."

"Did you expect that I'd just walk out on you and never see you again? If you did, then you don't know me at all."

She looked up at him, the first time this morning that she'd met his gaze directly. A tremulous smile curved her lips. "That's right. We don't know each other at all. So I have no right to expect anything from you. I don't think you should feel obligated to—"

"You don't want anything beyond what we shared last night?" he asked.

"What I want doesn't make a difference. You see, it's all a matter of mathematical probabilities," she said.

Nick looked at her, dumbfounded. Whenever she felt nervous or ill-prepared, she always retreated to her ordered little world of formulas and computer models. But what the hell did math have to do with what they shared in bed? "All right, I'll bite. Explain, Professor Marshall."

"Over the past few days, I've been working on a probability table. I found some data on the Internet and I created a model using divorce rates. Did you know the most prevalent reason for divorce is incompatibility?"

"So?"

"Well, we're clearly incompatible," Jillie said. "You know nothing about the Goldbach conjecture and I know nothing about power drills."

"What the hell does this have to do with anything? From where I sit, we get along pretty damn well."

"Maybe we get along now, but sooner or later, we won't. According to my charts, the probabilities of our forming a lasting relationship are approximately nine thousand, six hundred and thirty-seven to one. It—it's simple mathematics," she said. "I can show you the charts if you want."

"Forget the charts, Jillie," he said. "Tell me how you feel."

"About what?"

"Us. Together. Jillie, last night we made love. More than once, if you remember."

"My research says that when good sex is factored into a relationship, it doesn't significantly affect the compatibility ratios."

"All right," he said, his frustration nearing the breaking point. "Let me make it very plain. Are we going to see each other again after I walk out today?"

"Do you want to see me?" Jillie asked.

"Do you want to see me?" Nick countered. She thought about her answer a bit longer than he would have liked and Nick sighed. "What are you afraid of?"

"I'm not afraid," she answered, her chin tipped up defiantly.

"You hide behind all your numbers and formulas. Why don't you just say it? You don't want to fall in love with some working class slob who gets his hands dirty at work. You're a snob, Jillie." He pushed out of his chair and paced the length of the kitchen.

"I'm just a realist," she murmured.

"Hah! You're a fraidy-cat," he said.

Jillie gasped. "A fraidy-cat? Where did you get that from? Andy?"

"Let's be honest, Jillie. You're afraid of how you feel. You're falling in love with me and you don't know what to do. How will you introduce me to your egghead friends? What will you do if we can't discuss irrational numbers over breakfast? How will we ever live on my measly salary building bookshelves?"

"That's not the reason," she said. "I'm simply using my common sense."

"I think the past week has proved one thing and that is, you don't have an ounce of common sense—not when it comes to the boys and certainly not when it comes to me."

"We barely know each other," she snapped. "I met you nine days ago. How can you possibly expect me to make a life decision based on nine days?"

"I'm not asking you to marry me," he said. "I just want a damn date."

This stopped her cold. She opened her mouth, but it took a few seconds for the words to come out. "A—a date? Like dinner or a movie?"

"That's a start," he said. "Maybe if we did something more than just change diapers and sweep up Cheerios, we might find we're pretty compatible after all."

"All right," she said. She grabbed a pad of paper from beside the refrigerator and scribbled down her address. "I'm going to be home tomorrow night. Pick me up at seven. We'll…go out. And I'll prove to you that I'm right. This will probably be the worst date you've ever had."

Nick grinned, satisfied that he'd finally gotten through to her. One date was all he needed to prove his point. They belonged together. "It's a plan, then." He stepped in front of her and grabbed her around the waist, yanking her body against his. Without giving her a chance to speak, he kissed her long and hard, making sure it was a kiss that would last until they saw each other next. When he pulled back, he reached up and cupped her cheek in his palm, forcing her eyes to meet his.

"As hard as you'll work to prove that you're right," he murmured, "I'm going to work twice as hard to prove that you're wrong."

JILLIAN OPENED HER EYES long after the sun had peeked over the horizon. She'd had trouble sleeping and drifted off sometime in the wee hours of the morning. After only one night in Nick's arms, she suddenly found it difficult to sleep alone. Maybe it was more than that. After all, he'd been close by for all those days and now he was miles away. She didn't feel as safe and secure without him near.

She rolled over and groaned softly. She shouldn't have worried about sleeping alone. The boys had been awake before dawn and she'd brought all three into bed with her as well as Duke, who had taken up Nick's spot, his big head resting on the pillow. Even with a bed full of warm bodies, she still missed him.

In truth, Jillian half-expected him to be there when she wandered downstairs, a coffee mug in his hand and a boyish grin on his face. He'd be dressed in his typical jeans and T-shirt, casual yet incredibly sexy. She'd been so accustomed to the rumpled look of academia, the tweed jackets and khaki pants, the dull colors, that she found Nick a refreshing break in a world of rather mundane men.

But was that all he was? A break? A brief interlude? A vacation fling? Now that he was gone, Jillian had expected to put him right out of her mind. But instead, she couldn't stop thinking about him. Suddenly all the reasons for not loving Nick had turned into the exact reasons why she loved him so deeply.

They had absolutely nothing in common, yet she found him endlessly fascinating. Though he was just a regular guy, she'd come to see him as a hero of sorts, a kind and honorable man, a man she could count on in a crisis. And there was no denying that the physical aspect of their relationship was as close to perfect as she could imagine.

So what was holding her back? Why had she fallen back on her formulas to scare him away? And why was she so uneasy about their date tonight? They were the same people they'd been all week. The only thing that would change was geography. Perhaps it was because their week at the lake house had been like a week on a deserted island. The real world had been kept at bay, and they'd been able to enjoy each other's company without life interfering.

Back in Boston, she wouldn't be Aunt Jillie, inept baby-sitter and instigator of domestic disasters, damsel in distress. She'd be Dr. Jillian Marshall, brilliant mathematician, career woman. And he wouldn't be her white knight, riding in to the rescue. He'd just be…

Jillian cursed softly, then punched at her pillow. The truth was, she didn't know him at all, beyond the fact that he made her knees weak with his kisses and her body burn with his lovemaking. Maybe she'd been right to accept a date with him. By the end of the evening tonight, her doubts should be put to rest. And then she could go on with her life as if she'd never met him…and never fallen in love.

She snuggled back down beneath the covers and closed her eyes. There was no use worrying about that now. She'd have plenty to worry about once her mother arrived. She'd have to clean up the house and dress the boys and get them ready for Greg and Roxy's arrival this afternoon. Though she'd first intended to leave before they got home, Jillian had decided to cancel her afternoon appointments with her graduate students and face the music like an adult. She owed Roxy a big apology and she intended to tell her sister everything that happened—except all the parts about Nick.

Jillian only wanted to doze for a few minutes but the next time she opened her eyes, she found Roxy and Greg standing in the doorway of the bedroom. "We're home, we're home!" Duke lifted his head and barked, and the boys pushed up from the bed and rubbed their sleepy eyes. A few moments later, screams of delight filled the room, and Roxy threw herself onto the bed and hugged her sons.

Stunned, Jillian ran a hand through her tangled hair. "What are you doing home so early? I thought your flight didn't get in until two."

"We caught an earlier flight," Greg said, grabbing Andy and tossing him up, before giving him a bear hug. "Rox couldn't stand to be away a moment longer, so we took the red-eye from L.A. How have my boys been?"

Zach and Sam scrambled over their mother and threw themselves at Greg. "I see the house is still standing," he said with a grin.

Jillian smiled sheepishly. "I'm sorry about the mess. Mother was going to come over and watch them so I could clean up. I wanted to have them all bathed and dressed in their best."

Roxy rolled over on her back and laid her head on Duke's hip. "Don't be silly," she said. "The house looks fine, and so do the boys." She leaned over and hugged Jillian. "And you look good. You've got some color."

Jillian reached up and touched her cheeks. "We—we spent a lot of time outside. The weather was perfect."

Roxy frowned, fixing her with a shrewd look. "There's something else," she said.

Jillian threw the covers back and jumped out of bed. Running her fingers through her tangled hair again, she searched for her robe, tripping over the boys as they scampered around the room. Was it that obvious? Could Roxy tell she'd made love to a man the night before last? Or was her sister sensing something else? "So how was your flight?" Jillian asked, deftly changing the subject.

"Endless," Roxy said, snagging Zach around the waist and nuzzling his neck. "I am so glad to be home. Paradise is nice for a few days, but the silence was beginning to drive me crazy.'' She sighed contentedly. "So, how were they? Tell me the truth.''

"We had a great time,'' Jillian said, picking up a brush. "They're a handful but we got along fine.''

Roxy raised her eyebrow. "Is there anything else you'd like to tell me about?''

Greg cleared his throat, then gathered up the boys. "I'll get the monsters some breakfast while you two talk.''

Roxy sent him a grateful smile, then turned her attention back to Jillian. She pushed up from the bed, crossed the room to the dresser and stared at Jillian's reflection in the mirror. Jillian kept brushing her hair, thankful for the distraction. "I didn't notice Nick's truck in the driveway. Is he gone?''

Jillian shrugged nonchalantly. "I don't know. I think he finished the library, but I don't keep track of his schedule.''

Roxy grabbed the brush from Jillian's hand, set it on the dresser and drew her over to the bed. "Talk,'' she ordered.

Jillian took a deep breath, then forced a smile. "There is one thing I should say to you right away. I'm sorry I underestimated what it takes to be a mother. And if I said anything to make you feel bad, I'm sorry for that, too. It takes so much more than organization to keep this household running and I know that now.'' Jillian bent forward and hugged Roxy. "And I'm so glad you're back.''

Roxy chuckled. "I noticed the downstairs bathroom ceiling was freshly painted and I've got a new wallpaper border. Let me guess. The bathtub upstairs ran over and wrecked the ceiling?''

"The toilet,'' Jillian said. "Hot Wheels.''

"Hmm. Three weeks ago it was every towel in the linen cupboard tossed into a tub full of water and bubbles. That's the closest I've ever come to putting all three of them up for adoption.''

"Really?" Jillian said, warmed by the news that she wasn't the only one to suffer the occasional domestic meltdown. "That makes me feel better. I might as well tell you that I've also become intimately acquainted with the volunteer fire department. They rescued Sammy when he got locked in the bathroom. After I tried to crawl through the window, wrecked the screen and sprained my ankle."

"Sounds like it was a pretty normal week around here," Roxy said.

"I don't know what I would have done without Nick," Jillian murmured, staring down at her fingers.

Roxy leaned down and caught Jillian's gaze with hers. "I was wondering when you were going to mention him," she said.

"He did a great job on the bookshelves," Jillian said. "He's a very good carpenter."

"Yeah," Roxy said. "And the fact that we don't have to pay him makes him even better."

"What?" Jillian said. "You mean you didn't hire him to build the bookshelves?"

"If I paid him what he was worth," Roxy said with a chuckle, "those bookshelves would have cost about as much as the house. We invited him to stay in the guest cottage after he broke up with Claire and he returned the favor by building the bookcases. I guess he likes to work with his hands every now and then. It probably relaxes him."

"I—I don't understand," Jillian said. "I thought he was a carpenter. And—and who is Claire?"

Roxy blinked in surprise, before an uneasy look crossed her face. "Didn't Nick tell you what he does?"

Jillian shook her head. What was he hiding? Was he some kind of criminal, a drug runner or a mob boss? What could be so bad that he'd keep it from her? And who the hell was Claire?

"That's odd," Roxy said. "He's not a carpenter, he's an industrial engineer and architect. Pretty famous, too. He designs factories all over the world. A few years ago he designed a vehicle assembly building for NASA. He designed our house as a wedding present when he couldn't be here for the wedding."

"But—but, I thought he was just some ordinary guy."

Roxy giggled. "Nick? Ordinary? Oh, he must have found that amusing. He can be such a tease. And he hates it when women go on and on about all his fame and fortune. I think if he could have been a carpenter, he would have. He just likes to build things for relaxation. He has a pretty high-powered job."

Jillian felt a surge of anger burn in her brain. Was that what this had been to him—an amusement? A little charade? She'd admitted that she barely knew him, but now she wondered if anything she'd believed about him was true. Jillian swallowed hard. "Who is Claire?" she demanded. "His wife? His mistress? Or is she like me—someone he sleeps with on occasion?"

"You slept with Nick Callahan?" Roxy asked, with a gasp.

Jillian jumped up and paced the room, her hands twisted in the belt of her robe. "God, I can't believe I was stupid enough to go to bed with him! I—I thought he was sweet and honorable. And now I find out he was lying to me all the time!"

Roxy reached out and grabbed her hand, stopping her restless movement. "Jillie, what's going on between you two? Are you in love with Nick Callahan?"

"I—I thought he was just some ordinary guy, a guy I could never be serious about. And I was going to write the whole thing off as a little fling. But then I let myself believe that he was something more.''

She snatched up her clothes from around the room, then stripped off the bathrobe and nightgown. "In love with Nick Callahan?'' Jillian laughed sharply as she began to dress. "I may have thought I was—for a few minutes. But now that I look back on it, maybe it was just temporary insanity.''

A GRAY MIST SKIMMED across the choppy surface of Narragansett Bay and clouds hung low in the sky, threatening a warm summer rain. Nick stood on a bluff above the water, breathing deeply of the tangy salt air. His thoughts drifted back to the lake house and he glanced at his watch. By his estimate, Jillie should probably be on her way back to Boston by now.

In a few hours, he'd drive up to Cambridge, ring her doorbell and they'd begin their future together. Thoughts of Jillie had teased at his mind constantly over the past twenty-four hours. During daylight hours, he'd lapse into silly fantasies, and last night, those fantasies had become his dreams. Already, he missed having her in his bed, close enough to touch in his sleep.

Even this morning, during his business meeting, he'd caught himself wondering what she was doing, whether the boys had woken her up before dawn, what they'd eaten for breakfast, whether she'd bothered to comb her mussed hair before coming downstairs. He'd finished his meeting in Hartford before noon, a successful presentation for a new bottling plant he'd been hoping to design, and then moved on to an appointment with his real estate broker, Ken Carlisle, that he'd arranged long before his visit to the cottage.

"What do you think?'' Ken now asked.

"It's a beautiful piece of property,'' Nick replied. In

truth, he could already imagine the house sitting high above the water. He'd use stone and cedar, as if it grew right out of the rugged landscape. But the more he tried to convince himself that he'd found exactly what he was looking for, the more doubts he had.

"I'm not sure," Nick murmured.

"You're not going to find a piece of property this large on the Bay," Ken said. "If we don't make an offer today, it will be gone tomorrow."

"It's just so…" Nick sighed. What was it? So secluded? There were houses just down the road. And it was a quick drive in to Providence. It would be the perfect spot for his new home, except…

"How far would you say we are from Boston?" Nick asked.

"Boston?" Ken shrugged. "I don't know. Maybe an hour. Probably a lot longer in rush hour."

Jillie lived in Boston. If he was at all optimistic about a future with her, then this would be the wrong choice. Sooner or later, he'd grow impatient with the hour wasted in the car, an hour not spent in Jillie's arms, an hour wishing they were already together. And she might not want to stay overnight with him, not on nights when she had classes the next day. Rush-hour traffic into Boston would turn a one-hour drive into two or three. And what if she didn't like the property? Or the house he'd built? Building something new was an awfully big investment for a guy who wasn't sure what the future held.

Maybe he was being too optimistic. After all, they'd only known each other a little more than a week. A person couldn't make life decisions after such a short time—isn't that what she'd said? He'd seen her in just one situation and she barcly knew anything about him. Hell, this whole thing could fall apart after just one date.

"Even if you don't build, this could be a great investment," Ken said. "You could hold it for awhile, then sell it at a profit."

Nick shook his head. "I don't think this is the right place for me."

"Well, I suppose you don't have to make a move right away. It's not like you're homeless since Claire moved out of the house a couple of days ago."

Nick glanced over at him, startled by the mention of her name. He'd lived with her for nearly a year, and now, after only a couple of months apart, her name brought absolutely no feelings at all—no anger, no regret, nothing. "Actually, I'm glad you brought that up. I want you to list the Providence house. Price it to move quickly."

"But where are you going to live?"

He shrugged. "I've been sleeping on the sofa in my office since I got back from New Hampshire. I'll look for an apartment in a few days. I just don't want to go back to that house. It's like another man's life and another man's home. You can sell it, can't you?"

Ken frowned. "Sure. It's a very desirable piece of property. In the meantime, I could show you some condos downtown. It's got to be better than sleeping on your office sofa."

Nick shook his head. "Nah, I think I'll wait. I'm not ready to make any permanent decisions right now."

Damn it, he hated living in limbo. He wanted his life settled, his future laid out for him. Was what happened with Jillie just a passing fling? Or was the emotion he saw in her eyes when they made love meant to last? Nick knew what he wanted. He wanted Jillie Marshall in his life. Now, next week and for years to come.

He wasn't quite sure when he'd fallen in love with her, but it was probably in the midst of one of her disasters. He knew it for certain a few nights ago in the hospital, when he realized he never wanted Jillie to feel scared or worried again. He wanted to be there to protect her—for the rest of her life.

How he knew this was a complete mystery. Hell, he'd lived with Claire for a year and he'd never been quite this sure of his feelings. He'd known Jillie for nine days and there was absolutely no doubt in his mind that she was the one he was supposed to spend his life loving.

Her feelings were another matter. In bed, her passion took over and he could easily believe that the feelings were mutual. He *wanted* to believe. But the next morning, nothing had seemed the same. When he'd touched her, she stiffened slightly and when he'd tried to bring up their future, she found some math topic to discuss.

At first, he'd thought she was simply keeping their relationship from the boys. But now he wasn't sure. Knowing Jillie, she'd probably convinced herself that what they shared was only possible in the atmosphere of the lake house and nowhere else. In the outside world, she was a respected mathematician with high standards for a potential mate. And he was just a...a "carpenter guy."

Nick cursed beneath his breath. He'd tell her tonight and let the chips fall where they may. But would the truth be good enough for her? After all, he wasn't a rocket scientist, although he had designed a building for NASA a few years back. And though he'd gone through his college level math classes with ease, he couldn't do quadratic equations in his head.

He would tell her tonight, over a candlelit dinner and good bottle of wine. He'd patiently explain himself, his concerns, his doubts about her feelings, and then he'd get her to admit her feelings for him. Only then could their life together really begin.

9

THOUGH SHE'D BEEN expecting the sound for the past half hour, Jillian jumped when she heard the intercom buzz. She sat in the center of her bed, her knees tucked up under her chin, waiting, wondering how many times Nick would buzz before he went away.

She felt like a fool, a naive twit who had been duped by a more worldly and sophisticated man. To hear Roxy tell it, Nick Callahan was quite the ladies' man. He'd dated all types of beautiful women, from models to flight attendants, even an actress from New York. Sure, he'd settled down with Claire what's-her-name for a year or so, but, after that ended, Jillian had become just the first in what would undoubtedly be another long line of lovers.

Though she didn't consider herself beautiful, Jillian knew she'd at least been convenient. A willing woman close at hand, a plaything for Nick Callahan's amusement. At first, she'd been hurt, but now she was just angry. How could she have let herself believe that they could share anything worthwhile? She should have trusted her instincts.

Roxy had a completely different opinion of the situation, a view that Jillian couldn't understand. Maybe her sister chose to give Nick the benefit of the doubt because they were such good friends. But Jillian couldn't believe that Nick deceived her for anything but perverse motives. Sure, she may have been a little pretentious, a little snooty at first. But after they'd become friends, he could have told her the truth. It certainly would have saved her making a fool of herself time and time again.

She thought back to all the conversations she'd had with him. "Oh, God, I told him he should go back to school and become an architect. He must have gotten such a laugh. And all that babbling about the importance of bookshelves. He must have thought I was such a dope."

The buzzer sounded again and she ground her teeth and fought the urge to let him in. She'd love just two minutes to tell him exactly what she thought of his little games. Jillian hugged her knees to her chest and slowly counted to ten, then twenty and thirty. The apartment remained silent.

Relief mixed with disappointment. Jillian was happy that he'd finally gone, yet strangely frustrated by the fact that he hadn't tried just a little harder to see her. In truth, she had wanted to be pushed, to find an excuse to see him again. She missed his handsome face and the warmth of his smile. With a soft sigh, she crawled off the bed and wandered toward the kitchen. But as she passed the front door, a knock rattled the hinges. Startled, she cried out, then pressed her hand to her rapidly thudding heart.

"Jillie?"

The sound of his voice, even muffled by the door, still had the capacity to turn her knees weak and make her head swim. The memory of that same voice, deepened by passion, flitted through her mind and she blushed as she recalled the things he'd said to her as they made love.

She tiptoed up to the door and peeked through the peephole. A soft moan slipped from her lips. Why did he have to look so damn handsome? Jillian spun away from the door, her emotions at war inside her. Could there be an explanation for his lies? She tried in vain to think of a reason she might find forgivable, but she couldn't come up with anything even remotely plausible.

He knocked again. "Jillie, are you in there?"

"Go away!" she called. "I don't want to talk to you." The moment the words were out of her mouth, she regretted them. She should have remained silent. Sooner or later, he would have given up.

"Jillie, let me in. Come on, I thought we were supposed to have a date."

Her temper tested, Jillian flipped the locks, pulled off the chain and yanked the door open. Her breath caught in her throat the moment her eyes came to rest on Nick. Gone was his usual wardrobe of faded jeans and a formfitting T-shirt. Instead, he was dressed in an impeccably tailored suit, a white shirt that set off his deep tan and a conservative silk tie. But then she shouldn't have been surprised, since Nick really wasn't the carpenter she'd believed him to be.

With a charming smile, he produced a huge bouquet of flowers from behind his back. "I've been thinking about you every minute since we last saw each other." His gaze scanned her outfit, baggy sweatpants and an old cotton sweater. "You look beautiful."

Jillian grabbed the flowers from his hand then swung them at him, hitting the top of his head with a shower of petals and leaves. "You can take your flowers and your devil-may-care smile and your—your handsome face and you can leave!" She grabbed the edge of the door, intending to slam it in his face, but his hand shot out to stop her.

He gave her a long look. "Would you like to tell me what's wrong?" he asked, in a deceptively even voice.

"I only opened the door because I wanted to tell you face-to-face that we won't be going on any dates. Not now. Not ever."

A frown marred his perfect features. Then he drew in a sharp breath and took a step back. A soft curse slipped from his lips. "You talked to Roxy and Greg."

"Of course I did," she sneered. "What did you expect? That your little joke would just continue? Is that why you asked me out? So you could make an ever bigger fool out of me?"

"Jillie, that's not what I meant to do. And I was planning to tell you this morning. But then, when you said you'd be leaving before Greg and Roxy got home, I decided we should be alone when we talked." He raked his hands through his hair. "Hell, maybe I wanted them to tell you— to spare me from having to tell you myself."

"I don't want to hear anything you have to say!" She made to close the door again, but this time, he stepped around her and walked into her apartment.

"Don't you want to hear my explanation?"

"What possible reason could you have for lying to me?"

He slowly walked around the perimeter of her living room, gazing at paintings and knickknacks and the wall of awards above her desk. The mere presence of him in her apartment, so strong and determined, caused a shiver to run down her spine.

"At first, I didn't think it made a difference," he said, picking up a small plaque and examining it closely. "I didn't expect to fall in love with you."

His admission struck Jillian like a punch to the stomach. She opened her mouth to draw a breath, but she couldn't. Her head began to swim and, at first, she thought she must have misunderstood. Nick Callahan loved her? Jillian shook her head, unable to believe what he'd just admitted. If he loved her, then why had he lied?

"But you made it clear, time after time, that you couldn't possibly love me," he continued. "Not just me, the carpenter, but Nick Callahan, the man. So I let it go on. And when I fell in love with you, I thought I could use it to prove that you truly loved me." He glanced up at her and for a moment all her anger dissolved as his gaze probed hers. "I figured if you could love a man that you were dead set against loving, then maybe we had a chance."

He'd been right. She'd fought against loving him, convinced herself that nothing they'd shared was meant to last. And yet now, even after his deception, she still fought it. Why couldn't she keep herself from loving Nick Callahan?

Nick stared at a painting on the wall. "I know this doesn't make a lot of sense, but everything happened so fast and I wasn't always thinking clearly when it came to you. I just didn't want it to make a difference, and I convinced myself it wouldn't."

"Is—is that it?" Jillian asked.

"Not by a long shot." He loosened his tie, then unbuttoned the collar of his shirt. "I'm not going to leave until we get this settled."

Jillian shook her head, confused by all that had passed in such a short time. "As far as I'm concerned, it is settled. I don't have anything more to say to you."

"Why not? Because your computers and your number theories and your probabilities have already written us off? Or is it because this is something you can't control? Chaos theory at work again."

"I can trust my numbers. I can't trust you."

"Come on, Jillie, you know that's not true." He slowly made his way across the room, taking a few tentative steps at a time toward her. "We love who we love. Do you think I planned to fall in love with a woman who has already decided what she can and can't tolerate in a mate? Do you think I like being held up to some list of qualifications? Hell, I just broke up with Claire a few months ago. The last thing I expected—the last thing I *wanted*—was to have another woman in my life."

"I never made you any promises," Jillian said.

"No, you didn't. To you, I was just a working-class guy. It didn't matter how I made you feel or what we shared when we were together."

"Can't you see that we just weren't meant to be together?"

He slowly reached out and touched her hand, covering her fingers with his. Warmth seeped up her arm, like a drug, lulling her into a false sense of security.

Nick sighed. "The only thing I see is a woman scared of her feelings. You hide behind your numbers because they're orderly and logical. Love isn't logical, Jillie."

She took a ragged breath. How could these feelings be real? She and Nick had known each other barely ten days. A person couldn't fall in love that fast. *That* wasn't logical. "I think you should go," Jillian murmured, pulling the door open further. "I—I want you to go. Now."

Nick stared at her for a long moment, a mix of emotions flooding his expression. At first, she thought he might stay and press his point, but then he just shook his head and walked to the door. But as he passed, he stopped and turned to her.

A split second later, she was in his arms. His mouth covered hers and he kissed her like he'd never kissed her before. Jillian's legs went boneless and though she wanted to push him away, she couldn't seem to make her body do what her mind commanded. So she did the only thing she could do. Jillian kissed him back.

When he finally let her go, she stumbled, then grabbed onto the door. A slow smile curled the corners of Nick's mouth. He grabbed the bouquet from her white-knuckled hand and nodded. "I guess I found out what I needed to know," he said. "The next move is yours, Jillie."

With that, Nick turned on his heel and walked out, leaving Jillian to wonder just how she'd managed to do without his kisses for a whole twenty-four hours.

NICK GLANCED UP at the clock on the microwave, then rinsed his coffee cup in the sink. The boys were asleep in bed, tucked in by Roxy before she and Greg had left for a night out at the movies. The lake house was silent and he stretched out on the sofa and linked his hands behind his head.

He'd been at the lake for the past few days, soaking up the last rays of summer and helping Greg out with a few projects. In truth, he'd come hoping to run into Jillie again. He'd considered paying a visit to the college or her apartment in Cambridge, but had decided to leave that as a last resort. For now, he was counting on Roxy's help. In the spirit of familial interference, Roxy had extended an invitation to Jillie to join the family at the lake house for the Labor Day weekend. Of course, she hadn't mentioned that Nick would be there.

Unfortunately, Jillie had begged off, citing an overwhelming work schedule. Disappointed, Nick had decided to make the best of the holiday weekend. The boys had been thrilled to see him and he and Greg had taken them for endless rides around the lake in Greg's speedboat. Roxy had chatted on and on about Jillie, filling him in on her life since he'd seen her last, almost three weeks ago.

Nick closed his eyes, listening to the soft whir of the ceiling fan above his head. He'd have to come up with another plan, a way to convince Jillie that they belonged together—that they were *good* together. He allowed his thoughts to drift to more sensual subject matter. An image of Jillie swam in his mind, her body naked, moving sinuously above him, her hair tumbled around her face. Nick sighed softly, remembering the silken feel of her skin, the sweet taste of her mouth....

He wasn't sure whether he'd fallen asleep or not, but he sat up when a thudding sound from the front of the house interrupted his nap. He glanced at the clock and noticed that only fifteen minutes had passed. Greg and Roxy weren't due home for another hour or two.

He levered off the sofa and quietly walked to the stairway, listening for the boys. But another thud from the direction of the living room drew him into the dark foyer. He peered inside the archway to see a shadow dance by one of the windows. "What's this?" he murmured. He strode back to the kitchen and dialed the police, gave his location and explained the situation.

As he hurried back to the living room, Nick grabbed the first weapon he could find, a plastic baseball bat. He got there just in time to see the sash being raised. He thought about heading to the boys' room and protecting them until the cops came. Or turning the lights on and trying to scare the intruder away. But what if the guy had a—

A tightly held breath slipped from his lips as a head popped through the window. Soft brunette hair shone in the feeble light from the porch. She grunted, then cursed softly. "This is what you get for changing your mind," she muttered to herself.

"Jillie," he murmured, so softly she didn't hear. His heart twisted in his chest and Nick fought the urge to cross the room and pull her into his arms. He'd missed her so much and now that she was near, he wanted nothing more than to kiss her and touch her without hesitation.

She struggled through the window, tumbling onto the floor, her feet flying above her head. Another curse reverberated through the silent room. Her eyes hadn't adjusted to the light by the time she stood up and she tripped over a footstool. Nick took a quick step toward her, catching her in his arms before she fell. "You could have rung the bell," he said.

Jillian screamed and threw her arm out, whacking him in the nose. Nick let out a vivid oath, dropped the bat and cupped his nose with his hand. He felt the warmth of blood on his palm and groaned. "Damn it, Jillie, either you're going to kill yourself or you're going to kill me."

"Nick?" She stumbled over to a nearby lamp and flipped it on. Light flooded the room and he squinted. "You're bleeding!" she cried. Jillie rushed to his side, then tried to staunch the flow with the cuff of her jacket.

Nick gently pushed her arm away. "I'm all right." He tipped his head back and pinched his nose. "What the hell are you doing here?"

"What the hell are *you* doing here?" she countered.

"I was invited," Nick said.

Jillie frowned suspiciously. "So was I."

"Usually invited guests come through the front door."

"I—I didn't think anyone was home," Jillie said. "Roxy called me yesterday to ask if I'd come up for a visit. When I arrived, all the lights were off. I didn't realize until I got here that I'd left the key to the house back at my apartment. I figured everyone was in bed and I didn't want to wake the boys and—" She drew in a sharp breath. "Did you know I was coming?"

"I knew you were invited," Nick replied. "But until you broke in and—damn!" He turned and ran back to the kitchen, then dialed the police again. While he was waiting for the operator, he grabbed a paper towel and held it up to his nose. But before he could ask the operator to call off the squad car, he heard the sound of sirens out on the road.

Jillie came rushing in. "You called the police?"

"I thought you were a burglar! But then I don't have to explain that mistake to you."

"I don't believe this," Jillie said. "This just gets worse and worse."

Nick stepped around her and walked back to the foyer. Jillie followed hard on his heels. They both walked outside to meet the police. To Nick's surprise, the police recognized him from the last time they'd visited the Hunter household. A quick explanation was all it took to send them on their way. Jillie waited until they'd turned out of the driveway before she headed to her car.

"Where are you going?" Nick called.

"Back to Cambridge. I'm not staying here—not with you."

"Jillie, it's late. Don't be silly. You'll be staying in the house and I'm in the cottage."

"Don't be silly?" Jillie repeated. "Isn't that what you counted on? A few more laughs from Jillian Marshall."

He reached out and grabbed her arm. "Jillie, don't do this. Just stay, get a good night's sleep and tomorrow we'll talk. I'm glad you came."

Jillie stared up at him for a long moment, then nodded. "I am tired."

Nick opened the car door, reached in and grabbed her bag. Then he slipped his arm around her shoulders. "Roxy will be glad to see you. And the boys have been in fine form. They gave Duke a new look."

"Duke?"

"They smeared his fur with a jar of marshmallow cream. Roxy didn't find out until it was dry. The boys were covered with sticky dog hair and Duke looked as if the Sta-Puf man just exploded in his dog house."

Jillie smiled. "I'm glad things haven't changed around

here. Now that I've arrived, it's bound to get more interesting.''

They reached the bottom of the stairs and Nick gave her the overnight bag. Then he pressed a quick kiss to her forehead. ''I really am glad you're here,'' he murmured. ''I was hoping I'd see you this weekend.''

Jillie nodded, then turned to climb the stairs. The temptation to follow her up to the bedroom was undeniable. He'd gently push her back onto the bed and make love to her until the sun came up in the morning. But he wasn't about to take a chance. He would let Jillie come to him. And when she did, he'd never let her walk away again.

JILLIAN STOOD in the window of the guest bedroom and stared down at the lake. It was nearly midnight and the moon was just coming up over the water. Roxy and Greg had come home a half hour ago. Her sister had peeked in the room and called her name, but Jillian had pretended to be sleeping. Jillian could almost imagine the smug smile on her sister's face, her attempts at matchmaking a rousing success. A few moments later, she'd crawled out of bed and hurried to the window, hoping to watch Nick walk back down to the lake.

The light in the cottage was already on and Jillian tried to picture him inside, undressing for bed. The night was warm. Maybe he'd sleep outside as he had the last time he'd been to the lake house. She thought of the time she'd caught him swimming in the lake, how he'd emerged from the water, wet and naked, like some ancient Greek god. And how they'd made love later that night.

Drawn by some invisible force, Jillian tugged off her nightgown, then rummaged through her bag for the light cotton dress she'd packed. When she found what she was looking for, she pulled the dress over her naked body and ran her fingers through her hair. She couldn't sleep. Perhaps a short walk and some fresh air would help.

The house was silent as she tiptoed down the stairs and through the kitchen. She slowly opened the back door and stepped out into the warm night, the breeze fluttering over her skin. The grass was damp beneath her feet as she strolled toward the lake. She paused near the spot where they'd first discovered their desire for each other, remembering how they'd nearly made love right there in the middle of a thunderstorm.

She'd come here now looking for the moon on the surface of the lake, for the sound of the water lapping at the shore. But she'd really hoped to find Nick. Jillian stepped up onto the dock and walked to the end. But the dock was empty and the raft bobbed silently on the surface of the lake. With a soft sigh, she sat down and dangled her feet in the warm water.

A few minutes later, she heard footsteps. Jillian didn't turn around, just waited, her eyes closed, her heart slamming against the inside of her chest. She knew he'd come. She'd been counting on it. When she felt his presence behind her, she spoke. "I couldn't sleep." The words sounded so contrived, but she was past caring. She'd done everything she could to push him away, but no longer.

"Neither could I," Nick replied. He squatted down beside her, clasping his hands in front of him as he stared out at the lake. He was wearing a pair of jeans but no shirt. The soft light from the moon gleamed on his smooth skin and Jillian fought the urge to reach out and touch him.

"It's a beautiful night," he said. "There's an owl up in that tree. He'll hoot all night and keep me awake. Listen."

Jillian closed her eyes and let the night sounds penetrate her brain. Like a drug, the sounds soothed her nerves and focused her mind. "I can hear him." She glanced over a

Nick. "When Greg and Roxy bought this property, I thought they were crazy, living way out here, away from the city. But now I can see the appeal. I was glad when Roxy invited me out for the weekend. I really wanted to come."

"A few weeks ago, I looked at some property on Narragansett Bay," Nick said, sitting down beside her. "I was thinking of building a new house." He glanced over at her. "But then I changed my mind."

The conversation came so easily between them. Gone was the tension and the apprehension. Jillian loved to listen to the sound of his voice and she wondered if they'd ever run out of things to talk about. She couldn't imagine a time like that. "You don't want to build a new house?"

Nick shook his head. "I do. But not that house. Not there."

"Then where?" Jillian asked.

"Closer to Boston," he said, reaching out to take her hand. "Closer to you."

Jillian swallowed hard, tears suddenly pushing at the corners of her eyes. Why had this taken so long? Had she simply needed to come to it on her own? The short time they'd known each other suddenly didn't make a difference. If she'd known Nick for ten years, she wouldn't feel any less love for him. "Really?"

"Jillie, I was standing on this gorgeous bluff overlooking the Bay and, suddenly, I realized I didn't want to build a house that you weren't going to live in. I didn't want to make decisions about cabinets and fixtures and appliances because I wanted you to make those decisions with me. I wanted to build a home for us both."

"Nick, I—"

"I know," he said, pressing a finger to her lips. "We

barely know each other. But I do know that I've never felt this way before. And I never will again.''

''I—I've never felt this way either,'' Jillian said softly, staring down at the water. She pulled her legs up and wrapped her arms around her knees. ''Remember when I told you about the perfect numbers. How I thought that was what love was like?''

Nick nodded.

''Maybe I was right all along. We were two factors just waiting to meet, waiting to become a perfect number. With someone else, we would have been ordinary. But when we're together, we become something special.''

''And I was thinking it might be fate that brought us together,'' Nick said.

''Actually, I was hoping you'd be here this weekend,'' Jillian said with a smile. ''In fact, I kind of figured that we'd probably...run into each other.''

''This is where it all started,'' Nick said, looking up at the sky, ''and ended.''

''Maybe we could start over again?'' Jillian asked, hope flooding her voice until it nearly trembled with emotion.

''Maybe we could,'' Nick said. He held out his hand to her. ''Hi, I'm Nick Callahan. I'm a friend of Roxy and Greg's. I'm an industrial engineer from Providence. I have no idea what my IQ is. I got an A in college calculus but I have to use a calculator to divide eighty-four by six.''

She laughed. ''Hi, my name is Jillian Marshall. I'm Roxy's sister and I'm a college mathematics professor. I don't care what my IQ is, I dropped out of my college calculus course and I think it's charming that you can't divide.''

He leaned closer and brushed a kiss across her lips. ''I'm Nick Callahan,'' he murmured, ''and I'm in love with you, Jillie Marshall. And sometime soon, after we've had a few days to get to know each other, I have every intention of asking you to marry me.''

Jillian reached up to touch his face, her palm soft against his beard-roughened cheek. ''I'm Jillian Marshall and I love you, Nick Callahan. And sometime soon, when you ask me to marry you, I just might accept.''

''So I guess that's all settled,'' Nick said. ''Now what should we do?''

''I'm not sure,'' Jillian said.

''We could always take a swim,'' he teased, pulling her down onto the dock and nuzzling her neck.

''I don't have a suit,'' Jillian replied, wriggling against him.

Nick gave her a wicked grin. ''You don't need a suit, sweetheart.''

''I'm not a strong swimmer,'' she lied.

''Jillie, if you go under, all you have to know is that I'll always be there to hold you up.''

Jillian smiled, then wrapped her arms around his neck. With deliberate leisure, she kissed him, nibbling at his lower lip before trailing a line of kisses along his jaw. How quickly her life had changed. One minute she was alone and the next, her whole life lay before her, Nick Callahan at the center of it. She had found a man whom she could love forever and all she wanted now was for their life to-gether to begin.

''I love you, Nick,'' she murmured, kissing him softly.

Nick pressed his forehead to hers and stared into her eyes. ''And I love you, Jillie.''

With a laugh, Jillian pushed up to her feet and began a tantalizing striptease for Nick. Bunching her skirt up in her fists, she slowly raised it along her thighs. Then, in one quick movement, she tugged her dress over her head. ''Race you to the raft," she said in the moment before she jumped in the lake.

Nick shouted her name as she smoothly cut through the water. Jillian glanced back over her shoulder to watch him strip out of his clothes and dive into the lake. In a few short strokes, he caught up to her. Grabbing her around the waist, he pulled her body against his.

"I thought you couldn't swim."

Jillian splashed water at him. "There's a lot you don't know about me, Nick Callahan."

"I've got plenty of time to learn. I'm never going to let you get away from me again, Jillie."

She laughed, tipping her head back in sheer joy, the sound echoing off the water. Nick needn't have worried. Jillian didn't plan to do any more running. She'd found her future in the arms of Nick Callahan and nothing could be more perfect than the love they shared.

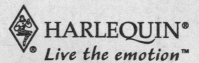

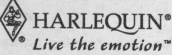

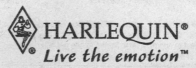